PENGUIN BOOKS

Authors' Choice

AUTHORS' CHOICE

Leading New Zealand writers
choose their favourite stories
—and explain why

Edited by
Owen Marshall

PENGUIN BOOKS

PENGUIN BOOKS

Penguin Books (NZ) Ltd, cnr Airborne and Rosedale Roads, Albany,
Auckland 1310, New Zealand
Penguin Books Ltd, 27 Wrights Lane, London W8 5TZ, England
Penguin Putnam Inc, 375 Hudson Street, New York, NY 10014, United States
Penguin Books Australia Ltd, 487 Maroondah Highway, Ringwood,
Australia 3134
Penguin Books Canada Ltd, 10 Alcorn Avenue, Toronto, Ontario,
Canada M4V 3B2
Penguin Books (South Africa) Pty Ltd, 5 Watkins Street, Denver Ext 4, 2094,
South Africa
Penguin Books India (P) Ltd, 11, Community Centre, Panchsheel Park,
New Delhi 110 017, India

Penguin Books Ltd, Registered Offices: Harmondsworth, Middlesex, England

First published by Penguin Books (NZ) Ltd, 2001

1 3 5 7 9 10 8 6 4 2

Designed by Mary Egan
Typeset by Egan-Reid Ltd
Printed in Australia by Australian Print Group, Maryborough

ISBN: 0 14 100529 7

www.penguin.com

CONTENTS

INTRODUCTION

S HORT STORIES HAVE a strong tradition in this country's writing
and, despite the preference in the marketplace for novels, they
continue to be produced in large numbers, given prominence by well-
established national competitions, featured in school and university
courses, and gathered into collections. They form a resilient genre
with its own idiosyncratic pulse of literary energy. At one extreme it
may be seen as the preserve of the literary purist, at the other the
best opportunity for the aspiring novice.

Selections of New Zealand short fiction are reassuringly common,
and often edited by our leading writers and literary commentators. I
am aware of most of these anthologies, have edited two myself and,
until recently, saw little reason to add another.

An important feature of such collections is the literary vision of the
editor, or editors, which often gives unity and a sense of direction to the
accumulation of work, and, perhaps, challenges convention. Sometimes
the editor is lauded as an arbiter of taste, at least for the time being:
sometimes he, or she, is vigorously criticised by all manner of people,
for all manner of perceived deficiencies. Both responses, and those that
fall between these two extremes, are part of a healthy literature.

It occurred to me, however, that it might be an interesting
experiment to relax the editorial agenda, to allow writers themselves
to decide which of their stories they would like to put before the
reading public. It is not a new idea, but one that has not been much
followed in New Zealand. I hope that readers will find it a fresh and
rewarding approach.

As an editor I felt both exhilaration and apprehension in the free fall of authors' choice. It is hard to let go, and sometimes, as the selections came in, I felt a pang that particular writers had not chosen my personal favourite from among their stories. But that, of course, is the very point of the exercise: to stand aside and give greater opportunity to the authors themselves. For that reason, too, despite my enthusiasm for these writers, I bit my editorial tongue, and resisted the usual commentary upon individual stories, the tidy classification, the identification of literary ancestors, the augury for the future.

To emphasise the degree of the authors' involvement, and to allow readers a special insight into the stories, I wanted also a comment from each writer about the basis of selection. Maybe a story is chosen because the writer thinks it has been unfairly neglected, maybe the writer gives warning that he, or she, is not to be pigeon-holed, maybe it is the author's darling, or maybe it is a chance to air important new work — and I am delighted at the number and quality of hitherto unpublished stories. Some authors share candidly the special significance a piece of writing has in their lives. Each context enriches the story itself, and I thank all the contributors for their willingness to give this extra, personal disclosure.

But even in such a book, the editor takes only one step back, though it is a considerable one that quite alters the contents. It was still my privilege and responsibility to decide which writers to approach. I chose on the basis of ability in the short story form, not in fiction overall, and so some of our foremost novelists do not appear. They have their own opportunities. As with all such selections, considerable subjectivity is involved. There are excellent New Zealand short story writers who are not represented in the collection because of lack of space, but I believe that those included clearly deserve a place.

I thank Geoff Walker of Penguin for his enthusiastic support, for his knowledgeable suggestions, and for allowing me the freedom of choice that I gave the contributors. Above all I thank the authors of these stories for their mastery of the craft, and their willingness for it to be demonstrated here.

Owen Marshall

SHONAGH KOEA

The whole subject of being possessed by literature interests me. I have often wandered about the ordinary world deeply upset by what I have read in works of fiction, or have been much elevated by such things. I remember in the 1980s I somehow, briefly, had a copy of *Hotel du Lac* by Anita Brookner and then had it taken away from me — perhaps someone lent it to me, I do not remember now — and for weeks afterwards I wandered about, intermittently as if in a dream. There was no getting any real sense out of me until another volume had been magically obtained which, in time, it was. I did not feel able to be a member of the so-called real world until I had found out what happened to Edith Hope, the main character in *Hotel du Lac*.

I also remember being very carried away by *A Dance To The Music of Time* by Anthony Powell. The business of a person being deeply possessed and influenced by processes in fictional literature is a thing I find very fascinating, and in the story called 'Longing' I have tried to embrace that curious idea.

LONGING

YOU KNOW YOU'RE ON the skids when you start using a duster as a bookmark. The novel she was reading was about a sergeant who shot himself, the volume a fictional but definitive analysis of the reasons for living and dying. Placing the ripped half of an old tea towel between pages 101 and 102, she set off on foot, already late, for the café at the bottom of the hill.

Yesterday it had seemed a quaintly nonconformist tiny outing to plan, just something inconsequential like buying French apricot jam at the supermarket instead of the usual brand, something you would forget later and would not even think about much at the time. Yesterday it had seemed not entirely invalid to think of what the Clarks had said.

He's a very nice little man, they said. An ex-headmaster. With a good superannuation scheme, they said. It wouldn't do any harm, would it, just to say hello now would it? Widen your circle a bit? And she had said, rather slowly, possibly not. Possibly it would do no harm at all, and ten in the morning would be quite okay. Ten in the morning would be quite okay to meet someone just for a cup of coffee. She had a cup of coffee then anyway, she said, so she could go down the hill and say hello to him, to this man they knew, without any harm done at all.

That was what she had said then, but today the truth was different. Today she did not want to go and say hello to a stranger. Today she had no telephone number to ring to cancel the whole thing so there she was, setting off in a light drizzle that showed signs of turning into a downpour, clutching a tartan umbrella and with a fur blazer slung around her shoulders. Today it all seemed unnecessarily intrusive, and silly. Perhaps just silly.

'A fur blazer?' he had said on the telephone when he asked her what she would be wearing. His small neat voice rose faintly on a small neat note of astonishment. We'll give him your number, the Clarks had said, so he can give you a tinkle. A what? she had answered. A tinkle. He'll give you a tinkle. He'll ring to confirm. I see — a tinkle. Her voice had sounded slow with despair.

'Yes. You'll recognise me because I'll be wearing a fur blazer.' She had listened to her own gritty little voice, wondering if he might be a greenie or just a man who knew nothing about women's clothes, nothing about women at all. 'And my hair tied up with a red ribbon.' She waited for the small extravagance of that to sink in. 'And I'm quite tall. Five foot nine at least, possibly even ten.' He rang off quickly without leaving his own number, or even a proper name.

'My name?' he had said when she asked. 'Alan. Didn't the Clarks tell you?' But he had not given a surname, nothing she could look up in the telephone book, nothing at all. We've given him your number, the Clarks had said. Hope you don't mind. How tall are you? I don't know, I'm the same height I've always been. You've seen me. You know how tall I am. I'm however tall I've always been. You'd be five eight, five nine, they said. He wants five two, and he wants someone more his own age group. You'd be a bit young, really, but time marches on and we're all getting older by the minute, aren't we. Are we? She was suddenly frightened. Behave in an older kind of way if you can. No giggling. Don't tell any silly stories. Don't go teetering along on those high heels, dear, definitely not them. Wear a sensible warm coat and sensible footwear, nothing silly. Maybe a darker colour, not pink. Be very circumspect. Don't laugh. Please remember there's Christmas coming up. We think it might be nice if you had someone to spend Christmas with. We've said you're five four so wear very flat shoes and sit down a lot. Slump if you can. And no earrings, dear, definitely no earrings. What? she had said. But they had gone.

In the morning she telephoned them as clouds rolled in from the north and an oily scud seemed to cover the sea. It would be a rough day, she thought. An excuse not to go out. She coughed, the sound a faint experiment. Perhaps she could say she was ill.

'Hello — you've reached the Clarks' residence. Please record a message after the signal —' She rang off. The answerphone was no use to her at all.

The café was at the bottom of the main street, enclosed in an arcade that led nowhere, with shabby boutiques jostling for the space and a junk shop whose owner stacked old leather suitcases and bundles of outdated *Vogues* on the pavement. She went to the post office first and waited in a long queue to buy stamps to place on fluttery airmail letters to places far away. You have the oddest friendships, the Clarks often said. Whatever is the use of knowing people who live thousands of miles away? What use is that? She let two people go ahead of her at the post office, hoping she would be too late, innocently held up so the ex-headmaster would go home. The sergeant in the novel wrote letters, she thought. He wrote letters home to his faithless wife and no answer ever came because she was off and away with the neighbour.

'We are a distant breed,' she sometimes said at dinner parties when the talk drifted to families and what everyone was going to do for Christmas. 'Everyone has gone a long way away for some reason or another. We write, of course, and send parcels. It seems a strange thing but years ago, at the beginning of it all, I was the brightest and the best and everyone thought I would be the one to go away and do something remarkable somewhere but somehow I have stayed at home and looked after things —' Sometimes she did not even get that far before someone interrupted.

'Why do you talk about the past?' Jennifer Clark had said just last week. 'I've known you for years so I feel I can tell you that you're often a bore, and I mean that with all the affection in the world. Someone has to tell you and Marky and I both think it's best coming from a loving and concerned old friend. We've talked about it, and that's what we've decided.' Was that last week, or the week before? Time had become slightly blurred since 'Silent Night' started to be played over the intercom at the supermarket, and her thoughts became violently blurred as well as she contemplated the arrival of the cards in the post that said our kindest thoughts are with you even though we will be far away on holiday and cannot ring you on the magic day due to the Brenchleys' beach house not having enough phones to cope with the load on Christmas Day. Not Christmas again so soon?

she had thought.

'I talk about the past,' she had said to Jennifer, 'because I don't see that I have a present.'

'What nonsense. There's always a little something under the tree for you, you know that, and we just don't ask you to dinner on the day because of all the noise and the crowds and everything. I've always said you're much better to come later on, more towards New Year and then we can just sit quietly and have something cold — there's usually still some turkey to pick at — and there's not the fuss. It's all much nicer then.'

'Yes,' she had said. 'Of course.'

'And maybe you'd better hurry off home, hadn't you?'

When she stood up, suddenly startled, Jennifer said, 'You'll have to think about your hair, won't you, and a few things like that. What you're going to wear, for instance. I don't,' she had said, 'think the jeans again, do you, dear?' So she had said no definitely not the jeans and had gone home. In the bathroom mirror her face was palely reflected, featureless, bleached of expression and her hair thinner than she had thought it was.

'Perhaps a different style?' Jennifer's tone had been persuasive. 'Give Chanteuse a call.' She had pressed a card into her hand. 'Here's her number. She's an absolute marvel. I think something shorter and snappier, don't you? And perhaps a colour rinse, something to give you a bit of pizazz ready to meet you know who. Tell her I sent you. You could trust her with your life.'

Stanley, her Chinese hairdresser, had managed to fit her in yesterday.

'Just a trim?' He had combed her long hair over his hands before picking up the scissors. 'Very good hair. Good condition.'

She sat on the black plastic chair and held the clips Stanley sometimes handed to her. He ran the salon all on his own now, had only one client at a time these days.

'Can't cope with pressure any more,' Stanley used to say. 'Nerves shot. Another clip, thank you.'

'We're getting along fine, aren't we, Stanley,' she would say. 'My hair's going to be okay, isn't it Stanley? What I really mean is — things aren't so bad, are they, Stanley, and my hair's not the worst hair you're going to cut today or anything like that, is it, Stanley?' He used to gaze deeply at her reflection in the mirror as she held out another clip.

'Hair very good. Everything's fine.'

'Thank you, Stanley. I feel better now.'

'I read in a magazine the other day,' she said as he cut her hair ready for the ex-headmaster, 'that in Beijing, even now, people digging up the roads find quite wonderful pieces of Ming porcelain. There's a market somewhere on the outskirts of Beijing where you can buy them. People have stalls and have pieces of Ming for sale. Wouldn't that be marvellous, Stanley, to go and buy some Ming for hardly anything, to find something really precious?'

Stanley snipped carefully under her left ear.

'Trouble is,' he said, 'not going to Beijing.' He held a lock of her hair against the line of her jaw for a long moment. 'Right length,' he said and began to cut again. When he was doing the back, after he had clipped most of her hair on top of her head and was cutting just a few strands at a time, he said, 'I miss Fred. I trim Fred's beard for how many years — ten? Fifteen? Fred is very good customer, lovely man to talk to. Tears are good,' he said, watching her in the mirror. 'Tears clean eyes. Tears are good.'

Outside the café a small man was waiting. He was wearing a tracksuit vividly striped in scarlet and the short sleeves of the top showed muscular and deeply tanned arms. The day was freezing. A maverick cold front had brought unseasonal snow to some parts of the country and the temperatures had rivalled those of mid-winter.

'You must be Evelyn.' He stepped forward. The street seemed deserted except for the two of them. 'You're number five.' He spoke with terrifying clarity. 'And I've got another three to look at, one a day for the next three days. I think it's best to be quite straightforward, don't you? I don't drink tea or coffee but let's go and find something, shall we? Usually I just have a glass of water.' He ushered her through the doors of the arcade. 'But I'd better have something just to be sociable.'

'A glass of water? Isn't that a bit kind of cold?' The soles of her Spanish riding boots tapped desperately on the linoleum floor of the arcade like the tiny hooves of an elk fleeing before a storm. 'On a day like this?' Outside the waves were being blown against the sea wall and a fine mist of stinging spray clouded the windows of the passage to the shops. 'Do you drink Milo perhaps, or Ovaltine?' For heaven's sake, Jennifer had said, make an effort. Don't talk about the past. Don't talk about Fred. Been there, done that. Fred's dead. Face it. I'm sorry to seem brutal but that's just how it is, Evie. Talk about other people's interests. Don't be boring, Evelyn. Please try not to be boring.

'Ovaltine is supposed to be a healthy drink and lots of people say it's delicious.' She was pacing herself beside him now, taking slightly longer strides so she sank down further with each step and looked, perhaps, a bit shorter. Taking deep slow breaths to a count of four, breathing out slowly to a count of four, anything to stop that rising sense of panic and horror. It is only coffee, she thought. Only an hour, perhaps only half an hour, each word sharply separate in her thoughts like pills taken from a bottle, nothing slurred about the action or the thoughts. It would be exactly the same, she thought, if she had decided to buy a cup of coffee in a crowded restaurant and had to share a table with a stranger. Nice place, isn't it. Yes, quite good really. Do you come here often? No, I just nipped in for a moment in rather a hurry. How strange, so did I and, speaking of being in a hurry, I must rush.

No, said the ex-headmaster, he did not drink Ovaltine. He never had a hot drink at all. Only water. And it was his Aunty Bridie who put him off tea all those years ago when he was a student. Have a cuppa, my dear boy, she said and dished up liquid brown boot polish or something similar in a cup.

'Put me off for life,' he said.

'How interesting. Sometimes things do that.' The café was only two doors away now. 'Something happens and it puts you right off something forever. You've probably got a very sensitive nature, haven't you.'

'No,' said the ex-headmaster.

'Your Aunty Bridie — what a pretty name.' Evelyn was becoming desperate now. 'Was your Aunty Bridie's full name Bridget? What a lovely name. I've always liked the name Bridget. Irish, isn't it? Have you ever been to Ireland? Are you, perhaps, a traveller? Was Aunty Bridie your mother's sister or your father's?' So she had tried to talk about him, talk about his interests, and bought her own cup of coffee.

'I'm sorry,' she said at the counter, 'I've become very independent in recent years. I always buy my own, if you don't mind.'

15

'Suits me,' said the little man and he looked perfectly happy as he waited for a little tap on an automatic drinks machine to fill a paper cup with his own tiny measure of lemonade.

'Small,' he said firmly to the Chinese proprietor of the café and handed over a one dollar coin. 'You have to watch them,' he said to her, 'or they'll charge you for a large.'

'Will they? Oh really? Are you sure?' She was waiting while her own coffee was poured, the man's eyes dark, unfathomable. They contained, she thought the incomparable withdrawal and isolation of another creature exiled from everything that had once been familiar. 'Thank you,' she said and gave him the money.

'He'd be five seven, five eight, tall for a Chinese.' The little headmaster cocked his head towards the counter. 'Shall we sit over here?' She let herself be led over to some round tables beside a slightly open outside door through which rain had seeped, the view of the sea over his shoulder grim and grey. 'My wife,' he said as he went, 'died sixteen years ago.' She thought he made it sound as if it were a fault of character carried out entirely alone and out of selfishness.

'Perhaps she couldn't help it.' Evelyn sat down on a little chair that looked lower than the others by a millimetre or two. 'Perhaps she didn't want to die and she just couldn't help it.'

'Well, I've been on my own, anyway, for sixteen years.' He sat down and sipped the lemonade like a little bird. 'She was about five four, my wife. Perhaps,' he said, the voice tentative and experimental as if he had only just had the thought, 'she might have lost an inch or two as she got older. She might have ended up five three, five two, who knows.'

'Who indeed.' She watched him and thought he might be waiting for her to ask how his wife had died. Cancer, she thought, or a car accident. The silence lengthened.

'People have all sorts of interests,' she said at last, her voice very careful. 'Some people, for instance, are interested in cars.' She darted a look at him. He sipped his lemonade again, unperturbed.

'Not me. I'm not a car nut. Not a good investment, cars.'

So, she thought, it was cancer.

Outside the waves lapped the sea wall, the water oily with debris. There had been warnings over the radio about sewage pollution.

'I went out to dinner the night before last,' she said, speaking suddenly, like a person jumping out of her skin. 'To quite a New Yorky restaurant. One of those long thin ones that go a long way back from the street, only one table wide. The tablecloths were all white, most wonderfully starched. It was very stylish, really. I quite enjoyed it.' Don't talk about yourself, Jennifer had said. Think of others, Evelyn. Say something bright and sparkling, Evelyn, but not too funny. Be a companion. Be pleasant.

'When did your husband die?' The headmaster was undeterred, his small tanned hand firm upon the beaker of lemonade, his gaze cool and clear. Outside the waves began to beat suddenly against the sea wall like a great heart breaking. 'Was he a big man? Was he tall?'

'I've forgotten. I don't ever think about it.' You have to move on, Evelyn, Jennifer Clark had said. Fred is dead. Forget it. It's a long time ago. I can hardly remember what Fred looked like to be perfectly honest and actually if I'm to be perfectly honest again, Evelyn, I'd have to tell you that Marky really didn't like Fred that much. My Marky's a mover and shaker and that's why I've got where I am today. You've got to move on, dear. Don't say anything about Fred. No one wants to know, Evelyn.

'It's a long time ago,' she said. 'You have to move on, people say. People die and you move on.' There was another silence. 'He would have been six two, maybe six three. It's a long time ago and I've forgotten. I may just be imagining he was six two because it was a long time ago and it's gone right out of my mind.'

The ex-headmaster took another little sip of his drink.

'I cook a mean pasta,' he said. 'I went to cooking classes and I cook a mean pasta. You get sick of eating carbon, don't you.'

'I'm sure you do,' she said. 'So there's a wonderful skill you've got. How clever of you. How marvellous.' Pass compliments, Jennifer had said. Be nice, Evelyn. Put yourself out. 'At the restaurant I went to some of the people ordered pasta, various pasta dishes. I'm not sure what they were, but they looked very nice. I had fish,' she said. 'That was nice too. Do you, perhaps go out to dinner sometimes? What restaurant did you last go to? Was it nice? Did you like it?' Ask him where he's been, said Jennifer. Show an interest. You talk all the wrong way, Evelyn. You've got to draw people out of their shells. Right, she had said. Okay then. I'll try to talk differently.

'There's a place I go to where you can get a very nice roast dinner for nine dollars.' He took another sip of the lemonade. 'It's not worth cooking it for that, not with the dishes to wash and the gravy.'

'How wonderful. How clever of you.' You've got to tell them they're marvellous, Jennifer had said. Men have to be flattered, Evelyn, in my experience. I'm just going to the bother of having this tiny, tiny word with you out of the goodness of my heart because really, Evelyn, you're hopeless. 'I think this dinner I had might have cost more than nine dollars but it was just a business thing. The company paid. I'm sure your roast dinner's a much better buy, this roast dinner you have regularly.' She was making him out to be glamorous, darting out all the time, an habitué of nightspots where gravy was served constantly, possibly in silver jugs. She put her finger through the handle of her coffee cup and felt no warmth at all. The coffee would be cold by now, she thought. 'Your roast dinner sounds a much, much more brilliant buy, just brilliant, and probably much more nourishing and better all round. In those New Yorky kinds of places they don't give you many vegetables, do they? They're always rather short on the greens.'

'Can you cook?' He looked at her coolly. Restaurants, greens, starched tablecloths had meant nothing to him at all.

'Yes,' she said. 'I can cook.'

'I've got two children. They're both earning now. Both of them are bringing in a wage.'

'My goodness me, how splendid.' She watched him and he seemed to be waiting for something.

'Have you got any children?' He was peering into the depths of the beaker now. 'I think there's something in the bottom of this, a bit of insect or something.' He glared darkly at the café proprietor. 'You have to watch them,' he said, 'all the time.'

'Don't even think about it,' she said. 'That's the best way and you won't upset yourself. Don't even look at it or think about it for an instant. And, oh yes, you asked me about children. They're all grown up, and earning. They're earning.' Try not to talk in that silly way of yours, Jennifer had said. Try to talk like other people. Nobody knows what you're talking about half the time. 'Definitely,' she said, 'they're earning,' and felt the unfamiliar words fall easily. 'My oldest son is six four and he's earning. They're all earning.' She sat up very straight in the little chair. A seaside café is a melancholy place on a wintry day, she thought. 'And they've got a friend who's so tall that when you

18

open the front door you're looking at his shirt buttons and you can't even see his head.'

The headmaster stirred uneasily and looked out at the rising sea.

'And he's earning too,' she said. Try not to make silly comments, Jennifer said. Only Fred ever thought they were funny and we always said he had an extremely childish sense of humour, Evelyn. 'I'm sure his mother's pleased.'

'I've looked at four,' said the headmaster as if she had not spoken, 'and then the Clarks gave me your name which makes five. I thought it was only good manners to meet everyone and say hello, you know how you do.'

'Of course, of course.'

'I've been all over the place.' He named farflung suburbs many kilometres apart, some of them extremely hilly and perched on razorbacks.

'My,' she said, 'haven't you had a time of it.'

'I thought it was only good manners to do it,' he said again, 'even though it's used a lot of petrol and taken up a lot of my time. I thought it was only good manners.'

'It was, it was.' She was doubling up on things now, trying to provide an expansiveness of conversation. 'Thank you, thank you.' And when there was another of those silences she said quickly, 'Do they give you horseradish with the beef?'

'Beef?' he said. 'What beef?'

'With the roast dinners. Do they give you horseradish with the beef, and mint jelly with the lamb? At this restaurant you like — this one where you have those lovely roast dinners.'

'I don't like anything like that. I don't think I've ever had horseradish. I'm not fond of sauces. I don't like gravy. There's some kind of notice over the counter about a wine sauce but I've never asked for it. I don't have the extras. It all just adds to the cost and you don't need it.'

'How very wise,' she said. 'You're probably very wise. The thing I admire most in life is wisdom.'

'It's an extra two dollars.'

'Wisdom? Is it?'

'No — the wine sauce.'

'Oh,' she said.

'The Clarks said you said "Oh" a lot. They warned me about it. They said, "She says oh a lot but she's quite goodhearted and a good little worker." '

'Oh,' she said again.

'Goodbye,' he said at the doors of the arcade a moment later. 'I've got another one to look at tomorrow.' He mentioned a bay further north. 'It's an hour's drive at the very least,' he said. 'I'm going through the petrol like nobody's business, as I've already said. I'm doing one a day so after tomorrow I've got another two. You were number five.'

'Quite so.' She waited for a moment. 'Good luck. Take care.' It was raining heavily so she snapped up the tartan umbrella with a pert little bang. '*Bonne chance* with the pasta.' When he gave her a sideways glance she said, 'I mean good luck, just good luck ordinarily.'

Behind them the café proprietor was mopping the floor, sopping up the puddles of rain with wide and generous movements that were as rhythmic as a dance. The handle of the mop was firmly held in his beautiful hands as an oar of a quinquereme might have been grasped on a great journey over distant oceans a thousand years ago.

'Goodbye,' she called to him, turning her back on the street and the headmaster. 'The coffee was very nice, thank you. I hope business picks up for the rest of the day. Thank you.'

'They're everywhere,' said the headmaster.

'Oh I know,' she said. 'We're all everywhere, all of us, just everywhere.'

'He didn't like you.' That was Jennifer ringing in the evening. The day had deteriorated into a continuing storm, thunder rolling away to the north and the sky parched by lightning. 'He's just given us a bell and we thought you'd better be told. He found you very gushy. He said you were more gushy than he wanted.'

'Gushy?'

'Yes — gushy. He said you gushed.'

'I did not. All I said was that a few of the things he mentioned were marvellous. You told me to say things were marvellous.'

'I don't mean to be negative, Evelyn, but he didn't readily identify with you, anyway, and that's apart from the gushing. He wasn't at all impressed with you, not at all. He said you were far too tall and younger than he wanted and he didn't take very kindly to the clothes you wore. He said you looked unusual. His exact words to me just now were, "Is she a bit arty," he said, "I haven't seen anyone dressed like that before?" His exact words. He thought you were odd.'

'I thought he was odd.'

'Why, pray, did you think he was odd?' Jennifer's voice was rising now, getting an edge to it. 'Why would a headmaster be, as you say, odd?'

'Oh,' she said, sitting down at the foot of the stairs beside the little telephone, 'I thought he was odd because he wore a tracksuit with short sleeves on a freezing day on an outing to meet a lady he hadn't ever met before and it might have been nicer to be tidier, and I thought he was odd bunging on about his stupid drinks at such great length and only having a glass of lemonade, again on a freezing day, and I thought he was odd how he noticed how tall everyone was and commented on it and I thought he was rude and racist to the Chinese man in the café. I thought he was rude and odd and I thought the way he spoke about his wife was appalling.' Jennifer's breathing had become heavy now, she noticed. 'And so on,' she said dangerously, 'ad infinitum.'

'You didn't even go to meet him dressed how you said on the telephone. You'd said something about having a red ribbon in your hair and that's what he was looking out for but when you eventually arrived you didn't have one at all.'

'Oh that,' she said. 'I forgot.'

'You forgot?' The voice was rising again. 'And I wasn't going to mention this, Evelyn, but I've checked with Chanteuse and she says she's never heard of you. Whatever am I doing wasting my valuable time on someone who's so ungrateful? It isn't a small thing, you know, to have a good word to put in for you with a hairdresser of the calibre of Chanteuse. I suppose you went to that dreadful Stanley, did you?'

'I don't think there's any need to shout like that, Jennifer. Certainly I went to Stanley. Stanley trimmed up my ends just like he always does. I like Stanley. Stanley understands me. I was going to get him to trim up my ends anyway.'

In the night the thunder still rumbled occasionally, but without conviction, the storm slowly working its way across the city. The weather had exhausted itself and, exhausted as well, she slept in pale old silk pyjamas between white linen sheets that had once been embroidered with garlands of flowers, mythical beasts, all tattered now.

Sometime in the night, perhaps in the deepest darkest part when dreams become reality for a moment in the mind, she found herself in the New Yorky restaurant again. The tables were still in their rank marching one at a time towards the back wall, the maître d' more talkative than he really had been, the other guests quieter.

She found herself gliding forward with no worries of tripping slightly or sitting in the wrong place. 'You've got very clumsy,' Jennifer often said. 'It's because you don't stop to think. Do try to be less clumsy.' But in the dream she danced forward, her feet skimming the bare boards of the floor, the other diners respectful and kind, their heads bowed like those of acolytes, all music distant. The seat opposite hers was empty this time and when the door to the street swung open again a man entered. Frederick. Frederick walked through the doorway dressed in his best checked overcoat he had once bought in London, the one that disappeared from the cloakroom under the staircase after the funeral and people said they had never seen it there, not ever, not even once. Liars, she had thought. Liars, all of them.

He came straight up to the table to sit in the empty place opposite hers but she was already standing, already leaning over the narrow little table to place her arms around his neck, her cheek against his. 'Oh Frederico,' she said. 'Frederico, wherever have you been? I've looked and looked everywhere for you. I've been waiting so long, Frederico,' and her cries of joy echoed in her own ears like the shouts of the sergeant the night before he shot himself.

EMILY PERKINS

I've chosen 'We're Here, Anderson Says' because it feels like my best attempt yet at portraying a relationship in which two people are floundering, though they both, for the most part, want to make it work. These characters are struggling for love, but are wary of false sentiment, even when they fall prey to it. They are not sure what love is, and as long as they keep worrying about it, their chances of finding it are slim. I hope the story conveys their plight with sympathy as well as humour.

WE'RE HERE, ANDERSON SAYS

W E'RE HERE, ANDERSON SAYS, to see if our relationship is beyond repair. Or — as he professes to hope — if we can restore it. If it is retrievable. Anderson has taken a liking to R words. 'Our relationship may just be retrievable Angie, and I for one would like to give it a try.' Even though he said it in his fake-sincere American accent, trying to take the vulnerability out of the words, I couldn't help but see Anderson as a lolloping dog, golden and eager, snuffling to pick up our relationship between his friendly jaws from wherever it was I'd thrown it. I told Jane that and she laughed but I could tell she thought I was mean and hard. Jane is terminally single so what she thinks doesn't exactly count.

In reality Anderson looks nothing like a dog. He's more a cat person which is one of the things that drew me to him. He has almond-shaped eyes and sinewy arms and sleek black hair which he may well be losing. He is losing. When I wake up in the mornings one of the first things I do is brush the pillow free of his fallen-out hairs. He is losing it from the front and also from the crown of his head. Unusually for me, I am still with Anderson. Normally at the first sign of trouble or evidence of fallibility, I am running as fast as my little legs can carry me. 'Better no relationship than a bad relationship,' has been something I liked to say. But with Anderson it has seemed as though it might be all right to sort through the bad stuff, to try and see the whole. To love anyway. The fact that I am tipping thirty doubtless has something to do with all of this. Tick tick.

Anyway, things haven't been so hot lately. Anderson suspects this is my fault; I am convinced it is his. An example of our discontent would be that my habit of littering, while previously unnoticed or ignored, has now become the focal point for everything that is wrong with modern society. I exemplify contemporary apathy, Anderson says. I remain infantilised in my relationships with authority, I fear government, I will never be capable of effecting real change. Change for what, I say, and Change for the good, he replies. It's an empty crisp packet, I say, not a fucking ballot slip. Anderson can be pompous but it isn't his fault. His mother was a famous sixties figure — he was brought up on a diet of communal marijuana and indigestible bread. Once we went round to visit and Anderson's mother's boyfriend was putting lentils through the juicer. Anderson is, obviously, Anderson's last name. His first name is unrepeatable.

The littering thing is just one item in a list of complaints Anderson has about me. My theory is that he thinks he wants to improve me, but secretly he is drawn to the fact that I do not care. Whatever (I am trying to curb my inclination to over-analyse everything), his confusion results in a consistent tone of disapproval. In turn I become unconfident, then depressed, and then I rebel. This cycle can take place two or three times in an afternoon. I play the old songs a lot, especially when I am trying to behave against type by cleaning the house.

It was Anderson's idea to come away. I am grateful for it — he has made all the arrangements. He looked through brochures, he enquired about hotels, he found cheap flights. Neither of us has been on a holiday like this before, where all there is to do is lie around in the sunshine and relax. Anderson's holidays, a legacy from his mother, usually involve third-world countries, disadvantaged locals and potential-for-trade investigations, or walks in the rain in Wales. I am more of a city break person, preferring coffee bars, art galleries and shopping to the delights of the elements. But I am quite enjoying doing as I'm told.

We're here now, Anderson says. We had to get up at two-thirty this morning to be at the airport in time for check-in. I look like my passport photograph. We walk blinking off the plane but heat doesn't rush at us the way I had imagined it would. The other people from our flight look different from us. We stand cramped in a little oblong bus with controls at both ends and I try not to mind that they look different from us. If I were to mention this to a certain person, he would tell me I was an inveterate snob. Anderson truly believes we are all equal, even those with bad dress sense. I think his egalitarianism is rare. A lot of people pretend to believe this but generally, if you scratch the surface, they don't want their kids going to play-group with those other, allegedly equal kids. I know this is not an earth-shattering insight into human nature but I find it reassuring nevertheless. It means I'm not alone. But I love Anderson's goodness, even when it bugs me, like now, that if I were to point out the preponderance of shell-suits and gold chains on this bus, he wouldn't laugh.

The hotel is much nicer than I expected. Like me, it matches its photograph. Despite Anderson's investigations I'd been convinced that the image in the glossy brochure was a lie and we would arrive to find a building site with ants on the benches and rusty water. Instead we are in a creamy concreted apartment with crimson bougainvillaea running down the sides of our balcony walls. The hotel storeys are tiered so, though we're on the first floor, we look out over a small garden towards the pool. We dump our suitcases unopened on the double bed and run down the stairs towards the beach.

Some people set a lot of store by horizons. Personally I think they're all the same. So I let Anderson walk on the water side, getting a crick in his neck from staring out through his sunglasses at the barely distinguishable line between sky and sea. There are waves, and the sand is coarse and yellow. We walk on the wet sand past rows of black-and-orange striped deck chairs. We're walking towards a rock-covered curve in the beach. We can't see what's beyond it. It's warm, but not hot. I had thought it would be hot. The lines of deck chairs have ended and a wind picks up. It blows darts of dry sand at our legs. I sing some lines from a Joni Mitchell song. Anderson pushes me because if there's one thing he doesn't like about his mother it's the music of her generation. His mother claims an erstwhile acquaintance with Joni Mitchell. For a woman whose life has been devoted to the belief that everybody is equal, she has a great respect for the famous and invokes the names of celebrities she has met as often as possible. That Anderson hates hippie music is one of the things that I like about him.

I'm singing the song a bit and when I run out of the words I remember I start talking. 'It's so beautiful,' I say, 'look at those hotels down there, look at those houses, it's like how I imagine California.' We take off our sandals and, holding them, walk in the shallows so that the sand doesn't keep stinging our legs. 'Aren't those pink flowers amazing? Did you see that enormous cactus at the airport? I never imagined them to look so extraordinary, it was much better than a photograph.' I don't know if Anderson is listening but I keep talking because there's a scared, thrown-overboard feeling in my stomach that I'm trying not to think about. 'The water's so warm. Do you think it's very polluted?' This last one, I expect, will get a response from Anderson, but before he answers there's a big grinding noise and an aeroplane appears from nowhere, vast in the massive sky.

The plane, with its shark-grey underneath, swings over us and on towards the airport just north of the beach. It's a wonderful sight, romantic and modern. I feel happier. Anderson doesn't say anything.

Later, back in our room, we put on our swimsuits and laugh at each other. Our bodies are frightened and white. Anderson tries out the snorkel gear he has brought with him. He fits the mask tight over his face so that the skin bulges slightly on the outside of it. Then he squeezes the breathing pipe under the mask strap and tucks the mouthpiece into his mouth. I laugh in the spirit of us laughing at each other in our swimsuits, but inwardly I am cringing. Anderson walks slowly around the beige room motioning with his hands as if he's doing the breaststroke. Then he raises first one arm, then the other, dancing nineteen-sixties style. Now he's doing the mash, and that dance with the gestures like hitchhiking. I despair of Anderson. What will he look like, down at the pool?

I shouldn't worry. The poolside is not an intimidatingly fashionable spot. Most of the people are in family groups, couples with matching short flicky haircuts, garish T-shirts and young children. The pool itself is a pleasing organic shape, in keeping with the seventies style of the hotel. We find two blue sun-loungers and settle in with our towels, our tanning lotion and our books. Anderson's snorkel and mask lie under his sun-lounger like a small parcel of kelp. He isn't going to use them in the pool, he assures me, but maybe if he walks through the gate in the fence and across the road to the beach. I am trying to love Anderson but the effort of it is making me a bit weepy. I lie with my eyes shut and try not to feel dislocated, here on this remote island, cut-off and alone. Eventually, to the soft sound of waves on the beach behind me, I fall asleep.

We're not here, Anderson says, to spend all our time apart from each other. He says this when, back in the room, I want to go downstairs for a drink and he wants to lie down. I know what 'lie down' means.

'Who spent all this afternoon apart from me,' I say, 'at the beach? You did.'

'Or, equally, you spent it apart from me at the pool,' he answers.

'We were at the pool first. It was your choice to separate off and go to the beach.' I don't know why I'm saying this. I could care less that he spent the afternoon at the beach.

'And it was your choice not to come with me.'

'I was asleep.' I sense a new tack. 'Which is why I don't feel like lying down now. If you're tired after snorkelling why don't you have a nap and meet me in the bar later.'

'Ange. Angel.' He touches my arm. The feeling of his hand tingles. 'Come on. We're on holiday.'

It occurs to me that I should never have come on a holiday paid for by somebody else.

'All right,' I say. 'Just for a minute.'

Dinner looks like it will be a success. There's a little restaurant on the beachfront, past the rocks we walked to today. We sit under the striped awning and wrangle with large plates of seafood. When I met Anderson he was a vegetarian but that didn't last. I used to cook breakfasts on weekend mornings and I'm afraid he fell, unoriginally, for the temptations of sizzling bacon. At the time I enjoyed knowing that there were limits to Anderson's self-control. Now I'm not sure. Here at the restaurant, our langoustines are like something from a bad acid trip, with giant claws and long plated bodies. 'Imagine one of those in your pillow,' I say, and Anderson winces. He's going brown already. His mother has olive skin, and he tans easily. It's nice to see him across the table, by the candle with the red glass surround protecting it.

'Where are you?' Anderson says. The truth is I am preoccupied with work. Just because you go somewhere new, it doesn't mean you can instantly adapt. Everything that happened yesterday still only happened yesterday, even though we're now in a different time zone.

'You know, Harold is really out of order,' I say.

'Who?' Anderson's head twitches slightly, as if to look around for someone behind him. His prawns are all peeled, the shells to one side of his plate, the fleshy insides lying there naked and ready. I am eating mine as I go, and getting prawn juice all over my hands.

'Harold. The unit manager. He's a jerk. Yesterday he sent round —'

'Angie. Forget about it. We're supposed to be thinking about us.'

I can't believe those words just came out of Anderson's mouth. 'You sound as if you're in a soap opera.'

'Don't be a bitch.'

'Don't call me a bitch.'

On the way home we walk past a souvenir shop that is just closing up. There are racks of tea towels with maps of the island on them, and a wall of key rings. In a small cage is a large sad bird — maybe a macaw. It looks flyblown and manky. I don't point it out to Anderson. He'd probably start a fight with the owner.

It's windy the next morning. Anderson says that's good, that it'll blow the cloud cover away. We walk down to reception to hire a car. We're going exploring. I have only just passed my test so though I let Anderson put my name down too I do not intend to drive. They drive on the right, here. Anderson pulls out of the hotel car park and we almost hit a car, which is coming down the hotel drive the wrong way.

'Cunts,' I say.

'Please,' says Anderson.

There is a newly sealed road we can drive along to a beach at the south of the island. Everyone says this beach is secluded. Everyone says, 'No one knows about it.' I am on navigating but I have to stop looking at the map every so often because Anderson is driving badly. He takes bends way too fast and can't get into third smoothly at all. I comment on this and he says, 'I know. It's difficult with my right hand.'

The inland scenery is strange and beautiful. There are mountains everywhere, bare and scored with lava trails. Cacti stand weird and spiky, looking like some humans would if they took off their body-masks. Planes fly overhead frequently, comforting, safe. We drive through a resort settlement. Golden couples amble hand in hand across the road in front of us; palm trees clatter in the wind. A sign says *Turn Left For Reconstructed Native Village*. It strikes me as strange, that Anderson and I are here trying to find some truth about ourselves, in this place that is fabricated, a fairy tale, a lie.

The road to the secluded beach is unsealed. Red dust rises from our little car. Anderson was right — the wind has cleared the sky of clouds. When we arrive at the beach, which is beautiful but crowded, it is the middle of the day and the sun sits fat and high directly above us. The people on the beach look slightly more like us than the people by the hotel pool. There are no trees, just a deep stretch of white sand leading down to the ruffled sea. I leave Anderson lying on a towel with his book and go to stand knee-deep in the water, feeling the hot wind against my shoulders, looking down beyond the surface into the twisting yellow diamonds of sun underneath. Anderson and I have been together for three years. He has, to my knowledge, been faithful to me. I have not returned the favour. I want children, for ignoble reasons such as fear of loneliness and vanity. Anderson does not want children: he is an advocate of depopulation. This is a shame because Anderson, I think, would be a generous, excellent father. He has nieces and nephews who adore him and stand back warily from me. One of his sisters' twin boys used to scream, 'Get out get out get out!' whenever I entered a room he was in.

I walk further into the water until it is up to my waist. The sun is burning heavily into my back in almost an obliterating way. I wonder if I turned round to look at Anderson, what I would see. Maybe he's reaching over to pick up a ball and throw it back to some smiling child. Maybe he's lost in his book. Maybe he's explaining to someone how to get back to the main road. Anderson has the sort of manner that encourages people to stop and ask him directions. He looks as though he is at home, wherever he happens to be. Over by the rocks two boys are shouting, and splashing at each other. Drops of water catch the sun, like crystals scattered in the air. I bend my knees, push off with my feet, and swim.

'You're not even here,' Anderson says.

There isn't any point in acting dumb. 'I'm sorry,' I say. 'Shall I make us some snacks?'

We are on our hotel room balcony, tired and slightly burnt after a day at the beach. Though I've had a shower, I can still smell salt in my hair. There's a bottle of wine opened on the white plastic table and a bowl of pistachio nuts. I have bought some crackers, salami and cheese from the hotel store. I stand at the sink bench and slice and arrange.

'You think food preparation is the answer to everything,' Anderson says from the balcony.

It's a small room — he doesn't raise his voice.

'I'm sorry,' I say again. I take a plate of food out and put it on the table. I pour us some more wine. 'Maybe things just aren't working out.'

'Oh, shut up,' says Anderson. 'We're not going to have that conversation here.'

'Shall we write some postcards?' I ask.

We go through the usual jokes: wish you were her; weather's here, wish you were lovely, et cetera. I send a card to Jane, my parents and my anorexic brother. Anderson sends elegant descriptions of the native flora to his mother, to his sister, to his colleagues and to Nicholas his friend who works for Amnesty International. On this card he writes, *thank god we defeated fascism so privileged dilettantes like us can lie about in the sun without too much trouble from our consciences.* He eats some salami, wipes his hands and smiles at me. I love Anderson's smile. It is not the smile of a good person, which goes to show that physiognomy counts for nothing. It is a dirty, wicked smile. I wish I saw it more.

'I love you,' I say.

'Don't sound so relieved,' he answers.

We get a bit drunk and each try to think of something personal to tell the other that they didn't already know. I remember how when I was at school we had a forty-hour famine, where we had nothing but barley sugars and people sponsored us for each hour that we went hungry. The proceeds went to a charity organisation helping famine relief in Ethiopia. I get to this stage of the story and Anderson begins a tirade against corrupt and unwieldy charities. 'But,' I say, 'what I did was get the sponsorship and then I was too starving to go without food so I ate anyway, then I kept the money.'

'That,' says Anderson, 'is not funny. It's not even charming.'

'Anderson,' I say, 'tell me again how we got together.'

'You know this story. We're supposed to be telling new ones.'

'Go on. Tell me anyway.'

'We met,' Anderson tells me as he strokes my ankle, 'at a dinner party given by your college friend Jane. There were four or five other people there, including the man with the blue shirt.'

'The man who looked like his head had been squashed in a vice,' I say.

'The man in the blue shirt,' Anderson says, 'who you were sitting next to.'

'Because Jane fancied you for herself,' I say.

'Because Jane and I had sponsorship projects to talk about,' says Anderson.

'Because Jane wanted to get into your pants.'

'Who's telling this story?'

I smile.

'The man in the blue shirt talked to you all night.'

'At me. He talked at me.'

'And I talked with Jane about the sponsorship plans but the whole time I was looking across the table at you. And you knew I was looking.'

'I did!' I say, and arch my foot.

'You knew, and you purposely didn't look at me. You pretended to be really interested in what the man in the blue shirt —'

'— with the squashed head.'

'— was saying to you. I thought, well, that beautiful girl really likes that guy. And everyone had coffee and you stayed so I stayed but he stayed too —'

'— and Jane was hinting heavily that me and squash-head leave —'

'— and it was time to call for taxis and I said I was going north and you said you were going north too —'

'And Jane asked me if I'd moved and I told her I was minding my brother's place and she asked me if he'd moved and I said yes, north, he's moved north.'

Anderson holds my toes, tight. 'And squash-head was going west so we shared a taxi and you told me —'

'I told you —'

'You told me your brother hadn't moved but you just wanted the chance to have a conversation with me.'

'And that was that.'

'That was that,' Anderson says. 'And now we're here.'

We pack a picnic and set off for the crowded secluded beach again. Anderson's driving is really bad. 'Check your blind spot,' I remind him as he overtakes recklessly. 'And watch your following distance.'

'Angie. I'd never guess that you've just learned your road code.'

'Christ!' I exclaim as a car comes hooning towards us and changes sides at the last minute. 'No one around here can drive. Did you see that guy?'

'I'm identifying with him.'

'Are you sure this is the right road?'

'No. Are you looking at the map or what?'

'It's hard to tell just here,' I say. 'I think this is where we're supposed to be.'

'You think or you know?'

'I think I know.'

'Angie.'

'Don't pick on me.' My voice comes out more whiny than I mean it to.

'Fuck.' Anderson pulls over to the side of road, braking harder than is strictly necessary. He snatches the map from my hands.

'What?' I say. 'Relax.'

'I have to do fucking everything,' he says loudly. 'You're completely thoughtless, you're so wrapped up in your own head, Jesus. You're doing my fucking head in.'

'Why are you with me then?' I shout this. 'Why? Because you like the way I look? I mean, that's really noble isn't it, that's really admirable.'

'I'm sick of the fucking way you look,' he says. 'And don't fucking cry. There's nothing wrong with your life that a bit of selflessness wouldn't fix up.'

At this I get out of the car. I start walking down the road and as I walk I begin to feel better. There is red gravel under my feet and the sky is empty. The mountains on my left loom closer and further away, like an optical illusion, depending on the cast of their shadows. I slip down the straps of my tank top so as to avoid tan marks. Anderson pulls up alongside, in the car.

The two boys I saw playing on the beach yesterday are here again today. I float on my back and watch them throw a red, white and blue striped ball back and forth to one another. They are brown-skinned, maybe Spanish. The older, skinny one has a protruding jaw and bat-like ears that stick out at an angle. His younger brother is beautiful. They throw the ball and laugh and call out. I think I can see which couple on the beach is their parents: a woman with curly blonde hair, cut short, and a dark-haired man with large eyes. He is rubbing suntan lotion into her shoulders. I kick a bit in the clear water, and watch the birds gliding overhead. Then the ball lands next to me, splashing my face. I stand and lurch after it but its slick wet surface slips away from my touch. The older boy comes lunging towards me, a huge grin on his face, his hands flapping excitedly from the wrists, and I see that he has Down's syndrome. I push the ball towards him and it spins as it skims across the water into his arms, the coloured stripes rolling like a barber's pole.

'That boy's Down's syndrome,' I say when I flop back, dripping, on the towel next to Anderson. 'Or Mongol or whatever you say.'

'Down's syndrome,' says Anderson.

'His poor family,' I say, moving Anderson's snorkel from under my hip.

Anderson looks up from his book. 'Why?'

'Because. They must worry about him.'

'Not necessarily.' Anderson looks down again, and turns a page.

I would love to do some shopping while we're here but there really is nothing to buy. The resort shops peddle nasty sarongs and imitations of expensive watches. Electronic gadgets — personal organisers, portable CD players — are on sale everywhere but they don't do anything for me. There are no attractive local crafts. We walk past an outdoor leisure centre with a mini-golf course and Anderson gives me a history lesson. One of the men playing mini-golf leers at me. He's wearing Bermuda shorts. I wonder if Jane would ever tell Anderson about the affair that I had. She still has a thing for him.

'Blah blah colonisation,' says Anderson, and I act interested and try not to think about the last time Jared and I had sex, on the floor of a hotel room in Amsterdam. I start singing the Joni Mitchell song again. A plane roars overhead.

'We're here,' Anderson says, 'so we may as well make the most of what's going on.'

By 'what's going on' he means the family entertainment in the cavernous bar of our hotel. It starts after dinner, which is an all-you-can-eat buffet of so-called Chinese food. Anderson has decided that tonight we should eat in the hotel and attend the G-rated cabaret. I don't feel in a position to argue, as he hands over some money in exchange for our food vouchers. My entire daily budget has gone on pre-dinner drinks. I have trouble eating my chow mein without getting it on my chin.

Near the side of the bar we find wicker bucket seats and settle in with another drink each. Kids are running all over the place, squealing and giggling in instant holiday friendships. By the wall some teenagers in last summer's fashions are trying to act cool. The cabaret is instantly forgettable and involves several over-tanned holiday reps with bad haircuts lip-synching to hits from the 1980s. The children love it though and I notice one kid, the boy from the beach, bouncing in his chair and clapping along with great enthusiasm. His mother, next to him, drinks a coloured cocktail with an umbrella in the glass. His father wears a checked shirt and holds the youngest son on his knee. Because he's skinny, you almost wouldn't notice the boy is different. But he must be thirteen, too old to be jigging around and clapping in that happy way. I feel tears pricking my eyes.

We're in our hotel room. I'm kind of drunk. 'Did you see him,' I ask Anderson, 'that Mongoloid boy?'

He lets the incorrect label pass. 'No. I didn't notice.'

'It was so sad. His parents looked so brave. And his little brother's normal but they were playing together just like nothing was wrong.'

'Nothing is wrong. The kid's got Down's syndrome, that's all. Why are you so obsessed with it?'

I think of the boy's smiling face in the coloured lights from the stage and feel a rush of emotion. 'Because he — because he's got

35

something missing, he's defenceless, he's too soft. What's he going to do when his parents die?'

'Be fine. Fuck's sake, it's not a major disability. There are degrees. You're being sentimental and patronising.'

The fact that Anderson is probably right again makes me angry. 'I can't do anything right for you, can I?'

'Don't start.'

'I hate you.' I am overcome with a sudden desire to ruin our holiday. We've been here only three days but it feels like forever. And I do hate Anderson, for taking me away from my life, with all its distractions.

'You're drunk. Shut up.'

'You're a balding pompous cunt. I hate you.'

'Fuck off Angie. I'm not going to take you seriously when you're like this.'

'You never take me sleriously. Seriously.'

'You're drunk.'

'You're a prick. I hate you.' Then I imagine the boy again and how Anderson would be if he had a son like that, how selfless and kind and persuasively normal. Anderson believes in people's essential goodness. It doesn't occur to him not to because he is that way himself. 'I love you Anderson,' I say. It now seems to me that he's spent all this time with me as a sort of test. I want to be better, to make him feel that he hasn't failed. I want to live in a universe like his where we're all decent and equal, or could be if only we tried harder.

'I love you. I love you.'

'Oh Angie,' he says, and his face, his beautiful sun-tanned cat-like face, looks as if something has cleared from it. 'You do right now. But you're still drunk.'

I start to cry. 'What's going to happen to us?' I say. 'I'm frightened of being alone.' I don't say, and I'm frightened of you as well.

Anderson ignores my tears. He sounds tired. 'Don't be frightened angel. I'm here,' he says.

RUSSELL HALEY

When I was eight I designed a self-propelled trolley. One of the wheels turned a dynamo. That mechanism fed current to an electric motor. This engine drove the rear wheels of the cart and ... *spun the dynamo!* You gave the bogie a push, jumped on, and cruised wherever you pleased. Gordon, my brother, knew all about science. He said the design couldn't work. Of course he was right. Stories, though, need not obey the laws of physics.

For me, the fictional equivalent of a magic self-powered trolley was the invention of a comic character. Harry Rejekt escorted me to his cottage on a bluff above Lake Karapiro and I wrote the eighteen stories published in *A Spider-Web Season*.

Harry embodies my rediscovered sense of joy in writing. He makes me laugh out loud at his antics. Harry moves at ease through this absurd world and he illuminates, not unkindly, my own fragile and sometimes ludicrous self.

So, I have chosen 'Press Play Until You Find Silence' for this collection because ... well ... Harry Rejekt and I gave the bogie a push a couple of years ago. We jumped on the cart and it is still running.

PRESS PLAY UNTIL YOU FIND SILENCE

HARRY REJEKT STOOD ON his verandah and looked at the lawn. A few days ago he'd cleared a small circle of turf from around the base of the magnolia and bordered it with yellow bricks. The *stellata* was in flower. White petals, yellow bricks, green lawn, blue sky — perfection. Harry felt a burst of pride at his handiwork. The front garden looked decidedly handsome.

Harry stretched up on his toes and then dropped back on his heels. He did this small exercise ten times. Next, Harry placed his hands on his hips and gyrated. Clockwise ten. If you kept this up for years you might grow a little taller. You could walk down Queen Street in Cambridge examining the tops of people's heads. See which ones had the canvas showing through. The other way, ten.

Something clicked in his pelvis but there was no accompanying pain. Harry had heard somewhere that knee cracks and knuckle pops were caused by compressed natural gas. But what kind of vapour lurked inside your lower vertebrae? Carbon monoxide, probably, if you sat around in your car for too long with the engine running.

There. His limbering-up callisthenics were finished for the day. Years ago, Harry used to do those Canadian Air Force exercises, the 5BX system, or was it 10BX? Anyway, one was for men and the other for women. But Harry couldn't keep up with the recommendation that you dried yourself vigorously with a rough towel after your daily shower. At that time Harry was baching in a scungy room behind the Symonds Street shops in Auckland and the only washing facility was a cracked hand basin. His single brown towel was threadbare.

Today the sky was clear and the morning was cool but not cold. Harry breathed in deeply and heard a shrill whistling noise in his left nostril. He snorted and breathed again. Yes, the high-pitched squeak was still there. Harry blew his nose violently into his handkerchief but this peculiar sound did not appear to want to go away.

There are noises within your body, Harry thought, that only you may notice. Take your digestive processes, for example. The most extraordinary things go on in your stomach and deep down amongst all those coiled tubes and pipes. There are rumbles and hisses, plangent chords that never reach the outside world. But we don't walk around with an ear deliberately cocked for other people's organic music.

Of course, there's slippage. People break wind inadvertently. Going up or down flights of stairs can present real difficulties for those with gaseous incontinence.

Noises happen. Harry had once been bothered by a very audible click in his sinus cavities whenever he opened his mouth. The only cure for that had been regular nasal douching with warm salt water. Horrible. It had been like drowning in a tropical sea in order to be saved from your own indiscretions.

But was this nosy sound — there it came again — was it really something or nothing? When you needed a filling your tongue could turn the smallest cavity into a vast cavern. So this minor little pipsqueak could simply be being exaggerated by the bones of his face. It was possible that an outside observer, not an observer, a listener, might not be able to hear anything at all.

Harry strode off decisively towards his parked car. He kept a small Sanyo tape recorder in the glove compartment so he could make notes while he was driving. Pairs of semi-rhyming words that would never make their way into a poem. *Inorganic* and *morganatic*. *Foggy Peru* and *Brian Boru*. He recorded ideas about a future journey to South America. Take a walking stick made from manuka. Bring one back crafted from some local wood. And facts. Hiram Bingham thought he'd discovered Vilcabamba in 1912 but he was mistaken. The ruins were those of Machu Picchu. And Pablo Neruda always spelled the name of the ancient city differently. Harry rolled the tape and listened to his own voice. 'Pablo Neruda writes M-a-c-c-h-u with two cs.'

Harry kept pressing the 'Play' button until he found silence. Yes —
that was the way to solve the problem. He'd see if he could record this
whistle in his nose.

Then, if his olfactory organ really were issuing a tune for all the
outside world to hear, if people like his employer, Dougal Colophon,
or his friend Joseph Bartleby, could detect it, he might have to breathe
through his mouth and pack his nostrils, temporarily, with plugs of
cotton wool.

Because how could you look anyone in the face and try to have a
conversation with them if this crazy squeal kept coming from your
nozooma? Good-day, wheeee! How's it going, whooeeoo?

Nothing. Not a murmur on the tape. Good. It was all in his own head.
But was there a malfunction in the machine? Perhaps it wasn't
recording *anything*.

Harry Rejekt tramped across his front verandah, turned, and set off
back again. He tried recording his footsteps and the click of Sako's
claws on the boards.

Yes. There was a muffled thumping on the tape. That was all. Sako's
nails weren't there.

Harry squatted on the verandah. The dog sat by his feet. Sod it.
The Sanyo was obviously picky about what it would record. It could
do low but not high, dull but not sharp. So much for that experiment.
His nose shrilled again. Harry tried to ignore it.

The lawn definitely needed cutting but it was far too wet to get the
Victa out of the shed. It was seven-thirty and the grass was still heavy
with dew. Harry studied the hieroglyphic trails that he and Sako had
created when they went for their morning pee. The collie had almost
drawn a question mark but apart from that scrawl there was nothing
to decipher. Another set of marks showed how they'd gone over to the
Subaru.

Yes, there were much more important jobs to be done than lawn
mowing. Harry still had a tray of pine seedlings to plant on the edge
of his coppice. Every evening when Harry finished work at Dougal's
plantation he collected a couple of dozen two-inch trees and set them
in at home. When he reached his eightieth year there might be a bit
of a pension growing on that broken land. But the self-seeded *Pinus
radiata* would have to wait a little longer.

According to the calendar it was spring, the first day of September, but for Harry Rejekt it was Potato Day. His Red Rascals had been languishing in a cardboard box under his bed since the end of last season. Now the potatoes were sprouting nicely in the dark, in their layers of hay, and it was unlikely there would be any more frosts this side of next winter.

So, it was time to plant. Whistle. Ignore it. Nice deep furrows, spuds placed gently with their shoots upwards, then drizzle, yes, *drizzle* handfuls of good friable earth down over each individual potato making a rounded pyramid, keeping the new sprouts safe, then rake back the piled soil and wait.

By Christmas you could wriggle your fingers into the long mounded rows and bandicoot out a few firm little blushing creatures for that special dinner.

It didn't work the same with tomatoes. You planted them on Labour Day, October 25, one week exactly after Dog Whipping Day, but you'd be into January before you could make a salad with your own Sweet One Hundreds or Russian Reds.

But there was a problem. What with all the recent hard yakka in Dougal Colophon's plantation, Harry hadn't been able to get around to turning over his potato garden. He'd just finished another solid week on Dougal's pines and that meant he'd only had one break in the last fifteen days.

Though he did knock off a bit early yesterday to fix up the loan of a rotary hoe from his environmentalist mate, Thomas Wessen. Not that he'd got the machine yet. Thomas had promised to bring it around first thing in his truck but so far there was no sign of him.

'I've brought you the Katydid.' Thomas Wessen dropped the tailgate of his ute and smiled at Harry. 'Now you can work very hard.'

'Oh excellent,' Harry said. 'I'm going to get my potatoes in today.'

Harry helped his friend to lift out the scarlet machine. They put it down by the tarata hedge that lined the drive. Sako crept forward and sniffed the rotary hoe.

'It looks pretty complicated.' Harry shook his head. 'And bloody dangerous.'

'Total nonsense,' Thomas said and gave Harry the manufacturer's handbook. 'Just follow all the instructions.'

Sako wandered away. The red machine smelled of oil and petrol but it didn't have any comfortable velour seats like Harry's car.

'Have you got hearing protection and safety glasses?'

'Never go anywhere without them,' Harry said.

Thomas ran quickly through the starting procedure and how to use the machine safely.

'Don't lift it towards you when the motor's running and keep your feet out from under the tines. If it jams — stop the engine.' Thomas lifted the pickup's tailgate and slammed it closed.

'Yes, fine,' Harry told his friend. 'Er — could you do something else for me before you go?'

'If it's quick.' Thomas looked at his watch. 'I've got a conference call in half an hour. Noxious weeds.'

'It's easy,' Harry said. 'It'll only take a second. Come here and listen.'

'Listen to what, Harry?' Thomas looked towards the coppice where birds were calling and warbling. 'Those are magpies.'

'I know. I know. What I mean is — can you hear me breathing? I've got a funny . . . come a bit closer.'

Thomas Wessen laughed. 'Are you making a practical joke for me?'

'No, honestly. I woke up with this . . . with a kind of whistle in my nose but you can't hear it on a tape recorder.'

'You recorded your *nose*?'

'The *noise*, I tried to. But it wasn't there.'

Thomas leaned towards Harry. 'Okay. Big breath in. Right. Hold it. Out . . . No. Definitely there are no unusual sounds in your beak, my friend.'

Harry watched the Ford Courier until it was out of sight. Thomas Wessen made a good living as an environmental adviser. How to deal with blackberry without poisoning your land. Using gorse as a nurse plant. Which organic spray worked best on plum slug.

Harry Rejekt wished that he too could make some money by giving advice. But on what? Nasal composition for flute and oboe? Conducting intimate relationships with mythical female hitchhikers? How to become a forestry entrepreneur? Oh well — he'd be back toiling in Dougal Colophon's plantation tomorrow and that would bring him in another hundred, hundred and fifty under-the-counter dollars. So, he should get straight on with the potato garden.

The Katydid hoe actually did look like a mechanical insect. Long chrome handles with white grips rose from the business end of the machine. And it weighed about the same as a big sack of maize. Harry carried the machine from the driveway and set it down on his front lawn. He leaned against a verandah post and read the operating instructions.

There was no clutch. As soon as you pressed the throttle lever on the handle the blades would begin to churn. Suppose the accelerator cable jammed? Would the machine be powerful enough to drag you round and round the paddock until the petrol tank was dry? No. Not a chance. The hoe had an on/off switch right there by the throttle lever. You could just flick it and you killed the motor.

Right. It was time to make a start. But first he should put Sako inside the cottage and turn on the biggest radio for him. You never know. If the house were silent the dog would have his ears cocked for trouble. Sako might think that Harry was being attacked by a giant red grasshopper. So let him listen to *Morning Report*.

The engine fired with Harry's first pull and he pushed in the choke button. He wasn't wearing his ear-muffs yet. In his experience you never tried to start a two-stroke motor whilst wearing auditory protectors. With a chainsaw you absolutely *had* to hear that first cough and then you moved the choke lever one notch up, thinning the mixture. If you didn't do that you flooded the bastard and could spend the rest of the morning heating the spark plug with your Zippo, putting it back in the machine, trying again. Hopeless.

Harry let the hoe run to warm the engine before it had to exert itself. The machine ticked over very nicely and it wasn't too noisy. Sako whined from behind the orange-painted front door. Of course he could hear everything — the radio and the Katydid. Sorry boy but it's better this way. You wouldn't want to be chopped up by an enormous blender, would you? Harry put on his safety goggles and was about to settle the ear-muffs on his head.

But hang on . . . the potato patch was round the *back* of the cottage. What he ought to do was turn the machine off and carry it there. Start it up again when he was *in situ*. Though the back garden was still in shade. Harry didn't feel like moving from this sunny area.

Harry Rejekt gazed at the lush grass on his lawn. The *Magnolia*

43

stellata was almost dazzling in its whiteness and it had grown amazingly quickly. So it must be very fertile soil out here in front of the house. You could say that this area had been lying fallow for what. Eighty or a hundred years? Before that, Ngati Koroki would probably have had gardens in this place. So — you'd get an absolutely bumper crop if you tilled a few square metres of this greensward. And a vegetable patch out here would be very close and handy to the front door. The lemonwood hedge down the driveway made a bit of a shelter belt. On a late spring evening, early summer, you could sit on the verandah with a cool beer and contemplate your mounded rows. You'd admire your tomatoes and take delight in the aubergines.

Harry took a sighting on the trunk of the Cootamundra wattle. If he were going to cultivate the lawn then he was determined to cut straight furrows. Except where he had to bend around the magnolia.

Harry settled the muffs over his ears and squeezed the throttle lever. The blades rotated and sliced at the turf. He tried to push the machine forward but it jumped up and down in one place as though it had no intention of digging.

Shit! The thing wasn't working properly. The lawn was too compacted. Even with his ear-muffs on, Harry could hear Sako's frantic barking inside the house. The collie obviously thought that there was a fight to the death going on between Harry and the scarlet insect. Maybe he should quit while he was ahead.

Then, instinctively, Harry drew the machine *towards* him with the throttle open. Ah. The tines dug in. The hoe burrowed down deeply and, as Harry stepped slowly backwards, the revolving blades created a swathe of fine tilthy loam. Right! Of course there was a bit of chopped-up grass in there too but that didn't matter.

Harry lifted the Katydid carefully and turned so his back was towards the acacia. He'd have to take a sighting on where he'd come from. His orange front door would do. And he could keep glancing over his shoulder at the yellow Cootamundra. Easy as pie. He and the Katydid could make a garden out of a mown green desert.

'Yo, hoe, hoe,' Harry said and began to turn over his front lawn.

When Harry switched off the Katydid's engine the silence was like a balm and even the dog was quiet. But, Harry thought with a surge of guilt, Sako must be dying for a piss. It was long past lunch time and

Harry was starving. The poor dog had been locked inside the cottage for hours.

Harry clumped up on to the verandah and opened his front door. Sako skidded past him barking and leapt straight off the deck onto a ploughed field. The dog ran towards the rotary hoe and he barked at it furiously before crossing to his favourite rhododendron tree.

When he'd relieved himself, Sako made his way back to Harry. The dog didn't appear to have noticed anything unusual out in front of the cottage. If Harry had parked a naval frigate there, Sako would simply have run up and sniffed his way along the hull. That would have been it.

But Harry now had an immense vegetable plot and, since the verandah faced north, the potato patch would be in sun just about all day long.

Of course the garden was far too big for planting out a mere wine-box load of Red Rascal potatoes. There was room enough, in season, for sweet corn, beetroot, Mangere Pole beans and tomatoes. Yes, you could also put in capsicums and lettuce, silverbeet and rhubarb. Courgettes too. Harry had learned to cook these exotic things without turning the little marrows into a grey-green pulp. And that would still leave a huge area, Harry decided, where he could just step around lightly and broadcast carrot seed. It was all volcanic soil under what had once been his front lawn. That was all you needed really. Good earth, sunshine and a due measure of the gift of rain.

Harry Rejekt looked at the furrows that ran across his land in sinuous waves. Well, he didn't get his rows straight but they still looked like emblems of fertility to him. Later, perhaps at the end of the afternoon, and certainly when he and Sako had had something to eat, he'd get around to choosing a small special corner in this gigantic garden and there he'd plant the Red Rascal potatoes.

Harry was still lighting a fire on an evening. He sat in his brown chair and looked at the flames. Sako groaned from his Turkish rug. Harry breathed in through his mouth and exhaled through his nostrils. No. No unusual sounds. Nothing other than the faintest rush of air, a sigh of contentment.

The thing about unwelcome noises — the metronomic click on your radio when a nearby farmer has switched on an electric fence, a top-dressing aircraft droning in the distance — the thing about these annoyingly persistent and intrusive sounds is that eventually they go. They bugger off without a word. What's more, you don't even notice that they've disappeared. They're long gone before you suddenly remember that they were once there.

Oh yes — a fire on a cool spring night was a very comforting thing. Harry threw another stout log of tea-tree on the bed of glowing cinders. He watched the chunk of manuka as it caught alight. But perhaps the firewood wasn't properly seasoned because a bubbly froth lifted from the end grain and the log began to emit a high-pitched squeak.

Harry pushed in the fireplace damper and went to bed.

ROWAN METCALFE

How does an author choose a favourite? It's impossible, like choosing a favourite child. How to judge one's own work? My favourite might not be the reader's. This year's favourite might not be next year's.

But if it has to be so, then it must be one that most satisfies the writer's own criteria. The sharpest knife, the cleanest cut, the tightest knot. One that came together in concept and construction to make a complete whole. One that she can sit back and admire. Or is there always just one more word that could be changed?

'Perfume' emerged from its own first line. Within moments of typing it I realised that my main character was blind and I had to create a world without vision. Sound and smell and touch had to come out of the darkness. For me, Greg's world is mysterious and erotic and there are parts I enjoy reading again, finding they are still just right. The smells and sounds are all there. It has the sense of completeness. The edges do not fray. And it lingers like perfume.

PERFUME

H IS MOTHER CAME in late, laughing. Greg stiffened under the bedcovers, listening for more. Darkness shifted, bending under the weight. Next the fridge door and the tinkle of ice. Though he knew he must be imagining those, as there were too many walls and heavy doors in this house. They opened and closed in sequence when she was at home, kitchen, bathroom, bedroom. Solid kauri.

Sitting room. Late-night videos with her pager on the sofa arm. He wondered who it was. It could be her colleague, whom Greg thought of as Doctor John. Twin pagers. Greg suspected, was actually certain, that Doctor John was married, though she'd never said. She didn't get much chance to socialise outside of work, so it was usually Doctor John, but there'd been someone else lately, she hadn't so much as mentioned him but Greg had smelt him in the bathroom and there'd been hand-rolled butts in the sitting room ashtray. He knew it was Staffy. He slotted his phones into his ears, and reached under the pillow for the Walkman. His right hand caressed, Nirvana swelled in his blood, a frenzied beat, Kurt groaning between his ears, full of pain as always. It had never been like this with Doctor John.

In the morning she was gone. She usually was. He pressed 'Play' on the kitchen cassette machine and listened to his mother's voice. 'Hi Greg, sorry to miss you darling, early call, you were sound asleep. I bought some stuff for sandwiches, in the fridge. I'll be home to do dinner tonight.' She finished off with a smacky kiss sound. She always

48

made that smacky kiss sound at the end. He guessed she couldn't help it, she'd been doing it for so long. He felt around in the fridge and found some plastic tubs with potato salad and some sort of pickled sweetcorn and pepper and a sticky plastic bag with slices of ham. On the shelf below were two bottles of wine, one with a cork, one with a plastic champagne stopper, and the remains of a six-pack. He popped the cap off it and tasted. Staffy's favourite. He laid the food out on the table, untaped the plastic bread bag and spread out six slices. The butter was so soft it blobbed off the knife, he guessed it must be going on noon and the buttery knife reminded him of his mother and Staffy. He couldn't tell how many blobs missed the bread and got smeared on the table.

He took the plate of sandwiches out on the verandah, which was shaded until late afternoon. There was a nice southerly breeze blowing up, carrying whiffs of the city traffic and now and then a faint sniff of ocean. He thought he might get a bus downtown and go and sit near the waterfront somewhere, or he could work on his homework project which had to be in at the end of the holidays in a week's time. It was on famous blind men in history. Or listen to the two cassettes that had arrived in the post from his cousin in Sheffield yesterday. He sent him bootlegs of the newest discs and samplings off the radio stations there and in between he read out reviews from the music magazines in his weird Sheffield accent. The two cousins had never met, but Greg hoped they would one day. It seemed no distance really and sometimes with the tapes playing and his cousin's voice speaking to him in his ear he could forget they weren't right next to each other at one of the clubs or concerts he described.

Instead he heard a 737 pulling up over the harbour and across the city and thought about Staffy taking him down to the breakwater at the end of the airport runway to feel the planes coming in when he was in the third form, holding on to him in the heated roar of jet fuel, huge breakers smashing against the breakwater below their feet. Until then there'd been Ade Bignold who'd once told him that the electricity substation which emitted a continuous high-pitch hum at the end of his street was a sucker, 'a subterranean sucker' he'd said with authority, that would suck anyone in that got too close to it. He still didn't trust those things, sensing sometimes a vast labyrinthine underworld, dark like his own, peopled by dragged-in souls, people like Kurt, lost down there.

Staffy was different. Staffy had taken him out board riding in the southern swell, and had described the stars to him by punching through a big sheet of paper with a sharpened pencil then getting Greg to rub his fingertips over it. The stars had been pierced through Greg's paper night ever since, prickling at this fingertips. The Southern Cross, the Pointers, Orion's belt, even the tiny Pleiades' delicate pimples. Their texture overlaid the ceaseless creak and grind of cicadas which marked summer evenings.

His mother's garden was full of rustling leaves in all seasons, thick glossy leaves, soft furry ones, blades and needles. Not that his mother gardened any more. She got someone in once a week, a student who smoked hash among the flax and lemon trees and listened to his own walkman while he worked. Greg was apparently as invisible to him as he was to Greg. He'd rather it had been the student than Staffy. He could hear the wind stiffening in the bushes down the garden, feel the day's heat begin to stir and curdle, the traffic smells in saltier gusts. He picked up his plate and went back indoors. His mother's bedroom held the same charm it always had. She'd replaced the thick bedspread with a continental quilt, the furniture moved around now and then, there was a new chair with a silky upholstery, but the same quiet chimes hung in the breeze from an open window, and her cupboard door still slid open onto a long array of textures to run his fingers along, crêpe, velvet, crinkled cotton, lycra that stretched all ways. The fur jacket she'd worn when he was a child was exiled to the furthest end, skinned in plastic. He'd slide his fingers up under the protective sheath.

'What is it?' he'd asked her, aged six, when she came home in it one day, like a cat. He'd stroked her arms and back. There were no claws and no tail and inside it was his mother. He'd start with the jacket, still smelling of that extraordinary creature. He'd find the thing she'd worn most recently, impregnated with her essence, sometimes flung across the chair or tossed on the floor. Her nightdress hung on a hook behind the door. A long satin one today, other times a big T-shirt, in winter soft pyjamas that reeked in the crotch. Someone had been smoking in bed, his mother never did that. Doctor John never did that. The chimes twanged softly, they had always sounded as if they were telling secrets. He liked to finger her makeup, tiny cylinders and boxes with nifty catches. 'What are they for?' he'd asked.

'They make my face pretty,' she'd replied.

'What's pretty?'

A question she couldn't answer. Perfume was simple though. Pretty was what perfume looked like if you could see it. The bottle was heavy and square-cornered with a little press-down trigger. Pretty was on the air like the smell of tobacco flowers at dusk, like pressing your fingernail into a ripe fruit, like the flavour of coconut icecream but you couldn't eat it. Pretty was like a veil he was tangled up in, smelling of her.

When he went into the dairy the usual voice said, 'G'day Greg.'

He hung around near the sweet counter for a minute.

'Want an icecream?'

'Na,' said Greg and jingled his change in his pocket. Then he walked over to the magazine racks. It had been Ade Bignold that had told him what was kept on the top shelf. He reached up and ran his fingers along the folded ridges of paper. 'How do you mean, dirty?' he'd asked Ade.

'You know, chicks with nothing on, doing filthy stuff. They keep it up on the top shelf so kids can't get it.'

They were just blank sheets of paper to him. Rustling under the bushes in Ade's hideout, Ade breathing harder and harder, twigs catching in his hair, crown caps and can tabs in the grass under his bare knees.

He chose a thick, expensive feeling one with a squared off spine and took it to the counter. The guy said nothing as he rolled the magazine and slid a rubberband over it, pressed the change silently into his palm.

Later he pushed it into the satiny gap between his mother's mattress and bed base.

It was a couple of days before Staffy showed up again. A courier came with the boxed set of Nirvana singles he'd ordered and he stacked them up in the CD player and put it on continuous play. He didn't go out of the house in case he missed Staffy. When his mother came home he plugged in the phones and he didn't do anything on great blind men in history. He explored subterranean sucker land with Kurt instead. The stars were ripped from the sky like a page out of an exercise book.

'You got it then,' said Staffy as soon as he got in the door.

They went into Greg's room and listened to four of the six CDs. Staffy lay on the bed smoking roll-ups and after the fourth Greg said, 'Do you want to come into Mum's room?'

There was a moment's silence before Staffy replied. 'What for?'

'She's got this magazine.'

'Yeah?'

'It's under the mattress.'

Greg could hear him thinking about it.

'Do you want to check it out?' he offered.

'It could be, you know, a woman's magazine or something.'

'She's got this new boyfriend.'

He heard Staffy's Reeboks slide off the bed end.

He closed the door behind them. The chimes moved quietly, uttering only broken syllables. Staffy turned a few pages, slowly, then riffled through and opened it out on something, like Ade Bignold. 'Wow,' was all he said.

'What is it?' Greg asked.

'Do you think this is your old lady's?'

'It could be the new boyfriend's.'

'What's he like?'

'I don't know, she hasn't introduced me to him. What are the pictures of?'

'I thought she was going out with this other doctor for years.'

'She is. Stop holding out on me, what's the magazine?'

'You wouldn't understand it.'

'Try me.'

'It's explicit.'

'I want to see it. Describe it to me, that page you're looking at.'

'It's a woman, okay?'

'What's she doing?'

'I don't see the point of this.'

'Be my eyes. I want to see her.'

Staffy cleared his throat slightly and sighed. 'It could be frustrating for you, I warn you.'

'Just get on with it.'

'Okay. It's outdoors right, she's lying in the grass on her back, and she's gorgeous, long hair, really pretty face, not like some of them.'

'Pretty.' Greg's hand closed quietly round the perfume bottle on the dressing table. Its thick glass corners dented his palm.

'Yeah, like long eyelashes, big luscious lips, soft skin.'

'Would you say my mother was pretty?'

'Yeah.'

'As pretty as the girl in the picture?'

'Well, you know, she's older. But . . .'

'Do women get prettier as they get older?'

'Sort of. Some of them. I thought you wanted me to describe this picture to you.'

'Go on.'

'So she's lying in this garden, with her hair all spread out on the grass and she's got this sort of little top on but it's pulled up so her tits are showing.'

'Do they look pretty?'

'Yeah, but the prettiest thing is between her legs.'

He gripped the perfume bottle tightly, it seemed as big as a brick but slippery with perspiration. 'What does that look like?'

The chimes tingled in a passing breeze while Staffy considered his answer. 'Like a piece of screwed-up wet velvet,' he said at last. 'Only you want to taste it and smell it and suck it.'

He moved closer to Staffy. 'What does it taste of?' he asked.

'Like nothing you ever tasted before, like fish and flowers and wine all mixed up.'

He shifted the bottle in his hand so his finger could reach the trigger. He put his other hand on Staffy's shoulder. 'Like this?' he said as Staffy turned, and he pressed it. There was a low hiss, Staffy leapt up and pulled away, dropping the magazine, but Greg kept aiming and squirting until his mother's perfume, raw without the warmth of her body, soaked him like a gagging cloud. He kept his finger on the trigger, aiming into every corner of the room, until the bottle was empty and Staffy had fled stinking into the street shouting that he'd gone crazy. Then he tossed it on the bed and closed the bedroom door behind him.

JOHN CRANNA

I was wandering around Sicily some years ago when I came across a trio of Berliners who had about them a kind of driven fragility. As I got to know them, it struck me we shared a certain ambivalence towards the past.

I had been flatting with Maori activists in Wellington who told me that collectively amnesia afflicted white Kiwis. Germans are frequently accused of the same thing.

As I was drawn into the lives of these Germans, it became clear to me how the political history of a nation can leave its watermark in the personalities of its citizens.

HISTORY FOR BERLINERS

THE FIRST TIME I SAW Jan and Klaus they were standing naked together in a dormitory in Lipari. Jan faced the window, his arms stretched out to the sill, while Klaus rubbed scented oil into his back. They spoke to each other in rapid German, their conversation punctuated from time to time by Jan's high laughter, and seemed oblivious to the conventions of discretion and reserve that tend to be observed by strangers in hostel dormitories. It only occurred to me much later that this little scene was for the benefit of the other Germans in the dormitory, physics and geology students who had come to the islands in order to climb the volcanoes and who never appeared in anything less than their sturdy mountaineering underwear.

The previous day I had taken the ferry from Sicily with these students, straightforward, friendly men with beards and professional-looking rucksacks. There had been a slow swell on the sea and the day had been very clear, so clear that we could make out a smudge of black smoke on the horizon in the direction of the discontented Etna. At the time the papers were reporting a scheme to redirect the lava flow of the volcano through a series of controlled explosions. The students were discussing the plan, in English for my benefit, and when they had agreed that it was an ingenious notion, one of the Germans turned to me and said, 'But of course we are in Sicily. First the old men of Palermo must be certain they can make money from this plan.' It seemed appropriate, somehow, that here in their ancient homeland the influence of the Mafia extended even to the regulation of volcanic activity.

In the lee now of the island's ashy shore, we moved across a mirror sea. Behind me the Germans were gathering up their rucksacks and securing their geologists' hammers to thick leather belts. The climax of their expedition, they had told me, was to be an ascent of an active volcano on the outermost island of the group. They had brought with them an impressive amount of gear, and later, when I made my way up to the hostel through the narrow streets of the old port, the students preceded me like a train of Sherpas. I found myself feeling absurdly underequipped, as though by coming to the islands in order merely to lounge about and lie on the beach I was betraying the more serious geological obligations of the visitor to these parts.

In the morning the students rose early and either tramped into the interior of the island or caught ferries to the other islands in the group. After they had gone, I made my way down to the old port and sat with a cappuccino and a three-day-old English newspaper in a café. In order to avoid reading the newspaper, I watched an old man on the breakwater performing a mysterious operation with wine casks. Water was drained from the cask, fresh sea-water funnelled in, and a series of pebbles dropped through its bung hole. Each cask was then turned a little on its axis and wedged still against its neighbour. I had been watching this operation for half an hour, trying to decide whether it was a scientific procedure or an ancient superstitious practice, when a ferry drew in to the breakwater and unloaded its cargo of passengers. All of them, it appeared, were islanders returning from the mainland and they quickly dispersed along the waterfront, until the breakwater was empty again except for the old man and his wine casks.

At this point the two Germans from the dormitory emerged from a side street and ran down to the breakwater. When they saw the ferry, moored and empty, they stopped, looked up and down the waterfront, and hurried over to the old man filling his casks. It was plain from the old man's passivity and by the increasingly urgent gestures of the Germans that he was failing to provide them with the information they needed. Then one of the pair, the more serious-looking of the two, came across to the café to where I sat.

'Excuse me,' he said. 'We are looking for our friend. Her hair is cut like this,' he made a flat gesture across the crown of his head, 'And her eyes are not working.'

'You mean she's blind?'

'Sometimes she is blind, ja.' I thought of the steep drop from the breakwater into the harbour, but thought better of suggesting they look in the water. He continued, 'You were here when the ferry arrived?'

'I'm sure she wasn't on the ferry. I would have noticed her.'

He called in relief to his friend, who was still trying to communicate with the old man. I noticed that his friend didn't break off the encounter straight away, as though reluctant to abandon the interrogation before the old man had shown some willingness to help. When he came across to the café I was struck immediately by how absurdly good-looking he was. Dishevelled blond hair, fine high cheek-bones and the shadow of a pencil moustache — the whole effect of ambiguous Prussian beauty was underlined by a mole on his right cheek in precisely the place where an eighteenth-century lady would have worn her beauty spot.

The three of us discussed ferry times for a while, and agreed that their friend was likely to arrive on the afternoon sailing. Then Jan, the blond-haired one, said, 'Your accent . . . you're not English?'

'I'm a New Zealander.'

'So. Sir Edgar Hillary. Why then aren't you with our Bavarian friends on the side of one of the volcanoes?'

'Sometimes New Zealanders get tired of climbing mountains.' Jan laughed the high, tense laugh I had heard the night before in the dormitory; not so much, I felt, at my reply, but because of the opportunity to continue the mocking tone of the conversation.

'Perhaps you will not be too prejudiced against us,' he said. 'We are from East Berlin.' I looked at his friend, who gazed back at me as seriously as before.

'You've been very enterprising in getting to Sicily,' I said.

'So. You're suspicious because everyone knows we Communists are kept locked up behind our borders. However, the father of Klaus,' he laid his hand on his friend's shoulder as though introducing an asset of immeasurable worth, 'is an official of the Politburo of East Germany.' I looked again at his friend, at his brown, serious eyes and for an instant I saw the offspring of a dutiful high-ranking Communist. The story was implausible enough to be true. Only a month before, when hitchhiking near Turin, I had been picked up by two young Hungarians, a laconic pair who had driven their battered Skoda across the Appennines in a grip of a ferocious death wish. One was a teacher, the other a journalist. They told me that they were both members of the Hungarian Communist Party and presented me with their Party cards when I showed scepticism.

'And now,' said Jan, getting up from the café table, 'we will leave you to recover your strength, so that you may once again follow your national calling.'

'Thanks.'

'The island is not so big. The privacy of the Anglo-Saxon cannot always be guaranteed,' he added cryptically. 'Ciao!' I watched them make their way along the quay, Jan's hand on Klaus's shoulder, until they disappeared among the ochre hulls of upturned fishing boats.

In the evening I ate alone in a restaurant hung about with glass floats and fishing nets. Fastened to the walls were the remains of unnameable sea creatures, their bones gleaming in the candlelight from the tables. I had failed to charm the waiter with my crude Italian, the food was unexciting and as consolation I was nearing the bottom of a litre of red wine. I thought back over my Italian grand tour, the three months that were drawing to an end, and the images of a hundred towns unreeled themselves in my imagination, the memories of some already blurring a little . . . was it Vicenza or Cremona where I had seen a hearse run out of control in a crowded street? And the *pensione* where a tiny monkey had answered the door to guests — was that Siena or Perugia? I recalled a long train journey to Naples, of being immobilised in the aisle of a shabby carriage with the peasants taking produce to the city, wicker baskets and bundles of vegetables, white hens rocking with the movement of the train, their heads in fitted black hoods like condemned men . . . had I ever felt more free than on that train journey?

Behind me, near the door of the restaurant, I heard a commotion, voices arguing in German and then the unmistakable high laughter, a little drunken this time. I turned to see Jan threading his way among the tables. With him was Klaus, and behind them a slim woman with Slavonic features and closely cropped hair.

'Excuse us again,' said Jan. 'Please meet our friend Krista who after all did not drown in the harbour this morning.' The woman smiled a taut smile. She looked angry. Jan went on, 'Now we have the chance to celebrate this lack of a tragedy. We must buy you a drink.' Klaus, who was already drunk, but who still managed to look very serious, called the waiter over and ordered another bottle of wine.

'Una bottiglia grande,' he said with a large gesture. 'Una bottiglia rosso, alto, rotondo e profondo.'

Jan eyed him speculatively. 'When Klaus is drunk he likes to become the great Latin poet,' he said. Then, turning to me, 'We were having a small disagreement between friends. We need the views of someone who is unbiased.' Krista said something succinct in German that could have been obscene. Jan raised his hands in mock defence and grinned.

'Let me explain to you what has happened,' he said. Some time earlier the three of them have met a couple of Italians in a bar. The Italians, who appear to be very wealthy, are *en route* from Genoa to the Adriatic and their yacht is at present moored in the harbour. After an hour in the bar together the Italians excuse themselves, but invite their new friends to visit them later at the yacht, explaining that there is no shortage of room on the vessel and that they are welcome to stay overnight if they wish. It is apparent that one of the men has taken a fancy to Jan, and there is a suggestion that a little cocaine may become available.

'You see now the terrible temptations that are placed before the loyal Party member when he is abroad?' said Jan.

Krista broke in. 'So, another little joke. Let me guess that Jan has told you we are from East Berlin, perhaps also that Klaus is the son of the Party Secretary. But he has told these Italians that he and Klaus are the heirs to a West German newspaper empire and has invited them to visit him in the family villa on Lake Geneva. Unfortunately none of these things are true.'

Jan did not seem at all embarrassed by this disclosure. He spoke sadly to his wine glass.

'Krista can always bring the free spirit back to the earth when it thinks to fly too far away.' Then he looked up. 'It is good to try on other skins, don't you think?' I said that I didn't think it was too harmful. I was annoyed at myself for having believed Jan in the first place.

'We still have the problem of whether to visit these wealthy Italians and help them use up their expensive drugs,' said Jan. Krista said flatly that she was not going and Jan ordered another bottle of wine. While he was arguing over the price with the waiter, Krista told me that all three of them were students in West Berlin and that they had been coming to Lipari every summer for four years. By the time we finished the wine, Jan and Klaus had decided that they would take up the yachtsmen's invitation.

When they had gone, Krista and I faced each other a little awkwardly across the table. I asked her why Klaus seemed to get more gloomy the more he drank.

'Klaus is like that. Also he's trying to have a relationship with a girl here in Lipari. This would make anyone depressive. Even in these times the fathers of Sicily keep their daughters locked up like wild dogs.' She got up from the table. 'We must go. Soon the hostel will be closing for the night.'

The hostel lay in a Venetian fortress overlooking the bay. It was approached through a tangle of narrow streets that ran down to the harbour. At night, the streets all looked similar, and this fact, combined with the effects of the wine, made us unsure of our direction. Krista told me about her eyesight, which at present was reasonably good. She suffered from a condition which badly affected her vision during a severe attack, but whose name she did not know in English. She was explaining what brought on the attacks when I realised we were lost, and by the time we had retraced our steps and followed the correct route, the heavy doors of the hostel were closed. The institution was run by a sandy-haired Italian whose moods fluctuated according to invisible laws: when I first arrived he was exceptionally friendly; however, earlier that day he had been curt and scowling, and now as we banged on the great studded doors I was apprehensive of what we might provoke in him. In the event there was no response from inside, the hostel remained dark and silent.

Part of the grounds of the fortress were marked off as an archaeological site, and as the night was warm and still, it occurred to me that this might be the safest place to sleep.

'How do you feel about spending the night among the bones of medieval Sicilians?'

Krista shrugged. 'Dead Sicilians I don't mind so much. It's when they are alive that I have problems with them.'

I looked into the inky digging, obscurely offended on behalf of a people I had not yet got to know and among whose ancestors I was about to bed down.

'Why bother to come here at all then?'

Krista was silent, and then she said, 'The difficulties for women — Klaus's friend for example — and for myself when I was travelling, perhaps they make me too cynical.'

We made our way cautiously through a series of linked pits, until we found what appeared to be a sheltered part of the digging. We lay on our backs looking up at the opaque Mediterranean night while Krista spoke of her journey through mainland Sicily. She said that she had spent several weeks in the mountainous interior, where she had stayed in 'thirsty villages containing only doves and old men'. She described the countryside of the interior, its bluffs and barren valleys, its scattering of lemon and lime trees, fixed in their places in the harsh soil by an unrelenting sun.

It had begun to get cold, so we pressed together for warmth, and some time that night, with the accumulated history of Lipari laid bare but invisible in the darkness around us, Krista and I became lovers, although my memory of how this happened, or which of us initiated events, is not at all clear. I woke in the morning to a fine rain falling on my face. Krista lay huddled against the wall of the pit. Between us were dislodged wooden markers, and I was wondering how far we had set back local archaeological research in our blind stumblings of the night before, when Krista sat up abruptly and looked around her.

'*Scheisse*. I'm soaking with water. Why are sleeping in this stupid place?' She was looking at me with genuine anger. I wondered whether she had drunk more than I realised, and was beginning to remind her of our attempt to get into the hostel, when she got up, rubbed her eyes furiously with her fists and walked off through the site in the direction of the hostel. The sandy-haired Italian watched me without curiosity as I signed the register in a hand so damp that the violet ink ran all over the page.

I lie on a blinding pumice beach. Nothing moves and I let the light seep through to the shuttered eyeball. With my fingers I penetrate the skin of pumice until I touch the damp layer below, the first rain that has fallen on Lipari in four months, the rain that despite its warmth and lightness has apparently so upset Krista. Now, after the morning clouds have cleared, the day is very hot, and ten metres away the Tyrrhenian Sea meets the pumice in a train of benevolent slaps. I am expecting the Berliners, who have told me that because of its seclusion this beach is their favourite on the island.

Jan's laugh announces their arrival from some distance off. He is with Krista and they wave at me across the dazzling pumice. Jan looks unusually pleased with himself and Krista too seems to have cheered up since the morning.

'Good, good,' said Jan, squatting beside me and inspecting me approvingly. 'You are getting some colour on your sad pale body.' With the deft movements of practised sunbathers, Jan and Krista took off their clothes, folded them carefully and stretched out naked beside me. Jan settled into the pumice and let out a contented sigh.

'It is only the sun that can purify the body after the sins of the night,' he said.

After an appropriate pause, I asked, 'How were the Italians?'

'The Italians were very interesting. If all the people of Genoa are like these Italians then Genoa must be a very decadent place. Perhaps next year I will go to visit this city and its wonderful people.'

'First, however, you must entertain them at your villa on Lake Geneva,' said Krista.

Jan laughed his brilliant laugh. 'You're right, honey. First I must do that.' He took out a tube of lotion and began to rub the almond-scented liquid into his skin.

'For Klaus, the night was not so good,' he said. 'Klaus is drinking to forget the girl who is shut away from him in the evenings. After a little more wine, Klaus became very excited and made his big speech about the barbarian fathers of Italy, using much foul language. Fortunately when Klaus is excited his Italian is not so good, and I think our hosts did not fully understand this speech. However, they understand when he lies down on the floor of their expensive yacht and vomits his stomach into their carpet.'

'And after all this, they still believed you were the sons of a wealthy publishing family?' I asked.

'But of course,' said Jan seriously. 'This is absolutely correct behaviour for the sons of wealthy newspaper families.'

Krista pulled a face. 'It's also absolutely normal behaviour for Klaus,' she said. She got up and picked her way gingerly across the hot pumice to the sea. She stood in the shallows with the water lapping around her ankles.

Jan called to her. 'Honey, your string is hanging down.' Krista half turned towards us, looked down and then tucked her tampon string up between her legs. Jan went on, 'And if you go into the water leaking out blood you will attract all the sharks of Africa to this beach.'

Krista picked up a piece of pumice from the shoreline and threw it at him, the way boys are taught to throw, with a flick of the whole arm. Although the projectile had been aimed casually, it only narrowly missed Jan's head. Then Krista waded into the water and swam out into the bay with flat, even strokes. I told Jan that I thought he deserved to have been hit. He gave me a mocking smile.

'But you are such a gentleman.' He propped himself up on one elbow. 'You see, Krista and I have known each other for a very long time, since we were twelve years old in fact. At that time we made some sexual experiments with each other. However, these experiments were not so successful . . .' He trailed off, and for a moment I thought he was expecting me to offer my commiserations. 'Since this time we have been very close,' he continued. 'But we no longer allow sex to make any complications in our relationship.'

I lay on my back, absorbing the heat from the pumice, trying to imagine the desultory coupling of twelve-year-olds in that distant grey city, trying to picture Jan and Krista growing up in a place that existed for me only as a collection of newsreel images, and I felt an irrational wave of depression at the unimaginable difference of our childhoods.

Jan was saying, '. . . when Krista's eyesight began to cause problems, some very sensitive doctors told her that she could be starting to go blind. This is a particularly stupid thing to tell an angry person of sixteen years old. On this occasion, Krista also did something very stupid . . .' He trailed off again, as though concerned that he was being indiscreet, then said abruptly, 'Berlin in the winter is a city with great dangers for the soul.'

Krista was swimming back from the headland towards the beach. Several times, involuntarily, I caught myself searching the bay for moving shadows beneath the surface.

'This is our fourth year of coming to Lipari,' Jan said. 'We have some kind of *affaire* with this island, Klaus, Krista and myself. Perhaps it is the strange *affaire* of Germany and Italy, which has been going on for a long time now. In the winter of Berlin I dream of lying on this beach and watching Krista swimming in the green water, and of arguing with Klaus about his crazy lusting for the girl who is locked away.'

'Klaus has been after the same girl all this time?'

Jan nodded. 'Each year it is the same. Sometimes I think that Klaus was born to be the sadist to himself.' He looked down at his own perfectly tanned body and frowned, as though baffled by the sheer perversity of Klaus's obsession. 'I tell him to lust instead for the Italian boys, who are not locked away at all.'

Krista had come up from the water and was standing beside us, drying her shock of blond hair and listening to our conversation. Her laugh was muffled by the towel.

'And when you and this wealthy yachtsman from Genoa are lusting for each other, what is his friend the other yachtsman doing?' she said.

Jan smiled. 'He's getting a little jealous, perhaps. However, he is much older, and some of his hairs are falling out, so he must be careful not to drive his friend away into the arms of some beautiful young man.'

'Like yourself, perhaps,' said Krista.

'Honey, you are very kind.'

In the evening the three of us went to the bar where Jan had first met the Italians. A little while later they walked in, dressed in immaculate white and with cashmere sweaters knotted causally about their necks. The younger of the two, Fabio, a languid youth with long eyelashes and an easy laugh, quickly joined Jan in the joking conversation concerning Klaus's misadventures on the yacht. Jan explained with transparent condescension that Klaus was out on another of his doomed missions at that very moment. Krista and I, who had avoided saying anything significant to each other all day, sipped vermouths and listened to the conversation. The Italians seemed charmingly straightforward and I wondered whether the decadence that Jan had spoken of was another of his compulsive inventions.

Eneri, a well-preserved man with the manner of a successful

academic (he appeared to be Fabio's senior by at least fifteen years), even gave the impression of being progressive in his politics. As the evening wore on he spent some time explaining the tenacity of the Mafia in Sicily in terms of the protection given it by the right-wing political establishment. Jan, who was still playing up to his role as scion of the West German ruling classes, and who in any case was in competition with Eneri for the affections of his young friend, disagreed with his analysis, at first quite politely and then, when Eneri persisted, with a passion that became almost comical. It was undeniable, Jan declared, that the only serious threat to the Mafia had been during the Mussolini years, when Il Duce's man in Palermo had been unafraid to treat the families with proper savagery, to the point of throwing the wives and children of prominent Mafiosi into jail.

Eneri said mildly that the years of fascism had been a special case and that he had been speaking of the political establishment since the war.

Jan gripped his glass and sat up straight in his chair. 'So you think that fascism was a special case in the history of your country. This is also what Germans would like to believe . . .' Krista laid a hand on his arm. She spoke to the Italians as though excusing the behaviour of a brilliant child.

'Jan is an enthusiastic student of these matters, and it's dangerous to start on such discussions with him. Unless of course you're keen to hear about the whole of your history since the time of Garibaldi.'

Eneri said that he would be very interested to hear such an account of Italy's history, but perhaps, yes, it would be better to leave it for another occasion. Jan was not going to be deterred so easily. His pupils seemed unnaturally dilated and he spoke very fast.

'Perhaps you believe it's better that we push these things into a dark corner of the mind. Of course the Germans and Italians are afraid to look too hard at this part of their history. We like to think that the fascists were just very clever men who fooled the people with their brilliant propaganda.'

I said, 'Surely that's partly tr . . .'

Jan cut in. 'It is a lie. Fascism grew up within the culture of the nation. Our parents and grandparents have spent forty years trying to pretend this is not so. They prefer to believe that they were fooled by the evil genius of Goebbels and Hitler. Until they accept that they were guilty, the soul of Germany will stay with its poison.'

Fabio, who had given the appearance of being bored by the conversation, carefully inspected his fingernails and said that this might be true of Germany, but he did not think it was true of Italy. I was surprised by Jan's outburst, and it had clearly not endeared him to the Italians, who not long afterwards made their excuses and wandered off.

We sat at the bar in silence for some time. And then Jan said, 'This may be the last we see of the wealthy yachtsmen from Genoa.'

I ordered Jan another drink and Krista said, 'Think of the difficulties if you had fallen in love with Fabio.'

'Perhaps I have already fallen in love with Fabio,' said Jan with unconvincing defiance.

Krista linked her arm in mine. 'And perhaps I have fallen in love too.'

Jan looked from one to the other of us, visibly shocked. 'Is this true?'

'Of course it's not true. We have only known each other for a day or so.'

Jan smiled a wan smile, but he had already begun to look more cheerful. 'Honey, you should not play jokes at such moments.'

Krista and I spent a lot of time together in the next few days, although our previous intimacy was not discussed. We went on long walks on the deserted coastal roads, we passed the pumice quarries on the northern end of the island, their monolithic hoppers, mobile gantries and vaulted conveyer chains functioning without any sign of human intervention. A pall of white pumice dust hung over this end of the island, as though the land was throwing up a veil in order to decently obscure the violence being done to its geological heart. Often we walked in silence, intruders in a scene of studied monochrome, the sky empty of birds and the sea leaden and subdued.

In this part of the island, autumn in northern Europe did not seem so far away, and Krista talked of her return to Berlin, of the claustrophobia that overcame the city in winter, and of the deterioration of her eyesight that followed the cold.

'The problem with Berlin,' she said, 'is that there is no escape from the past. When Jan says the Germans refuse to look at their history, he's correct, but in Berlin itself we have the opposite problem.

Everywhere we go we encounter the past — in the form of a snake of concrete that runs through our city. So Berlin also has its sickness. Too much of this past is as bad as too little.'

We had come to a headland at the end of the island and the path we had been following ended suddenly before a long drop to the sea. I said to Krista that in Polynesia such places were considered to be stepping-off points for spirits on their way to the underworld. We looked over the sea to the spectral shapes of the outlying islands and I considered the idea that this anonymous piece of ocean was eventually continuous with the vivid Pacific.

Krista said, 'You're very lucky to come from a country which is too young to have the problems of Germany.'

'We have our own nightmares from the past,' I said. 'A country as far from anywhere as mine finds it easier to keep these nightmares secret.'

'I think these are quite small nightmares, in comparison.' Krista was standing near the edge of the bluff watching a boat at the base of the rocks. Far below, two men were lifting lobster pots from the sea. She moved a little closer to the edge, perhaps to obtain a better view of the fishermen.

'I like your story of departing spirits,' she said. 'As a spirit I would feel privileged to leave from this point.'

She was at the very edge of the cliff now, and she raised a finger to her lips as though listening for the sighs of departing wraiths. But it was very quiet up there on the bluff, and the only sound that broke the silence was the disembodied slap of oars from the base of the rocks.

Krista stepped back from the edge, threw her arms around my neck and cried, 'Today the spirits are staying at home!'

Making love in the white dust of an abandoned valley, Krista talked of the spirits she had listened to the last time we had been together, spirits that hummed in the chambers of the digging below the fortress. She told me she had stayed awake half that night while the history of the place had risen up around us in the dark. Now, moving together in the white dust, she talked of Arabs and Venetians, invaders who had come to the islands across the millennia, who had settled and died here, and whose bodies now fertilised the earth beneath us.

Fucking and talking like this, she said, was a medicine, but when I whispered, 'For what sickness?' she wouldn't answer me. Wraiths ourselves, with the pumice dust sticking to our skins, we followed the valley to a beach and washed it away in the dull sea.

Later, in a crowded café in the main town, Krista covered her eyes with a hand and spoke softly to herself in German. When I asked her what was wrong, she answered irritably, still in German, and wouldn't explain further. Jan and Klaus were consoling themselves with drink that evening, Klaus for the usual reasons, and Jan in preparation for the departure of his yachtsmen, who had been seen preparing their vessel for sailing. We sat on the terrace of a bar that overlooked the main harbour, while Jan and Klaus sang sentimental German folk-songs and we drank from the neck of a bottle of grappa.

'By next summer,' said Klaus, his voice thick with the grappa, 'I think this barbarian father will have forced his daughter to marry a Sicilian boy.'

Jan put an arm round his shoulders. 'This is very serious. We must look for another girl immediately. Without this lusting it is impossible to imagine a proper summer on Lipari.' Klaus shook his head and muttered that this girl was irreplaceable, he would go mad before he could forget her . . .

Jan passed me the grappa. 'You see now the optimism of the true native of Berlin.' I asked Klaus whether he had considered running away with the girl. He peered at me, bleary-eyed.

'That is out of the question,' he said with bleak finality.

Jan said, 'The barbarian father might arrange for the Mafia to search out the fleeing couple.' He seemed to savour the sheer infamy of the idea. Since the argument with the yachtsmen, speculation on the influence of the Mafia had been a regular feature of conversation. We spent some time discussing elaborate plans for releasing the girl from captivity and ruses for throwing the Mafia off the trail.

At last Klaus broke in. 'This is quite stupid. She would never agree to such crazy ideas.'

Krista shrugged. 'Then perhaps you're wasting your time with this girl.'

'However, we can't just abandon her to the savage father,' said Jan.

'If she won't consider escape,' said Krista, 'perhaps she's not so keen on this romance as you believe.'

Jan eyed her reproachfully. 'Honey, that is most unkind.'

Krista shrugged again. 'Perhaps it's time for Klaus to wake up from his dream.' Suddenly she sounded very angry. 'Perhaps it's time for all of us to wake up. Fantasies about the character of the Latins. Dreams of the beautiful Italians who can save us from ourselves. Is this how we are going to spend the rest of our lives?'

Jan bit his lip. 'So. Everything is clear. Italy is no longer good for us. The playing ground has been closed off. Next summer we will all make love to New Zealanders.' In an attempt to retrieve the situation, I tried a feeble joke.

'I'm afraid we only make love above certain altitudes.' But Jan and Krista were no longer listening.

'Why do we come here year after year?' said Krista. 'So we can gaze at the Italians and pretend to have exotic romances? Unfortunately these romances are always dead before they are born.'

Jan sat rigid in his chair. 'And of course you will be able to tell us why this is the case.'

Krista slammed her glass down on the table, her face suddenly ugly with despair.

'Are you so stupid that you can't see if for yourself?' Her movement had upset the bottle of grappa, and now it spun across the table and shattered on the tiles at our feet. We sat there immobilised, while the creamy dusk descended over the sea and settled among the cane tables and chairs of the bar. And then Krista was on her feet and away down the path from the terrace, while the rest of us sat and watched the dregs of the grappa disappear between the black and white tiles.

I looked for Krista at the hostel and at the bars in town. Then I checked the port area and the arms of the piers enclosing the harbour. I took the road along the coast, pausing to check the beach where we had gone to sunbathe. At dusk this part of the island was even more desolate and at intervals along the road, like the desiccated victims of a drought, stood the spindly shapes of prickly pears. Now I was half walking, half running. I passed the valley where we had made love in the white dust of pumice, past the remains of a boat beached far beyond the shoreline by an invisible hand, until eventually I approached the headland at the end of the island.

I could imagine now the sighs of wraiths, the whispers converging in a susurration that thickened the dusk. Krista's Arabs and Venetians, the foreigners who had voyaged to these islands down the ages, and whose histories of colonisation and death had returned to obsess her . . . I heard them as they rose on the air and flooded out towards that high point overlooking the sea. I was caught up among them now myself, impelled towards the headland on a tide of whispers that had taken on the strength of a steady breeze. I ran up the path that led from the road to the bluff and cast around in the half darkness. There was no sign of Krista. I called into the dusk, but my voice was snatched away by the eddies that moved swiftly over the headland. At the edge of the bluff I looked down to where the ocean sucked and drew on the rocks . . . but the light was fading now and the jumble of granite withdrew into the gloom. I stood there on the top of the bluff while a dark wind carrying the memories of Krista's labyrinthine fears blew past me on its way out to the horizon.

When the sea had turned black, I walked down the path to the road. The air was still, the whispers had faded with the light, and I walked in a cocoon of silence along the road towards the lights of the town. The effects of the grappa had worn off, and I felt dull and stripped of emotion. I passed the moonscape of the pumice quarries, their stark architecture pitched up against the night sky. Whatever happened, I knew that my time in Italy was over, and that I would leave the islands as soon as possible.

Krista was sitting on a sand-dune near the road, and I would have missed her in the gloom if she hadn't called out as I went by. Her voice seemed unnaturally loud. She said that she had been on her way to the headland when her eyesight and the failing light had prevented her from going on. She had watched me pass from the dunes above the beach. I had looked very grim, she said, and smiled. I stood there for a while in silence, thinking of the headland at dusk, and of the metallic sea that stretched away to the coast of Africa. Then she held out a hand, and I pulled her to her feet. 'Why don't you come and stay in Berlin for a while?' she said.

We walked arm in arm towards the lights of the town, while images from an old newsreel turned in my mind: women cleaning bricks among blackened churches, the Reichstag against a white sky . . . barbed wire, airlifts and the sluggish river Spree.

CHRISTINE JOHNSTON

Writing about childhood is always a challenge. More than ever the writer is working to make something utterly contrived appear effortless and 'natural', trying to capture a convincing child's voice and world view, but necessarily sifting and reshaping the experiences according to (adult) artistic criteria.

I wanted to re-enter the claustrophobic childhood world, where sibling rivalry and parental disapproval assume monumental proportions, and to reveal that world, not through the eyes of the so-called 'sensitive' child, but using as a narrator the blunt and down-to-earth Caroline. She is a child who makes adults feel uncomfortable, and I wanted some of this dis-ease to affect the reader.

Focusing on childhood brought all sorts of strange memories to the surface — X-ray machines in shoe shops, the prejudice against minced beef, the practice of dropping a key down someone's back to stop a nose bleed. What was commonplace and unquestioned then seems bizarre and hilarious now.

I chose this story because I have real affection for Caroline and admiration for her stoicism and insight. Her family is not my family, but seems familiar. Her childhood is not mine but runs parallel.

FUNERAL SHOES

BUNTY BRAITHWAITE WAS ON her way to the Dainty Dairy to buy gobstoppers, when she was hit by a Griffins biscuit truck. They said she had a handful of coins that she managed to hold on to even in death. Thereafter, though not before, my mother called her 'Caroline's little friend', and I didn't contradict her.

Bunty's classmates formed a guard of honour at her funeral. We sang 'Away in a Manger', which, although seasonal, was not especially appropriate. We knew it well, and we sang if not lustily, then at least tunefully, for we were well drilled. Even so, our voices sounded feeble in the open air. Some of the girls wept. One boy uttered a strange cry which could have been a sob, a hiccup or even a laugh. No one was sure.

That was my first funeral. I didn't know when the next would be, but I had encountered death. I saw for the first time that, although we stride purposefully through life, the potential for death is all around us. The biscuit truck is never far away.

I lived with my parents and my brother in an old house which had once been a grocer's shop. Although it lacked a front garden, there was a generous area at the back with several outhouses. The bedrooms were upstairs, mine overlooking the back yard with its strip of lawn, flanked by gooseberry and blackcurrant bushes. I attended the local convent school and had made my First Communion.

My maternal grandparents, Nana and Pop McGrath, lived a few streets away. Old but fit, they had grown to resemble each other. When Tom was younger he had called them individually and jointly

'Nananpop', as if they were two sides of the one coin.

They gripped you firmly and delivered brisk, dry kisses. They would lead you into their immaculate garden, to pull radishes and baby carrots. Nana shook the soil from the vegetables, and Pop wiped them on his sleeve before popping them into your mouth. You tried to ignore the grit which sounded like gravel between your teeth. A scarecrow leaned jauntily over their vegetable patch, wearing a pyjama top of Pop's, an old straw hat of Nana's, and a pair of her slacks. Their house was modest, simply furnished, clean, but not excessively so. In their later years all their energies were directed towards the garden.

When Nana became ill and Pop was looking after her, their vegetables went to seed. My brother and I were sent out to pick peas, while the grown-ups had a conference, but there were none to be found. Unwatered, their plants had yellowed and died. Only the pumpkins thrived, claiming the whole vegetable patch, even sprawling over the concrete path. We came back too soon, to hear the adults arguing. My father, a reasonable man, was in favour of hospital. Pop was sobbing that Nana wanted to die at home.

'Not in front of the children,' my mother exclaimed when she saw us in the doorway.

Nana, who had heard the argument got out of bed and came into the kitchen, wearing pyjamas. Her large, veined feet were bare, her hair unkempt, her face yellow. She looked uncannily like the scarecrow as she leaned on the kitchen bench.

'I'd love a cuppa,' she said.

The adults tried to persuade her to return to bed, but she refused, and my mother set about making tea. Nana sat on a kitchen chair and ordered Tom and me to stand on either side of her. Her long arms encircled us; her hands, softened by weeks of illness, stroked our skin. I looked down at her feet with their extraordinary reptilian toenails. She was already becoming unrecognisable. Breathing heavily, she didn't speak. No one spoke, and the clock on the wall ticked loudly. On the other side of the table Pop was blowing his nose. My father put his hand on Pop's shoulder.

'Whatever you want,' he said.

Later my brother said, 'Nana isn't going to die.' He kept saying it. My parents turned their faces away, so that he couldn't read their dismay. They said, 'Well, no, maybe not. We hope not.'

When he said it to me, I replied, 'Yes, she is,' and he said, 'No, she's not,' and I repeated, 'Yes, she is.' He started crying and went to find Mum. I called him a baby and a sissy. I found it contemptible, this denial of death. I knew already. About Bunty Braithwaite. About the biscuit truck. I knew it could happen. The thing that happened to birds and mice and Mrs Law's old spaniel, also happened to people. Even Nana McGrath. Especially Nana McGrath, now that she was turning into the scarecrow.

Mum slapped me for making my brother cry. I knew they preferred Tom. They said he was a sensitive little boy. He was also better-looking. My mother's friends exclaimed over his beautiful hair and his long eyelashes. They put a lot of store by long eyelashes in a boy. I knew that in the normal course of events they should be exclaiming over me. I was the *girl*, after all.

We got new shoes for the funeral. Purchased in haste, they didn't fit for long, but while they lasted I thought of them as my funeral shoes. The shoe shop had an X-ray machine you could look inside to see the bones of your feet, though it was hard to accept that those bones were really yours. I thought my X-ray feet looked like Nana McGrath's, but I knew better than to point this out to my mother.

It was winter by then and bitterly cold. I remember how my new shoes stomped the fresh hail on the cemetery path. Mum's heels kept sinking into the damp lawn and the mud clung to them, but she hardly noticed. She and Pop, leaning on each other, wept without restraint. For the first time I saw my father cry. I cried too, and I noted that it endeared me to people. Aunty Jean held me tight and almost smothered me with her bosom.

After the funeral people filled our house to overflowing. There was a lot of drinking. Pop's large hand cradled a tiny glass into which people kept pouring whisky. I hated the smell of it. The women brought date loaves. I never saw so many date loaves in one place, before or since. When the caterers came with trays of hot sausage rolls, Tom and I filled our pockets. At my suggestion we went out into the washhouse and stuffed ourselves.

'Nana will go to heaven,' said Tom.

'Yes, I said, but *you* won't.'

He started crying. I told him to stop and pinched his thigh. He cried all the more.

'I hate you, Caroline,' he said.

That made me think about Bunty Braithwaite. Those had been her last words to me; and mine to her had been in similar vein. The next day she was silenced by the Griffins biscuit truck.

'I'm sorry,' I said.

'No, you're not.'

'Yes, I am.'

'No, you're not.'

To prove it I pinched him again. It was too easy to torment Tom — he wouldn't put up a fight. The door opened and Mum came in.

'There you are! What are you doing in here, you two?'

'Tom's been crying,' I said compassionately, my pinching hand now stroking his tousled curls.

'Will I go to heaven, Mum?' he asked.

'Yes, darling.'

'He'll have to go to Purgatory first,' I chipped in.

'You must be famished, you poor darlings,' said Mum, giving us a cuddle. She was softened by whisky. 'Come on, I've saved you some sausage rolls.'

The passage was choked with people. Pop was being lead upstairs, but he kept declaiming to those below — something about a marriage made in heaven and everyone was agreeing with him. He saw me and called my name.

I knew that Pop liked me. He would wink at me and call me 'a hard case'. With Tom he used a gruff voice and manner, and although they engaged in play fights, Pop could not conceal his irritation at Tom's timidity. I suspected that Pop, alone among my extended family, preferred me to Tom.

I went to him on the landing and he hugged me roughly, his prickly face scouring mine. Then he began singing in a trembly cracked voice: 'Nothing could be finer than to be in Carolina in the morning.' This play on my name was our private joke. I joined in. 'No one could be sweeter than my sweetie when I meet her . . .'

Suddenly everyone around was silent and the only voice to be heard was mine. Pop's face was crumpling, his mouth twitching and his eyes streaming. My cheeks were burning, but I kept on going: 'If

I had Aladdin's lamp for only a day . . .' When I finished, everyone clapped and my uncle hauled him off to bed.

That night as I lay awake, listening to the grown-ups downstairs becoming louder and more intoxicated, it came to me that Pop McGrath would also die, and soon. The idea took my breath away. They were such a pair, Nananpop. I knew that he could not live without her, and that he no longer wanted to. 'Nothing could be finer than to be in Carolina . . .' I knew what that meant.

I got up and went into Tom's room where a bed had been made up for Pop. Both of them were sound asleep. Tom had kicked off his covers and lay with his face in the pillow. Pop slept on his back, snoring softly, his arms folded on his chest. I smelt the whisky smell. I thought about the biscuit truck. Once you died there was no come-back. You could be in Heaven, or Purgatory, or wherever, but you were, to all intents and purposes, out of circulation. Tom would never understand about death, I thought, looking down on his angelic features. Death was too tough and uncompromising a concept for my little brother. At that particular moment it was almost too much for *me* to bear.

I went back to bed and lay awake in the dark. Downstairs they were singing, 'Danny Boy, the pipes, the pipes are calling.' I thought about Bunty. I could conjure up her round face with its scattering of freckles, her little green eyes, her pale eyebrows and lashes, her orange hair. I could recall the touch of her hand, how it could linger caressingly as it sought the optimum place on your thigh for a horse-bite. Her nails were bitten down but she could pinch long and hard. When she sensed victory she smiled, showing oversized new teeth, while her cheeks inflated and her eyes became slits.

I had called her every bad name I knew — 'fat-face', 'freckle-face', 'slit-eyes', 'ginger', 'carrots', 'fatty', 'shorty', 'piggy', 'bitch'. I had said that she was an orphan, that she was adopted, that her father was in jail, that her mother was in the loony bin, although I knew that none of it was true. She had said that my father put his hands down the toilet, and that he smelt like shit. (He was a plumber.) She told my friends that my brother wet the bed. (I wondered how she knew.) She had taken my pencilcase and broken all my new pencils. I had kicked her shoe down the bank and into a slimy ditch. She had thrown my beret up into a tree. I had stomped on her school bag and squashed her sandwiches.

Bunty Braithwaite was my enemy. She hated me and wanted me to suffer, and I felt the same way about her. The boys loved to see us fight and would wind us up. The girls waited to betray us to the nuns. 'I'm telling,' one would cry and run off. That was the only thing that deflected us. We turned our backs on each other and walked away. Until the next time.

But Bunty was dead, most likely in Purgatory, I thought kindly, though Hell seemed entirely justified. At her funeral there had been talk of her going straight into the arms of Jesus. How ignorant they were. Wherever her soul was, she was dead, and I had no reason to fear her lurking in the cloakroom. Nor would she be waiting with her cronies to waylay me on the walk home. I no longer dreaded spelling tests in which my superior results would prove a provocation to Bunty. Bunty was dead and death was permanent. (Of course, on the Last Day we would all rise again to be judged, but that prospect seemed comfortably far off.)

After Bunty's death something was missing in my life. My mortal enemy was gone, but I knew what it was like to be hated, and to hate. When my mother referred to Bunty Braithwaite in sugared tones as 'Caroline's little friend', I was silent. When others spoke of 'poor little Bunty', I composed my face solemnly, saying nothing.

Tom was to start school. While my parents told him how much he would enjoy it, I held my tongue. I had two months to toughen him up. He was not really interested, but I locked the washhouse and put the key beyond his reach. Whenever our mother went out and left us in the care of our father, I took advantage of the lack of vigilance. (Dad only vaguely kept an eye on us while he set about fixing things.)

Tom's first lesson involved not crying. I administered some mild tortures and offered bribes if he could hold back the tears. Although he was pretty hopeless to start with, he gradually improved. I exaggerated the humiliations in store for sissies. (At least I *thought* I did. I learnt subsequently that the practice of dunking in the toilet bowl was *not* my fiction.) I showed him how to pinch and give horse-bites and Chinese burns. That was all right for girls, but he needed more. He had to learn how to make a fist and punch. He resisted but I was staunch. He had no one to practise on but me.

One afternoon when Mum was out and Dad was up a ladder cleaning out the gutters, Tom was genuinely roused to anger, probably for the first time ever, and punched me on the nose. We both heard the crack. He turned terribly pale seeing the bright red blood gushing forth, colouring my blouse. I thought he was going to faint, but he overcame the urge. I grabbed a towel, one of the tatty ones Mum kept in the washhouse. I couldn't speak. The pain was extraordinary. The blood was out of control.

At that very moment my father's face appeared at the window.

'What's going on in there? Open up, Caroline.'

Then he saw me and tugged on the door handle.

'Unlock the door! What the hell are you up to?'

Tom started to cry. I felt that I should be pinching him to make him stop but I had my hands full. Dad quickly found a spare key. (We were an organised family, ready for all emergencies.) When the door opened, Tom fled sobbing. My father wanted to pursue him, but the sight of my blood stopped him in his tracks.

'What have you done to yourself, Caroline?'

It was clearly inconceivable that *Tom* might have inflicted the injury on me. Dad set about dealing with my bleeding nose. There were several different approaches and he tried them all, except applying pressure to the bridge of the nose which I would not allow. He sat me on a chair, while the blood rained into a bucket on my knee. The plumber in him rebelled against that, and he lay me down on my back — on the lawn mercifully — with a cold face-cloth on my forehead. After ten minutes I vomited a stomachful of blood. Then he dropped a key down my back. (Even *I* could tell that wouldn't work.) He was worried about Tom who had not reappeared, and so was I.

When Mum arrived home, Dad immediately went out, returning for a torch as it was getting dark. I was suddenly fearful of biscuit trucks. I could imagine Tom, blinded by tears, running under their wheels. If only he wasn't such a crybaby. I reasoned that if I had taught him anything, he would survive.

Hours passed and my mother became desperate. She berated me for driving him away. She called me an 'unnatural' sister. Though the bleeding had stopped, I continued my silence. She went out into the back yard to make a bargain with God. Tom heard her prayer and emerged from the blackcurrants. In the shaft of light from the kitchen door I saw how she knelt on the lawn and opened her arms for him. In spite of myself I was moved.

Tom lacked the guile to lie, but my parents could not believe that he had broken my nose.

'I was teaching him to fight,' I said, my first communication since the event.

They turned to Tom for confirmation.

'I can punch now,' he said, quietly proud.

They stared at him and shook their heads. He was their lamb who had been lost and was found. They looked at me and smelt deceit. Yet I was the one bloodied and broken.

My parents were worried about Pop McGrath who was said to be going downhill. When we had him over for meals, he complained about the food, pouring scorn on Mum's savoury mince.

'Did you get this out of a tin?' he asked.

Mum's face went bright red, but she controlled herself. I had never before encountered an adult who didn't leave a clean plate. When we visited him my mother tried to bundle up Nana's things, but he wouldn't allow it. He was grumpy and sour. He said I had a voice like a foghorn. He said Tom was tied to his mother's apron strings. He told Mum to run along home and do her own housework. He sat unshaven in the mess and the muddle of the kitchen with tea stains on his shirt. Something about his eyes was different. They were watery but devoid of sparkle. Moving his false teeth around with his tongue, he created a grotesque mask of his face, so that Tom was overcome with fear and wet himself.

I tried singing 'Nothing could be finer . . .' but it didn't work. He brought his big fist down on the table, making all the dirty cups and saucers and glasses jump.

'Cut the racket, girlie,' he bellowed.

Amazingly Mum ignored the puddle of pee. She moved very slowly, signalling us to go outside by pointing at the door. Even as we closed the door we could hear her going crook. 'You should be ashamed of yourself, raising your voice to a wee girl who was just trying . . .'

I wondered for a second who she meant before realising it was me. I wasn't used to hearing myself referred to in this way, and I didn't consider myself to be a *wee* girl. Tom was wee. I was big.

We went to the far corner of the garden, a jungle by then, and sat on the concrete wall. Tom was shaken, but he didn't cry. He shuddered every now and again. I held his hand for a while, but he stank of urine and I moved away.

Mum hardly paused for breath. We heard 'filthy, disgusting state of the kitchen'. We heard 'wallowing in self-pity . . .' and we heard 'Mum must be turning in her grave . . .' (I found this last remark appalling.) Mum's voice rose in pitch and in decibels. We heard 'What about me?' And 'I've lost my darling mother, while you, you, you . . .' We heard sobbing.

Tom was upset and started kicking the concrete wall.

'You'll wreck your funeral shoes,' I said. He didn't seem to care.

I discovered some convolvulus climbing over the fence from next door and showed him the 'granny-pop-out-of-bed' thing. He didn't get it. He kept asking why and how and where is the granny. I gave up.

After hours and hours Mum appeared and led us back into Pop's house. The puddle of pee had gone. The table was cleared and all the dirty dishes washed. Pop had changed his shirt and was putting the vacuum cleaner away. He greeted us with a forced heartiness.

'How are the best kids in the world? Come and give your grumpy old Pop a hug.'

He hugged us and whispered 'Sorry' in our ears. I noticed his hands were shaking. Pale and red-eyed, Mum stood back with a tight smile on her face.

'We'll be off now, Pop. See you tonight.'

Mum had told him off, but she wasn't pleased with herself. She cried later when she was telling Dad. When Pop came for tea he was terribly jolly to start with, but soon fell silent. He ate everything on his plate and went home early.

'It's knocked the stuffing out of him,' Dad said.

The next week it was Nana's birthday and everyone remembered that she was dead, and cried again. Then it was their wedding anniversary, which Mum said would have been a golden wedding. More tears.

Pop tidied up his garden and planted some scarlet runners, but his heart wasn't in it. He said he wouldn't bother with much else, but

Mum kept giving him plants to fill up the vegetable patch. Dad suggested a glasshouse, but Pop shook his head. Too much work, he said. He got tired and was reluctant to come over for meals. Mum made pies and stews and delivered them. She became frantic, cooking and cleaning at home and doing the same at Pop's. When Tom wet the bed she smacked him and made him wash his sheets.

'You're not to help him, Caroline,' she decreed, but I did.

I went to visit Pop after school. The house smelt of bacon and burnt toast. He was sitting at the table going through the photo albums. He showed me a group of smiling soldiers with bottles of beer. One of them was Pop.

'Where are you, Pop?'

'In France, girlie.'

His finger touched the faces of three of the men.

'All dead,' he said. 'Blown to smithereens.'

I looked at the soldiers who had died, at their wide smiles, their exuberant gestures with cigarettes and beer. I suddenly had the urge to confess to Pop my true feelings for Bunty Braithwaite.

'Bunty died,' I began, leaning on his shoulder. 'She was run over.'

'Yep,' said Pop, closing the album. 'The biscuit truck. And were you sad?'

I hesitated. 'No,' I said at last.

He looked at me for a long time. My heart was thumping and I thought he might tell me off, but he just nodded and put his big hand on mine.

'You're a tough customer, Carolina,' he said. 'Just like your Nana.'

That sounded like praise.

'Pop, remember the scarecrow? What happened to it?'

'The scarecrow? It just fell over and rotted.'

'Rotted?'

'Yeah. When I found it the weeds were growing through it.'

'But the clothes, Pop? It had clothes and everything.'

I started crying. I didn't know why I was crying for the scarecrow. I was convulsed by huge hiccuping sobs. Pop put his hand on my head.

'Caroline. What's wrong?'

I stopped. I suddenly felt embarrassed, and wanted to go home. I left him abruptly.

The next day Mum turned up at school in the middle of the morning and took me home. Pop was dead. I wasn't surprised; it was as if he had died already. He had suffered a heart attack, she said, which seemed to me to suggest a physical assault, but no; no one had attacked him. He had died in the garden. He was kneeling, staking his beans, when he keeled over. Aunty Jean said that he had died of a broken heart. I remembered my broken nose — the pain and the blood. His heart just stopped, Mum said. He felt no pain. It was for the best.

We put on our funeral shoes and went to the church which was full of strangers — men from the RSA and from the trucking firm where he had once worked. We sat up the front near the coffin, and Dad helped carry it out. Then we drove up the hill to the wind-swept cemetery. People said, 'It was just a few months ago . . .' They were sombre but dry-eyed.

Although it was spring, the day was cold as we stood beside the gaping grave. I expected to see Pop there. I shut my eyes tight and tried to construct him — his tweed coat, coarse to the touch, his tartan scarf and his hat with a feather in the band. His shoes the colour of toffee and as shiny. His pullover, his woollen tie, his trousers with their pressed crease. So far so good. But where was Pop? It was like putting clothes on a scarecrow.

'Caroline,' hissed Mum. 'Would you take Tom to the toilet?'

I took him behind a tree. When we got back the coffin was in the hole and the priest was praying. People stood there looking at their shoes.

Everyone was invited to the RSA for a sandwich and a cup of tea, though they actually drank whisky. There were lots of photos on the walls. I looked for the one of Pop, but without success.

With Pop it was a different sort of sadness — a blank and empty feeling. And a kind of relief. At home Mum became vague and unfocused. She stood at the sink, running water and looking out the window. She put her hand under the hot water and scalded it.

'You're shell-shocked, Rosalie,' said Dad.

She cried at last — great choking sobs but no tears.

'Who else will die?' Tom kept asking.

'No one else,' Mum said. The next time he asked, she sighed, 'Who knows?' Another time she said, 'Everyone has to die some time.'

Tom was shocked but he was coming to grips with it.

They were together again. We were sure of that. The entity that was Nananpop, violated by death, was restored by death. But it was lost to us.

Tom started school. I kept an eye on him, but to my surprise no one menaced him. Little girls pursued him and little boys fought to be his friend. That shook me in some way.

There was a new girl in my class — a Dutch girl called Ana Van der El. Sister Thomas asked me to be her friend, which turned out to be a full-time job, as she spoke no English and was the shyest girl I had ever met. (I wondered if I should teach her how to fight, but I decided not to risk it.) I composed a list of all the words she needed to know (284 in all) and made her learn some every night. Her parents were touchingly grateful. I was showered with spicy biscuits and given a Dutch doll with yellow plaits and little clogs, and was the envy of every girl in my class.

When my mother began calling Ana 'Caroline's little friend', I experienced an unexpected flush of pleasure. Bunty Braithwaite was not forgotten, but she had lost her sting.

MICHAEL MORRISSEY

I discovered Grafton, Auckland's then bohemian and student-oriented suburb, shortly after I enrolled as a student at the University of Auckland in the early sixties. I soon heard the word 'existentialism', a wonderfully un-New Zealand term that I found engaging and baffling. I bought a copy of *Being and Nothingness* by Jean-Paul Sartre, a 812-page tome I have yet to read.

With Grafton came not only existentialism but coffee, Dave Brubeck, poozling (removing furniture from deserted houses) and later LSD, marijuana, and parties where personalities like Neil Ilingworth, John Yelash, David Gailbraith, Rodney Kirk-Smith, David Mitchell and probably Anna Hoffman took centre stage. I have tried to capture some of these elements in 'Existential Kissing' and also of course the powerful grave-studded presence of Grafton gully itself.

The Bay of Pigs invasion had just occurred, America and the Soviet Union were stockpiling missiles. Mouth to mouth resuscitation was coming into vogue. We would discuss communism, getting drunk, and the films of Ingmar Bergman and Federico Fellini. Young men attempted beards and donned duffle-coats. Girls doing Bachelor of Arts degrees wore black stockings.

This reconstructed memory of my impressionable youth is a favourite of mine.

I wrote it at one sitting.

EXISTENTIAL KISSING

I T IS MID-1961 — the epoch of Holyoake is in full swing and the Beatles have not yet arrived. But there are consolations. I am about to give and (hopefully) receive my first kiss, which will be French and may even be existential.

The kissee (like me) is seventeen years old, a precocious first-year university student, devoted reader of Camus and Sartre, fan of Dave Brubeck and an inhabitant of deepest Grafton. Her name is Marilyn Cox. (Sexy name don't you think?) My name is Paul Satchell but I have already earned the nickname 'Jean' for my enthusiasm for Mr Sartre's causes. Sneeringly witty graffiti signed JPS have been appearing in the male toilet of the university clocktower building.

So here we are on a mild May night in 1961, Paul and Marilyn, sitting on some battered old cushions, not yet of the velvety psychedelic variety, drinking beer while Dave Brubeck is saying Take Five, Take Five, Take Five. Marilyn is wearing *black stockings*. Not impressed? In 1961 very few post-school-age girls wear *black stockings*. What is normal at school is considered very daring, very risqué, very French when worn after leaving school. Marilyn is pale, we Grafton existentialists are very pale, very Brubecky. Intellectually sexy as the Brubeck is, I am wondering if the Little Richard single I have secreted in my briefcase will do the job even faster, but on the whole I feel Marilyn is the Brubeck type. She is, after all, wearing a black polo-neck jumper. (I am wearing heavy, black, horn-rimmed spectacles.)

I mentioned Marilyn's lips but actually I know very little about them. Hers or anyone else's. She is about five feet away from me but it may as well be five hundred miles. Yet I remain convinced that my First Real Kiss is about to occur.

You will notice I haven't mentioned Sexual Intercourse. This most existential of acts is as yet a far-off terrain, a foreign land to Jean Paul Satchell. It does not, as they say nowadays, compute. There are no porno magazines, not even a *Penthouse*, let alone a blue movie to help me out. So far I have only male rumour and dirty jokes to go on. I have heard of French postcards (very naughty, very explicit) photographed in deepest Paris — but I haven't seen any. Nor do I know anyone French. No matter — I have read copious amounts of Camus and Jean Paul Sartre, even a little François Sagan. I am told that Miss Sagan is fond of driving cars at ninety miles an hour while barefoot. The idea of Marilyn emulating Miss Sagan is vaguely exciting, but according to the norms of the day it is the man who drives, not the woman. I have failed my norms.

On the kissing front I can boast a grand total of three. Three whole girls kissed by Jean Paul Satchell! One at a school ball, one at a bus stop and one in the back seat of a cinema — all of their mouths jammed tight as though stitched up by sewing machines. But there is (male rumour speaks the truth this time) a type of kissing called French kissing where tongues touch and entangle. *Existential kissing*. (Or so it has been named by Jean Paul Satchell.)

Much as I admire Mr Sartre's mind, I don't envy Simone de Beauvoir for having to kiss his lips. Mr Sartre doesn't look like the Latin lover type but you can't be sure about these cross-eyed specimens. He and Simone Live Together In Defiance of the Bourgeois Convention of Marriage. (I don't know anyone who does this either.)

But to get back to Marilyn's lips. They have an insouciant Bardotesque droop as though demanding to be kissed (but only by the right man, a certain Jean Paul Satchell, leading Grafton existentialist). Has Marilyn had her first tongue-entangling existential kiss? I've an awful feeling she has and a good idea who has given it to her; naturally, I hope Earl Hope is lying.

Earl Hope? A beard-wearing communist, reputed voluptuary and beer drinker of some renown. Much as I hate to admit it, Mr Hope has made himself into an even more notorious campus character than myself. Bulkier, more boomy of voice, his massive chest runs to a bountiful stomach that can spew whole paragraphs without the breath of a comma, never pausing to refuel saliva ducts as he spits and fumes politics. Politics! Politics! Politics! As Earl grows more indignant his voice ascends in pitch until he sounds like one of those famed Vatican castrati — so powerfully screamy he could shatter stained-glass windows.

Earl comes on like a fifty-year-old professor — sweeping general-isations backed up by stacks of carefully manipulated statistics, intimate anecdotes about the great revolutionaries that sound personally confided into his hirsute, oystery ear. (Why am I thinking about Mr Hope's ears? I should be focusing on Marilyn's lips.) Earl's being a communist is a highly predictable defensive strategy. His father is a filthy-rich, clean-shaven capitalist — ergo, to preserve his identity Earl has become a spitting, fuming, bearded communist.

Don't get me wrong. I don't hate Earl (though I may despise him). Some days I even admire the guy — his attacks on the domino theory, the nonstop quotations from Marx and Lenin, Bakunin and Proudhon ('Property is theft!') and the grisly details about imperialist genocide in Angola, Algeria and South Africa are all very impressive. What worries me is that Marilyn may take everything he says as gospel.

Concentrate, Satchell. There are legs close by; how do you get to them? Mr Brubeck isn't helping one bit. What an absurdity! *Get near the legs.* You're dreaming, Satchell. The lips must come first. But the lips are five hundred miles away . . . Mr Morello is packing away his drums, Mr Desmond folds away his sax and Mr Brubeck gives his last caress to the ivories — time to flip the disk and inch a little closer. Four more changes of the record and body contact will be achieved. Too slow, Satchell, be bold. Think *legs*.

These are pre-massage times remember. Grafton existentialists haven't heard of Swedish massage; rolfing has not yet been invented. There are no reasons why I, randy but shy Jean Paul Satchell, should actually *touch* Marilyn Cox . . . but just watch. My lower body is doing a dry snake-like inching along the floor as though I had an Avondale spider in my corduroys. Give her another drink and start on the ears. I have heard that ears are a good place to start. But if lips (and ultimately legs) are the goal, why start with the ears? Go for the lips! Go over to the window, pretend to be absorbed by the view (ferns, ferns, ferns) and sit down a yard closer. Do it, Satchell!

The strategy for lip contact is clear. A drink, two drinks, three, four. Marilyn gets tipsy.

Marilyn's mouth lolls open. Satchell's mouth moves forward . . . but first the drinks. Any man (especially a seventeen-year-old existentialist man) ought to be able to outdrink a communist girl with full pale lips, green eyes and black stockings. Black stockings may look good (they look *very* good) but they don't absorb alcohol . . . Marilyn's lips are pouting again. She looks like Brigitte Bardot with a PhD in Grafton existentialism. Wanting so much to kiss those luscious pale lips I raise my arm — which should be sneaking around Marilyn's waist — and let if fall lightly but it hits the floor with a weirdly loud thump. Startled by my oafishness, Marilyn's lips purse into a deliciously shaped bud, Mr Brubeck jumps a note — but I am closer.

When I next rise to change the record the horrible truth dawns that it is not Marilyn that is tipsy but I, Jean Paul Satchell, who is nearly drunk. The fact is I am (unlike Mr Earl Hope) not used to drinking. I sit, missing the padding of the cushion, jarring my spine. Twelve inches from Marilyn's black-stockinged legs! Thankfully she is oblivious to my efforts; lying back as though meditating (nobody meditates yet), staring at the ceiling, smoking, smoking, smoking. No one's that worried about smoking and cancer in 1961. Fidel Castro smokes doesn't he?

What is Marilyn thinking about? Come to think of it, what do young women think about? Do they have a different mental geometry from young men's thoughts? Do they ever consider what young existential men have *hidden* in their corduroys? I am *deeply absorbed* in what lies *beyond* Marilyn's black stockings. Somewhere beneath that gym slip of a skirt the stockings *stop*, a suspender belt intervenes and the pale untouchable existential thighs of Marilyn Cox take over. But why should they be untouchable? Why shouldn't I, Jean Paul Satchell, reach out and touch them?

I glance over at Marilyn. She has closed her eyes. Has Brubeck sent her to sleep? This is the big moment, Satchell. Lean over and meet the lips of Marilyn Cox, seventeen-year-old existential Grafton goddess —

'Open up! KGB!' A voice like a platoon of raping soldiers batters down the door. It's big beefy Earl Hope, bearded communist. Faster than a striking snake I shrink back from the prone form of Marilyn. By the time her eyes are open I am gazing with fake intensity through the jammed sash window at the Stygian Grafton night.

'Mr Hope I presume,' says Marilyn. The 'Mister' seems to imply both mockery and respect. Mustering up a false comradely smile, I made a competitive reassessment of Earl's physical attractiveness. Though no more than nineteen, Earl looks at least thirty-five — gargantuanly meaty forearms, a gravid belly, porcine waist, and a formidably Marxian beard descending almost to his naval.

In the grand manner of a duchess settling her skirts, Earl seats himself in the centre of the room. Marilyn offers a cup of coffee, that sixties aphrodisiac. Earl eyes my beer so thirstily I am obliged to offer him a bottle; he removes the top with an accomplished working-class flourish. Even though I may not be the audience he had in mind, I am a pair of ears — all he needs for verbal blast-off.

Cuba is his subject. The abortive Bay of Pigs invasion has just occurred. Earl has all the information at his command — in just 72 hours the 1500 CIA-trained Cuban stooges, inflamed by Samoza's exhortation to 'Bring back a couple of hairs from Castro's beard!', were defeated by the local militia and a battalion of the Revolutionary Armed Forces stationed at the Australian sugar mill on the edge of the Zapata swamp; and the 1197 prisoners were treated with scrupulous fairness. American deceit and conceit revealed for all the world's gaze. Castro wins against the might of Uncle Sam! With blinding statistical virtuosity Earl reels off the professions of the prisoners — 100 plantation owners, 67 landlords, 74 large property owners, 112 big businessmen, 194 soldiers of Batista's regime, 35 industrial magnates and 179 idle rich. There is a public debate on television and many of the prisoners defect to Castro. And why not? They are Cubans after all — they just backed the wrong side.

How is Marilyn taking all this? If I was in her shoes (or her stockings) I would be bored stiff. But her eyes are wide open. What can I add to Earl's impressive barrage? Of course! — Jean Paul Sartre visited Cuba in 1960, befriended Castro and acclaimed Che Guevara, 'the most complete man of his age'. With this nugget I hope to steer the conversation away from Cuba (of which I know little) back to Jean Paul Sartre (of whom I know much).

Suddenly, Marilyn opens her Bardotesque lips: 'Of course Sartre visited Cuba as a communist not as an existentialist.'

The brilliance of this remark hits me between the eyes like a poisoned arrow, paralysing speech. Earl's beard is nodding sagely yes, yes, yes. From where I am sitting on the floor (us Grafton existentialists always sit on the floor), Earl's beard is Castroesque and his fingers mime the holding of a fat missile-shaped cigar.

'That's right! Absolutely!' To wrap things up, Earl tells us how Senor Guevara (Alfredo not Erneste), director of the Cuban Film Institute, accused decadent publications like *Lunes* and *Revolution* of being *enemies* of the Soviet Union — of being spokesmen of Surrealism, Bourgeois Decadence, Elitism and Existentialism. It would appear that Earl agrees with Senor Guevara. Existentialism condemned! Sartre a communist! They both look over at me in pitying triumph.

'Enough of Mr Brubeck,' Marilyn declares firmly. My record is arrested in mid-track, John Lee Hooker takes over. Defeated on all fronts (musically and ideologically), I stare out into the Grafton night which is beginning to look like the Dark Night of the Soul. Earl is in full cry. Speaking in a Wagnerian bellow, he stabs holes in the air with an iron-foundry worker's proletarian forefinger — 'The true significance of the Cuban revolution is that it was the first revolution led by the working class! Castro was no intellectual — he only got to page 370 of *Das Kapital*!'

What is the appropriate scenario for New Zealand? Where are the millions of starving peasants? Where is the hugely discontented middle class? Where are the revolutionary intellectuals? The 1961 Holyoake government is as stable as pig iron. The military are imperialist lackeys who will fight any war suggested to them by Britain or the United States of America. The Boer War! World War I! World War II! The Malaya Emergency! The Korean War! — bayonets fixed, New Zealand boys will be there! They will fight any and every war except the revolutionary war at home. The climate for revolution looks hopeless. Everyone has a job and everyone is politically content. It's outrageous! How can two million people be happy?

I, Jean Paul Satchell, am not happy. Nor will I be until I receive a hot existential kiss from Marilyn Cox. Earl has finally veered off Cuba, and though I am eager to switch the conversation back to Jean Paul Sartre and existentialism, the bearded communist has shrewdly diverted the subject to the British Empire. He is winding us up into a revolutionary fury over how these proud green acres of Aotearoa, all sixty-six million of them, are still technically owned by the Queen. Frothing in grand style, his beard catching small amounts of orator's spittle, Earl's eloquence has Marilyn's chest heaving; even I am short of breath.

Soon we are all seething about Queen and Empire and assorted atrocities perpetrated by Great (ha!) Britain on Ireland, France, Africa, Germany and China. And while the brave little nation of Cuba has resisted American imperialism, what have we in New Zealand ever done to resist British imperialism? Not a thing. Nothing! The shame of the docile Pakeha!

In the cinemas, people still stand stiffly to attention like toy soldiers — all for the Queen! Disgraceful! But Earl has fought against this shame by heroically refusing to stand — not even when a Battle of the Somme veteran pulled his hair. Earl tells how he turned and said, 'I am a communist!' The cinema goes deathly quiet but for the veteran muttering darkly about King and country (even though the Queen now reigns). When the usherette is called, valiant Queen-defying Earl stands, or rather sits, his ground, insisting that he has every *right* to watch the movie from his seat (which he had paid for). Any attempt to remove him would be *grievous bodily assault*. That was political courage first-class in Auckland, New Zealand, 1961.

The beer, coffee and Earl's rhetoric have done the trick. We are all angry now. I have (almost) forgotten about kissing Marilyn. We are ready, she and I, to join in whatever scheme comrade Hope has dreamt up. And there is a scheme — a revolutionary plot! Just across the great green gulf of Grafton gully lies the grave of Governor Hobson. The Queen's representative is complacently *undefiled* in our neighbourhood. How dare he! What can be done? Explosives aren't part of our arsenal — not yet. 'But there are other means — human means at our disposal.' I am not quite sure what Earl means by this. Nonetheless he has raised his side-of-beef arm in an utterly convincing revolutionary gesture — 'To Hobson's grave!'

In a few moments we are standing at the bottom of Ferncroft Street peering down into the bush. In 1961, Grafton gully resembles an Amazon jungle, a near mile-long picket of dense fern and flax, honeysuckle and convolvulus set right in the heart of our city. Onward comrades! *Communist Hardy and existential Laurel descend into the ferny depths.* And it's Marilyn who has just made this intolerably witty parallel; unoffended, Earl rocks with laughter so Friar Tuckishly he trips and rolls into a cushioning entangle of convolvulus. Up he comes, bedecked with purple flowers, laughing his great belly laugh.

Deep in the gizzard of the gully we encounter a small trickle of a stream (our Zapata swamp). Above us looms the great arch of Grafton Bridge which Earl informs us was the largest single-span concrete bridge in the world when it was built in 1910. By day, traffic booms eerily down the hollow centre of the supporting column but at this witching hour all is quiet as we stumble up into the rusting iron fences and mouldering tombstones of Grafton cemetery.

Soon we are gathered around Hobson's grave. Earl is temporarily out of breath but eager to do battle with this Altar of Imperialism. A pox and a pestilence upon Hobson! Death to the Imperialist shrines of British orthodoxy! Long live the Grafton People's Revolutionary Army!

But what exactly are we going to do? We have no dynamite or gelignite, no chisels or sledge hammers, not even a spray can (not yet invented). We are now, as Earl said earlier, thrown back on human resources . . . Earl leads the way, unzipping his trousers he produces a steel worker's massive proletarian prick, engorged with urine. No sooner has his green stream splashed onto the old concrete, than Marilyn squats down with a giggle and, after a deft manoeuvre of stocking and skirt, produces a copious gush of her own. My own bladder being traitorously dry, I content myself with a spit and a kick. High with revolutionary glee at one o'clock in the morning (the street lights have just winked off) we stand triumphant over the tomb of Hobson now desecrated by the urine of the Grafton people's Revolutionary Army.

As we move off, Earl trips on the side of Hobson's grave and falls heavily. I laugh (though it is no laughing matter) as Comrade Earl's head is struck by the concrete. The Imperialist forces have struck back! Earl may be down but he is not out. Rising to his feet, forehead grazed crimson, he kicks savagely at the militant grave — 'Bloody imperialist!'

Though it would be easier to climb the steps and walk along

Grafton Bridge, a People's Revolutionary Army should stick to the guerrilla terrain of the gully. With the street lights off, it is awfully dark down in the cemetery, though Marilyn's green eyes seem gifted with a tigery keenness. If we follow the line of the bridge we cannot get lost, yet we stumble, laughing as we lurch. The Grafton People's Revolutionary Army returns from its first strike!

Suddenly Earl trips again, falls heavily into the stream. Seconds later we turn him over; he looks ghastly. I grope for his wrists. Nothing, no pulse. No, there is something, a dull beat. When we drag him out of the stream he looks a bluish-purple colour. Can nineteen-year-old communists have heart attacks? Earl looks half drowned as well (how long does it take to drown?). I know what to do — pump his arms back and forth in the Holger-Nielsen method.

'No — not like that,' hisses Marilyn. 'There's a better way!' She pulls open Earl's mouth and clamps her mouth to his. Has she gone mad? What good is kissing Earl going to do? The kiss doesn't sound normal — it's noisy, breathy. What is she trying to accomplish? Suck back all the water in Earl's lungs? Despite the life-death situation we are trapped in, I am thinking with drunken lucidity: Earl is getting a French kiss, a deep existential mouth job, and he doesn't know it. Marilyn persists with fierce energy, breathing in, breathing out. Abruptly Earl coughs and splutters, his eyes flicker open.

'Shit,' I say. 'You were nearly dead. But Marilyn . . .'

'It's called the Kiss of Life,' Marilyn explains. 'It's a new technique my father taught me to save drowned people. I've never had the chance to try it out before — but it works!'

'Did your life flash before you?' I foolishly ask.

'I don't think so,' Earl shakes his head groggily. He is sober now, we are all sober. (Was Marilyn ever drunk?) She is laughing again, her mouth opens, there's the wondrous life-giving tongue lolling about. I consider picking up a rock to knock myself unconscious so that I can drop into this small Grafton stream face downwards, jaw slacked open to drown, just so that Marilyn can work her lippy magic and bring me back to life with an existential kiss . . .

As we near Grafton Road, brush with death forgotten, Earl recovers his political wit. (How about his brush with Marilyn's life-giving mouth?) High in the slowly wheeling night sky above, a lone meteor flares briefly. 'Gagarin!' I cry, though he is already back on earth. Safely back in Marilyn's flat we drink our eighth cup of coffee for the day, smoke cigarettes and listen to Little Richard sing *Tutti Frutti aaaawwwlll Rooti*.

I never kissed Marilyn. I stayed friends with her until her first real romance with a footballer accountant who had no detectable communist tendencies. My affair with existentialism came to an abrupt halt with my first real girlfriend. Jane studied organic chemistry and played the cello. She kissed with musical virtuosity. We never discussed Jean Paul Sartre.

LINDA BURGESS

Choosing a personal favourite is like Sophie's Choice for me — just give me a few minutes to tell the rejected stories that they're all special. I'm very attached to all my stories because, though it's my favourite genre, I haven't written very many. Usually I get an idea and it gestates, sometimes for months, and the story is often complete in my head before I sit down to write it.

This story is special because it started during my mother's funeral a year ago. I was speaking of my mother, and how we had a sort of controlled freedom, a wonderful way to grow up. I spoke of the time I went on a bike ride with friends, consumed with guilt because I'd gone further than I was allowed to. This bike ride is not that bike ride, but it did seem that journeys are appropriate images to associate with growing up; with knowing who you are and where you fit.

One thing I love about writing is the way images collect and group when a story is coming properly. Short stories need to be more than just the situation they are describing, and that is the real joy of writing them.

BIKE RIDE

GAYLE'S BEEN TELLING Jennifer all about how she's going round with Neville, whose parents own the other fish and chip shop, and when she turns back she says, *Whoops*, then, How do you like your fish and chips? Well done?

Jennifer feels flattered right to the back of her throat as she says, casually, Yes, she does like them well done.

Gayle whips out the basket, hangs it above the steaming fat to drain for a second or two, brings it down with a *thwack* then another *thwack* on the edge of the stainless steel vat then they sprawl on to a square of greaseproof paper through which smirk last week's brides in the *Daily News*. Big crisp chunks of fish, shocking pink hotdogs bulging out of their batter, and chips chips chips. Gayle's sprayed salt all over them, whoosh swish *whoosh* from the big glass container with holes made by nails hammered through the metal top. Sauce? she asks but Jennifer says, No, they have some at home. Just the *smell*. She can taste it on her lips.

The pong in the kitchen. It almost ruins the fish and chips, but only almost, because nothing can ruin them, not really. Mum's cooking tripe for Dad, she does it once a month on a Friday, and it's stale nappies with onions and milk, it makes Jennifer want to throw up, but the good thing is it does mean they get fish and chips, which doesn't happen all that often because Mum doesn't believe in them. Dad's home and he's moaning about work again, how the Post Office is never going to promote him now because he turned down that move. Mum says, Well they like it here, so what's the problem and anyway she'd rather have him in charge of only four staff than have to move to Taihape even if it is a bigger branch. We can't keep moving the kids, she says flatly, with Murray at high school now and Jennifer due to start next year. And Evan only just starting school. They're small schools but good schools here, she says. And the kids have got their friends.

Jennifer and Murray and Evan have spread the fish and chips out on the kitchen table though Mum and Dad will be eating their tea through in the dining room, as Mum likes to, with serving bowls, and the plates warmed, and their own napkin rolled neatly in their own silver napkin ring. It's because her own mother served straight from the pot, she says, and she always wished she didn't. Fish and chips can be eaten from the newspaper with the tomato sauce, made by Mum in the huge preserving pan at the end of each summer, and put back into the bottles that the vinegar was in, after she's done the cases of Golden Queens which are sent on the train from Hawke's Bay. One hundred and fifty jars she makes, and the same of pears a couple of months later, enough to keep them in puddings all year.

Evan says, Yum *yum* pig's *bum* and Mum says, *Evan*.

Dad says he's had another bloody letter from head office and —

Mum says she's had it up to here with the Post Office and Dad should either leave or just — shut up about it.

Dad says, What's got on *her* wick then?

And Murray says, Hey these are *burnt*, and Jennifer says, No they're *not* and Evan says no they're *not* they're yum yum —

And Mum says, *E-van*.

Mum points to a letter which sits on the bench. It's the same Croxley notepaper that Grandma uses and Jennifer has assumed it's from Grandma but when she looks over she sees it's not Grandma's thick blue-black writing, it's finer, a paler blue and a bit wobbly as if the writer isn't holding the pen tightly enough.

Mrs Holdaway has written, says Mum.

What's that old trout want? says Dad and Mum gives him her not-in-front-of-the-children look.

Dad's been wandering again, she says, and her voice sounds as if her throat is holding on to it. They found him down at the Davis' this time. In his pyjamas. Mrs Davis brought him home, but . . .

Dad has moved over to Mum and he's holding the top of her arm, hard.

Don't, she says.

Do you want to put through a toll call? he says, letting go of her, and Jennifer's thinking, he's only trying to say he's sorry about Granddad.

I should, she says. Then she says, I should *go*. I feel so . . . Mrs Holdaway says he should be in a Home, she says.

What? says Evan, and Murray says Why? but Mum just says, Oh, it's complicated Murray. Don't worry about it.

Go up at Labour weekend, says Dad. Take the train. We'll be okay.

I should go sooner, says Mum. She lifts the lid off, just stares in at the tripe and closes it again. There's a waft of fetid air and Jennifer wills her nostrils closed and concentrates on her chips.

It's so unfair, Mum says.

Poor *Mum*, she says.

At least Dad doesn't know, she says.

Then she says, It's bound to catch up with you, marrying someone old enough to be your father.

Can I come? says Evan. On the train?

It seems a good idea that Jennifer waits until the next morning to ask about the bike ride. Mostly, as long as you ask Mum first you're allowed to do what you like. But sometimes she just says no, and nothing you can say makes any difference. You don't even bother saying that all the other mothers have said yes, because you know what she'll say to that.

Jennifer tells her they're going on a bike ride. Me, and Joanne, and Pauline, she says.

Where to? says Mum. She looks tired this morning, dark thumbprints under her sad eyes.

Joanne's farm, says Jennifer, and her fingers are crossed so hard behind her back that the one underneath starts to ache.

Too far, says Mum, as if there's no more to say.

Mum, says Jennifer.

Jennifer, says Mum. It's too far. It's ten miles.

Jennifer doesn't say anything. Mum's voice goes softer, but

underneath there's rock. No further than the Carthews', says Mum. Okay?

Jennifer doesn't want her voice to sound like Mrs Holdaway's handwriting so she's silent.

Okay? Jennifer? Okay? says Mum.

Joanne's at the front and she's riding no hands.

Look Mum no hands! shouts Pauline.

Look Mum no teef! says Jennifer, and it's their old joke but they all laugh.

It's so easy that soon the three of them are doing it. You hold on again when you have to stand up to pedal up the hills but down the hills you fly, no feet as your pedals spin with a life of their own, then feet back on and no hands. They're past the Carthews' in a flash and Jennifer doesn't even look. It's not much more than an hour later that they're juddering over the cattlestop and up the rutted dirt drive — all hands on handgrips now — to Joanne's farm. Joanne's Mum and Dad live in town where her father drives a taxi, since the house on the farm burnt down. Joanne says it was the kerosene heater and Pauline says, Sure it wasn't your smokes? and Jennifer feels the sun on her throat as she tips her head back to laugh. Not that it's a joke really. Joanne looks such a goody-goody; with her neat blonde hair, smooth brown skin and pale blue eyes, she's teacher's pet, but last year when they went on guide camp it was Joanne who'd brought the cigarettes. And Pauline who'd got the blame.

Joanne's brothers still live at the farm, in what used to be the worker's cottage. They're keeping things going. It's one room with a lean-to kitchen. In the room there are two beds, a formica table with an ashtray spewing filthy butts and a couple of packets of cigarettes on top of a pale green fly-spotted radio. There are two chairs at the table and two grubby beige fireside chairs with chrome arms.

Connie Francis, oh how *neat*, says Pauline sarcastically and Joanne says that picture's left over from the last people, as in Rosemary Clooney, someone they've never even heard of.

Hey but look at this, says Joanne and she closes the door which they've left open because it's warm in here, and a bit stale-smelling too, the faded stench of smoked cigarettes and with something else in the air, an odour Jennifer doesn't quite recognise, though it reminds

103

her of Murray, a bit. On the back of the door there's a big picture, a girl with the hugest bosoms Jennifer has ever seen, and she's pushing them together with her arms to make them look even bigger. She's wearing a gingham shirt that's far too small for her and she's sitting on a motorbike, leaning forward, and she's in a barn. There's some darling little fluffy yellow chickens next to her on the seat.

I'm hungry, says Pauline and Joanne says, the boys'll have something here, they won't mind, and she opens a cupboard and in it there's three double loaves of bread, coming together in soft white Vs. Joanne rips one of them in half, puts the two pieces on the formica table, kicks the chair which is holding the fridge door shut aside with her foot and gets some butter and a huge jar of blackberry jelly from the fridge. With her arm extended she carries the jar over to the table, the jam streaking its outside, her nose a feral, fastidious little point.

Damn, she says, there's only beer, we should've brought some Coke.

Beer'll do me, says Pauline, and she lies brazenly on one of the beds, one ankle propped on her raised knee, and her shirt gaping open, enough so you can see she's got a bra.

Instead of getting anything to drink Joanne cuts off a slab of bread with a vicious-looking hunting knife that she takes from the bench in its sheath. She tries to spread the butter though it's so hard the bread gets holes in it. She slaps on blackberry jelly and says to Pauline, Get your gob round this.

Ugh, says Pauline. A big splodge of purple jelly has fallen on her front, in the gap in her shirt made when she lay down, and is lying partly on her bra and partly on her skin, in the flat place in the middle. She digs with her finger, scooping it up and licking if off with a damp suck.

I could do with a fag, she says. Your brothers won't mind will they?

Joanne says, Well what they don't know won't hurt them, though she looks less than sure. Pauline tips two cigarettes out of one packet and one from the other and tosses one to each of them.

No thanks, says Jennifer, throwing hers back.

Pauline has lit hers with the one match left in the box. Have a monkey, she says to Joanne, and the ends of their cigarettes touch and Joanne draws in deeply. They lie side by side on the bed, sucking in their cheeks and puffing out. Soon there are wisps of smoke in quavery little rings hovering tentatively in the air above the bed; Joanne says her brother showed her how. Show *me*, says Pauline but in the end they both get the giggles, Pauline laughing so hard she falls off the bed, taking the eiderdown and Joanne with her. They're both lying on the floor looking coolly into each other's faces and suddenly Joanne's rolled over and she's spitting on her finger and dabbing at the smouldering tiny hole in the eiderdown and saying, Crikey, *watch out*, we'll burn the place down if we're not careful. Jennifer's holding the cold arms of the chair tightly, concentrating on keeping her eyes wide open, not even blinking so she won't do anything silly like bawling, and she looks at the little chickens in the picture and wishes wishes wishes that they were really there so she could touch them.

Joanne says that she supposes Jennifer has to go home as her mummy will be wondering where she is.

Jennifer says she supposes she should, and Pauline gives a sniggery little laugh.

On the way home Pauline and Joanne ride two abreast, no hands.

Look Mum no hands, says Jennifer, but they don't even turn around. Outside the Carthews' place there's a whole crate of full milk bottles sitting there, for the factory to pick up, Jennifer supposes. Or perhaps the dairy factory has dropped them off. She doesn't know which way round it would be. But Joanne has jumped off her bike while it's still moving, letting it fall into the long grass. I'm friggin' thirsty, she says and she grabs a bottle and drains half of it, without even stopping. The rest she gives to Pauline who finishes it off then chucks the bottle with the long and lazy lob into the boxthorn hedge.

Jennifer could sandpaper her mouth with her tongue she's so dry. She stands astride her bike, just waiting. She could easily just hop off and get a bottle, Mrs Carthew would never know it was her.

Instead she bikes off. They're behind her she supposes, but she's the leader. She rides so fast up the hill that she could cruise down the other side and halfway up the next if she wanted to, before having to pedal at all. But going downhill she stands up and really goes for it.

Down the hill she flies, her feet only just keeping up with the frantically turning pedals. It's the wind that's making her bawl. And she's yelling out for all the cows to hear, for all the world to hear, *I like my fish and chips well done.*

WITI IHIMAERA

'Life and Death in Calcutta' was one of two stories I wrote during a week in Kuala Lumpur in 1998. (The other was 'A History of New Zealand Literature Through Selected Texts'.) I was sitting at the poolside of the hotel with a stranger from India and asked, 'What is life like in Calcutta?' The response was the inspiration for this story.

With every story one writes, one is always in search of a particular excellence that will best suit the story. With this one, I wanted to find a polished surface that would reflect what are for me the most important aspects of my artistry — aesthetics and politics — within a deliberately low-key narrative and style. The story is not my favourite one but it has helped me in pursuit of a way of telling my next novel, *The Prisoner of the Glittering Tower*.

The story was printed in a volume which honoured the wonderful French scholar and friend of New Zealand literature, Jacqueline Bardolph.

LIFE AND DEATH IN CALCUTTA

TWO FRIENDS HAD INVITED a third to have drinks with them beside the pool of the exclusive hotel where they were guests. The pool was on the roof of the hotel, which was not in Calcutta but in a city far removed from the Indian continent. When, on his arrival, the third friend expressed his amazement at the pool's rooftop location, an engineering feat that must have cost much more than had the pool been placed on the ground floor, his two friends exchanged smiles of understanding. After all, their third friend had not been successful in industry as they were and therefore his lack of understanding of the appurtenances of five star living needed to be indulged. They watched as he stripped to his shorts and dived into the pool. They themselves had yet to wet themselves in the water, preferring to sip their cocktails and watch shaded by an umbrella from the sun.

The third friend was a teacher in Calcutta and after he had finished his swim and was towelling himself beside the pool, his two friends began to ask him questions about his life in India. They did this more out of politeness than interest. Noting his surroundings, and surmising that his friends would never ever set foot in a Third World country, the invited friend responded gently that there were hotels in Calcutta similar to the one they were in and that if they so wished to visit India in the five star manner, then they would find life exactly as it was anywhere else. However if they wished to see the real Calcutta, all they would need to do was venture a few steps into an alley off the main street and there they would find twenty beggars within hands' reach. His two friends expressed sympathy at the poverty of life their third friend conveyed, and one made a chance remark of the kind we all do that he always kept some change in his pocket just in case he was confronted with a beggar on a city street. At this point the invited friend closed his eyes and then posed the following parable to his friends.

'There was once a man in a white suit,' he began, 'who in his hurry to return to his hotel, took a detour and found himself in a street full of beggars. At once surrounded, the man brushed the outreaching hands aside but failing to escape, put a silver coin in one of the hands and proceeded on. As he departed he heard a commotion and realised that the other beggars were trying to wrest the silver coin from the one who had been given it. As well, a second group were now in his pursuit. Luckily the man in the white suit was quick on his feet and was able to elude his pursuers, all, that is, except one who caught up with him as he rounded the corner and touched his sleeve to detain him. "Kind sir," the beggar said, "you have given a silver coin to my colleague. It was my hand that was uppermost and should have received the coin. However, in a moment of jostling my hand was pushed to one side and, in that split second, the coin span away and into the hand which received it." '

The friends to whom the parable was being told looked at each other. 'The second beggar was unlucky,' one of them shrugged. 'He was in the right place at the right time but his was not the right palm. This is life. There are winners and there are losers.'

The invited friend nodded in agreement. 'Yes, and the second beggar was aware of this. He had been prepared to accept the whim of Fate. However, when he had seen his colleague in possession of the coin his first thought had been, "Why him? Why not me?" '

'For that matter,' one of the friends interjected the storyteller, 'why not any of the other twenty beggars in the street? The man in the white suit should not be blamed for an act of charity which albeit privileged one beggar over the others.'

'Indeed,' the invited guest agreed. 'Why not any of the other beggars? It was random chance that had dropped the silver coin in one palm and not another — and the second beggar realised this. But acting in hope he had run after the man in the white suit and, upon catching up with him, now wished to offer him the great gift of dispensing his bounty by choice what he had earlier done by chance. "Sir," the beggar said, "I wonder if you would also consider giving a silver coin to me. You see, Sir, I have a wife who is ill and four children who have not eaten for five days whereas the man to whom you have given the silver coin does not have a wife or children and has only his own mouth to feed." '

'But how does one know,' one of the friends interrupted, 'that any story told by a beggar is true?'

'Yes,' his companion nodded. 'Simply because one person says it is so does not mean that it is so. Not only that but one cannot give silver coins to every beggar that one meets. Justice is blind, the world is a random place, these things happen.'

'You are being too defensive,' the invited guest said. 'My point is not to criticise the man in the white suit but to engage a story of his moral dilemma and questions of responsibility. Previously the man in the white suit had given his silver coin unthinkingly and now he was being asked to give another silver coin on trust, on faith, on the presumption of truth. The beggar pressed on, "I am pleading with you, kind Sir, to honour me with your bounty," and, as it happened, the man in the white suit did have a second silver coin in his pocket, which he could easily have given. Indeed, he was on the point of reaching in to give it to the beggar until he thought he saw something in the beggar's eyes. A glint of triumph, perhaps, a touch of contempt that the man in the white suit had believed his story — or was it merely that sunlight reflected in a second-storey window had lodged in the beggar's eyes and made them seem to be those of a thief, a liar, a dissembler? It was simply a moment, as ephemeral as that same moment when the man in the white suit had dropped his first silver coin into that lucky hand, but it was enough to make the man in the white suit revert not to trust but to distrust. There is nothing so contemptuous to a man to think he is being made a fool of. Thus it was that he made his choice and thereby his second decision —'

'What was his first?'

'Agreed, his first was perhaps unconsciously applied when he gave a silver coin to a beggar, possibly the wrong beggar at that. But this second was consciously applied when he decided not to believe the beggar's story. Thus, the man in the white suit pushed the second beggar aside, passed on and entered his hotel.'

The storyteller lapsed into silence. His two friends signalled a waiter and ordered him to refresh their drinks. But their invited friend had no intention of letting them escape the narrative he was telling them.

'When the man in the white suit entered the hotel, that was the end of the story, insofar as it applied to him, but it wasn't the end of the story for the beggar. As it happened he did indeed have a wife who was dying and four starving children. Life and death in Calcutta does indeed often turn on who is given a silver coin and who is not. Should the man in the white suit be expected to take responsibility for the one who does not receive a silver coin as well as the one who does? Even if the man in the white suit had given him a silver coin that might not have prevented the death of the wife though it may well have prolonged the life of his children.'

'What are you trying to say?' one of the storyteller's friends asked with some impatience. 'First you imply that the second beggar should have been given a silver coin and now you indicate that, even if he had been given one it would have made no difference?'

The invited guest shook his head. 'Although at that level of existence the choice of prolonging life or not is equally deplorable, the possibility of maintaining life is so precious that it must surely be sought over the terminality of death — but that's not what I am trying to say.'

The storyteller's friends waited for him to elaborate.

'This is not a story about the beggar,' he explained. 'It is about the man in the white suit.'

The two friends of the storyteller were fortunate to be in a country where afternoon showers were common because at that moment they noted that such a shower was about to begin. They decided it would be best to adjourn to an inside bar, thanked their invited friend for coming, quickly collected their clothes and left.

The invited friend stayed by the pool. He had not meant to offend his friends but had merely wanted to respond to a chance remark about keeping change in your pocket for beggars in the street. He decided to have one last dip before leaving. He stepped to the edge of the pool and dived in. When he resurfaced the water was dimpled with raindrops.

CATHERINE CHIDGEY

There is nothing like a deadline to get the pen moving across the page. I wrote 'The Sundial of Human Involvement' in 1997 for the *Listener* Women's Book Festival short-story competition. The maximum length was seven hundred and fifty words, the opening sentence was provided by Fiona Kidman and there was a strict deadline.

The day the letter arrived telling me I had won my first competition (and my only one, come to think of it) I was doing my first reading in public. All of a sudden, the thing I had done in secret — writing — was being exposed to the world (well, to *Listener* readers and to the smallish audience at Wellington's City Gallery, anyway). It was terrifying, but it was also a lesson in the power of publicity — the story was published just before the release of my first novel, *In a fishbone church*, and gave the book invaluable exposure.

Being a full-time writer is a job which involves making up one's own rules and then trying to stick to them; playing both parent and child, if you like. It's wonderful, but sometimes I crave the sort of discipline imposed by that short-story competition. Any good opening lines, Fiona?

THE SUNDIAL OF HUMAN INVOLVEMENT

A T FIRST GLANCE, IT MIGHT easily be thought that the room was empty. This is the essence of waiting: an empty room, filled only with longing. Sara had been waiting for months.

She wrote him light notes — the garden, the weather, the horrible bridesmaid's dress — her pen hardly touching the veined paper. It reminded her of fingers on sleeping skin, this lightness of touch; messages for someone to decode as their own dream.

She tried not to go on about him, but only aroused curiosity.

'When's he coming, is he coming soon, it can't be long now,' they kept saying at the office. 'Is his English good, has he got a work permit, it wasn't just a holiday fling, was it?'

On the first of December her boss asked her to do the Christmas display. All day she wrapped empty boxes, arranged them as gifts.

I miss you so terribly, his postcard of Notre Dame said. *Should I bring warm clothes? An umbrella?*

When he arrived she warned him of earthquakes and showed him the largest wooden building in the southern hemisphere.

'This is the old shoreline,' she said, stopping at the door of a bank. Then she told him about the recent tremors, and how she had noticed that things in her room had moved ever so slightly: reading glasses right at the edge of a shelf, perfume bottles inched out of line.

He laughed. 'This is a strange place,' he said, 'where wood masquerades as stone.'

That night she showed him the bottled water, the torch, the blankets, just in case.

He gave her a present, duty free. He liked her to wear it, rewarded her for doing so. He'd say, 'I like the Obsession on you today.' A kiss, a smile.

His interview was a success, he said. They'd liked the idea of someone from overseas. He took her to a wine bar to meet his new colleagues; scented businessmen who leaned in close to tell her secrets above the clink and sip of other firms. She could make out tiny indentations in their earlobes. After she'd seen these pin dots, inverse Braille, she relaxed. She knew what these men would have been like when they were teenagers, and wore acid-wash jeans and ear studs and went to nightclubs to meet girls who would pretend to understand them above Talking Heads and Erasure.

When she was coming back from the toilet she saw them nudging him, grinning.

'Tasty, tasty.' they were saying.

She sat down again and one of them bought her another drink and she said thank you into his closed-over ear.

'You've never seen this before?' he said, amazed how little she knew of her own city. 'There's one in Amsterdam, it's wonderful. Stand on the date. Feet together.'

Her toes skimmed brass letters, numerals. She felt uneasy, moving so quickly through months, years, but he was laughing and the tulips were out and she had little choice.

'Arms up like a steeple.'

Her shadow fell on the time. He held up his watch in triumph, tick tick, so close to her face she could hear its tiny silver hands scissoring the day into shrewd portions.

'Now you,' she said, grabbing his hands and dragging him into the tiny space of that day, which was too narrow for two. She moved one day ahead to make room. She wanted to make sure he would cast the same shadow.

Four days for the North Island were not enough.

'There is always so little time,' he began, but she changed the subject.

She showed him the Devil's Bath, Diamond Geyser, Bridal Veil Falls. They took photos of steam, not realising their own shadows would appear on the prints, solid against the rising haze.

The floor between them was covered with coins. He had surplus francs, marks, a few Irish pounds. She had lighter currencies depicting flowers and ships.

She said, 'I like those two-tone ones, silver rimmed with gold. They're like the moon passing over the sun.'

He gave her one to keep; her own eclipse. She gave him leftovers from Singapore, for the trip back. He could buy something small, perhaps, to prove he had been there. A key ring, or an orchid sealed in glass.

At the station he wheeled his case across the stone compass, bumping it over brass arrows, promising to write. She pretended to ignore the unchanging nature of direction, the absence of a needle spinning anywhere, anywhere.

PATRICIA GRACE

I've chosen 'The Day of the Egg' because it's been sitting there with its hand up and has never been chosen before. I like the characters, the way they contrast with each other and the way they have come out of the text for me. I'm pleased with Phil the pharmacist who hasn't been given many words at all, but has revealed himself in spaces. Dropping the egg was Dorothy's 'good luck', when prepared words became other words. A decision changed and she dumped Phil. Good on her. Maybe there are now other decisions she will make on her own behalf. I enjoyed writing 'The Day of the Egg' and still like reading it.

THE DAY OF THE EGG

DOROTHY WENT TO THE fridge and took out an egg, holding it between the tips of three fingers and thumb. She was going to cook it with a slice of bacon and a few chips for the old man who she could hear in the bathroom watering his face. And when he came in she was going to tell him. The cat in the tree was the last thing.

Sam was a mate of her father's whom Dorothy had known since she was eight. It was usually on a Friday night that Sam would arrive with her father, both of them primed. They'd bring beer and pigs' heads and spend the weekend boozing. Not just the two of them. In the end there'd be a crowd. Dorothy and her brothers and sisters would go to sleep listening to the songs running into one another, the feet thumping, the uke and mandolin going to town, the teaspoon ringing in the neck of a bottle, the big spoons clacking. Now and then in the middle of the night there'd be a row, shouting and a scuffle, someone going headlong out the door.

In the morning the kitchen would be sour-smelling, and there'd be an array of sleeping bodies — one or two seated at the table with their heads among the bottles, glasses and cigarette ash, another stretched out on the kitchen settee, sometimes one or two on the floor.

Dorothy and her brothers and sisters would start cleaning up and eventually the sleepers would get up and go outside — find a way home, or prop themselves against a tree ready to start drinking again.

The kids would clear the table first, then get themselves Weetbix and hot water. They'd find the tin of condensed milk and dribble that over their Weetbix. If there was no Weetbix they'd make a drink with the condensed milk instead.

After breakfast they'd take all the bottles out and stack them behind the shed, make a fire for the rubbish, wash the glasses and dishes and floors. Their mother would get up eventually and come out into the kitchen croaky and sore, shiny from a cold-water wash. They knew she wouldn't say anything about the tin of condensed milk. Their father would go out to the wash-house to see if he'd remembered to hide a flagon or two there.

On Sunday afternoons Sam would go home to his wife and daughters, that is until his wife and daughters put his belongings out on the footpath one Sunday and locked the door. After that he came to live in an army hut on a farm property nearby.

Dorothy left home when she was seventeen and found work in a pharmacy in the city. When she was twenty she married a pharmacist called Phil.

Dorothy and Phil had been married for ten years and had two children when Dorothy's father died and her mother asked them to come and live in the house with her. In fact her mother wanted to give them the house as long as she could live there too — she and her cat, for the rest of their days. Dorothy talked to Phil who jumped at the chance of taking ownership of a freehold house, while at the same time hoping he wouldn't have to spend too much money doing it up. It was a bit of a dump. They did some renovations and moved in.

It was a morose, unattractive cat that Dorothy's mother had attached to herself. It was a square-faced tabby tom with chewed ears that put its stink all through the house. Phil thought of bringing it home a pill. It wasn't just that it was ugly, stinking and bad-tempered, but also it ate too much according to him.

Ever since Sam had come to live in the hut nearby, Dorothy's mother had done his washing, which she would go and collect from him once a week. In return he would chop and stack wood. Usually when her mother returned the clothes to him she'd stay and have a whisky because Sam liked the company, but apart from that her mother had given up drink. Her father, while he was alive, had toned his drinking down too over the years, even though he still went on a bender once in a while.

Sam, on the other hand, had stepped up his intake. After his retirement he would get up each day at six, walk across to the yard and work on the wood for an hour, then he'd fill his bucket with water, which was as much as he needed for the day, make himself a cup of tea and tidy his hut. At nine he'd be on the road with his bag over his shoulder, walking the four kilometres to the local. He'd return at four, pickled, with a bottle in his swag to keep him company for the night. Dorothy's mother and father worried about his habit of smoking in bed.

And one night the hut did go up in flames, but Sam managed to get out with a few minor burns.

After the fire, Dorothy's parents wanted Sam to come and live with them, but all Sam wanted was to move into the old wash-house, which is where he had often bunked down in the old days. So they fixed the wash-house up for him and life went on much the same as it had before, except that Dorothy's mother would go out each night before she went to bed to check that Sam had put his cigarette out before going to sleep.

It was soon after Dorothy and Phil moved into the house that Sam started seeing spiders. These were as big as plates and came out of the walls at him, or if he tried to escape outside they dropped down on him out of the bushes. Dorothy and Phil would hear him yelling, fighting them off out in his bunkhouse or crashing about yelling in the trees. At first Dorothy's mother tried to help him but soon found there was nothing she could do, so she left him to it. But every morning she'd cook him breakfast and make sure he ate it. Breakfast was his one meal of the day.

So when Dorothy's mother died, Dorothy and Phil inherited the house, the unfavoured cat, and Sam. At about that time too, Dorothy gave birth to an unplanned daughter, whose conception Phil had been sour about, wondering how it was that Dorothy, wife of a pharmacist, could have been so careless and so stupid.

The cat never came into the house once Dorothy's mother had gone. It went wild and at night they'd hear it growling and howling out in the trees.

Not long after Dorothy's mother's death Phil began to talk about Sam being moved. It wasn't the deetees he objected to, although that did come into the discussion. It wasn't the fact that Sam messed himself now and again or wet the bed, because that was Dorothy's problem. If she wanted to clean up those sorts of stinks it was up to her. What Phil objected to was the price of breakfast.

In truth Dorothy was disgusted with Sam too, sick of cleaning him up, sick of his smell, sick of his dingbats. She knew that the kids were ashamed of having someone like that around, and that Sam was the reason they never brought friends home to play.

'But he's got nowhere else to go,' Dorothy said.

'There's the Savvies,' said Phil. 'We'll drop him off at the Savs. He's just a freeloader. Everything goes on the booze. Nothing for Muggins.' Then he changed his voice to a sing-song squeak, 'Nothing for Muggins but Muggins does him a breakfast every morning.' Actually Dorothy was sick of Phil too.

It was when she found the cat hanging in the tree out by the wash-house with Sam's belt round its neck that Dorothy knew Sam would have to go. She took the cat down from the tree and buried it before the children got up, and when she went back into the kitchen and told Phil he delivered an ultimatum. 'Get him out of here,' he said, 'or I'm off. Have something arranged by the time I get home tonight, or that's it, I'm going, you can pack my bags.' He went out the door and Dorothy held her breath until she heard him backing the car down the drive. Then she let her breath go, slowly, thinking about what she would say to Sam, which words to use to tell him.

When she heard Sam coming she went to the fridge and took out the egg, and as he came in she turned towards the stove where the pan was heating. With her back to him it was easier to start talking.

'Uncle Sam, there's something important we have to talk about,' she said.

Then she dropped the egg.

And there was the egg staring up at her from the middle of a polyurethaned cork tile. The broken shell of the egg had distanced itself, standing off like a misshapen eyebrow. For a moment she looked at it, thinking about what it might be staring at, what it could be seeing — like herself standing above it, looking down, one hand poised holding a tight space between fingers and a thumb, lips parted ready for speech, prepared for an outflow of words that were important.

It was seeing Jenny, stopped in the doorway with Neddy behind, their eyes moving from her face to the floor and back again. It was taking in baby Harriet who was crawling quickly from under the table, laughing, reaching a fat finger to poke. It was seeing Sam with his hand on the door handle and the door half closed. The hand was bluish and flaky and had the shakes. Sam's face, turned towards her words and the sound of her voice, was frightened, the lower jaw was hanging and dribbly, and the bottom lids of his eyes had turned inside out and were meatish-looking.

Then Dorothy put her lips together, turned and reached for a paper towel. Jenny and Neddy came in asking questions and laughing, the baby poked the egg-eye and smacked a spread hand down on the shell eyebrow. Sam finished shutting the door, turned with his shoulders hunched forward and his hands loose by his sides and said, 'What, Dotty?'

But her words, the carefully thought out words, the words of importance, had been cut off, swallowed, under, or over, the stare of the egg. And during the process the words had changed and become other words.

She finished cleaning up, turned the pan off and shifted it from the element, pushed muesli under the noses of the two older children, picked up the baby and sat down.

'What, Dotty?' he said again.

'Phil's leaving,' said her changed words. 'Tonight after work. I'm moving you into Mum and Dad's old room. It's no good someone your age, someone sick like you, sleeping out in a dump of a shed. Actually I'm having that shed pulled down,' she said, though she'd only just thought of it.

She stood, shifting Harriet on to her hip where she felt as light as could be, flipped the stove switch, shifted the pan across.

'So that's it. All I have to do is pack his things, after I've made us some breakfast.'

BARBARA ANDERSON

'The places and the people whom we knew when we were young stay with us and haunt us till we die,' said John Mulgan in *Report on Experience*. I was interested, on rereading 'The Girls' thirteen years after it was written, to find that my vague agreement with Mulgan's words has deepened into conviction.

The older and more haunted perhaps? Or more rationally, the stronger the impact, the longer retained.

I lived in a small town as a child but I knew several farms.

The different world of country children fascinated me. The casual question from the sink, 'Are you killing today, Ronnie?' filled me with awe. The bleak concrete or wooden killing sheds made a deep impression. These stark images, surrounded by space and light and solitude, are with me still.

I also wanted to write about the difference between country and town lives in those days. The independence and self-assurance of friends who had 'been giving Dad a hand' since infancy seemed to melt when they came to town. They couldn't understand the serials at the flicks. They were useless in traffic.

They got their own back though, these country cousins. The dumb townie didn't like the killing sheds.

THE GIRLS

ALL THE GIRLS COULD KILL. Their father taught them. — Stand astride grip with the knees yank the head, knife in. Speed's the thing. They smell blood.

All the girls did too. Blood, the sour smell of concrete and later the stench of guts. A gantry with a pulley was positioned above the sump. There was a tap with a length of blue hose attached. A naked light bulb hung from the ceiling, the shadows were sharp. Years later when Ellespie saw an interrogation scene in an old black-and-white she smelled the shed and moved her lover's hand from her thigh. His beard loomed. — What's wrong? She shook her head and stared at the face of the victim which filled the screen.

The killing shed was an exact square of concrete blocks. It squatted beside the woolshed in direct line with house.

— Couldn't you screen it or something their mother said.

— Plant a bloody rose on if you like said their father but she never got round to it.

She came from Argyll, a small woman with thin ankles and tiny paw-like hands. He fell without volition, a sinker plummeting. She maddened him, called him insane names, seemed amused, teased him with distance and flair. Sometimes in despair he could almost imagine grabbing that red-blond bush of hair, twisting it at the back, jerking.

— You'll have to marry me Elspeth he said.

She did, and hated everything about the place: the mountains which lay too near, slanting in long diagonals against the sky; the trim little cottage which became less so as the hot pink paint faded to

124

blush and the tide of grime mounted.

She chanted the Highland expatriate's song to herself, grinding it into her mind. 'Yet still the blood is strong, the heart is Highland. And we in dreams behold the Hebrides.' Except that the blood was not and the dream an ache in the mouth.

Why did she marry him then? She knew her own mind, a source of interest and pleasure to her, so why had she drifted into it? Not because he insisted, demanded, standing with legs tensed as though he might spring at her. — I don't think I love you, I mean . . . He slammed his hands together. — Love! Christ, I've got enough for a harem he said.

She tried with the girls. — I did try. She had dreamt of a romance in which she starred as Mother; of lovable infants tumbling at her feet, not four lean and hungry whippets. Shona, Fiona, Ellespie and Jean.

He slaved on the place which was barely a viable unit. Shona heard and told them. — The farm's barely a viable unit she whispered. Oh, they said. He was a hard worker. Elspeth, even her mother in a brief disastrous visit, granted him that dour colonial accolade. She watched him one evening as he fed the dogs from the dog tucker safe which stood on four legs beside the chopping board. His knife slashed and hacked, she could see it glinting in the dusk as the dogs strained at the ends of their chains, their barks screaming yelps, their leaping bodies twisted. He had been out since six that morning with one brief marauding stop at the house for food. Elspeth's mother watched in silence until each dog had been flung its share. She turned from the window and plonked stiff-kneed on the flowered sofa, pulling the knitting needle from the coil of hair on her neck. — He's honest, he's a hard worker, you married him now get on with it she said.

Elspeth knew she had tried to shatter the cool mother tradition she had been born to. Had tried to break the mould, which unless smashed, sets each daughter in her mother's attitudes. As soon as she pushed each daughter out to scream its arrival into the world, she tried. She cuddled each newborn, as emaciated as a Christ child in a fifteenth century Dutch painting. She suckled each grabbing mouth. She smiled and cooed at each set of grey eyes which stared unblinkingly at the centre of her forehead. And she gave up.

She took to little rests. As long as the girls could remember mother had a rest each afternoon. After lunch, once she'd got him out of the house again. Shona, Fiona, Ellespie and Jean, called Jinny, learnt early that you got them out of the house, though Dad leapt always, his hand reaching for his yellow towelling hat from the top of the fridge as she stacked the dishes and covered them with a tea towel, tucking in the corners because of the blowies.

— Look after Jean she said as usual one day in the school holidays.

— I'm going to have a rest.

— Ssssh Shona warned as they crept beneath the bedroom window.

— Ssssh snarled Fiona and Ellespie, lips contorted against wrinkled noses with the effort. Jinny picked up the cat which emitted the ghost of a burp. It followed them across the chaffy grass most afternoons to the woolshed where they played involved and hierarchical games. — And Jinny can be the baby they said. Jinny rebelled. She was punting her behind along the oiled floor beneath the wood sorters' table crooning to herself. Her scream brought them running. She had gouged her hand on the rusty shearing comb which hung from her palm. Shona yanked it out, blinked at the beads of blood welling to streams, picked up the hiccoughing child and ran. She was half way across the home paddock before she remembered. When Elspeth came out she found them all waiting on the back step, Jinny asleep in her sister's sharp arms, a stained tea towel around the hand.

— Why didn't you wake me!

— Shona's pinched face was blank. — You were having a Rest. You said!

— Mad . . . Mad.

Ellespie wanted to know what her mother did there. The girls were down at the creek after school, hunting for koura and she was sick of it, turning over stones and nothing there. — I want to go to the toilet she said. — Go here said Fiona. — No. She left them squatting in the chill water and ran up the hill, skipping the cowpats with precision. She dragged an empty apple box from the wash house, scrambled onto it and peered in. Her eyes met those of her mother who lay on her side of the bed, eyes open wide, wide. Ellespie toppled off the box and ran. Not even reading!

This one's the reader, Dad told Miss Pennelly, his hand on Ellespie's shoulder at school evenings to discuss progress. Their mother had gone too, originally.

— The Scotch, not Scottish, Scotch, have always known the importance of Education. Their public school education, and I mean *public*, is the best in the world. Bar none she told them firmly. — My mother is Scotch said Ellespie. — Scottish corrected Miss Pennelly. Ellespie let her have it.

But again she drifted from them. As it were. — You go Stan. Not tonight. I couldn't. She smiled up at him, her hair bright as sparks under the lamp though dimmed to faded ginger by day. He stood silent, hair slicked back. All ready. A muscle at the left side of his mouth jerked sideways as he shrugged into his whiskery sports coat. — All right you lot. Into the car. Not you Jinny. He lifted her from his feet, clenched her to him for a moment then handed the kicking child to Elspeth. — I want to go too! Legs threshing, stick arms thrust upwards to deny purchase, Jinny 'performed'. Elspeth dropped her on the floor and picked up the Fair Isle pattern as the door shut; she kept them all in jerseys. — You're too little she told the sodden heap bawling at her feet, her words drowned by the noise of the Chrysler's gears crashing as it slammed down the track.

All the girls had to earn the right to work with him.

— I'll show you once. Right? he'd say, and they nodded. Many things they knew because they had always known, the same way they knew the door at the Farmer's Co-op with the powder puff and mirror was theirs and Dad's the one with the top hat. They knew which way each gate opened, how to saddle up, whether it was a stray sheep on the Tops, or that plant thing. How to feed out. He yelled at them, his face twisted with rage, if they did anything stupid. He never praised them, except Jinny. Occasionally there was a wink as the last pen filled or they were cut out in the sheds. Or as they jolted home in silence, the scent of horse sweat heavy in the air. Killing was the last thing he taught them, when they were about fifteen.

Ellespie was older. — I don't want to. I just don't want to. Shona and Fiona had their own knives by now which hung in the shed for when they were home.

— You don't have to Ellespie said her mother. She pressed the palm of a hand against her black hair and pushed it into shape.

— It's completely barbaric. I can't think how I ever allowed it.

— You were probably having a rest Mum said Jinny.

— Don't cut your toast Jean. Break it.

— Why?

— Because. Elspeth demonstrated, her little paws tearing the toast into large pieces.

— Of course she has to learn said their father. He was puzzled, searching his wife's face for a clue. — What would you do if I was ill?

Elspeth laughed, toast crumbs spurting from her lips.

— You! You wouldn't know how.

So Jinny the smallest, wiriest of them all learnt next. She reminded Ellespie of a game little Shorthorn calf. Tough orange curls bunched above her forehead. Although nimble, she seemed to stand four square, planted, her eyes steady in her pale face. She came back from the shed the first time in silence. — What was it like? whispered Ellespie. The grey eyes stared as though identifying her. Every freckle showed. — All right said Jinny.

When they left school Shona and Fiona flatted in town. Shona had style, an unexpected bonus. She cased her angular body in luminous trousers so tight they seemed painted on. Pelvic bones jutted either side of the concave dish of her stomach, her hair was swathed and hidden in scarves. Scarves like those worn by where-are-they-now actresses, though most are dead. Gloria Swanson say. She worked as a receptionist for two years (The Doctor will see you now) then married a young thruster from Christchurch who was giving the place a go to consolidate. Elspeth was slightly in awe of her eldest child. — Shona is a strong woman she said and you could make what you liked of it.

To the end of their days Shona and Fiona remained essential to each other. A matrix of trust and ambivalent memories united them. Happy? Unhappy? They discussed it endlessly. Spent hours telling each other things they already knew.

— Jinny was the rider of course said Shona.

— Oh of course said Fiona.

— I never was.

— No you weren't.

— Still it was fun wasn't it? tried Shona.

Fiona considered her verdict. — We-ell she said.

— I mean a lot of it.

— Oh yes, a *lot* of it.

They wrote frequent letters telling each other what the recipient was doing, as though she had no way of knowing otherwise and would find the information useful. 'It is Thursday and you will be busy with the party for Doug's conference,' wrote Fiona. 'Wednesday so you'll have your spinning group,' replied Shona. Shona 'slipped away for a few days with Fif' whenever she could manage to park the children.

— Do you think it would have been better if she'd left? Gone back? she asked one day, her breath puffing a drift of icing sugar from the top of Fiona's Blow Away Sponge. Fiona took a long sip of tea and replaced the cup in its saucer before replying.

— Well there you are. She sighed in elegiac sorrow for all remembered childhoods. — Who's to say? she said.

Fiona had married a high country farmer. She took her knife with her just in case. If Bruce or the shepherd or whoever couldn't kill. But of course it never was needed and rusted, wreathed in fluff behind scuffed shoes, deep in the back of the master wardrobe. Years later she wrapped it in newspaper and took it to the farm tip because of the children. It gave her a weird feeling as she flung it from her. That poem. King Arthur's sword, a hand coming up from the lake. The sword though would otherwise have sunk, whereas she had to clamber onto the uncertain surface of the tip to bury the knife. She covered it with over-age or unidentifiable objects from the deepfreeze clean-out which had shared the wheelbarrow ride up from the house. Then lightened, at ease with the world, she pushed the empty barrow down the track in time for the school bus, singing *Jesu, joy of man's desiring* to the surrounding hills.

Shona's knife stayed in the shed. She seldom mentioned the farm. People were surprised. — You! On a farm?

Jinny used hers. She remained on the farm which she never had any intention of leaving. She was sweet as a nut, ageless as unticked time. As her mother drifted further further away she took over the housekeeping as well, such as it was. She slammed a joint of mutton in the oven when necessary. She swept the kitchen floor when the thistle seed puffs in the corners had accumulated to tremulous quivering heaps. She and Stan sat together each evening. Elspeth was in bed by eight. They gave up the television. The picture, never the best because of the mountains, now lurched continuously, rolling them into its world of home life and splattered violence, its marvels of nature, sport, and innovative advertising. ,

— It's a good advertisement though, said Jinny one night before they flagged the whole thing away in disgust. They stared at a lavatory seat lid quacking between rolls. — You remember a talking lavatory seat.

Stan located his matches and relit his pipe. — You remember the talking seat he said. — Not the product. So it's not.

— Mmm said Jinny. She put out a hand, palm upwards in silent expectation of his box of matches.

The next day she nailed a loop of leather strap either side of the fireplace so she and Stan could hang their feet as they dozed, smoked or listened to The Weather. Shona and Fiona never discussed with Jinny what would happen, you know. Later.

Ellespie never had a knife. It hadn't seemed worth it though she learnt eventually. She continued reading and went North to Training College. The lines on her father's forehead creased in concentration when she showed him the letter. He snapped his glasses back in their case. — Why d'y'want to go up North? he said.

Ellespie felt as though she had been caught red-handed, the jam spoon dripping on the storeroom floor.

— Oh well she said. — You know Stan.

— Know what?

— See the world. All that.

He drove her to the bus in silence but that was nothing new.

Everything about it was good. The tugging wind trapped and cornered by buildings, steep short cuts bordered by Garden Escapes, precipitous gullies where throttling green creepers blanketed the trees beneath. And Bruno. Occasionally if she woke in the night when he'd yanked the duvet off her she thought of Stan, how he seemed impervious to heat or cold, an automaton programmed for work.

— My father doesn't trust town men she told Bruno one day.

— Christ in concrete he yelled with delight. — Where've you been! It's like living with someone from the Lost City of Atlantis. She twisted the sludge-coloured mug so the crack was on the other side. — I don't know about the Lost City of Atlantis she muttered. — I've got a book about it somewhere he said.

He had a book about everything. They lay in bed all Sundays reading, swapping occasionally. — Read this bit. — The man's a wanker. — Yeah but . . . His arms were beautiful hairy triangles to support his thrusting head.

— God I'm hungry he moaned. It was a test, a gamble. Who gave in first, who crawled groaning from the low bed to pull on something and grope to the dairy. She had seen Dustin Hoffman in *Kramer versus Kramer* zip his jeans like that. Not looking.

On Saturdays if they weren't reading or making love they went to the gym. They sweated with the righteous, each cocooned in her/his personal individualised workout programme. Self-absorbed as Narcissus they searched for themselves in ten foot mirrors, faces blank or contorted with loathing not love. They heaved and grunted, pulled and swung. Tab the flab. No gain without pain. Stan, Stan, it's me.

Bruno despised joggers. — Yon Cassius hath a lean and hungry look he roared. She looked it up in the *Dictionary of Quotations* under Cassius. — Give me men about me that have muscles! He seized her, squashing her nose against his Save the Whales. She loved him heart crutch mind and belly. He was a huge man, a towering hairy giant. His shape filled the doorway outlined in flame from the light in the hall as he groped to the bed and fell on her. — Where's the light. — It's shot she gasped. — Oh well I guess we'll make it. When she thought of Bruce and Doug, oh well never mind.

She wrote careful letters home. — A friend of mine Bevan and I went . . . Bevan, I call him Bruno, says . . . Jinny answered in her large looping scrawl. — Who's this Bevan/Bruno? Stan wrote occasionally, painful lined one-pagers. — It's been hosing down since Mon. But we need the feed. How are your studies? All the best. Dad.

They were discussing abortion in the abstract when the telephone rang.

— I don't approve of it said Bruno, slipping a new insole into his gym shoe.

— You don't what? she said.

— I said I don't . . . He stood up. — OK, OK I'm coming he snarled. He clumped to the telephone hobbling on one shoe and lifted the receiver.

— Yeah. Yeah she's here. Hang on. He turned and waved the receiver vaguely in the air.

Ellespie slid along the dinette seat. — Who is it?

— Didn't say. He handed her the receiver and plonked down again to concentrate on his insole, smoothing it in place with careful splayed fingers.

— Ellie here.

— Ellespie? The voice was faint. The line bad.

— Jinny! Toll calls, like kisses, were for crises. — What is it? she said.

— Dad. He rolled the truck.

— Is he all right?

— He's dead, the flat voice answered.

— Jinny! gasped Ellespie. Bruno's head lifted. — I'll come straight away she said.

— You don't have to. Not straight away. Shona and Fif. They're . . .

— I'll come tonight.

— OK. Thanks.

— Jinny?

— Yes.

— How are you?

— I'll meet the plane then, said Jinny. — Unless I hear.

Jinny picked her up at five o'clock. The foothills were unattainable golden lands, the mountains hidden by cloud. The airport was a paddock equipped with aeronautical essentials. Its air of makeshift impermanence was enhanced by the knowledge that the slab-like hut (office, lounge, conveniences) was opened only once a day for the arrival of this plane. As she came down the steps Ellespie saw Jinny scowling into the sun, hands thrust deep in her pockets. She didn't move to meet Ellespie, kissed her, but avoided her sweeping hug. She picked up her sister's small pack and they marched meshed in silence to the car. This is totally one hundred per cent insane thought Ellespie. — Tell me about it Jinny she said a few

132

minutes later as the Holden swung onto the farm road.

So Jinny told her. How he needn't have gone to town on Tuesday. Not really. There was nothing vital. Where it happened. That turn by Berenson's woolshed I'll show you. How Stan climbed out, he must have thought he was all right. I mean he stopped Ivan in the paper car, told him about the rolling. Ivan had seen the truck anyway, recognised it of course, checked it was empty. Dad had seemed OK. Ivan said. He died ten minutes later. Ivan had been very decent. Everyone had. Rushing over with food. There had been a postmortem and all that. A haemorrhage of the brain. It can happen like that sometimes they said. Jinny's voice drained on, her eyes pulled straight ahead.

— And how's Mum?

The eyes flicked at her for a second.

— Just the same.

— But does she . . . ?

— It's hard to know.

— Jinny does she know he's dead?

—Oh yes said Jinny. — She knows he's dead. She sits with him.

I have all the arrangements in train Jinny said later, her mouth grimacing to emphasise the euphemism. — Guess what the undertaker said! Her laughter was a crow of delight. Ellespie shook her head in silence.

— He squeezed my hand said Jinny, and said he regretted we had to meet in such tragic circumstances! God in heaven! Do you reckon they do a course?

She told Ellespie that they would have the morning together before Shona, Fiona and husbands appeared, having made child-minding arrangements. But her room was empty when Ellespie opened the door early next day.

Ellespie sat with her mother who seemed pleased to see her and asked after her children. — I've always liked the Air Force she said. — There was a camp near us at home. Absolute charmers. Yes. She sat serene and vacant, even her knitting fingers stilled. — Have you seen your Father she said suddenly. — Yes said Ellespie.

She made macaroni cheese hoping she remembered correctly that it was Jinny's favourite not Stan's. She removed his towelling hat from the top of the fridge and hid it in the woolshed behind the pine logs, then corrected this absurdity and put it back.

The coffin rested on small trestles. It stood in the closed-in sunporch beside the lumpy divan, level with the Indian cotton curtains she had run up last time. Ellespie gazed at the effigy of her father which lay cushioned in white satin.

The skin was dragged tight over the beak nose, mounded eyelids sealed the eyes. Ellespie stared at the face against the shiny stuff and thought of Jinny.

At twelve-thirty she went into the living room. Her mother was sunk in the rioting flowers of the sofa, her hands folded over the *Journal of Agriculture* open on her knees at Poultry Notes. Ellespie touched one of the still hands. — I'll be back soon Mum she said. I'm going to find Jinny. Her mother's sandy eyelashes blinked. — What's for lunch? she said.

Tracks fanned out from the back door. To the sheds, the vegetable garden, the hens, the garage. Jinny's old roan was tethered to the fence by the concrete shed, his head hanging. Ellespie ran across the paddock and fell in the door. Jinny was leaning against the wall smoking a cigarette.

— Hi she said.

Ellespie's shoes scuffed the concrete as she moved to her.

Relaxed, indolent, Jinny flicked the butt down the sump and heaved herself upright. She shrugged, the slightest lift of the shoulders. — Oh well.

At the door she turned to Ellespie.

— Come on, she said.

C. K. STEAD

This story hasn't appeared in any New Zealand anthology before, and I suspect (though I may be wrong) that this is not because it doesn't work, but because its central episode has such a raw edge of the real about it, it makes our cultural arbiters uncomfortable.

Recently John Tamihere said that Tariana Turia had 'a romantic view' of whanau and iwi. That view is found also in the work of Patricia Grace and Witi Ihimaera. In fact, until Alan Duff came along, modern New Zealand fiction by and about Maori was dominated by it. I don't say it's a 'wrong' view and Duff's is 'right'; only that the picture has been less than complete.

The central event in my story — the Pakeha policeman chasing the Maori burglar through the night — is based on something that happened. Like my young novelist Angela McIlroy, I tried various ways of writing it and found that whatever way it's told, it seems to take on a symbolic quality. It is Pakeha law and Maori pride that are being asserted, neither with complete success. How will it end? There is no end, because this is history — 'to be continued'.

A SHORT HISTORY OF NEW ZEALAND

HE WAS 52 AND HAD THAT London look — dry hair (he ran his fingers through it, glancing at himself in the lift mirror), tired eyes, something unhealthy about the skin; the suggestion of less than perfect cleanliness, which, like Lady MacBeth's 'damned spot', no amount of washing would quite remove. Was there a word for it? 'Careworn' sounded too Victorian and virtuous. 'Stressed' was its modern and equally self-serving equivalent.

Within himself he felt little of this — only allowed the recognition to run through his mind, thinking it was how she, a 26-year-old fresh from New Zealand, would see him. As the lift doors opened he caught sight of her sitting in Reception. It was her knees that registered first, primly side by side, in dark stockings, with neat knee-caps and a fine curve away from each side, cut off by the line of the skirt. Good strong Kiwi legs, he thought; and then remembered how when he'd first come to England it had seemed to him that young Englishwomen had no calf muscles. It wasn't true any longer. In the intervening decades Europe had become athletic.

She looked in his direction and must have guessed he was the man she was to meet, but he went first to the desk and said he would be out until three.

'James Barrett,' he said taking the hand she held out to him. 'And you're Angela McIlroy.'

Out in the street she'd lost her bearings. He pointed down Farringdon Street to where the figure of Justice over the Old Bailey lifted sword and scales against the dome of St Paul's. The sun glared down through the haze, casting no decisive shadows. The thump of a 24-hour disco came up through a basement grating. Believing he knew how dingy and confusing these streets must seem to her, he hailed a taxi and gave directions.

They were settled at a table under a tree in a pub yard near the British Museum and had made their choices before he took the little tape machine from his pocket and propped it between the pepper and salt.

'You won't mind, will you?' he asked, and she shook her head. She was unassertive, making no attempt to impress him. Shy, he decided; slightly apprehensive, but self-contained — and he made a mental note of these descriptions.

No need to turn on the machine yet; no need to begin at once with her novel, which was the purpose of the interview. Better to begin — where else? — at their common beginning. She knew he'd grown up in New Zealand? — left as a young man intending to return, but had married an Englishwoman and . . .

Yes, she knew all that. She'd been told. 'Interesting,' she added, nodding and smiling — but he could see it was something other than interest she felt. Disapproval, perhaps? Or was it just indifference?

'I've been back, of course, but only for short stays — three weeks at most. There were eighteen years I never set foot in the place. By then it was too late.'

She'd ordered a salade niçoise. He watched her struggling to cut the lettuce in its bowl. Her drink was mineral water.

'Quite sure?' he asked, lifting his bottle of Italian white.

She held up one hand, like a policeman. Her mouth was full of salad. He filled his glass.

'Oh dammit,' she said, draining the mineral water and holding out her glass. 'Why not?'

'Why not?' he agreed, filling her glass.

'I'm not abstemious,' she said. 'Not especially. But jet-lag and wine . . .'

He nodded. 'Here's to *A Short History of New Zealand*.'

They touched glasses and drank, but the naming of her novel seemed to bring back that wariness which just for a moment he'd thought was about to be cast aside. She fell silent, waiting for him to lead their conversation.

'I read a large part of it coming down on the train this morning. It's quite a grim picture.'

She inclined her head.

'And a true one, so far as I can judge.' And then, almost without meaning to, he began to talk as the expatriate. Once started, it was hard to stop. Some part of his mind was detached. Was this the way to go about it? But then, why not? Somehow he had to get a response out of her.

His view of New Zealand was almost entirely negative, and at first, from the way she met his eyes, nodded, murmured assent, he could see he was taking her with him. But then he went too far. He felt it himself, and saw it in her eyes. Even New Zealand's weather, it seemed, was now inferior. This was London's third good summer in succession. She put her hand over her mouth, and her eyes were smiling.

He looked down at the tablecloth and thought for a moment. 'I'm a journalist,' he said firmly. 'Sometimes when I get a twinge of the old nostalgia I just let myself think what it would have been like working on the *Herald* or the *Dom* or the *Press*, or the *ODT* for God's sake — just imagine it! — dealing with local cow and sheep stories, while all the world stuff was coming in on the wire, written by someone else.'

She nodded, but with such a blank face he began to feel irritation. Did she want him to write about her book? Did she understand that he was doing her a favour? 'My paper has a million readers,' he said.

Her face softened, as if there was something she understood. 'You've done well,' she said.

Her novel, *A Short History of New Zealand*, began with these sentences:

'One's name is Brent and the other is Hemi. One is white and one brown, and they are running under the moon. Ahead and behind and in all directions stretches away the landscape of the plains. You could say they are the cop and the robber. You could say they are the colonist and the colonised. You could say they are the Pakeha and the Maori.

'They are running through most of a long night. Sometimes they stop for breath. Sometimes Hemi reaches the end of his tether and turns on Brent. Pursuer is pursued, back over the same ground. But then it resumes, the other way. They run and keep running.'

The novel is set in a very small town — what used to be called a settlement — in the North Island. It has one cop, a young man who belongs to the local rugby club and takes long training runs with his team-mates. One night he's taking a last look around when he hears something in a storage shed. He goes looking. There are some tense moments in the silence and darkness of the shed — he's sure someone's there but can't find him — and then the burglar, a Maori, makes a break for it, straight out and down the wide main street, the cop in pursuit. In a couple of minutes they've left the town behind. They're out on the open road, running under the moon through that empty landscape, sometimes on the road, sometimes across ploughed fields, through bush, along stream-beds, back to the road again.

The Pakeha sprints. So does the Maori. They slow to jogging, recovering breath. The Maori sprints and the Pakeha almost loses him — but not for long. Sometimes the pursuit slows to a walk, or stops. They talk back and forth across a safe gap, reason with one another, threaten, shout insults.

Then they run again.

With the Sunday papers tucked under one arm he walked back from the village, over ploughed fields, skirting the wood where pheasants, bred for the annual shoot, scuttled away into the undergrowth. The gamekeeper had set snares for foxes, simple loops of fine wire along the edges of pathways. James tripped them as he went. He liked the sight of foxes appearing on his lawn. Why shouldn't those handsome predators, as well as the tweedy kind for whose sport it was intended, have game for supper?

Anne was waiting for him on the gravel outside the front door. He could see by the way she held her hands, and then by her anxious expression, that something was wrong. There had been a phone call from New Zealand. It was bad news. His mother . . .

He flew non-stop. There was no choice if he was to be there for the funeral. It meant eleven hours in the air to Los Angeles, a stop of two hours, and then on again — another twelve to Auckland. His grief was confused with jet-lag and a dread of finding himself among relatives with whom he believed he could have nothing in common. But after the service, when they'd gathered at his sister's Mt Eden house, drinking and eating and talking on the verandah and out on the back lawn, it came over him how much he was enjoying himself. The hugs of cousins he didn't at first recognise brought surges of old affection. Trivial reminiscences gave him pleasure. It even pleased him to be called Jamie. He'd expected to find himself behaving in a way that would be judged aloof, unfriendly, superior, but it wasn't like that at all. In his strange, jet-lagged state it was as though he saw it all from the outside — saw a different self emerge and take over — warm, outgoing, filial, fraternal, avuncular.

Once or twice in his life a death and funeral had had this effect. He hadn't wept. He'd become an actor on a public stage. But this time it was different — something to do with these people, and with the green of the plum tree in new leaf, and the white of pear-blossom, and the freshness of air and light and water. How long was it since he'd felt such uncomplicated happiness?

He remembered that when he was a boy he would meet his mother unexpectedly in a room or in the garden and they would smile — not anxiously, just with the pleasure each felt at seeing the other. The sadness of that thought didn't spoil his happiness. It was part of it.

Late in the day he was asked the inevitable question: how was he finding New Zealand? It would have been easy to evade — to say it was only hours since he'd stepped off the plane. But what came out was 'great' and 'super' and 'wonderful to be home'. He knew it was the right answer; but it was as if, at least for that moment, it was true.

His questioner smiled, glad to hear it, but then shook his head. 'This country's a mess, Jamie. I don't like to say it, but the fact is *you're better off where you are.*'

That night he crashed asleep while the others were still drinking and talking, then woke in the early hours of the morning. He was in the back room of his sister's house, with wide windows looking out on the garden that was overhung with pongas and cabbage trees. The silence was so complete he strained for something that would prove he hadn't lost his hearing. A floorboard creaked — that was all. These wooden houses shifted with the changes in temperature.

A light shower began to fall, whispering on the iron roof. In childhood rain on the roof had always brought sleep, but now he lay listening, soothed but wide awake, his body still on London time.

He turned on the bedside lamp and looked in his bag for Angela McIlroy's novel, and beside it his tape recorder. He put the machine close to his ear, switched it on, and put out the light.

'The framework of your novel's the chase, but in alternating chapters you go back into the lives of the two men — family history, childhood, schooling . . . Did you feel you could do that equally — I mean with confidence . . .'

'I don't think I felt confident about any of it. I just jumped in and hoped I wouldn't sink.'

'Well, clearly you didn't sink. It's rather unusual, from a woman novelist. Not about . . . Not the usual sub . . .'

'They have mothers and sisters.'

'Yes, but the central characters . . .'

'You don't find them convincing?'

'Oh yes, I think so. Sure. As for the, ah — the Maori background . . . Well, I guess — who knows? I think only a Maori could say.'

'I'm not sure . . . I don't think I agree with that. I mean anyone, Maori or Pakeha, could say they felt it was right. Or they felt it was wrong. If you're talking about feeling, that is. Of course if facts are wrong, that's different. But no one . . .'

'No, I'm not suggesting that.'

There was a break. In the background could be heard the clatter of plates, the murmur of other conversations, a burst of loud laughter.

'Look, I don't know how to put this — I'm just feeling my way towards something. It's certainly not a criticism of your novel which I think is well written and well shaped. But the way it's done touches on something . . .'

'Delicate?'

'Delicate — yes. But I think I mean . . . big. I'm not making myself clear, am I.'

'Keep going.'

'It's there in the title — a short history of New Zealand. That's quite a claim. Quite an indictment.'

'Oh an indictment. Is that what it is?' There was the sound of her laughter. 'I think I plead the fifth.'

It was no longer a matter of law and order, or crime and punishment. It had become a question of who was fitter, stronger, cleverer; who would out-run, or out-fox, the other; who would win.

Those roads are long and straight, and when Brent saw headlights in the far distance he thought here was his chance. He would flag down the driver and tell him to call in help. But even while he was thinking this there was the twanging of fence wire and the Maori was off overland. He got a bit of a break on there, and quite soon, after crossing a couple of paddocks, he was in a field of corn. Something had happened to the crop. It was head-high but it seemed to be dried out, dead on the stalk and unpicked. The Maori plunged into it and disappeared. Brent hunted and then stopped. It was such a still night you couldn't move in there and not be heard. If there'd been a wind the Maori could have moved under cover of the rustling, but there was none. And the moon was bright. So Brent waited and rested. When the Maori made a break for it the chase was on again.

They ran through empty fields, through flocks of sheep, through cow-paddocks, through stubble, through crops of swedes and potatoes and cabbages, always well clear of farmhouses. Dogs barked in the distance. A nightbird sounded as they ran through the edges of a swamp. They came back to a road and ran on it. Then there was again the twanging of fence-wire and they were off over a field of onions. The onions had been turned up by a mechanical digger — they were lying on top of the soil, waiting to be collected, and they made it hard going. The Maori seemed to go over on one. It must have rolled under his foot, his ankle twisted, and for just a moment he went down.

Now you bastard, Brent thought. And then he wondered, What the fuck am I going to do with him? How'm I going to bring him in?

When he got to him the Maori was up on one knee, holding a knife. 'Come and get it, Dog-breath,' he said.

On the tape they sounded at first hesitant with one another, wary. He'd known it was because she distrusted him as an expatriate, expected him to be patronising. It had made it hard for him to get to the more difficult, and therefore more interesting, questions. But as the lunch went on, and she shared his wine, the exchanges had become more frank, less hesitant.

He ran the tape forward, and listened again.

142

'I keep coming back to your title . . .'

'Yes, it's bold, I know.'

'And it makes how the thing ends important.'

'Don't tell me about it. Terribly important. I spent so many months agonising over all that. Then I'd give away the title — look for something more modest. But that seemed the easy way out. The cowardly . . . You see I'd had the title in mind right from the start — before I'd written a word. That, and the basic story of the all-night chase, which was something that happened. I read about it in the paper, and straight away I thought this is a short history of New Zealand. But it had such symbolic force — too much. Pakeha chases Maori through his own land to enforce British law. Every now and then Maori rebels and turns on Pakeha, but then it's back to the old chase. That was okay in a way — as a story — because it was real. It happened, and it was believable. But if it was to carry that symbolic load . . .'

'That's why the end . . .'

'Yes, because it's not finished, is it? I mean the history's not. It goes on . . . So the end of the novel has to be — what's the word?'

'Tentative? Not definitive?'

'Yes, that's right, but . . . *Provisional*. That's the word. I had it on a piece of paper pinned over my desk. The ending had to be provisional. The first version ended with an arrest. They ran all night and then early in the morning Hemi just lost heart and gave up. Well, that might be how it would happen — but as symbol . . .'

'No good. I can see that. They haven't given up.'

'And then I had him get away. No good again, you see. Too easy. Sentimental. Because the real history . . .'

'Yes, it's tougher than that.'

'Then I had them fight it out. But how does that end? Pakeha kills Maori? Maori kills Pakeha? They're both killed? They make friends and walk off hand in hand into the sunrise? You see? Nothing seemed to fit.'

'Not as things are right now. But they're all possible, aren't they?'

'You mean in reality.'

'I mean — what do I mean? They're possible ends, most of them, if you think just of the two men. Maybe the problem is there's too much conflict, d'you think? The story sets them too much in opposition. After all, it hasn't always been like that. If you think of our history . . .'

'Our?'

'Yes . . . Oh, I see. You think as an expatriate it's not mine any more.'

And there the tape ran out.

'Come and get it,' the Maori repeated, holding the knife out in front of him. And then suddenly he was up and running, not away this time, but straight at his pursuer. Brent turned and ran.

The sprint didn't last long. They had run too many miles; but when they stopped the Maori must have felt he was on top.

'Okay', he said. 'Just fuck off and I'll let you keep your balls.'

He turned and walked in the opposite direction. It can't have been long before he heard footsteps coming after him, keeping a safe distance. Brent wasn't going to give up now. If he couldn't arrest the bugger, he'd stick with him until daylight.

It took a few runs this way and that before the new rules were established. When the Maori chased, Brent ran. Once it was so close he felt his shirt slashed, and a strange sensation — not pain, a sort of coldness — down his back. He didn't think the knife had cut him, but later he felt a trickle of blood. After that he kept his distance; but as the Maori turned and headed off, he followed.

Now the Maori ran again, effortlessly, as if he was doing it to suit himself. He didn't look back. They came to a stopbank — it loomed up high and straight above the plain on one side and the river on the other, with a flat grassy path along the top. They went up on to it and kept running, heading down-river towards the sea.

After half an hour they ran off the stopbank and down a road, and there, opening out in front of them, was the coast — dunes and sand all scattered over with huge white logs and driftwood that had come down the river over the years and gone out to sea only to be washed back by the westerlies. Under the moon it looked like a huge boneyard, with the sea thundering against it.

The Maori seemed to know where he was going now. He stopped short of the dunes and headed north over fields until he came to another road. It was there he went into a pine grove. Brent lost him briefly, and for the first time thought he should give up. He was now a long way from home, and nobody would know where. He might be ambushed and knifed. You could bury a body in the piles of needles and it might not be found for years.

But he kept going, relying on his ears and on the stillness of the night. He stood with his back against a pine trunk and listened. When the Maori moved, Brent went after him.

They came to a clearing and stopped. They were on either side of it, the moon coming through so they could see one another. They rested, sizing one another up. After a while the Maori said, 'You got a wife and kids?'

Brent told him he had a wife, no kids yet.

The Maori turned the knife-blade this way and that on his palm, as if his hand were a razor strop.

'What about you,' Brent asked.

The Maori said, 'Soon I'll introduce you to my mates. They're Rastas.'

Brent didn't reply.

'Where I'm taking you,' the Maori said, 'we got a big hole in the ground, like a cave, eh. We call it a tomo. You ever seen a tomo, Dog-breath? They drop dead calves down there. Sometimes a whole cow. Not even the stink comes up.'

He turned, out of the clearing, and began walking through the pines. He came to a fence and climbed over it. Over his shoulder he called, 'Come on Pakeha. Let's get there before the sun comes up.'

She'd solved her problem by adding a second layer — the story of the writer writing the story. It was what James had liked least about her novel, but he could see why she'd done it. There could be no end, so there had to be many ends — many possibilities, all left open. It was called 'meta-fiction' these days and it was very fashionable, but how could you get around the basic human appetite that every story should have a beginning a middle and an end, and that to be enjoyed it had to be believed?

The rain was getting heavier. The whisper on the roof became a rustling, and briefly a roar. There was the sound of water rushing along gutterings and through down-spouts, and dripping from ponga fronds on to the lawn. Then it died away again to a gentle hissing.

He thought of his Northamptonshire garden, the roses and

hollyhocks, the woods across fields with crows circling and crying. At last drowsiness returned, and sleep.

He dreamed that he was talking to Angela McIlroy over lunch, or rather, listening while she talked. She spoke in fluent Maori, though words like niçoise and frascati were mixed up in it. Now and then she paused in her monologue to turn the blade of her knife back and forth across her open palm.

He strained to catch what it was she was telling him, certain that he did understand — that he was capable of it — but never quite making sense of it. It was like something just beyond reach, or a word on the tip of the tongue.

FIONA KIDMAN

My travels abroad did not begin until I was in my mid-forties. Of all the places I was dreaming of going, Greece came first. Family ties made it my most important destination.

From the time that I arrived in Athens just towards sunset, with too much luggage, and too much to say for myself to the taxi driver, the trip took unexpected and sometimes alarming turns. As a woman travelling alone, I had to learn how to compose myself and act with unaccustomed restraint, and yet, at the same time, be prepared to stand up for myself.

I went to Greece carrying my father's camera. But I am no photographer, and I hardly used it at all. Instead, I found myself looking at the landscape as my father would have done and my eyes became my camera, the weight of the camera my father's memory.

What happened on that trip coalesced into a story which contains elements of these events; undoubtedly, the character is based upon myself. But 'The Whiteness' is a fiction, rather than an account, the character a person I can look at and reflect upon, and know better than when I started to write the story.

THE WHITENESS

WHEN IT IS EASTER SUNDAY somewhere in the world but not in the country where you are, a mile down into the ravine at Samaria does not seem a bad place to contemplate one's spirituality.

Or for that matter, one's mortality. The Samaria Gorge is the longest and deepest in the world, running between the White Mountains. To get to the Mountains one must go by bus, then for those who are fit enough there is a walk through the Gorge, a distance of nine miles. The traveller who makes this walk emerges on the other side of Crete to catch a boat back to Chania.

That is not possible all through the year, because of snow in the winter, or, in the spring when I was there, melting snows can cause flash floods in the Gorge. If you begin to go down and then find that the way is impassable, there is only one way to leave, and that is by the way you came, back up the rough mountain path.

The sign at the bus depot said that the Gorge was closed, but the woman who sold the tickets said that it was open. She wanted me to buy a ticket for the entire journey. I pointed to the sign and she laughed. There were young Germans with blond hair and flashing white teeth waiting in the queue. They were wearing mountain boots and they were impatient to buy their tickets. I looked at their boots and asked the woman about my shoes.

She did not understand. I took off my soft slip-on sneaker and held it up. Was it suitable? She laughed again, and took off one of her own shoes, a little high-heeled pump. She shook her head at her own shoe — *ochi*, no. She clicked her teeth with disapproval at her offending

148

footwear. Then she nodded at mine. '*Endaxi*. Okay. Understand?'

The Germans were muttering to each other. I bought my ticket and boarded the bus.

In the Mountains I looked for a guide, but there was none. When you go into Samaria you are on your own. I think that that is as it should be. The silence of the Mountains becomes your own silence. Each decision you make belongs only to you.

What you can, or cannot, or will not endure becomes something for which you are responsible.

It may be that you will make the wrong decision in the Mountains and then I believe it would be possible to die. But this would have been your mistake, an inability to judge elements and your capabilities in the face of them.

Oh well, yes, you may say, that is all very well, that is what mountaineers and white water rafters and adventurers of one kind or another do all the time.

That is so, but theirs is a calculated risk, a knowledgeable gamble; they are not tourists thrown suddenly and unexpectedly for a day into a primitive wilderness.

I do not pretend that I was anything else. 'Dear little Ellen,' murmured the English woman in the bar, the night before, 'do go, I'm sure you will love Samaria.' She and her husband claimed they knew I was a New Zealander the moment I opened my mouth but I did not believe them, for they did not say so until I told her from where I came. We may recognise each other's curious flat vowels but Londoners who visit the same place each year, year in and year out (even Chania), and read important literary works as they sit beside the window looking into the bay where the fisherman lifts his lines by night flares, do not know about us. I do not think they know much about anything.

They thought I would not go to Samaria. They had smiled at each other in the way of people who know better. I nearly didn't go, because of them.

Two miles or more down into the Gorge, there is a tiny monastery. If I get as far as that, I said to myself, I will have done well.

For, although it is good to be alone in the Mountains, there was also a confusion in the air that day. Certainly there is an aloneness of spirit there, but it would be untrue to suggest that I didn't encounter any other human beings. I had not gone very far along the path when I began to meet people who were coming back up it. They had begun earlier in the day. Nobody seemed to be certain whether the Gorge was open or not, and while some (people who, like the Germans, were wearing heavy boots) had gone on and not returned, others who were already tired just from going down were beginning to understand the enormity of their peril, the distance, the sheer climb back that would be entailed if they kept going and then found the Gorge impassable. Some had gone too far, and quite young people were coming back, their faces contorted with distress. It seemed impossible that some of the old ones would ever get back.

I said to a young woman, who was crawling back — this is true, the heat of the day had come upon the mountain, and she would walk a few feet forward then fall on her knees on the jagged path and crawl a short painful way — 'How far did you go?'

She looked at me with glazed eyes, and said, 'Don't go any further, for God's sake, don't go on.'

So that when she and her companions had gone, I sat down in the White Mountains, and I looked at the way that I had come and the way that there was to go, and I thought that I could die in the Mountains if I carried on to the monastery. Sometimes on this journey I had wondered if I would ever reach home again, sometimes I had been afraid. I had left home believing that I was a self-contained person. I was not certain any more. I was often lonely. Other days I felt ill. I am forty-five and my health is no better and no worse than that of many women of my age whose bones are beginning to feel the edge of change.

In the White Mountains I was not afraid, or lonely, or sick. I did not feel that I had to challenge myself to some limit beyond my endurance. The choice was simple which is not to say that the route back was. The heat was pouring between the rocks and midday came and passed and still I climbed back the way I had come. But I would not die in the mountains, I would return from them, and go on.

At two o'clock in the afternoon, at the top of the ravine, there are not too many places to turn. A canteen, and a rest house where a considerable crowd of tourists milled around knowing each other, and that was all.

And no transport until six o'clock that night.

I knew the way we had come, across the Plain of Omalos. It stretched away before me, a plateau about five miles across in the middle of the Mountains, and on the far side of it, a mountain village. If I were to test myself, this was how I would do it. I would cross the plain on foot. I would move close to the Greek earth, yet surrounded by clear ground. I would put myself in the middle of that wide space where I would not be touched. I am not afraid of space.

The sun had dropped more than I realised when I set out, or perhaps there was cloud descending on the Mountains. It was much colder than it had been in the ravine. I told myself it was bracing.

I would not have seen the things I did that afternoon if I had not walked across the plain.

At ground level, and obscured by the dead winter foliage from the bus where we had passed before, I could see whole carpets of blue and red anemones. I took out my camera and aimed it in the general direction of the flowers. I felt ridiculous at first, thinking that the flowers would see how inept I was at using a camera, and then laughed at myself, at the silliness of shooting off picture after picture at such crazy angles and without consideration for the way the light fell. I had not used the camera before. It had been my father's and it had been insisted by my family that I carry a camera. I had not wanted to take it because I cannot take photographs. I have resisted learning because I am afraid I will not take the very best of photographs. Oh, that is quite true. That is how I am.

What I did not think of then, but do now, is that my father had used the camera to take pictures of flowers which he would later paint. Subtle little watercolours. He was old when he began to paint but even then, he was not bad. No, better than that, he was good, but he left it too late to be the best. I think he might have been if he had begun when he was young. That was his tragedy you see, to have failed at so many things, when he might have been the best at this one thing. The very best I mean. I do not exaggerate.

Anyway, that was what I photographed on my travels, that and nothing else. Flowers hidden under dead branches. Months have passed and I have still not had the film developed. Perhaps there will be nothing there. Maybe I won't have it developed.

On the flat fields, shepherds minded flocks of rangy sheep. And hundreds of people collected wild vegetables and herbs, tiny plants which emerge in the spring and have to be burrowed for in the earth. The vegetable gatherers sought the tiny *stawyagathi*, each one no longer than a finger, yet they carried bulging sacks. As I passed, their glances would flick across me but their expressions changed little.

So I arrived at Omalos, a little after four, and sat outside the *taverna* to watch the people of the village. I watched discreetly and from a distance, I did not cast bold glances in their direction. They filled the centre of the village and it appeared as if a celebration was in progress. On the tables stood bowls of freesias and irises. Slanting-eyed girls were learning to flirt. I wondered how long this would last, for I had observed that women in Greece were grave and industrious and worked while their men sat in the sun and looked at women tourists.

A tractor hauled a trailer load of young men backwards and forwards through the village past the girls. The girls peeked and giggled.

At length, a man approached me, and offered food and a glass of *retsina*. He said that the food was special — it was a dish of something that looked like curious little batter pancakes with proved to be filled with a mixture of very strong herbs and a cheese-like substance. They were quite delicious. I accepted this food with modesty and downcast eyes, not looking at him — or not very much, although I did see that he had blue eyes, which in itself was exceptional. But I was careful, for I did not wish to antagonise the women. That care was to no avail.

The party folded, the air grew colder with mountain chill, and I moved inside the *taverna* which was run by a very strong-looking though quiet young woman. Many people came and went as the afternoon wore on and she entertained them, offered hospitality, but not one inch would she give to me. I asked for, and paid for food, I asked for the use of the toilets and she pretended not to understand me. I showed her my phrase book — 'Ghinekon, ghinekon parakalo.' She tossed her head. 'Lavatory please, please your lavatory.' I said.

She pointed over her shoulder and looked the other way. If she looked at me at all that afternoon, her look was always cold.

The man came back with more food. I refused him. I smiled, but I sat very still, not accepting him at all by movement or gesture.

No one else spoke to me.

A young French couple, dressed as in the time of hippies, came in.

They had hitched up from the town. They hired a room for the night above the *taverna* for three hundred drachmas. I asked them if they spoke English. A little, they said, and we talked but not for long. They had not come to talk to strangers, only to each other. The villagers welcomed them. I could see that it was because they were a man and a woman together, a couple. No matter how they looked or dressed, it was this togetherness that was understood.

The cold began to frighten me. This was deep biting mountain cold. My kidneys ached.

New Zealanders who fought in the war are buried in Crete. They fought on the beaches alongside the Greek people. At school, a girl in my class was called Crete, and her little brother, Maleme. I asked the woman for a brandy and she told her son to fetch it for me. I said to her, 'Eema Naya Zeelandya.' I am a New Zealander. A special kind of pleading. She appeared not to have heard me and I did not say it again.

Her legs were perfectly clad in dark stockings and she wore neat laceup shoes but her feet danced when she moved and she never missed her step no matter how much she was carrying from table to table. She continued this dancing unfaltering step as she walked away from me.

The bus came at last, sounding its high fluting horn as it crossed the plain which led to Omalos. The bus was full of vegetable pickers from the plain, and we descended from the mountains, moving into hairpin bends as if to pass over the edge of each cliff, and then as we came to the valleys the strong heavy scent of the orange groves came up to meet us, and the temperature rose again.

I ate, as I did every night, at one of the waterfront restaurants, surrounded by the hordes of tiny half-crazed and mangy cats which hunt in packs on the Chania waterfront, and I waited for the scarlet sun to fall into the sea.

But I chose a different kind of restaurant that evening, one which sold bland Americanised food. I liked to eat Greek but my stomach was in rebellion. I asked for a half bottle of wine such as I had every evening on the waterfront, but this restaurant did not have half bottles, only a large carafe-shaped jar. For those who travelled alone, the choices were to be dry or drunk or out of pocket. As I was about to refuse the jar, a woman at the next table spoke to me.

She said she had bought one of the jars but she did not need all the wine either. She asked me to share it with her, and that was how I came to join her.

Her name was Anneliese, a Dutch woman with long straight iron grey hair and wide cheekbones. Her face was clean of make-up. She spoke flawed but elegant English, and she asked me if I minded her smoking roll-your-own cigarettes. I reminded her that I was her guest.

She too travelled alone.

The waiter brought two meals although she had already eaten and I had ordered only one. I said I would buy her the fresh dinner if she would help me drink the jar of wine. She said she was still hungry and, like me, she had come here because her stomach needed a rest from oil.

We ate and drank and sat by the lapping water and the night submerged us.

I told Anneliese about my children and her face grew sad.

She smoked awhile, then said: 'I would like to adopt a child.'

'Why can't you?' I asked.

'Because I am not married.'

'Can you not have a child?' I asked.

'I've thought about that, but I could not carry a child without love for the father. I could love a child for itself.'

'Have you never loved a man?'

'Oh yes,' she told me. 'For twelve years, and I thought he didn't want a child, and neither did he think so then. Then he went away, and he had a child whom he loves with a woman that he does not love. He wants to come back to me.' Her voice was full of tears, but she did not seem to be a self-pitying kind of person.

'Won't you take him back?'

'No. Because I cannot take him from his child.' She shook her head, as if in disbelief.

'It seems like a muddle,' I said. 'But yes,' I added hurriedly, for she looked at me as if I had not understood. 'I can see you're doing the right thing.'

'It's no good, soon I will be too old to have a child and too old for the authorities to allow me to adopt one. I would take any child, any child in the world that has nowhere to go. I would take a black child, a brown one, a sick one, if it had no parents. It doesn't have to be like me, I don't seek my own image.'

I said that in my country adoptive parents were not always held in high regard, that there was a backlash towards women who took other people's children, that it was regarded as a political act against natural mothers, to take and adopt their children. I said this with a trace of bitterness.

She regarded me intently. 'So there are no lonely or abandoned children in your country?' she marvelled.

We both smiled, relaxed from the wine, and a little lazy about following up absurdities, although not so much that we did not, mutually, remain inscrutable about our position in relation to the absurd.

'Are you a feminist?' she asked.

'I suppose so,' I said. 'Aren't you?'

'Well . . . I believe so. What else is there . . . ?' She hesitated. 'It's hard to know what one is here.'

She had long cat-like eyes. I thought she was beautiful. She made me think of my friend in New Zealand who wrote to me care of each poste restante, good, vigorous, loving letters. And other friends. Those of us who touched, trusted, moved up to each other and away, protected and protested on each other's behalf, in our own ways. I thought of the dark Greek woman with dancing feet and of the blue-eyed man at Omalos. Had she been protecting someone? Was she like us, after all? But if that was so, why had she not seen me as I wanted her to? Why had she sat in judgment upon me, and why had I failed?

'What are you looking for in Greece?' I asked Anneliese.

'I don't know,' she said, as if startled. 'What are you?'

I shook my head. 'I'm not certain. I see things and they go away.'

It was true, and even now it comes back to me only in flashes of brightness, and a whiteness in the mountains. There is little to hold on to. I thought I would write to my friend that night and tell her about this, and about my day. Only days before she had said in a letter that she had come to the conclusion that it is moments lived most intensely that are often soon forgotten, or somehow erased. They leave their mark, she said, but the edges become blurred.

I did not write the letter and she will have to make do with this, after all. It is the nearest I can come — to holding on I suppose.

When I parted with Anneliese we looked searchingly at each other. I was going to give her an easy kiss on the cheek and I think that that was what she had in mind too, certainly I would have embraced her, if we had not, at the same moment, changed our minds and withdrawn from each other. I cannot be certain what she thought then, but I suppose she may have considered, as I did, that it was not as simple as that.

We shook hands, firmly and gravely, and looked at each other in order to remember, as best we could, what we saw. We walked separately into the Greek night on a Sunday that wasn't Easter.

VINCENT O'SULLIVAN

One doesn't live in Wellington for long, especially in the inner suburbs which carry so good-humouredly their cultural and bureaucratic freight, without suspecting that satire and reality are comfortable coffee companions, and at times even bed-fellows. I enjoy the pretentiousness of some New Zealanders because we're not very good at it, rather as private school accents don't quite do the job those high fees would like to guarantee. We are a people who are easily inflated and easily let down, as the sports pages on any Monday morning brings home. But we don't always distinguish between the two — the earnest puff and the seeping loss of air.

'Success, and the Oral Archive' touches, I would hope, the edge of some of this. It is, of course, nowhere near the nerve-centre where the national pysche ticks, and which waits its long, cool, implacable probe. My narrator would tell you that she quite appreciates why this is so, and perhaps quote Mansfield at you, advising how lies are part of a larger truth.

SUCCESS, AND THE ORAL ARCHIVE

W HY DID I CHANGE MY MIND, Lois, about the interviews? When you rang the third time. That's what did it. In the politest way you said simply no, I'm asking you yet again. You see how I admire persistence? Although what that in itself tells you about the grain of women's lives is another matter! So. That thesis topic, again? *Partners of powerful men: an investigation.* We'd never have thought of asking that at one time would we? But then sociology, political studies, personal intrusion — you need a doctorate even to know where one ends and the other begins. You're Management Studies? A feminist perspective? Really? No, you've been very sweet.

You'd want me to begin at the beginning, I expect? I've read stories that pretend they don't begin there but of course they always do. Although if there's no trick these days it's hardly a story is it? You don't read much fiction? Not in your line of study? I was *reared* on it, unfortunately. Life was what we did when we weren't reading. There was a gang of us at school who used to get the hots for Katherine Mansfield. You still use that expression? Each one of us thought she was a little closer, knew just that little bit more, about Big K as we called her, than any of the others. Libby, who was not the brightest of us but read the most books, went on to become what Tom called a muff-muncher *extraordinaire* and wrote an article on her years ago at the centenary which the only people who read it mentioned in their own articles apparently as being, in a word, pretty ho-hum stuff. Yes, still teaching I expect, what else? And who were the others? Kim who in our innocence we believed was rich because she was the only one

158

of the gang who didn't live in a state house. Julia was part Italian and prettier than the rest of us, and gave up being a Catholic to dedicate herself to 'human kind'. Her own words, those. A Mother Teresa without the veil kind of thing. Julia was killed by a mad bomber in a hospital in Bosnia. Carol Dempsey, dumpy and *quelle ordinaire* whose mother baked brilliantly. None of us said so at the time, but that was why she was one of us. Those were still the years when a sponge cake was the spiritual centre of New Zealand life, why shouldn't rosy-cheeked Carol derive some fall-out from that? And myself. Five of us who sat apart, drawing as much attention to ourselves as we could, talking of K as if she was number six. We reeled off paragraphs we learned by heart, we kept journals that were full of rage at Hamilton and the tearing winds that in fact hardly blew there but were an essential prop, like the magnolia in the backyard lashed with blades of light. We doted on sensations I suspect we had only because a self-centred consumptive made so much of them sixty years before.

Libby said one day that Big K had written only weeks before she died, how she wanted to be so clear the light shone through her, she wanted to be dead straight, she wanted to be *true*. The gang turned itself into a glut of transparency. We told each other, frankly, our innermost thoughts. Libby kissed Julia on the lips. Kim said sometimes, yes, she did look down on Silverdale a little, but there were times she envied us too because our lives were simpler and more honest, because her mother was the only one of all our mothers who was having an *affaire*. Julia said she didn't believe in Holy Communion, which was the most outrageous thing she had ever worked herself up to say. Carol's cheeks blazed like a grate when she said she had lied about the King's College boy touching her up in the Auckland Domain over the Christmas holidays, she has said it only because K has written in her journal that she'd been foolish several times with Siegfried E in the Botanical Gardens. None of us was transparent enough to say we never believed he had, Carol, not for a moment. But I played the trump card. I said I didn't really believe in Big K as I used to, that I thought I was growing a little tired of her, *enfin*. It was something that came into my head that very minute, because I knew *nothing* could equal it for a secret you'd never want divulged, and so they would believe me absolutely. I was translucence itself. It jarred the others too because they knew something had shattered. The gang would never again be quite the same, how could it? Catholics would go on without Julia believing, that was no great deal theologically. Carol's lies didn't matter even when she was telling them. Libby's tongue, well, did anyone care whose mouth she put it in? But from the moment I said that, the magic was shot. I could see the loss in their faces. There was a *frisson*, a charge that went through me. I can't tell you how exciting it was to say something so appalling, something that now sprang the five of us apart. As soon as I said it I saw the colour run *from* Carol Dempsey's cheeks, I saw Libby lost for words and Kim pick at the back of her expensive watchband, and refuse to look up. Julia tried to console me by running her hand across my neck, to ease the bereavement. And I knew that the rest of them would never know it, of course, but at that moment I was closer to K than any of them. No wonder I grew out of her. No wonder when Libby sent me that essay of hers years later in its 'prestige journal' as she called it, I didn't finish reading it. It had nothing to do with K, everything to do with Libby in full prance. I tried to read a few of the famous stories again when we were stuck in Nice after Ivan ate tainted shellfish, and they simply didn't work. Because I read them as I did in sixth form. I couldn't read them as a grown-up. So there was no bridge, was there, from then to now, from me to her?

The point, you see, is to know where we start. To know, and then forget about it completely. I can't stand a successful man — John for example is one who comes to mind — a successful man who can't wait to tell you he began on the other side of the tracks. Then you wait for the next line which is always the same — *but baby, look at me now!* As if the Dow Jones gives a leap because a shares portfolio took its first tottering steps in a backyard with a plastic play-pool and a car with stolen hub-caps! It's as fraudulent as David starting with so many privileges he had to pretend they were ever greater than they were, two silver spoons instead of one.

I know you've done your homework, Lois, so I don't need to tell you David was my first husband and Tom my second and may well be my next now that Ivan has put on his trinkets and minced off with his Otaki dentist. All these years of 'Open wide' has to pay off sooner or later surely and Ivan was the man to prove it. Ivan's? Hard to say what quite. He's inclined to move his capital about so that only his friendly lawyer in Monaco is really up with the play. If he lost Gordon's e-mail

I suspect he'd be a pauper. But I'll let you in on something that may be worth jotting down. The one thing I *have* learned, either through my own husbands or other people's if it comes to that, is that it's not poverty that's the great leveller. It's money. The leveller to beat them all. The more someone has of it the more he is like someone else who has the same amount. Money's a tad like sex, isn't it really? A matter of back-lighting, isn't that what they call it in the theatre?

I'm not one for parables Lois but let me tell you about an aunt of mine, an unmarried nursing sister who recalled a flasher when she was training in Waikato way back in the fifties. A flasher who prided himself on his size. He'd step out from behind the trees at the side of the Nurses' Home and open a garberdine coat. There you are, my dear, get an eyeful of that. No nastiness, no dirty talk, just the flash simple, the opened coat, the heroic member fronting them in the frosty Waikato night. And the girl who solved it did it so simply it was next thing to genius. She stopped, quite unfazed, look at it with some attention, then said very politely, 'No thank you very much, I don't smoke.' Imagine the disappointment of that, the droop of overweening pride. I learned nothing from my aunt except that, but it was well worth learning. Another girl might have stepped back, hands raised, shrieked, and then flattered him into another dozen exposures. There's an American poet isn't there who said, 'All the fun's in how you say a thing'? Say rich, Lois, it looks rich. Don't say it, and the day after the crash you wouldn't smoke it for breakfast.

But what line is there between the girl I began as, with the clarity at least to see through truth, while her friends were blindfolded, so to speak, hoping their extended hands would bump into it if only they were sincere enough — between that girl and the woman I am now? Yes, fifty, if you must be brutal about it. But you know the general illusion, Lois? Because I have had three rich husbands they assume I must have carried sex through to an art form. The reverse is the case, seeing it's accuracy you're after. Those girls I mentioned earlier who were in the gang. I've had fewer lovers than any of them. Libby I hear goes to a conference a year and comes up smelling of roses, *new* roses, every time. Carol Dempsey, Carol-of-the-cheeks, has never married and never been without a man younger than herself since sixth form. Her cheeks still glow, to look at her you wouldn't think sin would melt in her mouth. Pretty Julia, I don't know about and never will now of course. And if Kim had notched her belt even in our student days in Auckland then whatever the belt was holding up would well and truly have fallen by the time she finished Honours. And so it goes. But I am the only one the public wants to gawp at. George from *Metro* snaps me at a party and there I am in the social mug-shots, the chink of lucre in the background because that is my ambience, my aura, whatever they like to call it.

They? Think of it like this, Lois. There is a kind of wheeling, self-perpetuating mass that congeals, flows, absorbs, discards. It has a dynamic that can't quite be worked out and that is why it seems so fascinating, because it's never precisely understood. Novelists worth reading, as far as I can make out, are interested finally in little else — how the social act is performed, who is acceptable, where the lines of exclusion are drawn. No, I don't mean I have a theory about it, Lois. Theories are for those *outside*, isn't that so? Theory is always a strategy to *possess*. If you're there, why bother?

It is amazing though — I'm on a different tack, is that alright? — how much can be achieved, how much destroyed or *raised up* — another Big K phrase, remember? — by hints, by indirection. By smiling slightly at the precisely suitable time. By looking from a window, bored, for even a second. That first evening I met David. A dinner party for a property speculator whose fortune began by wiring commercial buildings below cost and wiring them so badly there was a court case ten years later after an accidental death. But by then he was into fishing lodges and chair-lifts and so left quite different fingerprints. Two other women at the dinner hung on his very word. If he'd thrown a length across the table they'd have climbed along it like Jill and the beanstalk. David and the other males laughed a lot and in fact said very little. The failed electrician demonstrated how to cast an irresistible fly in tricky river conditions, absorbing things like that. There was a pause when I put my hand on the sleeve of the man next to me. The man happened to be David, although I would have done the same whoever it might have been. I said quietly, as though intimacy was the very thing I was after, 'It's the intelligence of *not* doing those things that appeals to me.' I feigned surprise when the table looked at me, when my apparent rudeness faded before the fact that I was so genuinely attentive to the quiet man whose arm I touched. The other men rather liked me for it. The women seethed of course. And David was mine as surely as if I had used a stun-gun.

I don't take any pride in telling that story, but I feel no awkwardness either. It tells you simply the way things were, the way they panned out, the way the dust settled. I can't help thinking of Robert Frost today, can I?

> And I was one of the children told
> Some of the dust was really gold.

Last week Lois I explained about David getting ill and the row with his brother and how their friend Tom tried to smooth things out, I told you that? Until David's illness became too much. Tom was a brick, as my mother would have said, right through. He's pure kindness, Tom, but he's kind to everyone in pretty much the same way so it actually becomes unkindness to the last person who believed it was something special towards her. 'The sadism of easy comfort', now there's something you might work on one day. Kind and a touch predatory in a mild enough way. I watch Rachel Fisher when she's reading the *Late News* in one of those jackets that looks as though it was *hewn* rather than sewn and one can't help wondering, you know, whether he raises her foot as though it's pure treasure, his mouth wet across it and under it and biting her heel before he props her back and gallops away on her stockinged leg in a way she'd have no more considered an erotic peak than I did, and then it's run of the mill. Twanging garters which is one side of him just as another is his wine club on second Thursdays or his tapping on suburban doors in Braille Week, his biblical turn as I used to call it, 'Dives helping the blind to see'. Rotary loves it, naturally. 'Sir Thomas helping again this year?' A little shiver knowing they'll work together. And of course he does. Of course he arranges her, sets the cushions under her, kneels in his satin dressing gown as he *slowly* rolls her stocking, the sole of her foot resting on his chest. I know Lois, it isn't the detail you're quite after. Dear expansive Tom, I don't believe there's any great merit in *not* discussing things fully, mind. You must know *Fleuri*, along from the Gardens? If you overheard us there my dear you'd know what detail was! Sit there with my friend Laura, say, and she knows more combinations than a safe-cracker. What do I mean? Last week in the couple of hours we're chatting there a dozen or so women come in, several groups at different tables. Laura knew nine of them. Of those nine, six were in their second marriages, two in their third. Two were now married to men who had formerly been married to three other women out of the nine. Simply from the gossip mills she also knew of four men who had undergone *affaires* with members of the nine, and two well-known netball coaches — one of them *très élégante*, you'd never so much as guess — had been involved with the woman who sat at the next table. That friend's husband oddly enough had told Laura's husband how another of them, always hanging about St Michael's apparently for all the difference it made, had taken him in hand at a PTA party of Kelburn Normal School. She was chair of the school board so had a key to the infirmary. It *is* an excellent school though, Laura says. All of which is to say, Lois, what a rich communal life we have although I know it's fashionable to say we don't. No, I'm not, as you'd say, taking the piss. See, you *are* smiling even when it's not thesis-friendly!

Back to frankness then, is it? I hinted to Laura in confidence I must say about Tom's *penchant* for fishnet. Is there any man I wondered who doesn't have a kink somewhere? Josh doesn't, Laura said, almost snapped it out, actually. I never doubted that, I said. I *didn't* say you only have to think of Josh in the cable car each morning, nine o'clock exactly, his paper folded so neatly he may well have pressed it before he left home. And the ties he wears, that merest bit behind what is just going out of fashion? Laura must see something, I suppose. You keep in touch, she asked me, you and Tom? We'll always be friends, I told her, he even asked me what he might get Rachel for Christmas! I told Laura that. Their first together you see and the poor man wasn't quite sure if she'd appreciate too much of a fuss. *Christian* fuss, which rather took the wind from Laura's sails. It never occurred to her that Rachel *practised*, if that's the word. These things, she said. Christianity. Judaism. 'Thank God they don't cut much ice with *my* family', not a flicker of irony in the dear woman. But knowing she and Rachel's cousin were such friends I made a point of telling her how Tom would try his hardest, I knew that, there wasn't a mean bone in his body, but I doubt the poor girl knew *quite* what she's in for. I know it doesn't paint me in the nicest colours does it but it was like lighting a fuse telling Laura that. I could see her in a week's time, her eyes raised above the cappuccino, confiding how she was so *worried* about Rachel, she so *hoped* things would turn out well. Tom's such a sweetie, she would say, but there is a history apparently, the less said. And the steam would rise from her cup like fumes round the sybil and those big brown eyes of hers widening with concern. And further along the fuse as Rachel's cousin talks to Rachel herself. Tom's *amour* will give her famous throaty laugh. But she will feel angry when her cousin leaves, and then calmly cold, that what she had believed was intimacy is worse even than common knowledge. It gets *pity* as well. She knows Laura is good at pity. She will tell Tom of course, make no mistake. There will be a row, then they will make up. Tom will insist they eat out the night the sports commentator fills in for her with the *News*. People will look at them and know they are putting things together. Later he will tongue as reverently as ever the French imported stocking, she knows how sorry they both are. But the fault line has already stirred. They both know that. The runnel of sand that will bring the cliff down. Rachel's cousin and Laura and whoever else Laura has been so worried with, you would hardly credit the threads that extend from *Fleuri*, Lois. The filaments and infiltrations, the returning tremors of the web. I'm sure Big K has an image for it if I rummaged around! What? Me? I'll wait for the phone to ring and Tom to say where would I like to have lunch then, and he will not want me to say *François'*, but that is what I shall certainly say because we went there so often. He will agree because he will be touched by what he takes for my nostalgia, and I know it is where we are most likely to be seen by those who used to see us. Next thing who else won't know?

Yes, I know Lois, I'm the last one who wants to call our little chats off. But I did feel I rather prattled on last time. No, I did. That stuff about the holiday in Cairo and *my* ideas on the pyramids, hardly riveting stuff. Edit the transcripts? I wouldn't think of asking you to do that. Surely it wouldn't be *authentic* research in that case? People fiddling the record after the event? No, I don't mean forever, not at all. I'll be in Melbourne early November then the Reef but I do promise, I do, the moment I'm back. There's an e-mail so of course you can get in touch. <u>Sirtom@ihug</u>. I'm assuming though you'll use other names when you write it up? You do? I'd need to insist on that. Discretion, when the chips are down, trite as that sounds. Yes, we'll talk more about business next time, I promise. Shares. Whatever you like. You know you can ask me anything, Lois.

165

OWEN MARSHALL

I wrote this story a decade ago, and even then I was thinking of rural men I'd known as a young man. Some I had worked for in vacations, some I had played sport with, some were my relatives, or my wife's relatives. Perhaps now characters like Tucker and Neville are far less typical of the farming community, but I still recognise the attitudes and backgrounds in some heartland people I meet today. Rural communities are more resistant to change, and the effects of that can be positive as well as negative. Prejudices can be entrenched, but so also can virtues.

The story has a gloss of satirical humour, but it is mild satire, and sympathetic humour, I hope. Sophistication may be lacking in country and small-town Kiwis, but many of them make shrewd assessments of their fellow citizens whether from cities or farms, and most of them in my experience have a sense of fair play and a basic good will. I laugh at these characters, but also with them.

As well I must admit to seeing something of myself in Tucker Locke, and my daughters assure me that I'm right to do so.

HEATING THE WORLD

TUCKER LOCKE WASN'T married until he was forty-two. A cheerful woman from the Taieri with good legs and three daughters finally decided to move north for the sun and take him in hand. Before that Tucker was one of a group of bachelor farmers so typical of the New Zealand heartland that they form a subspecies of the population.

After his mother died, Tucker had done for himself, as the saying goes, and with his cooking he just about did for anybody else who called as well. He had lived in traditional rural simplicity rather than poverty. He had an average downland mixed farm worth about half a million in bad years, and camped in his own home — a tartan rug on the porch bed, a laundry that still had a copper, and yesterday's paper as a tablecloth at breakfast as he read today's.

It wasn't that Tucker was a failure as a farmer, not at all, but his financial priorities and lifestyle were congenial. Super and drench, a new post-hole digger, or drill, the best stock and certified seed, were the natural expenses of life, but to buy a new lampshade, or replace the kitchen lino for reason of colour co-ordination, would no more enter his head than to dine at the Victor Hugo restaurant in town when he had food in his own home. A four and a half thousand dollar skeet gun on the other hand, or an irrigation mule at twenty thousand, were perfectly justifiable purchases.

The subspecies of rural bachelordom is perpetually renewed of course by the very process of attrition which reduces its contemporary generation. By the time he was forty even Tucker had become aware

168

that he was no longer typical amongst his acquaintances, and that there were deficiencies in a comparative sense. At the tables of his married friends he developed a taste for lasagne and apple strudel. His devotion to cold mutton, mashed potato and swede was somewhat undermined, and the sight of children forced him to consider the fact that his farm had no heir. So, advised by his friend Neville O'Doone who had taken the plunge a few years before, Tucker began the display which indicated that he was willing as well as eligible. He appeared in the retail area of his local town, wore a woollen tie with his sportscoat, and attended a few mixed gender events such as the trots and the show.

The community considered Tucker very fortunate in his marriage, and so did Tucker, nevertheless he had no knowledge of modern women and the marriage brought changes he had not predicted. Neville O'Doone was his counsel in such things, always in the informal and off-hand way that the subspecies deals with the deepest matters of the psyche.

Tucker and Neville were travelling together to an open day on shelter belt trials at Methven when Tucker first sought advice from his friend. They had been commenting on the management and condition of the properties they passed, doubtful of the future for Romney wool, when Tucker abruptly referred to Neville's wife. 'Margaret likes soap, I suppose,' he said.

'Soap?'

'Women like soaps: a variety of soaps and things,' said Tucker. 'I counted seven along the bath last night, and all partly used you know.' His laugh had good-humoured ease as its intention, but conveyed bewilderment instead. Neville told him that he meant shampoos. 'Shampoos, all different colours,' agreed Tucker. 'One oily, one normal, one dry, a body shampoo, a protein conditioner, an apricot facial scrub, and one enriched with the natural soil of some sort of pretzel which grows only in the Orinoco. And soft, pink soap which turns to a slush without use like snow, and vanishes as rapidly.'

Neville could recall Tucker's bathroom before his marriage: one block of yellow soap on which it was easier to work up a sweat than a lather, and with dirt settled into its seams as it weathered so that it was grained like a metamorphic rock. 'It's mostly liquid stuff they buy,' said Tucker sadly. 'It just runs away. You've no idea, it just runs away down the plughole. And women don't like to share a bath, do they. We've put in a shower as well. I could dip a mob of two-tooths in the time my girls take to shower.' In a half-hearted way Neville tried to persuade Tucker that shampoos and conditioners weren't really soaps. 'All do soap's job,' affirmed Tucker. 'Can you believe seven different bottles, and others besides. Bath salts and that.'

'Oh, yes,' said Neville, but then he'd been married some years before Tucker. He felt a little superior, the sort of superiority you feel when up to your waist in quicksand, but observing someone else in up to his neck. 'But you wouldn't want to go back to being single again would you, Tucker?'

'Oh, no. Hell no,' said Tucker, but his face was pensive, as if regarding a mountain of expensive saponaceous products degrading in natural atmospheric humidity.

They were together at the gun-club when next Tucker raised his home life. Neville had commented on a flash, wine shirt his friend was wearing. 'Pull,' said Tucker, and fired. 'Yes, Dianne thinks I should have some new things. My clothes seem to be wearing out more rapidly these days.'

'How come?' Neville hadn't noticed Tucker working any harder than usual.

'I reckon my stuff is getting worn away in the washing machine,' said Tucker guardedly. 'Women love to get the clothes from my back.'

'Do they indeed, you old dog.'

'I mean for washing. I've always felt myself it takes a day or two to feel comfortable in what you're wearing, but Dianne has it into the machine before I'm hardly used to it. Continual washing is bad for the stitching I'd say, and seems to be shrinking the waistbands, but there's no telling her. I'm getting quite a wardrobe now you know.'

It was true. For twenty years Neville had identified Tucker off his own property by his blue check sports jacket, but he was becoming more difficult to spot since marriage, as his colouration varied. 'Women have a good deal of clothes, you know,' said Tucker with some vehemence.

'I know.'

'My daughters have a drawer of pants each. Whole drawers of pants.' Tucker lifted his hands to emphasize the incredibility of it, then let them fall helplessly to his side. Tucker had been accustomed to maintain three pairs of underpants — one to wear, one to wash and one to change into. He couldn't comprehend the necessity of any other regime. 'Scores of them,' he whispered absently. It was axiomatic for Tucker that clothes were used until they were worn out, the same sensible approach he took to cull ewes, or tarpaulins for the hay shed, yet he was confronted with a philosophy which discarded garments because puce was no longer in fashion, or because the pleats had a tendency to accentuate the hips. 'Margaret buys a fair amount of clothes?' asked Tucker.

'From time to time. Yes,' said Neville. Tucker's expression lightened. If headlong expense was universal in wives, he was human enough to feel pleased that he had company in being a witness and somewhat reluctant backer.

'You're getting to understand why women look better than men. One reason, anyway,' said Neville.

'I guess you're right,' said Tucker. 'I've got two suits myself now, though I can't see that people are going to die regularly enough for me to need to alternate them.'

Tucker still shot well however, despite his financial concern, Neville noted ruefully. He has an eye like a stinking eel, Tucker has. He shot everything out of the air with almost vindictive skill and won another top gun sash and a side of hogget. Neither he nor Neville thought to relate the cost of their day to the conversation.

Tucker and Neville met on sale days at the Dobb Hotel, the only one in town that hadn't put in a barbecue and outdoor seating. Tucker drank draught beer, but slipped in a Glenfiddich every now and again as a chaser. It was in the Dobb that Tucker confided further in Neville concerning his personal life. They had been talking about the Celtic-Old Boys game, and Neville said Ransumeen wasn't talented enough to bring on the oranges at half-time. 'I've rather gone off fruit,' said Tucker after a pause, during which they both watched through the window Gus McPhedron trying to climb into the back of his utility for a nap. Neville found it difficult to follow Tucker's claim, for old Mrs Locke had been a great one for utilising their own orchard, and her pantry had held rows of bottle plums, peaches, and quince jam. She had showed them even, in the produce section of the A & P show. There had been boxes of wrinkled, autumn apples in the laundry, and Tucker normally had one or two in his pocket, or the glove compartment of the truck. He had a kelpie once which liked eating them, but Tucker had shot it for biting his best ram in a costly fashion. Neville said something of all that. 'No, no,' said Tucker. 'You don't understand. There's bought fruit, see.' His tone was one of shocked disclosure. Fruit was nature's bounty, something that arose naturally from one's land without great attention and with no mercenary aspects. Ah, but since his marriage Tucker had been introduced to mandarins and melons, pawpaws and peppers, passionfruit, oranges and kiwifruit.

'Do you know how much a feijoa costs?'

'Well, ah,' said Neville.

'Much more,' said Tucker. 'We have bananas often in a bowl together with oranges and pears.' Tucker was half defiant, half distraught, convinced that such hubris would bring his ruin. 'This morning I looked at the ticket on one of the bananas. They each have their own ticket you know. It had come from Ecuador. Ec-u-a-dor!' Tucker was silent after his syllabic exclamation, which had drawn looks from other tables. He was considering the number of chargeable exchanges and activities needed to get a banana from the plantations of Ecuador to his wooden fruit bowl in Te Tarehi. Gus McPhedron was asleep in the ute outside, the tail-gate down, the sun glinting on his tan stock boots. 'And the thing is, see, that often fruit goes off before it's eaten and has to be thrown out.' The concept of produce purchased from the ends of the earth and then thrown out was arsenic to Tucker's peace of mind. Almost bitterly he downed another Glenfiddich. 'No one bothers to eat a quince, or a plum, these days,' he told a sagely nodding Neville. 'The whole crop lies beneath the trees in the orchard for the wasps and the birds.'

'But what's that against all the advantages of marriage,' asked Neville.

'Oh, you're right there,' said Tucker. 'Of course I wouldn't change for the world.'

Yet at the Town versus Country game, in the first half, when the action was mainly down the other end, Tucker voiced further anxiety. He had picked up his family from town the night before and unfortunately been exposed to some of the prices. 'You know how much a lipstick costs, just one?' he asked. Neville was embarrassed in case some of their mates heard, but they were too busy abusing the town ref. 'Twenty-nine dollars thirty-nine,' said Tucker. 'It's true. It's true. And how often do you see a tube used right up. Answer me that.'

'You're blind and bloody half-witted with it,' shouted Neville.

'And Sarah wanted some shoes for aerobatics,' said Tucker as the Town took their penalty.

'You mean aerobics,' Neville said.

'Right.'

'You see aerobatics is —'

'Okay,' said Tucker.

'So she wanted sports shoes.'

'I went in with her myself,' said Tucker. 'Reddickers had a sale and I found a decent pair reduced to fifty-five dollars.'

'That's reasonable enough,' said Neville.

'Oh, but they wouldn't do. Not enough heel cushioning for the effects of aerobics the woman said. A lot of people did structural damage to their feet that way, she said, and Sarah said her friends had different ones. You wouldn't believe what I had to pay before I got out of that shop.'

'Tell me,' said Neville. 'Back up your man, Cecil, for Christ's sake. That boy's all prick.' But Tucker couldn't bear to mention the actual amount in all its grotesque enormity.

'Six lambs at today's schedule prices,' he said, and even the sight of the Town's captain being taken off on a stretcher barely lightened his spirits. 'Six lambs, can you credit it. And all for jumping about in.'

On their way back from the match, Neville and Tucker heard on the car radio that there was progress at the great power summit. 'They're wanting more changes,' said Tucker pensively. Neville thought he was referring to the world leaders, but after some confusion realised that Tucker was meaning his wife and daughters. Perhaps it was just a matter of scale after all, though. 'Interior renovations,' said Tucker, as if giving Neville a medical diagnosis of some significance.

'So?' said Neville.

'First grade Axminster, designer wallpaper, new drapes.' Tucker was marking them off on his fingers as he spoke, and steering with upward pressure of his knees. It seemed that Tucker's wife was determined that the good room get the works. 'Ceiling repainted, pelmets removed, droop light fittings and new fire surround tiles of

Tuscan red. We'll use the room a good deal more because of it, of course,' said Tucker to console himself, yet the car shimmied because Tucker's knees were trembling.

'It's improving your asset, Tucker,' said Neville. 'There's that as well.'

'That's true,' said Tucker. Neville's considerate response encouraged him to further revelation. 'We have all duvets now,' he continued, his tone wavering between pride and defensiveness. 'Yes, duvets on all the beds, and now we have a double dozen unused blankets folded in the cupboard.' Tucker had pressed past anxiety to a state almost of awe. The grandeur of the extravagance conditioned him to expect some providential punishment. All those blankets that had provided sensible warmth for generations of Lockes, now stored with good wear still in them, and duvets purchased in their stead. It couldn't be right in the view of a Calvinistic god. 'Of course I'm a believer in progress,' said Tucker stoutly.

'A lot of the improvements have been on you though, haven't they?' said Neville. 'I mean Dianne's done you up proud since you've been married.'

'True, true,' said Tucker. Neville was thinking of Tucker's wet-weather gear. In the old dairy next to the back door there had been an array of Locke coats going back into rural antiquity. Tucker's favourite had been a sou-wester which must have defied the last ice-age, and although the cuffs were frayed completely away, the coat itself remained so stiff that if Tucker took it off between cloud bursts, it would stand like a tent in the wet grass. And it blended in with the landscape so well that even the wiliest mallard couldn't pick Tucker out in the mai-mai.

'That new nylon parka for example,' said Neville.

'An anorak,' said Tucker. 'You ever heard of an anorak?'

'Oh yes,' said Neville complacently as a well-married man.

'A bright, red anorak.'

'Very fetching.'

In frosty July Tucker and Neville went to an euchre evening at Wally Tamahana's. Afterwards as they stood in the moonlight to enrich the nitrogenous content of the lawn, Tucker spoke with unease of the range of alternative milks with which he was forced to become familiar since he had been persuaded to abandon a house cow. Red tops, blue tops, green tops, banded tops, low fat, non-lipid, reduced cholesterol, anti-coagulate, mineral free. Tucker claimed he could see a logical trend in it all: the more things were removed from the milk the more the product cost. 'You know,' he said to Neville, 'soon we'll pay the highest price of the lot for milk with everything extracted — and it'll be water.'

'It's all progress I suppose,' said Neville, but he too could remember the cream jug of his boyhood in which the spoon would stand upright.

'Right. Right. Of course I wouldn't have it any other way,' said Tucker bitterly.

Neville was deliberately cheerful as he drove Tucker home, but Tucker, having lost fifty-seven dollars at the euchre to Wally Tamahana, was in a mood to resent any hint of extravagance in others. They rattled over the cowstop at the entrance to Tucker's farm and drove up the track. The median grass not yet brittle with frost whispered beneath the car, and the lights and the moon picked out the massed stinging nettles by the hen house and sheep yards. Tucker's house was a focus of activity and warmth, every room seemed to be lit and one of Tucker's new daughters was singing along with her cassette player. Neville thought it grandly welcoming, but Tucker gave a whimper. 'The door. Ah, god.' The back door was open in defiance to the vast, surrounding winter night, and the glow of double bar heaters could be seen. 'Look, look,' said Tucker brokenly. 'We're heating the world.'

ALBERT WENDT

I've chosen this story because it's a recent one and set in Auckland, where I now live. It explores middle age, unemployment, racism, and what they can do to an individual, his family and community.

I kept seeing this lonely, middle-aged Samoan man who's been made redundant, and I kept hearing a woman's voice saying, 'The eyes have it.' With these, I started writing, focusing on the 'eyes' as a central way of seeing. Most of the characters, streets and places have names which mean one form of sight or another.

That took me into a family, an aiga, full of love and loyalty, and what happens to it when the father/husband begins to fail, lose his self-esteem.

I like the story because there are mysterious, sometimes dark, forces weaving through it. I like the final design of it, the ways I've woven 'eyes' and 'sight' into the story. I identify deeply with the characters, and I'm proud of the strange ending which I didn't contrive. The story itself arrived at that ending, and even though I don't understand it fully, it does make 'sense'.

By the way, Pacific Islands people suffer the worst unemployment in Aotearoa.

THE EYES HAVE IT

'*The eyes have it!*' A woman's voice, a high-pitched childlike voice, stops him. Fiavaai looks around. The current of shoppers weaves past him, avoiding his scrutiny. He continues walking. '*A e fia iloa uiga o se kagaka, kilokilo i maka!*' His mother Fofoga. But why now? Why in the thick of this winter morning? Then to emphasise she's fluent in English — she'd graduated from Samoa College — '*If you want to know the true ways of a person, look into her eyes. The eyes have it!*' For over thirty years he's not remembered her saying that. She'd died in 1967, two days before Christmas, during a sudden rainstorm that had erupted out of the west and thundered across Sapepe and up to the mountain range, taking her last breath with it. He'd left for Auckland a year later, his brothers in Auckland paying his fare. Most people had considered her a strange person because she said very little and, when she did, she spoke in pithy aphorisms in her unusual childlike voice which she was ashamed of, and which he and his brothers and sisters were ashamed of too.

Fiavaai turns up the furred collar of his jacket to cover the back of his neck and ears. Head down, he avoids the puddles, the passers-by and his mother as he turns into Sighte Street and heads for Manukau Harbour, away from the main street and traffic. A cold, black light lies like sharkskin across the mudflats.

Mataola, their church and hall, and their pastor's house occupy the corner of Wideye and Ispy Streets, looking across the road and over the seawall, mudflats, harbour, the suburbs, towards Hillsborough

Cemetery sprawled across the hills on the other side. To his right are the wharves, storage silos and Mangere Bridge.

The front gates of the church are open. He can't see anyone about as he hurries up the driveway past the church to the house and the keys under the front doormat.

Unlocking the garage door, he swings it up. Pastor Migao's two cars are out. He pulls out the motor mower and catcher.

Later, hot from mowing, he takes off his jacket, puts it on the church steps, and stands gazing across the harbour and sucking in the thick smell of mud and sea, the odour of his childhood in Sapepe. He spent his first two years in New Zealand in O'Neill Street, Ponsonby, living with his brother Vaaimamao and his family and working as a cleaner at the university and hating his job. When Tepa, his second brother, got him a job at the Sleeplite Factory where he worked, Fiavaai shifted to Mangere Bridge to stay with Tepa. Since 1970, this church, which he helped raise money for and build, has been the centre — the eye — of his and his aiga's life.

Ten days after joining the congregation he started noticing Fotu, Senior Deacon Tilotilo's oldest daughter. *My eyes were upon her!* he smiles as he unhitches the full catcher and starts scattering the cut grass over the flower beds round the church. *Yes, my eyes couldn't leave her.* He joined the church choir and the volleyball and kilikiti teams when he learned she was a member of those. Then he *felt* her eyes upon him though she pretended, like a well brought up Samoan woman should, that she wasn't interested in him. Every time he caught her looking at him, she looked away. She had the deepest brown eyes he'd ever beheld, a glowing fathomless brown into which he dropped, breathless, and was held for ever. His brothers cautioned that because Fotu had been raised in New Zealand since she was five, she wouldn't be 'a good Samoan wife', but the 'eyes of his heart' refused to shift from her. They married at the end of the second year, two days before Christmas, during a sudden rainstorm that swept across the harbour and over their church, drowning out the sound of their choir. It was a splendidly large and lavish wedding befitting Tilotilo's status as an ali'i and senior deacon. Fiavaai and his brothers paid for Pupulasa, their uncle and ali'i, to come from Samoa for the wedding.

Yes, for years and years, he and Fotu have lived and loved within each other's intense and utterly trusting gaze. At thirty-three, the Sunday their second daughter, Fay Fofoga, was baptised, Fiavaai was made a deacon, the youngest in their church. Three weeks later Mr John Falseye, manager of the Sleeplite Factory, promoted him to foreman. A month later they bought their first house, then at Christmas their first car, a black second-hand Holden stationwagon. Yes, we have been blessed in God's gaze! Blessed. Fotu and Michelle Mata and Fay Fofoga and myself. Blessed with happiness and success.

Two more rounds and he's finished mowing the lawns. Using the hose he washes the mower and puts it back in the garage. Glances at his watch. Almost 1 pm. He usually lunches with Pastor Migao and his wife Matamumu in their house at that time, but there's still no sign of them, so he gets out the weed trimmer, plugs it in and starts trimming the edges, the whirling sound of the trimmer cocooning him from everything else. Their daughters have Fotu's eyes: deep brown and flecked once — a tiny black spot — on the right edges of the pupils. Uncanny. And like Fotu, when they're angry or excited, the black flecks seem to glow. Still no sign of Migao and Matamumu. He rolls up the trimmer cord and returns it to the garage. As he re-emerges, he gazes up. The light stings his eyes; they start watering.

The lunchtime traffic on the main street is thick and loud. He unzips his jacket, and the slow breeze cools his body. An old man, hands folded over his walking-stick handle, sits motionless in the middle of the bench in front of Bestview Meats, Fiavaai's regular butcher shop. He nods to the old man but the old man's hooded gaze is fixed behind him on the summit of Mangere.

From the rotund, rosy-cheeked Mr Bleake Glare, his butcher, he buys pork sausages, mince and pigs' trotters. 'Thanks again, Chief!' Mr Glare says, as usual.

From the Golden Eye Superette next door he gets their week's groceries and, knowing they have a little extra in that week's budget, he treats his family to some green bananas and coconut cream for a fa'alifu, and a large piece of povi masima for their Sunday to'ona'i.

The smell of limes and coconut cream embraces him as soon as he opens the front door of their house. Last night's raw fish. And his mouth salivates, retasting the tangy marinated fish. Methodically, he stores his purchases away in the fridge and cupboards, lifts the hefty basket of dirty laundry, hurries to the washhouse at the back, fills the washing machine and turns it on. He then rearranges and cleans the washhouse shelves, sweeps the floor, and returns to the sitting room and starts vacuuming . . .

5.30 pm. He hears the Lancer sweeping up their driveway and into the garage. Car doors opening and shutting. Their voices, footsteps, to the back door. Door being pushed open. Fay, then Michelle, then Fotu, into the corridor.

'Hi, Papa!' Fay calls in English.

'How's things, Dad?' Michelle asks, as they trail into the kitchen. (As usual Fotu is off to the bedroom to change.)

'Plenty of work today?' he asks in Samoan.

Fay sighs, rolls her eyes, and says, 'Yeah, too much!'

Michelle heads for the stove, peers into the pots, and says, 'Smells great, Dad!'

'What's our meal?' Fay asks her.

'Pork sausages and gravy, peas, mashed potatoes,' Michelle itemises. 'Great, Dad!'

'After you change, you set out our dinner,' he instructs them.

'Yeah, Papa!' Fay says. They shuffle off to their bedrooms.

His brothers and the church elders keep telling him that he is blessed with loving, loyal, generous, 'very Samoan' daughters. With high-status, high-paying jobs as plastics engineers. Most of the other women of the same age in their church are onto their third or fourth child, but here are his daughters devoting all their spare time to teaching at the Sunday school and leading youth groups.

He's never grown used to his daughters' physical resemblance to his mother: short and compact in stature, with prominent foreheads, narrow faces and large eyes, long delicate hands; and, like his mother, they are well coordinated and excel in most sports and other physical activities.

He'd switched on the heater in the sitting room at 5 pm, so the room is now invitingly warm as he hurries into it and switches on the TV. He turns as Fotu enters in her red slippers, ie lavalava and black sweater. 'Ese le pisi o makou gei,' she says, kissing his left cheek. 'It's nice and warm.' He stops himself from embracing her. For almost thirty years she's worked as a nurse aid at Auckland Hospital. She's in charge of twelve nurse aids and loves her work, though it is very stressful. She sits down in her soft chair; he sits in the other one beside her. 'News soon,' she remarks. He nods. 'What did you do today?' He details his day, and stops when the news starts and her attention shifts to that.

He doesn't watch much television — the news and a few other programmes — and sports, especially rugby. Fotu and the girls watch hours of it, and he understands why — it's their relaxation and escape from their heavy, demanding work. He tries not to watch Fotu as she watches the news but he knows she knows she is in his adoring gaze and enjoying it. He loves it too when he is in her slow lingering gaze. She lays her hand gently on his arm; starts caressing it. Her whole presence, like a quiet and slow fire, spreads through him. Just before the end of the news he hears the girls setting the table in the dining room.

Seated round the dining table, they bow their heads and he says grace in Samoan, ending, 'Thank you again, Father, for protecting us today from harm and the temptations of this sinful world. Thank You for Your generosity in providing us with this food, Amen!' His daughters wait for him, he waits for Fotu, who smiles, and starts filling her plate. A few minutes later they begin eating. 'E magaia kele le kakou dinner,' Fotu compliments him.

'Yeah, Dad, you should be a chef in Ponsonby . . .' Fay echoes.

'. . . where they have all those fancy palagi restaurants,' Michelle adds.

He smiles. 'I mow the lawn at church today,' he says in English. 'Migao and Matamumu are not there. They usually are.'

'Without you, the loku'll collapse,' Fotu claims. 'You mow and clean the grounds and the falesa. You even help keep the church books . . .'

'Reverend Migao doesn't know any accounting,' Fay continues.

'And his wife can't even balance the Aoga Aso Sa accounts,' Michelle adds.

'It is *our* church,' he emphasises. 'We have to ensure it continues God's work well.'

Fotu and the girls move into an animated discussion of what they've done that day, and away from him. He finds he is no longer hungry, even though he's eaten only half a sausage and some of his mashed potato. He tries to concentrate on what they're saying but finds his attention can't grip it. Their sound vanishes and he watches their faces and mouths move in a voiceless mime . . .

'Are you okay, Dad?' Fay interrupts.

'Yeah, Dad, what's wrong?' Michelle echoes. He shakes his head, smiles, and continues eating, conscious — and uncomfortable about it — that Fotu is observing his every move.

Afterwards, Fotu and the girls wash and dry the dishes, and clean up the kitchen and dining room while he showers, using just enough hot water to take the cutting edge off the cold and saving on electricity. He avoids the mirrors and any other reflecting surface as he dries himself in the bathroom and then dresses in his blue ie lavalava and red sweatshirt which Fotu bought him the previous Christmas.

When he returns to the sitting room, the others are absorbed in the TV. They don't notice him as he sits down beside Fotu. Automatically she rests her hand on his arm, as if to reassure herself that he'll always be there.

'What's on tonight?' he asks.

'Your favourite programmes,' Fay replies.

'Yeah, *Millennium* and *X-Files*,' Michelle confirms. He remembers those aren't on until later. He tingles as Fotu's hand moves in one long slow caress from his wrist to his elbow. He stops himself from looking at her as she gazes headlong into the television.

'Got to go and continue writing my sermon,' he says. No one reacts. He gets up, pauses and gazes down at Fotu's head. The fingers of grey in her hair glisten in the TV's glare. 'Tell me when *Millennium* comes on,' he instructs. He turns and goes into their bedroom and his desk under the front windows.

He switches on the desk lamp. It is getting colder, so he puts on his woollen dressing gown that Michelle sewed for his fiftieth birthday, and sits down at his desk. Opening the quarto-size pad, he starts reading what he's already written of his sermon: *It is not enough to fear God. You must love Him for the blessing of His loving gaze is upon you* . . . His left hand slides down into his lap and through the parting in his dressing gown and around his penis . . .

On weeknights, Fotu and the girls usually go to bed about 10 pm. So when he returns to the sitting room, he finds only Fay there. He

183

can hear Fotu in the bathroom, brushing her teeth. A short way into 'The Blood of the Shark', an episode of *Millennium*, he reminds Fay that she has to work in the morning. She gets up slowly, yawning. 'Fa, Dad!' she mumbles, then kisses him on the cheek and leaves.

A long gurgling as the bathroom sink is unplugged, and he hears Fotu going into their bedroom.

Once again the episode is about a serial killer; this time a blond, cat-eyed youth who uses an old-fashioned razor to carve his initials into his gay victims' bellies after he sedates them with drug-laced drinks. He then imprisons them in a deserted cabin in the forested hills of the Napa Valley. As the fourth victim's throat is slashed from ear to ear and his blood gushes out and splatters across the screen and the cabin floor, Fiavaai gasps and sits up, surprised (and elated) because his penis is half-erect, fat and fairly hard. He grips it harder to try and retain the blood. It's been a long time. Another savage slash across the chest from nipple to nipple. As he watches the wound parting and the scarlet blood starting to ooze out, he grows hard and thick . . .

Fotu is purring audibly as he enters their bedroom; sleeping on her side with her back to him as he slides into bed and draws the duvet up to his chin. Careful not to touch her, he lies gazing up into the darkness.

His dreams are clogged with new blood that bubbles out of the killer's initials — E.Y.E; and the squealing of pigs being slaughtered with bushknives, outside the frame of his seeing.

Cereal. Tea and toast and boiled eggs. He's also made their lunches. 'When did you come to bed?' Fotu asks, as she butters her toast.

'Very late,' he mumbles, avoiding her eyes.

'Must've been a *really* bloody *Millennium*!' she smiles.

He nods once. 'Yeah, fat and full of blood exploding in a climax of police bullets piercing the killers insane eyes and brains!'

'Yuck, Dad!' laughs Fay.

Soon, as they scramble from the table to the car and work, 'Have a good day!' he calls to them.

'You too, Papa!' Michelle replies.

'Yeah, Dad, don't work too hard today!' Fay choruses.

After washing and putting away the breakfast dishes, he gets the morning paper, sits at the kitchen table and, scanning the job vacancies expertly, circles the ones he's interested in. Four in all. He'll ring them later in the morning. It's been almost five years since he accepted his redundancy package — enough money to pay the rest of their mortgage and other debts, leaving $15,000 to add to their savings account. Fotu, his daughters, his brothers, the Sleeplite manager and staff, and his union reps and workmates encouraged him to take it. With his experience and qualifications he'd walk into any number of new jobs, they told him . . .

He changes into his sweatshirt and pants, puts on his Nike Jordan's — Fotu's last birthday present — and, drawing the hood over his head, starts on his daily morning walk. One hour around the volcanic cone that is Mangere, through streets where he knows people won't recognise him, the pain easing from his joints. Walking at a pace that is brisk and strenuous enough to stop him from contemplating his position. Too dangerous . . . too upsetting. The slopes of Mangere are luminous with the mid-morning light. A lingering luminosity. Like breathing.

While he is still hot from his walk, he starts ringing . . .

After leaving Sleeplite, he relaxed for almost six months, repairing things round the house, gardening, going to the movies with his family and helping Reverend Migao. No need to hurry; he'd earned his retirement, Fotu kept telling him. His daughters filled in his unemployment forms, and he took them to the welfare office and got put on the unemployment benefit. He experienced no feeling of humiliation, believing he was returning to the workforce when he chose to. Then, when boredom set in and he *needed* to work, he realised, with mounting panic, that he didn't really know how to get another job — he'd never applied for work before. Fotu and the girls sat him down with the Saturday *Herald* and, discussing all the job possibilities advertised, they chose six they agreed would suit him best.

On Monday morning, they approved of the way he was dressed, wished him well, and left for work, with Fotu turning and waving to him through the rear window. He was so convinced he would get a job, he whistled and hummed as he drove to the first advertised vacancy, parked briskly in front of the office of Mangere Furniture, brushed back his hair and straightened his clothes, and then marched into the office.

The clean, tidy, prosperous-looking office impressed him. The middle-aged receptionist smiled as he approached the counter. Her dark blue eyes twinkled and welcomed him. 'What can I do for you, sir?' she greeted.

'I want to apply for the job advertised last Saturday.' She nodded and told him she'd get the personnel manager who came in a few minutes later and, after introducing himself, took him into his office.

'We have many of your people working here,' the youthful manager said. 'Very good workers. Two are foremen. Seemoreans, I think.' The manager was formal but welcoming in his questions about his work experience and background. 'We still have two vacancies, so fill in this form, and we'll let you know later.'

Enthusiastically, Fiavaai filled the form. The manager, smiling widely, shook his hand firmly and wished him well.

Fiavaai brimmed with confidence as he drove to the next vacancy: a small factory behind a row of large warehouses. Two pick-up trucks in the parking lot. The screeching of electric saws ripping through timber. The large sliding front door was open and he could see a small thin woman in a white blouse and jeans behind the desk, writing. He slipped into the office and stood looking at the woman. She glanced up. 'Hell!' she gasped. 'Did ya have to come in so — so . . . !'

'Sorry!' he heard himself apologising. When he caught the disdainful look in her grey eyes, he started sweating.

'Whadda ya want?' she asked.

'I come — I come to apply for the job . . .'

'It's been taken!' It was as if she'd slammed the door against his face, right against it, and was enjoying it.

He backed out, suddenly wanting to run, while she kept looking at him.

Once in his car, he gripped the steering wheel and sucked in air, deeply, to try to control his panic. He didn't want to believe she'd lied to him about the job being taken; he didn't want to believe she'd deliberately *attacked* him. And why?

He forced himself to drive to the next vacancy, and was drenched with sweat as he pulled up in front of the building. Trying to be invisible, he sidled up the corridor and into the office, avoiding the eyes of the workers who went by.

There were two young women at the counter. One was Polynesian. Samoan? he hoped. He went to her.

'Good morning!' she greeted. He couldn't look at her face.

'I come for the job in the paper,' he stammered. Without saying anything and smiling still, she pulled a form from under the counter and placed it in front of him.

'Please fill that out,' she said, handing him a ballpoint. She was considerate enough to move away and let him fill out the form. 'If you have any queries, just ask.'

His confidence started returning when he found he could fill out the form, easily. She returned and, for the first time, he could look at her directly. Trusting brown eyes, genuinely interested in him. 'O oe se Samoa?' he asked. She looked puzzled. 'Are you Samoan?' he translated.

Shaking her head, she said, 'I'm Tongan. I'll give your form to our manager and when they make a decision, we'll let you know.'

'Thank you,' he replied, meaning it, grateful she'd treated him well.

Another form to fill in at the next company. The male receptionist was polite but emotionless, which he found he didn't mind.

The owner of the next furniture company, a large, gruff palagi who stank of BO, let him get as far as telling him he'd spent twenty-plus years at Sleeplite, and then informed him the three advertised vacancies had been filled.

He dreaded going to the next one, and sped home, his heart pounding in his throat. That evening he told his family his interviews had gone well.

No one rang back.

That Saturday he pretended he was as enthusiastic and as hopeful as his daughters were as they went through the paper, listing more jobs he should apply for. They also wrote and sent three application letters for him. They coached him some more about interviews. 'Jus' sock it to those palagis!' Michelle and Fay encouraged him.

'They need you; you don't need them!' laughed Fotu.

On Monday he drove to the first vacancy, prepared and expecting to be *mistreated*. He was. The smileless Polynesian manager, after he told him what he'd come for, said, 'No, you've come too late,' and turned away and continued talking to the woman at the desk behind him. Once again, panic threatened to explode from his belly and out through all his veins as he sat in his car by Manukau Harbour, oblivious to the stench of the mudflats, trying to contain his disintegration with the hope that he'd again 'misread' the way he'd been treated. After all, Polynesians — Niuean, in this case? — didn't mistreat other Polynesians. When the possibility that he wasn't being considered seriously because he was middle-aged and Samoan (a Coconut) intruded, he rejected it. But he was too afraid to go to the other job vacancies on his list.

When he got home, he tried to garden to distract his fears. He couldn't. The soap operas on TV didn't work either. So for the first time in years he prepared their evening meal. As a youth in Sapepe he'd cooked for and served his elders; that skill returned, and he was consoled momentarily when his family declared his cooking was delicious. Again he lied to them that his interviews had gone well. After dinner he insisted on washing the dishes and cleaning the kitchen, so he wouldn't have to sit and watch TV with Fotu. After that, he disappeared into their bedroom on the pretext of working on a sermon. By the time Fotu came to bed, he was in bed pretending to be asleep.

He was awake at 6 am and, wanting to avoid his family's scrutiny, was into his sports gear and on his first morning walk, ever.

Within the next few weeks, they established and refined the routine of the weekend job search in the paper and the shortlisting of job prospects, his daughters writing a few applications, and then his round of visiting the companies and waiting for replies that rarely arrived. Part of that routine became his morning walk to avoid having to face his family; and his shopping for and cooking of the evening meal.

After he'd got his daughters to show him how to use the washing machine and vacuum cleaner, doing the laundry and house-cleaning became part of that too. At first he'd been tempted to escape the day and the job interviews by going to the pubs or billiard saloons or the TAB like many other unemployed Samoan men. One visit to each place confirmed his absolute lack of interest in such activities and the unemployed who participated in them. It was ridiculous trying to like alcohol — the taste made him want to vomit.

He felt vulnerable to ridicule at church the first few months he was unemployed, but when Fotu kept reminding him that three of the other deacons and over half the adult congregation were out of work, and as he spent more and more time helping Reverend Migao, that feeling disappeared.

By the end of the second year of his unemployment, he and his family accepted and honoured the routine; they also accepted that no one was ever to mention that the routine was never going to get him a job.

He is careful not to wake her as he slips under the duvet and puts out the bedside lamp. He now accepts, after a few years of it, that he won't be able to sleep for at least an hour. That hour he usually spends gazing up into the darkness and letting his thoughts wander. He lies as still as possible, as if he doesn't want his surroundings to know he's there.

His sexual relationship with Fotu had always been full, fairly uninhibited, and hugely enjoyable. But partway through the third year of his unemployment it had started to *falter* — his euphemism for it. He was shocked and ashamed to the knife-sharp quick of his pride when, while at full exhilarating stride, he started losing it. Desperately he tried to hold it but it faded to a limpness which he tried, unsuccessfully, to revive with his hand. 'Don't worry, you're just anxious and tired!' Fotu consoled him. He insisted on proving he was still able, by using his hand until he was hard and spurting over her belly. 'See, you're still okay,' she whispered.

But it happened again that Sunday night when, aroused by *X-Files*, he hurried to bed and an eager Fotu and discovered, to his humiliation, that his saliva-slippery hand and then her usually magic mouth couldn't get him strong enough to enter her. Believing her to be profoundly disappointed — though she insisted she wasn't — he used his mouth and hands to make her come.

Every time he failed (his description) — and it was now frequent — Fotu insisted it was because he was tired and stressed. Just relax, it'll come back! she assured him. But it worsened and he started avoiding any situation that might result in sex between them.

As he relaxes into sleep, he senses her moving up against his side. He tenses, hoping she'll fall asleep again. But she turns and presses her breasts and belly against him, and her hand over his left breast. *She's deliberately challenging me to fail again!* When she opens her thighs and places her right leg over his belly, he's convinced she wants to humiliate him further. She nestles her face into his neck; her tongue starts rippling across his skin.

'Just relax, darling!' she whispers in English. 'Don't worry, just let go!' He tries to, as her searching hand slides through his public hair and caresses his waking penis. 'See,' she murmurs, 'see, it's coming alive again.'

Anxiety starts invading again. No, he's not going to fail! No! Deliberately he opens his sight to the exuberant and intoxicating imagery of *Millennium*, a compelling, invigorating current of it. Fear. Blood. Torture. Slit throat. The beautiful naked corpse half-buried in rotting leaves in the winter darkness of a forest.

'It's hard, bloody hard, like a steel blade!' he imagines her inviting him. 'Kill me, go on, kill me!'

Triumphantly, charged to his every cell with power, he thrusts her legs open and plunges down . . .

'The eyes have it!' his mother whispers, her warm breath tickling the inside of his right ear. 'Yes, *their* eyes have it!' He opens his eyes; knows it's Saturday morning. Glances at Fotu who is on her side, her face only a few inches from his, her mouth slightly open. He turns away from the stench of her breath.

He brushes his teeth, dresses in his ie lavalava and a clean T-shirt, and hurries to the kitchen. He has to lock himself in the routine again before 'their eyes' expose him fully to his fears.

Bacon and tomatoes and butter out of the fridge. Element on. Slice the tomatoes. Butter into the heating frypan. Electric jug and toaster on. Teabags into the teapot . . .

As usual Fay is the first to come into the kitchen, the first to say, 'Hi, Dad, have a good sleep?' He nods once, turns his back to her as she starts getting out the crockery and cutlery and setting the table.

When he turns from the stove, his heart and ears zinging with the crackling of the bacon, Michelle is seated at the table, yawning repeatedly as she combs her hair. 'Smells great, Dad!' she says. 'I could eat a horse.'

'Then get up and help!' He can't believe he's just said that. Michelle looks surprised and hurt, but he finds he doesn't want to retract his criticism. 'That's what you do every Saturday morning: let your father and sister cook your bloody breakfast!' He can't believe he's capable of such severity, but he's glad, yes, glad of it. 'Yes, I must be the only stupid Samoan father who cooks for and serves his children and . . .' He stops, decides he likes it. '. . . and his wife! It's humiliating!' Thrusting the tongs at Michelle, he orders, 'You take that and help your sister cook the breakfast.' She pulls the tongs out of his grip and turns away, abruptly. 'Don't you bloody well treat me like that!' he hears himself shouting. He's glad when his arm rears up, fist clenched, ready to strike down at Michelle's head.

'Don't, Dad!' Fay's frantic plea grips his arm.

'I'm sick and tired of being treated as a woman and a bludger — yes, a useless bludger — in this family!' He wheels and stumbles towards the front door. Stops. Turns round again. Michelle is weeping into Fotu's shoulder. His mother stands with a protective arm round Fay, glaring at him. 'I've had enough of all of you watching me, spying on me, stripping me down to my — to my soul!' Arms wrapped around his head like shields, he crumples to his knees and listens to his sobbing filling the corridor and the accusing eyes of his daughters and wife, and his mother, who is trying to say, *'Your father's eyes have it but you never knew your father, did you?'*

KERI HULME

Your favourite is now, (the one you're working on — with).

Given that 'A Night Song for the Shining Cuckoo' was written in 1979, published in *Landfall* in 1981 (under a pen-name 'Kai Tainui'), why choose it above past — or, more particularly — current material?

I once had the experience of writing a short story that turned out to be the innards of a novel. That was 'Simon Peter's Shell', all copies of which I destroyed, but the thing had legs. It became *The Bone People*.

When 'Night Song' appeared, I was buoyed — and deflated. I am a feminist: it was irritating that the male persona I had taken on was so readily acceptable to 'the establishment' (we won't go into the Maori dimensions), but it was bloody allergic-reaction time when my female lead had her name arbitrarily feminised.

Maybe that's why Francis and Bird and Charlie hung round in my head for so long after. Or maybe they were really intriguing people and I wanted to know more about them. For I did: I pursued them down the years. It has turned out they were not innards, but the penumbra — the soul, wairua — of 'Bait'.

Kia ora tatou katoa.

NIGHTSONG FOR THE SHINING CUCKOO

I HEAR THEM SINGING in the hills, *kui kui kui, whiti whiti ora.* Rainbirds. I used to think, O hell, rain coming.

Charlie's strumming the guitar, humming the sad little nursery rhyme. The rainbirds set him wondering too.

I broke my back falling off a log. It was a nice log; I used it for crossing the stream between my place and the beach. At first it felt like I'd just sat down too hard. Then it didn't feel. Four hours later, a hiker chanced by, which was lucky, and pulled me out of the stream, which wasn't. I had plenty of time in hospital to moan about it. 'I would have died. I *should* have died. I'm gonna be a cripple. I'm gonna be useless.' I went through all the stages: self-pity; rage; why? why *me*? more rage; and finally, well, what do I do now?

There was one thing I wasn't going to do.

Sometimes in my old town you'd see them, blanket-lapped waists, wheeling through the streets. They sought a dark indoors, a drowning, to stay in gentle beer and gin. All the stares knew that beneath the blanket was maiming; bare scarred nubs, amputations. So they hid.

I didn't buy a blanket. I didn't hide. I didn't go back to my lonely beach. 'You're mad,' said the physiotherapist. 'You've never lived in a city have you? Why start now of all times? And I can't imagine anyone less like a shopkeeper, you old bush — ahh — person, you.'

I said, 'Not so old. I can change my ways. I have to, eh.'

I didn't say, 'Beneath the cage of ribs there's a bare scarred heart. My old life is smashed. I want a new way so different I won't have to think about what I was. In the city, I won't hear the sea, the bush-wind or the birds.'

'I'm looking forward to it,' I lied to the physio.

There's no future when your body has betrayed you.

They loaded me onto the plane by forklift, as though I was a container of freight. They loaded me off the same way. I'm strong in the shoulders and arms, stronger now than ever. I hauled myself into the back seat of the taxi; the driver folded my wheels into the boot.

'Where to, mate?'

I opened my eyes after a minute and looked at him. Would you believe Heaven, mate? Would you believe Hell?

But we went to the land agent's instead. The agent looked at me dubiously.

'It's got the space you required,' he says, 'but the area it's in . . . you're sure you want to — ahh — spend your money this way?'

Why don't you take a world cruise or join a Cripples' Home or retire somewhere out of sight, he meant.

The flat at the back of the shop could be altered to be adequate. The shop itself was the only dairy for five streets. The previous owners had made a mint, they said. You'll have to restock it, but it's a neat self-service operation ideal for . . . you. Particularly when you engage your assistant.

I nodded. In the glow of their figures, all profit no loss, I could see myself sitting smiling behind the counter, watching the till grow fat. I *would* get myself an assistant. I shook hands all round. I said I wanted to stay the night. I could manage until tomorrow when a carpenter would come and start changing the flat to meet my needs. They fussed. Then they went away smiling and left me staring at the present.

Bleak bare lights.

Spiders sneering from corners.

A nugget-black bug rollicked under the till.

Encrusted dirt I hadn't noticed until now.

Outside there's screams and a sound of breaking glass.

A dog goes yelping down the street Au! Au! Au!

Unholy, I can't do this all by myself.

There was a knock on my insect-freckled windows. I slewed the chair round. All I can see is a shadow watching me. Some bloody nosy kid, right, it's going to cop an earful, but by the time I get the door open, there is nobody there.

I wrote to Fraser asking for help, for the first time ever. Fraser wrote back. Fraser had priorities. He began,

> Dear Sister, good to hear from you. Glad to hear you're up and about again. Sorry we couldn't make it to see you, but we are particularly busy right now. I've just shifted the hydrangeas, and trimmed the wisteria, and begun a new rockery.

The garden details went on for two pages, plumeria, saxifrage, lobelia, and the letter ended,

> Sorry we can't make it up to see you in your new start in life, but you will realise the need for us to look after our own property. Madge has just got over The Change, and doesn't like even the thought of travel. However, Charles says he'll come and see you, but I've never known Charles to keep his word in anything. Your loving brother.

We never were close.

Poor Fraser. You adopt a child and try very hard to mould him into an image of your prim restricted self, and he leaks out of the mould. Wild, I can hear you say. Needs discipline, needs pruning.

Poor Madge. You adopt a child, wince that he smells, has a runny nose, orifices, but try very hard until the first time he bites you. Then you retreat into The Change of Life and don't come out of it until the dirty kid grows into a wild young man and leaves home.

Poor Fraser and poor Madge. Now you can huddle together in your trim tight garden, untroubled by further notes from me.

I poured myself another wine. Its label said, standard quaffing wine. I'd been quaffing. I raised the glass, Haere mai, Charlie, come quick.

My nephew and me are close.

He strolls in a couple of days later, and stops and stares at me chairbound.

'Jeez, are those radials?' I can't help a giggle.

Then he shakes, stretches, sighs.

'Bloody long hike, that.'

Comes and hugs me.

'Where you been this time? Commune? Nga Tama Toa? The wopwops?'

'Scrubcutting. You know, the employment scheme thing. I've chucked it in.'

'For here?'

'For a while.'

He's still got a wicked grin. At 19, he's nervous of the maimed, but he can smother it under a smile. He prowls round the flat, round the shop, a tall skinny fella in tight jeans, all cock and ribs like a musterer's dog.

'You really gonna live in this thing, really work it?'

'For a while,' I echo.

'OK, let's make it sing.'

'What'd you mean, make it sing? It's humming sweet now. More or less.'

'The less first.'

'Lifting and shifting stuff. I can do so much with my tongs, so much with my muscles. It takes a helluva time to stock the high shelves a tin at a time though.'

'So I can lift and shift. Anything else?'

'Noooo.'

'Meaning yes.'

'Well, I'm busy enough, and the trading figures the last owners gave me were honest enough, but I'm not making as much as I should. I've got a small plague of shoplifters.'

'What size of shoplifters?'

'All sizes. A couple of desperate pensioners, trying to eke their dole out. Schoolkids doing it for a dare. One blue-rinse matron, really snooty when I caught her. I dunno what to do.'

'I'll kick arses, auntie. Or we call the cops.'

'You kick, for a start. Or play heavy anyway.'

He grinned a mean grin.

'First one we catch tomorrow.'

Which was Bird.

I was sitting behind my new low counter when he crabbed into the shop. He stared. He has eyes full of the dark.

Charlie blinks in surprise when I cough.

I can see him thinking, That scarecrow? She means him?

I cough again, and nod. Charlie keeps his eyes skinned.

Now, over the past month, I've learned to watch people the way I used to watch whitebait. Keenly but not looking at them. Peripheral vision picks up things direct staring doesn't. Even so, I've never yet seen Bird actually lift anything. The stuff goes missing after he visits, but that is all I can swear to.

He has a routine.

'How much is that?'

'You got any money, Bird?'

'How much is that?'

'Too much for you, I think, fella.'

'How much is that?

He can keep up the unanswered question longer than I can refuse to answer it. His thin hard cheep wears my resistance away, even though I know — oath how I know! — his routine off by heart now.

'OK, it's a dollar forty.'

'Oh.'

He shifts to the next shelf, limp and creak.

'How much is that?'

And so on. He's never bought anything yet.

Today, he stares longer than usual, his eyes flicking from me to Charlie, from Charlie to me. Bird, being Bird, can smell trouble.

But Charlie turns his back on us after a moment, and stuffs his hands in his tight pockets, whistles nonchalantly, starts rocking back and forwards on the balls of his feet as though he wanted nothing more from life than to stare out the window into the grubby street.

So Bird starts up his routine, and we play it through until the last 'Oh'. And then he shuffles towards the door. And Charlie blocks it, and holds out his hand.

'I saw you swipe a torch battery and a peppermint bar. Give.'

'I didn't take anything.'

'There's a mirror up now boy, and I saw you taking all right.'

Bird swivels his head to look back above the window, and Charlie follows the move, grinning in mean triumph.

Bird snatches the nearest thing to hand off the shelf, heaves it, and lurches for the door.

The nearest thing to hand was a pound tin of spaghetti and it thumps Charlie hard in the belly. While he doubles up ooof! he doesn't shift from the door, and Bird stops. When Charlie straightens, he's lost his grin.

'Jeez you little bastard.'

He snatches, collars, shakes.

'Hey Charlie.'

Yeah, I'm sick of being preyed upon; yeah, I'm sick of Bird ripping me of all people off, but I don't think I can stomach seeing him made an example of — there's already three curious regulars watching from out in the street.

'Charlie, let him go. Bird, piss off. Don't come in here again.'

Charlie is very quiet for the rest of the day. We close up shop. We eat.

'You like a wine, Charlie? Or a beer?'

He is brooding over the fire.

'Nope.'

I pour myself a glass. It's more of the standard quaffing.

Charlie says suddenly,

'What was it? That he's a cripple too?'

That was meant to wound, and does.

My turn to nurse a silence.

'Look, we agreed last night, we catch a few and warn 'em off, one way or the other. You called him out, I acted. He deserved thumping for that, let alone hanging one on me. You never used to be soft, Francis.'

Serious if I'm getting my name instead of the auntie label I detest. So I try an explanation.

'I haven't started to decay, Charlie. Look, you remember Ally Wang who came in late this afternoon?'

'The fat wahine, the one with the old lady in tow?'

He's frowning.

'That's her. She and the old lady and Bird were the first three in here. I was open at eight in the morning, brand-new paint, sawdust and fresh plastic smells, waiting. They wandered in about lunch-time. Not so much customers then, as dogs sniffing out a new tree. But hell I loved them Charlie. I was beginning to think there was a neighbourhood black ban on paraplegics or something. So I gushed a bit. Wanted to know their names, were they from the neighbour-hood, all that kind of crap. And towards the end, when the boy had finally got himself inside, I asked, "And what's your little um, what's your child called?" Ally Wang looked blank. "Him? Bird. And he's not mine. I just look after him for my sister." And the old lady looked surprised. She said, "Bird? E tika?" Ally: "Kaore. Ko Te Pipiwharauroa tona ingoa." Old lady: "Kaore noa iho! Penei me te pipiwharauroa, ne?" And they sniggered. Your Maori good enough to follow that?'

'Nope.'

'OK, his given name is Te Pipiwharauroa. There's an old saying, Penei me te pipiwharauroa, which is a polite way of saying a child is a bastard, you know, a cuckoo's child laid in some other bird's nest. I followed all this with interest, and then made the mistake of looking at Bird. I can see how he looked now. I'll retain that expression of his while I breathe. But do you know what?'

'Nope.'

'He's made a game of that shame label. He calls himself Bird. He won't answer to his given name unless he thinks you're a friend. So that's one reason I wouldn't let you hide him. The other was his defence: I like guts and quick wits. I think if he had snivelled, I would have been happy for you to give him the message about thieving.'

'Francis, you haven't gone soft. You've gone bloody soppy.'

Have I?

Does city living eat away at your survival instinct?

Dunno.

The hard thing I find about the city is the dirt. I wheel out these days, down to the corner, back round the block. Not going anywhere, just getting acclimatised. Used to the filth. Greasy shreds of paper, dogturds, glass-splinters. People-spits, birdshit, grey wads of chewing gum studding the footpath. Clogged air, and too many people to breathe it. Even the rain is dirty here.

Charlie left after a week.

He stocked the shelves, and said he'd be back in a couple of weeks to do it again. Said to ring 'Mike in Hastings' if I needed him sooner. I didn't think he'd come back for months, if at all.

Bird came back in the shop the day after Charlie left. It can't have been coincidence. He must have been watching.

I said, 'Get the hell out of here,' full of sour self-pity that Charlie had gone.

'How much is that?'

'Out.'

'How much is that?'

I sped my wheels round the counter and came at him.

'Out Bird, or else.'

He stood his ground. He switched from pointing at the goodies on the shelf to pointing at me.

'How much is *that*?'

I stopped.

There was a smile in Bird's eyes, not reaching the rest of his face, but lighting the night of his stare.

So the city's made me soppy. So what?

'Ally, why doesn't Bird go to school?'

She shrugged her heavy shoulders.

'Bird's simple, you know, retard-ded.'

'O yeah? Who says?'

'The Welfare. Like the social people you know?'

'O. I know.'

But I don't.

Bird stopped playing the How-much-is-that? game. Now I mainly talk, and he listens. Poised foursquare between sticks and caged ungainly legs, head bent, while I waffle on and on. The house I built myself. The white pine posts I used to cut on contract. Whitebaiting September through to the last day of November. Trickles, shoals, runs of bait.

More and more, try to stop it as I do, I talk about walking south to the top of the world, south to where the surf makes a high bright haze.

Bird doesn't say anything. He listens, then looks with those lightened eyes, and then struggles away.

I think Bird may be smart, smart enough to hide all he feels and all he knows.

Nights that are never fully dark, mornings that feel used by dawn.

Business is wearisomely good. The shoplifting spree has diminished to an odd time or two a week. I rise early and stock; serve through the day and early evening; balance; clean up, and head for the comfort of the bottle.

I had quaffed to blurdom the night Charlie arrived back, two weeks to the day just like he said.

'Who's there?' I asked the knocker at the door.

'Auntie? You OK auntie?'

'Hell, Charlie!'

I unlocked the door.

''E good to see you again,' I was weeping into his hug.

He is frowning at the tears.

'I never seen you cry before.'

'It's the piss more than anything, Charlie. No worries, eh. Hey, it's *good* you're back, man, so good.'

He looks more worried still.

'You've got thinner, Francis.'

'Liquid diet, eh!'

'Ah hell, auntie. This sort of life isn't any good for you. Look, why not go home? I'll come back with you. I could lay a path. Concrete slabs right the way to the beach so you could wheel there and back, eh. Widen your doors. Bring the sink down. Do up the loo the same as this one's done. Make it so you can live properly at home. And I could —'

'Charlie, you don't know a shovel from a spade.'

'I could learn.'

'Yeah, yeah, yeah.'

He cooks tea in silence, but it is thoughtful silence, not sullen. After we eat he asks, 'Shop going alright?'

'Could use your help in some restocking. Otherwise, it's steady.'

'How's your shoplifting society?'

'About extinct. Well, what goes on now is tolerable. The business can stand it.'

He sipped some of my wine.

'Saw that Bird hanging round the shop door.'

'At this time of night? What was he doing?'

'Nothing. I clouted him, told him to push off home.'

My nephew grinned his lean wicked smile.

'I still remembered that can in the belly.'

That night I dreamed, and heard the rainbirds, the shining cuckoos whistle in the hills.

O Charlie, you and your talk . . .

I can hear his easy snoring.

I can hear a distant siren.

I can hear a dog suddenly yelp, head away down the street Au! Au! Au! May be the same dog I heard the first day . . .

'I'll give it another month, Charlie. Stay at least that long, and see if I can't get used to it.'

'OK. I'll stock you up this week, go south next week, and be back before your month's up. Just in case you want to leave early.'

So much for your resolutions, I told myself. So much for cutting yourself away from the old mobile past. Because I'm feeling drunken with nothing to drink at the thought of a month-to-go. A mere thirty days of exile and then maybe . . .

Nothing like shopwork to keep your wheels firmly on the ground. Mundane, materialistic, matter-of-fact. Fraser, you would be proud of me as I scoot about serving, smiling behind the counter, really watching the till grow fat. I keep my books in order; I prune myself, poor Fraser, in a way you wouldn't understand. You would see it as the sprouting of florid sprawling tendrils of self-will. Wine, and late nights, and too much giggling. Charlie rears his young strong shoulders, holds my world steady. He cooks for us both, cleans most of the place. The shelves are packed with stock. He serves in the shop, when I can't hold the giggles down.

I am out the back in the bathroom, cooling my flush with tap-water. If I keep feeling this high, I am gonna solve the immobility problem, Francis . . . I am just gonna float away out of this chair he he, and then I hear,

'Why don't you want to go back to Auckland?'

'It's dark there.'

'Go on, they burn more lights down there than the rest of us put together.'

'It's dark there. It's dark where I am.'

'You live in a hole or something?'

'It's dark there.'

'Ah come on Bird. I heard you say that three four times already.'

'Don't you understand English, Ngati DB?'

'You're Ngati DB yourself, come to that.'

'It is dark though.'

Charlie hrrmphs in disgust.

I hear Bird creak away out.

I sit looking at the mirror.

Pain eats flesh. So does fear, and hate, and worry. Thinness is never a virtue. My legs are shrunk to skin and hollows, but I been warned to expect that. Hollow eyes too. Death carving a skull already. But I am past fifty.

I had never thought before how thin Bird was.

Dirty, yes. His pale hair is pewter-coloured, matted with grime. But Ally is a sloven. Her bulk smells rancid, layer on layer of nightsweats. She doesn't take care of herself, let alone anyone else.

And I thought the dark in his eyes inhabited him, was not imposed from outside. You get some people born with the dark inside them.

Charlie comes through, whistling an odd little tune. He grins at me.

'Sober, auntie?'

'Yes . . . what's that piece of mournfulness you're mouthing?'

He grinned more widely.

'Something I'm going to sing that Bird before I go.'

'O yeah? Was that Bird in just now? You were talking to? You kissed and made up or something?'

'That was that Bird. I've been chatting him up . . . he! Whatchya do in Christchurch, Charlie? O chatted up a bird and that.'

He twirled around.

'He's cuckoo in more ways than one, eh? Heh heh!'

Heh heh heh.

Charlie tuned his guitar. Bird stood and stared. I sat immured in my chair. I was sick to death of that chair. Maybe my tiredness showed on my face. Maybe that stirred Charlie because he laid the guitar down before he played.

You got a favourite song, Bird?'

'No.'

'You like Maori songs, Bird?'

The boy shrugged.

Charlie picked up the guitar again, but uneasily. He looked at me. I looked into my wine. The jokiness had gone out of the air.

'Come into the back, Bird.'

Charlie had said before, 'You going away soon? So are we.'

He winked at me.

'Got a couple of presents for you. Here,' handing over a torch battery and a peppermint bar.

'Free,' says Charlie, beaming. 'No nasty questions asked either.'

Bird took them. Then he repositioned his sticks, and stood without moving a muscle. I got the feeling then that Bird would take whatever came to him, had done so all his life. But like me, when I sprawled for four hours underneath the nice log, he knew that some blows kill, and you can be killed piecemeal.

He hadn't so much braced himself, I realised after, as armoured himself, frozen himself, against what was coming. If you don't move, you won't seem alive. If you don't move, it'll pass over you. So Charlie played and sang to stillness.

    Pipi pipi manu e

I hadn't felt the dead half of me so heavy before.

    Pipiwharauroa,

The break between living and dead parts ached.

    E pi pi pi ana e

I wanted a knife of fire, to sever me, to free.

    Mo papa, mama wharauroa,

But only my lungs hurt, taut and strained because I wasn't breathing.

    Mo papa, mama wharauroa.

'It's a good song,' said Charlie sulkily. 'Good tune, good rhythm. And it's a nursery rhyme, for God's sake. It's not like I was singing him obscene words.'

He stuffed his last pair of jeans into his pack.

'I'll see you in May. Maybe.' He turned once on his way out. 'Francis, jeez it was a joke.'

I waited 'til he got out the door. Then I threw the standard quaffing bottle at it. Threw myself hard forward so the waist strap cut in and hurt something live.

Yeah, I know, Nineteen's not man-size. Nineteen is boy growing into man, still capable of a child's casual cruelty. I knew some kids once who sorted out their baby sister, stuck her in a cardboard box, and left it in the middle of a busy road. They giggled like hell when two cars hit it. Jeez Mum it was a joke.

Go away frozenness. Go away eyes.

I had another dream with rainbirds in it, but this time they weren't haunting the hills. I was near my bright surf, and I was walking, hobbling towards it. I was trying to kill it. I screamed.

> *I asked for riches.*
> *You gave me scavenging rights*
> *On a far beach.*
> *Now you have taken the rights away!*

Somebody laughed loudly.

Blessed are the people who expect nothing, for verily they shall get it.

I tried to ease my cramped chest by breathing crowd air. Wheeled myself four blocks down to the local tavern. A long distance sped by hands. The kerbs are murder, jolt the breakline, so I breathe hard. Doesn't undo the cramps, though.

The bar is ripe with smoke and noise. There are embarrassed edgings away from my wheels. I get a jug and steer towards a table. The crowd melts a wide hole round me. Now I'm one of the maimed, blanket and all. Like the tired old men wed to alcohol, their wives clasped in brown paper bags; left lonely in corners, dribbling in their love. I brood over the beer. Then,

'How yer gettin' on mate? Boxa birds, eh?'

'Boxa birds all right, mate. All shit and feathers, eh.'

He cranked a laugh out. Puffed red face. Full of the terrible instantaneous friendship drunks ladle out, I think. Then I see him groping round his crotch, unconscious he's doing it, and realise he's one of those weirdos turned on by cripples. He keeps on lipfarting away. Talk dull as dead cod eyes, thick as yesterday's porridge. I'm wedged against the table and can't wheel away.

I borrow Bird's defence and freeze. I don't notice when he goes.

Maybe the child's armour worked for him.

I say to Ally on my last day as a fat-till watcher, 'Bird sick or something?' Very casual.

'O me sister took him back,' says Ally, her face shuttered. 'Last week. Me sister got him then.'

'O yeah,' very casually indeed.

Bird sent back to Auckland, his smile still trapped in his eyes.

I hear them singing in the hills, *kui kui kui, whiti whiti ora*. There's a young bird calling out, a shining cuckoo, calling continually, for the father, the mother cuckoo. Rainbirds.

I used to think O hell.

SARAH QUIGLEY

When I look back at this story, it's like looking down a long tunnel. Although I wrote it a few years ago, it felt separate from me after only a few days, and I like this sense of distance.

A couple of real-life elements in the story, though, mean I can remember the actual writing of it. An opening I went to at the Saatchi Gallery in London became the white art gallery in the story. And a meeting with someone who invented crosswords for a living gave the character of Harman his job.

But essentially there are mysteries at the heart of 'Only Connect' that even I don't know the truth about, and I like not knowing. Oscar arrives from nowhere, Harman has somehow ended up with a life invisible to the outside world. And if I had to say what happens to both of them at the end — well, I suppose I could, but to state it would make it sound far bleaker than it actually is. Because if the story has a theme, it's that even though we keep such a large part of ourselves hidden, sometimes it's possible to reach out and make a connection with someone else.

ONLY CONNECT

IT TAKES HIM ALL DAY TO finish it. He watches the buttery light slide across the wall. When it reaches the doorway, it is evening. The day slips out of the room; he sits on the floor and waits for autumn.

Once autumn arrives quietly above his head, he will join Oscar. Once the leaves discard their supple silence and speak to him, then he will permit himself to be with Oscar.

The disadvantage of living in the inner city, Harman has found, is the absence of a corner shop. To the professional couple who live upstairs this is of minimal importance: their fridge holds wine instead of milk, in their apartment breakfast is a token of shameful domesticity. To Harman it is a twelve-year itch, an inconvenience which has never yet overcome inertia but which wakes him every morning like a persistent headache.

The maze of unrelenting streets is waiting for him even as he lingers in sleep. It sounds like an alarm bell in his cloudy mind.

It isn't as if he filters out the external world. Indeed, he has made it his policy to embrace the surrounding trivia. Seven days a week, 7 am sees him marching up Constitution Street towards the distant superette. Office blocks rear against a white sky, empty carparks yawn, but Harman walks on through the jaws of an expectant city to fetch his paper. There is a deep unease in him at the events the night has left behind — events he does not yet know of. This unease remains with him until he is seated at his table with the world's secrets spread before him.

It is fifteen and a half minutes to the superette: fourteen minutes home, after his bones have loosened and his skin has stretched. He could, of course, get his paper delivered. But the unpredictability! — the lying between stiff sheets, the waiting from second to second for the thudding blow on the doormat.

No, Harman dislikes being reliant on others. Instead he must plunge into the morning, must follow his charted route with purpose. His body splits the thin sunless air, his feet rise and fall like keys on a typewriter.

It is only later that his certainty leaves him. Later, when the disloyal day has opened itself to other people, when it has scattered into blowsy afternoon streets and disparate intentions. Then Harman stands eleven floors up, surveying the dusty map before him with something like despair. The movement below simulates panic, but it is this — he must force himself to remember — it is this which makes possible his orderly morning. Overnight, this frenetic movement is captured in black and white, restrained within rectangles: can be held in two hands. Once it lies in its new form on Harman's table, Harman is able to reassert his existence.

That early conviction. He ekes out its memory through the increasingly chaotic day until, with darkness, with relief, he can once more bar the doors to his eyes.

It is a Sunday afternoon when he is first aware of someone else on his floor. For nearly two years now, the lift has stopped at Floor 11 for Harman alone: rent has risen, superior apartment blocks have risen, expectations have risen. No longer floating on the crest of fashion, Hereford Towers is emptying like a slowly sinking ship.

Harman has devised ways to circumnavigate the irregularities of his home. Like a husband affecting to read while his wife undresses so as not to acknowledge her spreading stomach, the slackening of her arms, he looks away from its flaws. A tightly folded wad of newspaper under the fridge levels the buckling kitchen floor. Paper — also newsprint — is glued over the cracking plaster in the bathroom so that Harman can lie in the bath, can read and reread reviews of concerts he has never been to, films he will never see. His forays into a still, pre-blue world bear fruit years on.

211

The first he knows of his new neighbour is a repeated tapping: regular in its consistency, irregular in volume. It grows and fades, advances and recedes, until Harman's kitchen wall undulates in a green wave. Harman puts down his fork. He feels anxious, possessive, threatened. He feels fear.

Long after the tapping stops, it is still with him. The knock at the door: is it actual or anticipated? He shuffles his lunch around his plate and listens to a silence which swells in his ears.

His pasta is now beyond repair. Its blue-cheese sauce is wrinkled like the skin of an ill man, smells of promised decay. Harman scrapes it down the waste disposal unit.

Of course, he has his own life to lead. He sits eleven floors above the heads of the people he puzzles, and traces solutions to their origins. He has always lived life back to front, prefers retreat to advance, is known by a surname. At thirty-five, his body is already shrinking; his brogues have begun to float on his feet. He no longer sees his parents.

He coaxes success from his work with music. His voice is high and thin but he tackles an entire orchestra without hesitation. Rachmaninov, Tchaikovsky, Wagner: their passion lends itself to his network of words. The walls of his head stretch to take in the ages and wrap themselves around the globe. Seated at his tidy table, he calls up Greek deities, invokes blood-lust. He summons the roar of the twentieth century and the dust of the future.

The phone must be off the hook during working hours. He feels the possibility of interruption as an ache in his jaw, a stiffening in his fingertips. During bars of silence, he draws reassurance from the tiny hum of a disconnected line.

His editor communicates by letter. In the eight years of their relationship, he and Harman have never met. He delivers clichés in a sturdy black hand: *Keep up the good work. Well done old chap. Pull out all stops.*

Recently, however, he has dropped hints about computers, modems. Harman remains noncommittal. He dislikes the thought of his work being flushed away down a phone line. E-mail seems to him both the most vacuous and dangerous of mediums: a careless hurling about of words with little thought for consequences. At times he looks out his window and sees the sky cluttered with electronic junk mail.

In this age of boomerang conversations, he knows that time is a threatened commodity. Unconsciously his movements become slower. He is holding back the clock.

The landing is full of plants: orchids, miniature roses, cyclamens, ferns. Hastily, Harman unlocks his door, but before he can shut it behind him a large rubber tree sweeps out of the lift.

Hey neighbour. Oscar introduces himself. A scarlet bandanna is secured around his knotted neck. He is a florist from New York, London, or Milan: he has lived in many cities. His accent is a trans-Atlantic slide.

Harman grips the door handle. One foot is on familiar ground, one in no-man's land. His own voice sounds static, his welcome to Hereford Towers plants itself greyly among the greenery.

Oscar doesn't think he'll be around for long. *Hereford today, gone tomorrow,* he says. His laugh is as pliant as his voice.

Harman rejects an offer of herb tea on the grounds of work to be done. As he scours the inside of his oven, he hears Oscar and his plants rustling through the wall.

It is not until later that the tapping begins. Harman stiffens, continues to scrub the cracks in his tiled bench top with a toothbrush. He puts on the radio, a discussion on opera. The tapping carves the conversation into senseless structural units. Harman anticipates the crumbling of a twelve-year regime. It is alarm which propels him onto the landing.

Oscar answers his door promptly. There is a sheen on his high forehead and a pulse beats in his throat.

I'm disturbing you, he says. He invites Harman in, explaining that he has been spoilt, that his previous neighbour was hard of hearing.

A six-foot Statue of Liberty presides over Oscar's living-room. His bookshelves display many pairs of shoes: glitter platforms, luminous sneakers, cowboy boots, silver-toed Doc Martens. He doesn't read, he tells Harman, he's in too much of a hurry.

He seizes an enamel cigarette box, waves it at Harman who refuses. The doctor's always forecasting death, Oscar says, but why not enjoy the journey? The cigarillo in his mouth is as thin as his fingers, his fingers flick the lighter back and back into life. As he inhales, a moment of complete absorption happens in his face.

Politely, Harman broaches the subject of noise, of thin walls and the need for total concentration when he works. Oscar listens intently.

I'll change to slippers, he says.

He crosses the room to a huge chrome stereo. His red shoes flash, their built-up heels tap in a way already familiar to Harman.

You like Tchaik? he says.

He pulls the headphones from the stereo and music roars at Harman. Oscar snatches up a twig-like baton, strides from west to east.

I put my headphones on, he says. *I put my headphones on and lose myself.*

He continues to stride. Harman is beginning to feel homesick but hears himself accepting the offer of a drink. Oscar pours a pastis, asks what Harman does, expresses admiration. *Must have a brain on you*, he says, and he recites an Apache poem for Harman which he learnt from his grandmother. He's quarter Native American, he tells Harman, but where his parents ran with wolves, he just dances with fairies. He laughs again, with serious eyes.

Harman must go. He weaves his way to the door through rows of tomato plants. Their furry leaves conceal tiny green globes. Oscar says if they ripen in time, he'll give some to Harman.

He ushers Harman out into the hall with ceremony.

I'll wear slippers, he says.

The kitchen looks unnaturally tidy, as if withholding secrets learned while Harman was next door. When he puts the kettle on he realises he is still wearing his pink rubber gloves. Oscar's grave eyes stay with him for the rest of the evening.

When he goes to bed, his tongue is still scuffed with the taste of aniseed.

Oscar brings an arrangement which a customer has cancelled. It has red chillies on twisted stalks, and golden grasses which Oscar has dyed himself. He holds up his fingers: Midas-tipped.

I have a particular talent for dyeing, he says, and he laughs.

The arrangement sits on Harman's table, its exotic wings stretch over his morning paper. After two weeks the alien beige environment overcomes it; Harman must sweep away the remains.

There is no more tapping from next door, but Harman realises his ability to live noiselessly is unique. Doors and windows shake his concentration, laughter creeps through air vents. Now Harman works to the sound of Oscar living.

A friend of Oscar's is having a private viewing and Harman is to be Oscar's partner. He changes four times before putting back on what he has been wearing all day. Oscar wears his high red shoes and chequered flares. As they toil up one hill and down another, he commends Harman's choice of Hush Puppies.

The gallery is cool. White walls meet white floors so that Harman is not sure if he's on a lean or standing upright. Silver wrists clatter, mercury tongues slip through conversations. Like Harman, the paintings hang back waiting to be noticed.

Oscar introduces Harman to ten, fifteen, fifty people. They have names Harman cannot repeat without feeling self-conscious.

Meet my brilliant neighbour, Oscar says. He and his friends can only think visually, he tells Harman, so they're impressed by word people. He brings champagne and jellybeans.

Harman has entered the evening sideways but now he sees it as easily accessible. He imagines setting up his work table in the white barn: his sheets of paper stacked on the white floor, his dictionaries revealed by curtainless windows.

He could live here, or elsewhere.

Oscar's door opens and closes at all hours. Harman watches Oscar's figure being swallowed by the heat, emerging from it: striding towards town or returning from it: arms full of fish or flax leaves, arms full of nothing. When Harman sits down again at the table, his latest clue has lost some of its significance. His pencil grinds a little dust onto the grudging page.

It is an Indian summer. Oscar says it is thanks to his heritage that Hereford Towers still basks in April sun. The days are swollen with heat, they lie about under the trees and depart reluctantly when the shadows come. Harman leaves his door to the landing open so the air in his apartment is replaced regularly.

He continues to walk for the paper but his urgency has lessened. Sometimes it is 7.30 when he walks and sometimes it is 8. Sometimes Oscar's grasshopper legs are leaving the building as he returns. The heat has made his neighbour even thinner, has sucked the flesh from his face. He waves windmill arms at Harman and hopes the muse is kind.

It is late, it is Saturday, and Harman has not heard Oscar for forty-eight hours. He shuts his door, slides the bolt: hears an echoing, lengthier, thud.

Oscar lies on the landing. His scarlet bandanna is around his neck. His head is towards the lift but he hears Harman's horror behind him.

I might need some help, neighbour, he says. His voice hits the wall slowly, and slowly bounces back to Harman.

Harman approaches. He realises Oscar is not wearing his bandanna.

Get back, says Oscar. *Don't touch my head.*

His voice is imperative, un-Oscarly. He allows Harman to take his arm but holds his scarlet face and neck stiffly to one side. He lies on Harman's sofa until the bleeding stops.

Just bumped into the wrong people, he says.

He asks Harman to talk about anything, says Harman can be frank because he won't be around for long.

Harman starts, thinks of ambulances, doctors. Oscar says he's fine. *The incredible frivolity of the dying*, he says, then tells Harman that's a joke too.

Under cover of the night, before the bleaching sky reminds him who he is, Harman tells Oscar many things. He talks of ambition and of despair, of loneliness versus solitude and the temptations of madness. He talks of curried cod and the best way to clean an oven, and of the strangeness of getting up and going to bed three hundred and sixty-five times a year with no one else knowing.

Oscar listens until the stars turn themselves off, and the day starts to waver under the gaze of a new sun. *I'll be seeing you, neighbour*, he says. His walk to the door is slow but not unsteady.

Harman has kept all his morning papers. Every paper from the last twelve years sits neatly in his spare room. This is one thing he did not tell Oscar: why should he have?

There is a narrow aisle from the door to the window, which allows access to the back stacks. For a week Harman walks this aisle and listens for a sound on the landing. He walks and waits and listens, but he hears only the breathing of the fridge and the inaudible sound of his own ears. After three weeks he knows that waiting is no longer enough. His work has consisted of hints instead of happenings: has been compiled by absences, negations, implications. It is time to fill in the blanks. It is time to invert.

In his bath he mixes vast quantities of glue. He sits on the floor and rips up six months, one year, three years of news. When he glances out the window, he thinks Oscar's stick figure is striding in the park, but when he second-looks all he can see is trees.

He makes the trunk so large that he cannot reach around it. Two men might link arms about its newsprint bark but Harman does not aspire to do this himself. Its branches, made from many layered strips of 1986, stretch to the corners of the room.

The events of seven days and seven nights break over and around Hereford Towers but Harman remains oblivious, chooses to be uninformed. He turns down the challenge of each morning, spends quiet days in his living-room adding layer onto layer. In the hot yellow evenings, he ventures down to the park and gathers leaves which are newly fallen.

On the last day he completes his task. He stands on a kitchen stool to string the leaves. They form a green ceiling, bring a kind of coolness to his face. He is pleased to have finished. He sits down with his back to his tree and discards future and past with a quiet relief.

NORMAN BILBROUGH

Some stories are held in particular affection by their writers. Even though it is recent — written in 2000 — 'Down on the Corner' is like that for me.

It's always a challenge to write about men's feelings; they're usually so covert. In this case feelings are juxtaposed with male information — a field where men are always confident. But information, especially about love and women, is a tricky area, and when it's handed on to a son, it assumes a kind of fraught responsibility. But my affection for the story lies in the fact that I like the two men in it: they're grappling with experience, it's been tough, but they're brave too: they're trying to be brave and honest — and emotional.

DOWN ON THE CORNER

ALTHOUGH VINCE HAD NOT eaten meat for ten years when he first saw Rita dancing, there was a corner of him that had still contained an appetite for animal flesh; a corner that he did not admit existed, although periodically he found himself stalled before butchers' windows.

'Your mother was a terrific dancer,' he said in the burger bar after the movie.
    'You've told me that before,' Justin replied.
    'I want to say more. Girls like guys who can dance.'
    Justin screwed up his eyes. He wanted to think of himself as a good dancer, but sensed the truth might be otherwise. And he'd never danced with Kylie.

Vince had seen Rita dancing in the large country town where he worked on the local paper, and she had just opened a boutique. The band was playing 'Down on the Corner' and like a lot of men he was prepared to forgive the flat rendition because of Rita.

'She expressed herself dancing.'
    Justin fished the marshmallows from his hot chocolate. He was eighteen, and he didn't much want to hear how his parents had expressed themselves. As far as he could see his mother had been expressing herself all her life. But since he only saw his father twice a year he was prepared to tolerate a conversation that could feasibly

embarrass him. Also he was in a new city learning how to make pizzas instead of delivering them, and he was lonely.

Vince had not danced with Rita that night. He watched her from the sidelines, a girl with black electric hair and a body that seemed totally at ease with whatever music was thrown at it. Later he saw her devouring chicken drumsticks and drinking from a naked beer bottle.

Not my type, he thought.

He saw her again at a Summer Solstice festival. She wore a thin blue dress and she was dancing on the grass to a band that was making a halfway decent job of 'Natalia'. Although there had been many hot days her feet and legs were white. Vince couldn't take his eyes off her feet. He was surprised: he didn't know he had a thing about feet, and before he knew it he was circling her in the jerky tribalistic way that was the dancing of the time, and she was smiling at him. The number finished.

'Hey,' Rita said, 'you're a lousy dancer, what about buying me a drink?'

'If you're lucky the girl will take the first step,' he said to Justin.

'The first step to what?'

'To going out with you. She'll give the signal.'

Justin supposed Kylie had made the first step, but for the wrong reason.

'That guy in the jeans and before the movie,' he said angrily. 'He'd never score that girl with a haircut like that.'

Vince had drunk water while Rita gulped beer. He watched her white neck swallowing, and she said, 'You're an intellectual, aren't you?'

Vince wore glasses, and he sieved his experience of life through the medium of words: all sufficient to earn such a label in such a town. Later he discovered that any person concerned with print, from a sign-writer to a newsagent, was an intellectual in Rita's eyes.

'I don't like intellectuals,' she said.

'Although,' he warned his son, 'they sometimes say the opposite to what they mean.'

Justin was silent. Vince guessed that he was thinking of the movie, where a platoon of American soldiers had fought their way up a hill in the Pacific to find death and an embittered self-realisation at the top. He was irritated: there were more important things to explain other than why American planes had to buzz the beaches as the GIs were wading through the surf.

'I'm starving.' Justin fetched a hamburger and offered it with a grin to his father.

Vince refused with predictable distaste.

After the beer that summer's day, it was not sprouts or lentil balls or a respectable bean salad that Rita had gone for, but a pie. She ate how Vince had been taught not to eat — with her mouth wide open. The innards ran down her chin. And when Vince told her he was a vegetarian she looked at him in horror. 'You're not into all that hippie shit are you?'

He could not see what was particularly hippie about his taste, and if anything she looked more of a hippie than he did. He was intellectual, and she was . . . instinctual. The way she devoured the meat thing was instinctual.

Definitely not his type.

Then they had met in the main street where he was filling in for the shopping reporter who was off sick for a week, and she had run an antagonistic hand over his battered leather jacket.

'Very Yves Montand.' Rita had lived in France. 'Very intellectual. What books are you reading today?'

Vince should have denied he'd been reading anything. Or just said, *Siddhartha*, or Jean Paul Sartre. But he was reading *The Silver Chair*.

'What's that about? Furniture?'

'It's a kid's book.'

'You read kid's books?' Rita laughed loudly.

Vince was disappointed: nothing he said would be right in this woman's eyes. So he was surprised when she said, 'When are you going to take me out?'

Out? To a vegetarian restaurant?

They went to a pub where she drank beer and ate fish and chips, and he had lemonade and chips.

'You don't drink either?'

'I feel better if I don't.'

Rita looked at him, the sneer threatening to surface again. 'You need meat to feed all those brains.'

'Yes,' Vince sighed, 'and lettuces are traumatised when they are pulled from the ground.'

'What?'

'Nothing.'

'What sort of haircut did you have when you met Kylie?' He couldn't remember what haircut he wore when he first saw Rita dancing. Probably something long, but not unkempt.

'I didn't meet her. I knew her. Just a haircut.'

Justin had known her at school. From a distance, so to speak. But he had actually encountered her more intimately in a car park: a place where he spent a lot of time either arriving or departing at speed. Justin never drove moderately into a car park, browsing for a place. He arrived and put his foot down. Car parks, for his older passengers like Vince, were places more terrifying than a Japanese-occupied hill in the Pacific.

Kylie had seen the car first, then Justin.

'You got a new car,' she accused.

Justin shrugged, as if he had owned many cars.

'Cool steering wheel!'

Justin laughed. The steering wheel was covered in leopard skin: he couldn't go wrong with that cover. 'Can you drive?' He knew that for all Kylie's gum-chewing, platform-booted style she was a girl that experience had writ less large upon than himself. But despite this the sight of her brazen teeth, her wet gums and her small sharp tongue aroused him even more than accelerating across a car park and clipping a supermarket trolley.

'Nah.'

'I could teach you. Hop in.'

Of course Justin couldn't teach her, he was too aware of her pulsating mouth.

But Rita had taught Vince . . . After the pub she showed him her boutique, the back room of which was filled with a cutting table. She leaned him against it and kissed his lips. She tasted of shark and batter. She kissed him again.

'Girls like kissing,' Vince instructed. 'They like kissing for its own sake.'

Justin had had his first kiss after a screening of *The Matrix*, and hamburgers. Kylie had been chewing and talking under the eerie yellow light of the car park and Justin wondered how he was going to halt all the mouth movement and enact the kiss. It seemed a technical problem: a manoeuvring of cogs and wheels. But from the corner of her eye Kylie sensed his approach, and a great silence fell; a silence that Justin remembered about the kiss, and Kylie's reaction to it. He dropped his open mouth on hers and she threw it off.

'Shut your mouth!' So Justin had, and a pressing of lips followed. That had been arousing, but he had not known how to continue. The re-runs of *Baywatch* and *Beverly Hills 90210* gave no guidelines for further procedures.

And after the fourth fish and chips contact Vince's hand had gone to Rita's breast. She took his hand away, and climbed onto the table. Vince was glad it was not a trestle table: it surely would not have borne their weight. He lay on Rita, fully clothed, and although an intellectual he could read the signal in her eyes and the signal on her mouth, so he kept kissing her delicate seafood lips, her cheeks, her neck. They did nothing else that night.

'Kissing is erotic,' Vince said.
    'What's the big deal about it?' Then Justin said, 'You'll be saying that kissing is sex next.'
    'It is.'
    'Well, what happens after that?' Justin had picked up a knowledge of desired targets in the soccer changing room, but nothing instructional that bore a relationship to human beings.
    'It depends what happens between you two.'

Kylie had been in her last year at college, and for a fortnight Justin was allowed to pick her up after school. There was always a kind of withheld excitement for him when she appeared at the gate and scanned the cars for his. But what he mostly remembered were the phone calls where they talked endlessly about nothing. It was like turning out the contents of their pockets and examining every piece of accumulated trivia.

Then there was his heart. It blithered: it had grown into unruly proportions.

'If you fall in love, that solves a lot of the sex problems,' his father said.

Justin was still hungry. He wanted another hamburger, but felt mean. And Vince wouldn't buy it for him. 'How?'

'Love smooths out the body problems. Your body problems.'

Justin guessed the blithering heart had signalled he had entered the love territory, but it didn't seem to help the body problems. 'So if you fall in love sex isn't important?' The thought appalled him.

'Love helps sex,' Vince amended, 'especially if it comes first.'

After the table kissing Rita had looked through Vince's eyes as if she was examining the worms of his brain. 'Apart from reading books do you get to have any fun? Are you a fun animal?'

It sounded infantile to Vince, but to deny it might lessen her interest in him. 'Depends what you mean.'

Rita snuggled into him. 'If we're going to be serious let's not have sex for months and months. Sex as you know it.'

Vince gulped. 'Okay.' He was brave, and all those years without meat had taught him to be a stoic. Also there was something heroic about going to bed with a woman and not having sex.

'Women like to be wooed,' he said to Justin. 'Most of them don't want to be rushed. Men are in a terrible hurry. They don't understand Romance.'

Kylie had let Justin kiss her occasionally, with sealed lips, and he was allowed a good amount of nuzzling. Also she was not averse to hand holding. Then a gang of them drove out to a beach for a barbecue one Saturday night. It was a cold spring, but after booze and under-cooked sausages the oldest guy, Rick, the guy with the biggest laugh and the biggest stories, ran into the water fully clothed. Kylie laughed at him: she showed off her mouth. Justin didn't budge. He held her hand and wished they were away from the noise and the splashing so he could tell her she was lovely. He drank more instead, and threw sand over her legs.

'Burying somebody, you reckon that's romantic?' he asked Vince. 'You know, burying them up to their waist at the beach?'

'Depends on the sand.'

It had been clammy. Kylie pushed him away, and Justin lay down with Rick's big laugh in his ears. When he woke, Kylie was not beside him.

'Women,' Vince continued seriously, 'love Love.'

'How do you mean?'

'Love is terribly important to them. It's more important than sex.'

It had only taken a few weeks of petting and kissing — and sleeping chastely together — before Rita had said, 'Do you love me Vince?'

Vince broke his response down into components. He realised he had loved his mother, after she died. He had loved his dog, an awful spaniel called Tory. And once when he was a kid and his father had cooked him fresh salmon at the Rakaia rivermouth, he had loved him too.

His skin loved Rita, he loved watching her move, loved sniffing her. And he suspected she did not love him, but it was important for her to hear it.

'Yes, I love you.'

She looked at him critically. 'Good.'

But gradually a new feeling had grown in his heart — and his curly dominating brain seemed to have no say in the matter.

'I love you Rita,' he said without hesitation.

That was enough: Rita kissed him in a way that seemed like permission and they had crazy sex. And when they sprang apart, Rita said, 'You're a real puritan aren't you. All the horny ones are puritans.' Vince felt proud. 'Say you love me!'

'I love you Rita.'

But Justin hadn't been able to find Kylie. It was as if she had removed herself entirely from his life. His head ached, and when he blundered through the scrub on the edge of the sand he found kissing bodies, but not her. He searched up and down calling softly, and came upon two bodies struggling in the back of Rick's car. Justin was aghast: he had not realised sex could be so unstylish. He watched open-mouthed until Kylie sat up in the seat and gaped at him.

Justin's heart imploded, his lungs shut down and all his blood flooded through his tissues. It seemed even to pour from his eyes.

He could not remember the drive home except it was very short. It was a wonder he did not kill himself.

It's not true,' he said in a strangled voice, 'about love being more important than sex. It's not true!'

Kylie had not loved Rick. Justin was sure of that. In fact, as far as he knew she never went out with him again. And of course she didn't go out with Justin. A month later he drove his car away from her, and away from his expressive mother. He missed them both, terribly.

He looked at his father angrily. 'Why did you leave Mum?' he accused. 'If you're so shit-hot at handling women how come it didn't work out with her?'

Vince was startled: he reached for his son's hand, as Rita would have done, but Justin jerked away.

Vince looked at his own hands. He was tired. 'Your mother stopped dancing,' he said.

'What's that got to do with it?'

'After you were born she never danced again.'

Vince had been told that Rita's depression was post-natal, a common thing, but two years later she was still depressed. She bought the biggest television on the market and spent her weekends and evenings and some week mornings watching it. Justin grew up with a screen rather than a book, which in retrospect was probably how Rita wanted it. She knew Vince hated the slick illiteracy of television. Justin's first sentences were advertising jingles.

Then one morning when the television was pumping its mindless substance over the tiny boy in the next room, Rita gave Vince a look. One that said, *I don't like you. You come from another planet.* And Vince had looked back and seen an unhappy woman. A woman who didn't relish her bacon each morning — and worse, no longer joked about his sprouts and gutless salads. A woman who no longer had the energy to be vindictive.

'She didn't want to live with me. She wanted another type of man. She wanted to get *married*, but to somebody else.'

'She did get married. And she dances now. She dances with Tom. They dance to all that old stuff.'

'"Down on the Corner"?'

'Don't know that. They dance to Talking Heads.' Justin laughed. 'They even dance to The Vengaboys.' He looked at his father. 'You're crying.'

'I'm not!' Vince never cried, but when he put his hand up to his face he felt wetness. And his heart felt as if it had been horribly squeezed. He had killed Rita: he had taken the life from her. He blew his nose, and his son reached across and put his hand on his. And despite his tears and embarrassment, Vince said, 'I thought I couldn't dance because of my low blood sugar.' He laughed. They both laughed.

Two weeks after he had left Rita — remembering the relief on her face and the puzzlement on his son's — Vince had felt really low. He went into a restaurant and ordered a beer and ate a steak. He expected his spirits to lift beyond his sock line, but they didn't. The steak was dense and sinewy, and tasted like somebody's old flesh. He couldn't finish it. He drank half the beer and left the restaurant with indigestion. The meat corner never came back.

FIONA FARRELL

It's hard to choose a story since they each have meaning at the time of their composition. I've chosen this story for two reasons. It was written recently — and I'm a mean mother when it comes to a story. I feel no attachment whatsoever after a few months. The story might just as well have been written by someone else entirely. But this story is newborn so I still recognise it as mine. And it's about the place where I live and my current state of motherhood, with two daughters off in Nepal, Australia, South America, Thailand . . . So it's a kind of magic story, I suppose. It's acting out something I'm fearful of and offering me comfort at the same time, as all my stories do.

HEADS OR TAILS

THE PLANE CAME DOWN ON a routine flight from Santiago to Punta Arenas: spiralled from a clear sky like a spinning coin. Heads you lose, tails you lose.

They used such freak accidents as fillers back when she worked on the subs desk at *The Guardian*: bus plunges in the Himalayas, ferry sinkings in Bangladesh, plane crashes in the Andes — minor tragedies in distant places, lopping paragraphs from the bottom up. They kept a tally one year and got to 28: 19 bus plunges, 7 sinkings and 2 plane crashes, one with associated cannibalism. They became a joke, a running gag.

And now, her daughter has become the punch-line.

There is a god, you see, and he doesn't have much of a sense of humour. He's the tough old bastard of the patriarchs, demanding a perfect red cattle beast, pure ashes and a young woman without blemish as his due sacrifice. You can't fool with him.

So in a way, Christie has brought this on herself and on her child. She had thought as she sat at the subs desk in Ashburton happily pasting up other people's tragedies, that such things could not happen to her. She had elbowed aside the old man at the crossroads and laughed at fate and now the joke has risen up, as jokes do, and slapped her down.

This morning she is walking from west to east. It's a mile along the beach from one headland with its dark smudge of karaka to the swamp by the cliff at the other, and you can do it in either direction, walking into the sun or away from it. Today she walks into the sun at the sea's edge where the wet sand holds a perfect image of the sky so that with every step clouds break apart beneath her feet as if ushering in angels. There's a gull flying over by the rocks dropping a cockle from its beak. It lumbers up into the air, hovers, drops, swoops in to check for damage, lumbers aloft once more and the cockle smacks to earth. Over and over. Thwack . . . Thwack . . . Christie's eyes dazzle on this clear morning so she keeps her head down and walks slowly. Among those shells, could that be a fragment of bone? Could that tangle of seaweed be a hank of hair? Could those scraps of plastic have been torn from a backpack or a boot? She keeps her head down and her hands shoved in her jacket pockets, holding Molly close.

Molly is laughing. She had said she wanted something different for her passport, a photo that would cheer up the dreary old farts at airport immigration desks. She had had her friend Bridget photograph her with a daisy stuck in her wild hair. Molly laughs for the camera in the regulation 35 x 45 cm format, her hair flying in an electric frizz and if you looked really hard, behind the daisy there's a marijuana leaf.

'Isn't that a bit risky?' Christie had said. But Molly had shrugged, said nah, they'll never notice, you worry too much, Mum. And it was true: Christie did worry, though she tried to keep her worries within bounds, avoiding the gothic visions favoured by her own mother whose world had been an endlessly inventive and perilous place where you could be blinded by your own mascara wand, permanently paralysed by dubious restaurant food or infected with nameless horrors by the seats in public toilets. When Christie came home wearing her long blue-and-yellow university scarf, it was to learn that a young man known to her mother had died when just such a scarf had tangled in the wheels of his motorbike.

'Killed instantly,' she said, stirring her tea lugubriously. 'Neck snapped like a chicken.'

'I don't have a motorbike,' said Christie.

'It's those escalators I'd watch out for,' said her mother. 'I wouldn't get on one of those escalators in that scarf if I were you . . .'

You fought against the vision, but it changed things nevertheless: you wore that scarf a little less jauntily, you checked the chicken cacciatore surreptitiously, and you balanced with your bum several inches above the risky plastic rim.

Christie had tried to adhere to some notion of probability. She had surrounded her daughter with statistical reassurance: 98% of children get to school and back on their bikes unscathed, 80% of New Zealanders die of old age in their own beds, you're 1000 times more likely to be injured on your way to the corner dairy than to die in an air accident.

But here it is: that tiny aberration.

Death bursts in while you're watching the inflight movie at 30,000 feet, out of a clear blue sky.

There were no survivors, just seawrack and flotsam on an icy shore: airline cushions, plastic trays, scraps of clothing — and her daughter's passport, still dry and legible inside its plastic folder. Her daughter's face laughing among bureaucratic stamps and scribbling with a daisy and a marijuana leaf in her hair.

Christie had looked up the place on the atlas. The Peninsula de Taitao dips a misshapen toe into the Pacific where the continent shatters into desolate archipelagos and massive mountains. She could have gone to see if for herself. LANChile had offered her and other relatives a consolatory flight, for the victims were an international lot: Japanese, Australian, American. Molly had been the only New Zealander.

'Of course you should go,' Paul had said, and he had taken over the phone and spoken to the LANChile representative himself because his sister's voice had begun to crack dangerously. Whole words were plunging into crevices of silence.

'Yes,' he had said, in his sonorous talking-to-foreigners style. 'I think my sister might indeed welcome the opportunity to go.'

NO! mouthed Christie in the background. No! No!

'Si,' Paul said to the representative. (He liked to use little snippets of the foreigner's own tongue wherever possible, just for practice.) 'Si . . . I am sure such a visit would be of great assistance to her as she goes through the grieving process.'

Christie found her voice again. The words sprang from behind the palisade yapping and snarling. 'It's not a process,' she had said so loudly that Paul had placed one hand over the receiver. 'It's not a bloody course I'm on here, you know: step one, step two and away!'

'We'll be in touch,' said Paul to the receiver. 'Gracias. Adios.' He hung up.

'I'm not going,' said Christie.

But Paul had read *Coping with Sudden Loss* on the plane over from Sydney. Years of rolling round the planet on the international science conference circuit had rendered him adept at the rapid assimilation of facts between the complimentary martini and the miniaturised *boeuf bourgignon*. He knew that death must be 'normalised'.

'Think about it,' he said. 'You don't have to decide now. One of us could come with you.'

And then it was Marybeth's turn to say NO! NO! from her seat by the window where she was carefully picking out a petal in crimson chain stitch. You've got work to attend to back home, she said. Funding applications, the Chinese delegation, not to mention your own children who are no doubt running amok at this very moment, smoking, drinking and god knows what else. I want to go home, she said to Paul, away from this dreadful place where children die. I don't want to catch misfortune.

She had stood at the threshold on the night they arrived from Sydney two weeks ago, dragging her little suitcase on wheels, and the whole house had been in darkness.

'Hullo?' she had called. 'Hullo?' Then Paul had switched on the light and there was Christie sitting on the carpet in a room which seemed drained of all colour. A desolate place.

Marybeth prodded needle into linen, drawing the red thread like a trickle of blood. NO! NO!, she said to Paul, across the room. Please don't prolong this.

She said none of this aloud, of course. Everything was said in a minute shift of the head, a change in position. But Paul understood this language.

Christie had heard it too, though the words were scrambled by the yelling within her own head. She didn't want to fly anywhere. Flight offered no consolation. What she wanted to do right now was scream and smash things. She wanted to fling the coffee cup Marybeth had placed so solicitously by her elbow at the wall then take the pieces and slash herself as the old women used to. She wanted to crouch on the carpet and rock and wail. She wanted to shave her head and pluck off her eyebrows and hurt and howl till blood and snot and tears ran together. She wanted to hand herself over to grief, body and soul.

She picked up the coffee cup carefully and put it out in the kitchen before any harm could come to it.

'It's not a process,' she said, aiming for calm reasonableness. 'I just don't want to go. It's kind of you to offer to come with me but truly, I'll be fine.'

Good old Christie, thought Paul. She'd been bloody brilliant. Had a bit of cry when they planted the memorial totara up by Lion Rock where Molly had done her early climbing, but otherwise she had taken it on the chin as always. Just the way she used to when she was a kid, standing stock still while their mother dabbed on the mercurochrome which stung like a million bees. 'Who's a brave soldier?' their mother would say. 'Eh? Who's a brave soldier?' And 'Me,' Christie would say, then she'd march outside and kick that bike, that swing, that stupid inanimate thing that had hurt her. She'd really lay into it.

'I just want to be left,' she was saying to them now, 'to deal with it on my own.'

And finally they agreed. They packed the little suitcase on wheels and Christie drove them to the airport in plenty of time for the 10.35.

'We feel terrible leaving you like this,' Marybeth said, her face crinkled with anxiety.

'I'll be fine,' Christie said again. 'I've got plenty of support.'

She used the word deliberately: 'support'. Marybeth would understand that. She had, after all, spent the better part of an afternoon organising just that: a support network of Christie's closest friends who could be relied upon to call on an unobtrusive roster. Christie had heard her at it the day before when Marybeth thought she was safely out of the house buying cigarettes at the dairy. She wasn't at the dairy. She was curled up in Molly's old hideyhole under the camellias watching a spider wrapping up a bumblebee for later. She had meant to go to the dairy. She had run out of Rothmans and after years of not smoking they had become a necessity, made all the more essential by Marybeth's surreptitious move downwind to nudge open window or door.

Christie needed cigarettes and lots of them. But as she was walking down the path she had seen the camellia with its shining leaves and the hollow behind its trunk where Molly used to hide when she was three and already running away, already the explorer. She had bent down.

'Come in,' said Molly. 'Come into my house.'

She had crawled under the leaves and lain on smooth clay. Overhead she could hear Marybeth talking rapidly on the phone to Leah saying that Christie needed all the help she could get because well, you know what she's like, she puts a brave face on things while underneath she's a wreck.

'Are you a wreck, Mummy?' said Molly.

'No way,' said Christie.

'We're really worried about leaving her on her own,' said Marybeth, 'but we've got to get back because apart from anything else, our kids will be running wild . . .' She laughed lightly to deny it. So would Leah mind popping round occasionally — and if there were any problems, then please, let them know and they'd be over on the next plane.

There's a pause.

The bumblebee was tightly swaddled in thread but the spider spun on, turning and twisting, just to make sure.

'So full of life wasn't she?' said Marybeth in the funeral voice she had used all fortnight. 'It's impossible to believe she could be gone.'

'Who's gone, Mummy?' said Molly.

'You,' said Christie.

'Silly Mummy,' said Molly. 'I'm not gone. Look: I've made you a pink salad for our tea.' And she hands Christie a fistful of faded camellia petals.

Marybeth rang them all: Leah, Johnno, Neil, Jane.

And now she was leaving. She gave Christie a long caring hug. Over her shoulder Christie could see the boarding light blinking. Only a few more minutes and they'd both be gone.

'You're sure you don't want to come over and stay for a bit?' said Paul. And she said no, stop fussing Paulo, and he patted her on the shoulder, reassured by the old family name. She did indeed seem to be bearing up, still the brave soldier. He hadn't quite known what to expect. But his cellphone had rung three times in the car on the way to the airport. You couldn't leave a department to run itself.

'Well, sing out,' he said. 'We're only a phone call away.' And at last they were leaving, rising away on the escalator, waving. Their heads disappeared, their solid bodies and finally, their shoes.

So Christie drove home to a mercifully empty house where she crawled into Molly's wardrobe, hiding with Molly's skateboard pressed against her thigh, Molly's op shop fake fur jacket in her arms, Molly's passport tucked inside her bra against her bare skin. From time to time the phone rang and she let it go so that the answerphone clicked in and Molly's voice echoed down the hall.

'Hi. We're not in. Here's the beep.' She had never been one to waste words.

'You should answer,' Molly said. She had crawled in too, to play Sardines. 'Else people will get suspicious.' So Christie brought the phone in with them and when Leah or Johnno or Neil rang and said, 'Hullo, Christie, just thought I'd ring and see how you're getting on?' she'd say, 'Fine thanks, but do you mind if I don't talk right now? I've got visitors.'

'That's clever,' said Molly. 'Now everyone will think we're busy and no one will bother us.'

'Jingle bells jingle bells,' rang the doorbell Molly had bought her last year for Christmas.

'Jingle all the way.'

Once, twice. A pause.

'Mum,' said Molly. 'There's someone at the door.'

'Tell them to go away,' said Christie. 'They're a nuisance.'

Another pause. There's the click of heels on the floorboards in the kitchen and down the hall, then the wardrobe door opened.

'Christie,' said Jane. 'What are you doing?' She had the phone flex like the ball of wool in the labyrinth in one hand, and a bunch of dead chrysanthemums in the other.

'Tidying,' said Christie, backing out from coats and boots.

'I left these on the porch last week,' said Jane. 'And when I came by and they were still there, I thought I'd better check that you were OK.'

'Sorry,' said Christie. 'We never use the front door.'

Ooops. Jane noticed the 'we'. She'd have to make more of an effort she thought, as she went down the hall and tried to remember how the rest of it went.

'Would you like a cup of tea?' she said as she fumbled for the tea caddy.

'That'd be nice,' said Jane but she was watching carefully, alerted by the wardrobe and the milk which was curds in the carton and the mildewed pizza on the bench with '20 mins at 350°' on a bit of paper in Marybeth's neat handwriting.

Jane said she didn't mind whether she had milk or not and was everything all right?

'Sure,' said Christie. It was a sunny autumn day. Probably early morning. They sat on either side of the table to drink their tea. Molly was making a milkshake at the bench. One of those health blends she favoured when she was fourteen: milk, banana, yoghurt, wheatgerm. She was standing with her back to them, a grotesque grinning face on the back of her Freaky Tee and barefoot in shorts. Christie wanted to say, 'Don't use that milk, Molly. It's off. Go down to the dairy and get a fresh carton.' But Molly was already upending the curdled carton and milk was pouring out, fresh, white and unclotted, into the blender. So maybe it was OK after all?

Jane stirred a spoonful of sugar into her tea and Christie was aware suddenly of her quiet scrutiny. Did she look a mess? How long was it since she shampooed her hair, changed her clothes? Molly turned, sipping her health drink.

'You look awful, Mum,' she said. 'You should cut your hair like Paula Ryan. You should dye it. It's getting faded.'

'Gee, thanks,' Christie was about to reply but Jane said, 'Are you looking after yourself?' and the instant passed as Molly slipped away leaving only the dazzle of sunlight on the bench, so bright that Christie's eyes stung and watered.

'Of course,' said Christie.

Jane reached across and took Christie's hand.

'Come and stay with me,' she said.

'No,' said Christie.

Through the kitchen door she could hear Molly outside on the trampoline doing flips. Bounce, bounce, up and over.

'I'd love to,' she said. 'But I can't. I've got to be here.'

'For what?' said Jane. And Christie almost said, 'For Molly of course. I don't want her to come home to an empty house.' But she caught herself just in time and improvised.

'For the telephone and the fax and all the rest of it. That's how it is when you've chosen to go freelance: deadlines looming on all sides, and everyone's been patient, but I've got to get on with it. No work, no money. And it's good to be occupied . . .'

She was chattering now, but Jane looked less doubtful. A

bumblebee knocked at the kitchen window, let me out, let me out, and the sickly waxy smell of bumblebee panic filled the air. Jane had been reassured, but not completely.

'What about the evenings?' she said. 'Are they OK? Because you could work here during the day, but come round to stay at night.'

Christie couldn't bear it: the kindness, the concern, the bitter black tea, the bunch of withered flowers on the bench.

'No,' she found herself saying. 'Thanks. Actually, I'm going to go over to stay with Paul and Marybeth for a bit.'

'When?' said Jane. She was not easily deflected. Give me dates, facts, an estimated time of departure. Christie thought rapidly.

'Day after tomorrow,' she said. Molly looked up startled from her perch on the bench where she was sitting in the sun. She had sneaked back in when they weren't looking.

'Liar,' she said. 'Liar liar pants on fire.'

'Friday?' said Jane.

'Yes, Friday,' said Christie. 'At 10.35.'

'I'll give you a lift to the airport,' said Jane.

'No,' said Christie. 'It'll take too much time. I'll get a taxi.'

'If you're sure . . .' said Jane. It would take too much time. She knew without looking that she had an Open Home in Sumner on Friday at 11 am. And despite first impressions, Christie seemed to be coping OK. She'd be well looked after by that rather nerdy brother of hers and his awful earnest wife. So Jane could give her bereaved friend a hug, duty done, and leave with a clear conscience for a valuation in Sydenham.

As soon as her Toyota had backed out of the drive, Christie picked up the phone and, before she could lose the plot, called Paul. He was a little distracted. He was refereeing a fight between wife and daughter over a used condom found during the vacuuming.

'I've decided to go to South America after all,' said Christie, and Paul said, 'Good, good' over the escalating row in the background. ('At least I'm taking precautions,' Louise was yelling. 'Isn't that what you're always telling me to do?')

'Do you want company?' said Paul.

'No,' said Christie. 'I'll be fine. This is something I want to do myself.'

'Good, good,' said Paul over 'Do you want me to catch AIDS? Is that what you want?' while Marybeth signalled frantically across the kitchen: reinforcements, please. *Now.* 'Well, keep in touch and remember we're always here if you need us.'

'Sure,' said Christie, and as soon as he was off the line, she called Johnno, Neil, Leah — the entire support network — to say she was off to Australia to stay with her brother for an indefinite period.

'There. That's all arranged,' she said to Molly when she had finished, but Molly had skipped off down the hall the way she did these days on skinny little-girl legs. So Christie packed the car unaided with a random selection of bedding, laptop, whatever food was in the pantry and by mid-afternoon she was ready.

'I'm off,' she called to the house and to whatever or whoever it might hold. Then she drove out of the city which was bustling and busy and too alive to notice, out past the lake with its little floating islands which were preoccupied swans. Up the hill beyond Little River, zigzagging to the summit then a winding progress through late-afternoon sun along the ridge with the sea on either side ducking and diving from view, and finally at sunset she was driving down a spur and there was the beach between its twin headlands set down on the sea like the paws of some great tawny beast, and there was the farmhouse behind its palisade of macrocarpa, and there was Eric McFadgen and his dog Tess standing by the farm bike in a muddy yard.

'You want to rent it?' he said. 'The bach down there?'

'Yes,' said Christie. 'We rented it once, years ago.'

'That'd be at Christmas,' said Eric.

'Yes,' said Christie. 'At New Years.'

'S'a different story in the winter,' said Eric. '(Getouttathat, Tess.) There's nothing much in the way of heating, just the open fire. And the cooker's had it.'

Tess removed her nose from the exotic crevices of this stranger while the stranger was saying she didn't mind, she's brought camping gas and she prefers an open fire, she'll collect some driftwood, and Eric said she'd better have a word with Joyce.

Joyce was buffing her nails and dreaming of low maintenance in Hoon Hay with no mud and no cattle.

'It wouldn't suit me,' she said. 'Being down there on my own over winter.'

'I want a quiet place,' said Christie.

Through the window was the bay with its white breakers and the bach backed up to the cliff. If she wanted to gain admittance, she'd have to pass the entrance examination.

'I'm working on an article,' she said, thinking fast. 'I'm a journalist, freelance. I want to be somewhere where there won't be any distractions.'

'Well, you've come to the right place for that,' said Joyce.

'One of my aunties was a writer,' said Eric. 'She wrote a book. It's around here somewhere.'

He fumbled on the shelf behind the woodburner.

'Here you are,' he said. 'You might like a read of that.'

The McFadgens of Ngaionui by Alice M. McFadgen.

'Thanks,' said Christie.

Joyce meantime had been doing some rapid calculations. That was a late-model car at the gate and the coat had a weird cut that was probably designer label.

'Would $120 per week be acceptable?' she said. 'Eric could bring you a bit of dry firewood.'

'$120 would be fine,' said Christie. Whatever it took.

Joyce watched the Fiat bounce off down the track, the first $120 already folded away in her wallet. She buffed her nails and Hoon Hay edged a little closer with every scrape of the emery board.

The car jolted along the side of the creek to the bach. It did indeed look rough, rougher than she remembered, but Molly was unbothered. While Christie unloaded the car she could hear her daughter's laughter from the beach, a delighted squealing like the call of seabirds. She was always running off like that, under the hedge, over the fence, exploring wild places. Patagonia, for instance.

It was dark by the time everything was unpacked and the cold seeped in with the night from the sea. Christie made a cup of tea and climbed under her blankets.

'. . . when 25-year-old George McFadgen stepped ashore in Ngaio Bay in 1859 he found little evidence of Maori occupation. The disastrous visitations of the feared northern chief Te Rauparaha had . . .'

The words slid sideways on the page. She forced herself to focus.

'. . . only three women remained, the widows of men who had drowned in a drowned in a drowned in a . . .'

The words hopped like bed bugs. Meaningless dots and squiggles.

'. . . alone in the bay they maintained a devoted vigil waiting for the bones of their loved ones to wash ashore . . .'

The sea breathed.

In.

And out.

In.

And out.

The candle guttered and died. Christie lay in the dark on a saggy wirewove listening to the skittering of creatures outside in the marram grass conducting their busy nocturnal lives. She looked out the window at the night sky.

She was at the end of the line.

Draw a line from the Peninsula de Taitao straight across the Pacific and this was where you ended up: on this beach. This was where you must wait, the line tied round your little finger, awaiting the tug which meant you had caught something, living and dancing, at the other end. This was as close as you could get . . .

She woke to a muted morning. A great wall of sea mist had come down on the bay and when she walked on the beach it was as if she walked under a veil. Only a circle a few metres round was visible. Ahead of her she could sometimes glimpse the humpbacked headland, sometimes not. Behind her, the trail of her footprints disappeared into nothingness. She was invisible here, alone. When she turned to the sea and howled it was as if her mouth were tamped with cottonwool. She stood by grey water and drew the edge of a broken shell down the whole length of her arm and the pain oozed out in tiny red bubbles. She walked to the end of the beach feeling the tracery of pain under her jacket. She walked to the black rocks of the headland, split into the massive rectangles which had so entranced Molly, drawing her up to explore, to climb from crevice to crevice like a dancer.

'Come down!' Christie had called. 'Come down! You'll fall!'

But Molly had turned, was turning, was laughing and saying, 'Don't worry. I'll be fine!' And she climbed away from her into the fog.

Christie waited for her till the tide came lapping at her feet with its tentative tongues. Then she turned and walked the other way to the swamp. Back and forth between the paws of the beast which held the sea flat so that it slapped at the sand in a dreary repetitive *Take that.*

Take that. Walking till she was weary, holding Molly tight in her parka pocket and as she walked there were other people, other women, sometimes there, sometimes not, looking out to sea. She could hear the squeaking of their bare feet on the volcanic sand as they passed without speaking. She felt comforted by their presence. She was not the only one there, waiting.

Days converged. She made tea. She walked on the beach, sometimes in the southerlies which slammed into the bach, making it squeal and threatening to toss it up like so much kindling over the hillside. Sometimes in rain or fog when the place held her in the palm of its hand as if in kid gloves. Sometimes in dazzling sunlight where the air shimmered in layers above the beach and she had to squint, black flecks dancing in front of her eyes. Sometimes in the nun-colours, indigo blue, white and velvety black of the full moon. She slept at night holding tight to her line.

And one morning, here she is walking west to east, into the sun, from the swamp end. There are oystercatchers marching about with their hands clasped behind their backs irritably pecking at the world under their feet and the gull dropping a cockle — thwack — onto the rocks. She is walking at the sea's edge where the wet sand holds the image of clouds. The sun is full on, the wind blowing clean and chill from the pole and everything seems more than usually real. The karaka grove on the headland is present in every individual leaf. The rocks have perfect matching shadows. She has stopped and bent to pick up a piece of paua, a perfect circle with a hole just big enough for her little finger, and when she straightens the women are there, walking down the track by the karaka grove at the far end. Not quite visible, just dancing flecks, a mote in the eye, she has stood up too quickly, it's low blood pressure or some damn scientific thing. She slips the paua ring onto her finger and it fits perfectly. The flecks resolve to a single person who jumps down onto the beach and begins to walk toward her steadily through the morning sun. Christie twists the ring on her finger so that it gathers up some skin and hurts. She feels panic now, and if she could, she would turn and run, but she has grown roots, sent down white tendrils into the earth like those trees up there, her toes caught in solid rock. The approaching figure comes on, and she sees it raise its hand. And now Christie's breath is hard in her chest.

Is this how angels are supposed to be? In a blue parka with wild frizzy hair and torn satin trousers? Is this how they're supposed to feel, laughing and hugging with strong arms? Christie cannot hug her back. She stands still, trapped by her deep deep roots.

'Molly,' she says.

And it is Molly, and she isn't dead, and she's saying that some bastard nicked her passport and all her stuff, money, clothes, the lot while she was sick, really sick, hallucinating, vomiting, up in a village in Bolivia and there weren't any phones and you can't make collect calls from Bolivia anyway and it took her three weeks to get back and she had had no idea what had happened until she applied for the new passport and suddenly all hell let loose and then no one knew where Christie was, and everyone was saying she must have you know, killed herself or something. But I knew where you'd be. I knew you'd be here. I just knew it.

'So we're not dead, you see,' she says. Hugging her tight. 'We're not dead. We're both still here.' And now Christie has her arms around her daughter and they are standing together on the beach and there are other people approaching who may or may not be real.

But this is. And the sun spins above them, heads you win, tails you win.

And the line is tight around them all.

And the bones have all washed ashore and taken on their dear warm selves.

PETER WELLS

Normally I find myself pigeon-holed as a 'gay writer'. People often think fiction is thinly disguised autobiography. It always gives me pleasure to write a story which stands outside the area I'm most identified with. I wrote this story after I read an article in an English newspaper, *The Guardian*. It was about lost children and airports. Something about the situation intrigued me. Sometimes there's a freedom in just imagining how other lives might be.

Later I picked up a book called *Rwanda, Death, Despair and Defiance* and many of the first-hand accounts had a chilling authenticity and straightforwardness which stood beyond the artifice of fiction. Perhaps for this reason holocausts are so difficult to describe, except in terms of testimony. It is as if fiction cannot hope to equal the prosaic reality of horror. With 'The Friendly Stranger', I wanted to get some of the emotions of perplexity amid sorting out of information. This is common to all childhoods, and the larger picture, of violent change, and diaspora, could now happen in our own part of the world. It's a universal condition.

THE FRIENDLY STRANGER

MY FATHER TOOK HIS Rolex off. He played with it in his palm for a while, as if he were weighing something unseen. He sighed. He walked out of the room. The staff had already gone, apart from Luisa and she now walked round the kitchen quarters, carrying a machete. When she saw me looking at it, she raised it and grinned. I looked at her. For one moment, in the half-light, I thought she was threatening me. But she said, 'I will protect you, Baby Giraffe.' She had called me that since my childhood, when I was very thin and had big eyes.

Now I am fourteen, my mother dislikes this familiarity. She told Luisa to call me by my new name. 'Afraica — a good African name,' as my mother at that time said.

At this very moment, I don't seem to have a name. It is like everything, changing so swiftly it has become dangerous to say anything definite. The official bulletins were still saying the President would fight to the last. But Luisa said, 'The Old Cock has flown the coop.' She brought down her machete. The headless chook, she called him.

He was over the border. As many Ministers as possible and their families had gone with him.

I think this is what so depressed my father. He had been left behind. And he had, at one time, been a rather low-ranking Minister. Before he lost favour. But at least, as he said, he had come out of it with his head. And arms. And legs.

Our leader wasn't too picky when it came to limbs.

246

My mother came into the room now. She almost whispered in, she was so nervous. I hardly recognised her. She was taking the diamonds out of her ears. Chanel.

She had slumped into the deep leather armchairs and was sitting there, looking round the room like she didn't recognise anything any-more. I could see she was reverting bit by bit — she was changing back into who she had been, before she came to the city, and become a Minister's wife. She had been hard on the servants. She was not used to ordering people around. She suspected them of laughing behind her back, so she was extra-hard on them. At the same time the peasant in her meant she always inspected their work. They thought she was a tyrant. Perhaps that is the way it goes: a tyrant at the top, and tyrants down below. My mother was not above beating the servants herself. She said it made her feel better.

Now she was sitting there, half-whimpering as she massaged the holes in her ears — where the heavy diamonds had been.

'Baby Giraffe,' she said, and she indicated to me I should go to her. I hated her. She had beaten me also. When I would not go to the French Embassy parties, and later, when I didn't want to play squash with the President's children. I went towards her diffidently. When I got closer, she grabbed my wrists and held them, painfully. Her large eyes, faintly clouded with fear, I thought, looked all over my face as if she wanted to find in there something hidden.

'Issoufou. You will look after Issoufou, won't you?'

This was the first whisper I'd heard that my parents might be going away. 'Yes,' I said, in turn looking into my mother's face. It was then I noticed she had changed out of the outfits which always seemed as if they had come out of the magazines she liked leafing through.

I thought back to those moments of peace: when she got a new magazine from the airport. To start with these magazines were second-hand, filched from her employer, the Associate Minister's wife. They were stained with coffee or lipstick, the perfume samples all smelt. Then, when my father became an Under-Secretary, she bought the magazines herself. They were sent sea-mail so they were always a month or so out of date. My mother would sit in her chair, for hours, reading everything — or since her command of English was so bad (a fact which she went to ridiculous lengths to hide) she gazed at every page, studying the advertisements as much as the news articles.

I can remember when, at last, she had the magazines flown out. My father was Minister then and I remember my mother walking in so airily with the thick wad of magazines — *Vanity Fair, Tatler, Harper's Bazaar* — and her placing them down, just so, on the glass-and-marble table. When I went to look at them she got angry. She made me put on white gloves so as not to mark the pages.

'Little Miss Nobody from a village nobody knew from shit —' she said to me '— and look at me now.'

But one thing I always noticed. Nothing ever quite lived up to the thrill of putting on those clothes. She was always happiest when she got them out of her air-conditioned walk-in closet or when Norma, her maid, laid them out like they were priest's clothes.

'Norma was a prostitute,' my mother says now. 'She was selling my old clothes. She was a spy. Evil.' But at that time they were like best friends, Norma fussing over my mother as she zipped her up. 'Your mother's off to have lunch like Princess Di,' Norma said. But I always noticed my mother was quiet when she came home. I think other women had better labels, more diamonds. 'There's nobody to see me in this dump,' she would say to me, whispering violently, her breath hot against my skin.

The door opened and my father came in.

With him were two people, a man and a woman. I disliked them instantly. They were looking round the room, as if my father were offering the place for rent. My mother looked up. She was startled. She didn't know how to greet them, so she said nothing, except every so often a look of complete fear fastened over her features so I could tell she wasn't listening. In fact she seemed to be listening to sounds outside, as if she was expecting something. My father, I noticed, had already changed out of his Saville Row suit.

'Go outside, dear,' he said to me.

I looked at my father. He had become a sad man, weighed down with some unspecified grief, some sense of shame. I never really knew what he did. I mean not in detail. When I went to his office the men bowed and opened doors. Everyone smiled at my brother and me. Everything was done for us. But I could smell fear, I think, behind the smiles. Men were frightened of my father. Perhaps, I thought, looking at him now, he had had men's arms cut off, or legs. Or perhaps, since he was only a Minister, an ear, or fingers. Toes maybe.

'Wait outside dear,' he said to me in a kind voice. 'We won't be long.'

The two strangers looked at me from head to foot.

'Hello dearie,' the woman said to me. 'You're very grown-up for your age aren't you?'

Some shadow passed over my father's face.

'How old is she?' the man said.

'She's . . . twelve,' my father said, his voice low.

'I'm almost fourteen papa, you know that,' I said.

There was a brief silence.

'She speaks English good,' the man said.

'Go outside Baby Giraffe.'

It was my mother's voice. She didn't seem to realise she had used my childhood name. I felt a slow flush burn across my face. The woman, fingers running over the leather of the couch, looked at me closely. She had a half-smile on her face.

As I walked towards the door, the woman said, 'She'll work it OK.'

I listened from behind the door.

My father hardly talked at all and when he did his voice was tired, deeply tired. I heard him say, '. . . in cash.'

'What currency?' I heard the man say. This man's voice was honeyed, leisurely. He looked like he would take a long time to make a bargain — the choice of what he would have.

'American dollars,' I heard my father say. There was a sharp pause and then he said, 'But not much, a limited amount.'

I listened to the beetles banging into the lightbulb, sliding off.

'How much?' the man said.

My father named an amount.

A beetle dropped to the concrete. I crushed it underfoot.

There was silence.

It was then, in the distance, I heard what I remember to be the very first mortar fire. At the time I didn't really know what it was. It happened, and there was an outbreak of silence, as if everyone in that city stopped, and took a deep breath in and listened. It was as if everyone was thinking what it meant. Everyone was listening now.

'The price suddenly went up,' the woman said.

She laughed.

My mother said as if she hadn't heard, 'These diamonds, they're from Chanel. From Paris.'

The woman said, 'You can't eat diamond.'

'What's happening, Baby Giraffe?'

I nearly had a fit. I turned round and there was my brother, Issoufou, standing there looking up at me. He was dressed in all his American clothes — big baggy pants, the baseball cap back to front, his Nike shoes. They had been flown into our country, direct from New York. My brother is six.

I put my finger to my lips.

'There are some visitors,' I said, attempting to speak in an ordinary voice.

'I don't like them,' he said to me.

I looked down at his face. He was a too-pretty boy. It was like, at that age, he was pretending to be a boy. His hair was soft and his skin like chamois. He had his rollerblades hugged under his armpit.

'I want to go skating,' he said a little sullenly.

There was another sound, closer. I recognised it this time.

It was answered by a longer burst.

He looked at me.

'What's that?'

'A gun,' I said.

He was silent for a moment.

'Is it NYPD?'

He was excited.

'Not quite,' I said to him, 'but a bit like that.'

He ran and went to look out the window.

'Issy,' I said to him frightened. 'Keep away from the windows.'

He looked at me for a moment then he understood. He crouched down as he'd seen on television and crabwalked towards me.

'Have we got enough ammunition?' he asked me in a stage whisper.

'We don't have any guns,' I said to him, 'but we've got something better.'

'What's that?' he said to me brightly, but at the same time as if he doubted what I was saying.

I tapped my head.

'Brains,' I said to him.

He nodded as if he wasn't convinced.

The ugly man and woman left. They said they would return the following day at 5 am. We — the woman's eye moved over my brother and me — were to wait inside the garage downstairs. We were to have only one suitcase between us.

'You have to dress down,' she said, 'None of that **** American ****' and here she used a word I had never heard before in the house. But that is what it was like suddenly, things were inside the house before you could say anything, travelling on the air, life the sharp swerve of gunfire, or bad language. At this point we heard the sound of running feet.

The man and woman left quickly.

There was complete silence.

My father went out the door.

Issy looked at all this.

'Mamma,' he said in a wailing kind of voice, and began to take a step towards my mother.

She walked towards the door. She didn't turn round. Issy went to follow her. I caught him. I had to hold onto him because he was fighting hard.

'Leave her alone,' I said. 'She's busy.'

'But what . . .' he said to me, breathless. He was winded. He couldn't even cry. 'But what's going to happen to us?'

I said to him, 'We're going away. We're going to escape.'

When we were waiting at the airport I kept running my father's words again and again through my brain. I kept inspecting them, like they were a script in which lay all the hope of our survival.

'You are lucky Baby Giraffe,' he said. 'You speak good English. You will be able to make yourself understood over there.'

It was then I understood my brother and I were going to England.

'It is better for you both,' my father said, 'and we will soon join you. Once the troubles die down. Listen,' he said and he spoke quickly then, having looked over his shoulder at the door. 'Luisa is really your grandmother. She gave birth to your mother. Make sure you say goodbye before you leave.'

I blinked.

Then he said, 'Mr and Mrs Andreica will take you to the airport. They have false passports. Mrs Andreica will accompany you onto the plane. She will pretend to be your aunt. When you arrive at Heathrow, Mrs Andreica will hand you over to an embassy official, Mr Honeysnape. I have phoned him. He is a friend. He will look after you until your mother and I can get there. There will be no problems. We have money in an account in Switzerland.'

When he finished he made me repeat what he said. This wasn't difficult. I have a photographic memory.

Then he said, 'Your mother and I will get there as soon as possible.'

'Daddy,' I said.

He kissed me then, and he looked both ashamed and sad. He was ashamed to be back in native costume again, without his Rolex. There was an unsettling silence everywhere now.

The radio had stopped, as had the television.

There was just this sound, like animals or snakes crawling through the undergrowth. You had to listen, carefully.

When I went to say goodbye to Luisa, she wouldn't listen when I called her grandma. Perhaps it was too late. It was definitely too late, I see that now. Luisa said, 'I'll guard the house. If anyone tries to get in they have to get past me first.' She swung the machete. She laughed. I thought: she has gone mad. Then I thought: perhaps this is what is happening, everyone is going mad. Or: everyone has gone mad.

This cheered me up, as if I understood something for the first time.

Then I thought: if everyone has gone mad, anything can happen. The fear came back, and I thought: I want to go to the toilet. This urge overcame me so burningly all I could do was stand there, embarrassed. I went into my room and took down my posters, packed up my favourite CDs. I put these in my suitcase. Luisa — my grandmother — came in at the very last and held out her hand. Inside it was an amulet, it was carved out of bone. It was in the shape of a duck, plump, serene.

She brushed her lips against my hair making a strange groaning sound and I felt a kind of almost electric shock pass out of her and into me. I grabbed hold of her and tried to hold tight. She kept heaving and making these sounds as if she wanted to cry, but couldn't.

Out at the airport there were other kids from the diplomatic school. I could see from their faces how we probably looked — ashen, sullen, as if something was being taken away from us, which it was. I saw a girl who was my best friend, Naima. Now she was with a man I'd never seen before, and I could see she had been crying. She kept rubbing the inside of her leg. We sat opposite each other and every so often our eyes would meet — just meet and we would look at each other as if one of us was waiting to recognise the other. In between us walked a young soldier. He was probably only a year older than me. His face was carved. He had a compact, hunter's body. Sweat was pouring off him. He kept swinging his M16 round in a restless, wild way, as if he was anxious to use it. He is mad, too, I thought. He is as afraid as we are.

All the time they were playing martial music over the loudspeaker system, the national anthem again and again, as if they were afraid what would happen if it came to an end. Yet when it did there was only a crackling perimeter of silence, and we all waited, wondering what might happen next — then the anthem took up again.

After several hours, a bus brought American nationals to the airport. They got off and went and sat together. Issoufou had got hungry. He was used to always having his meals exactly on the prescribed dot, this was part of his life. I said to Mr and Mrs Andreica that Issoufou wanted something to eat. Both of them were reading paperback novels. His was a John Grisham and hers was a Jackie Collins. They looked up at me. Mrs Andreica had those glasses which enlarge the pupils. I could see the yellow conjunctivitis of her eyes, run all over by little red rivers of blood.

I repeated my statement. Mrs Andreica said, licking her broad cushion of a thumb, and turning a page, 'He'll eat on the plane.'

'When will the plane go?'

'When it goes,' Mrs Andreica said and the yellow tip of her fingernail began to drift along a line of print. Her tone of voice had so much contempt in it, I felt a great fear. I wanted at that moment to go back to the house, to maybe walk back. It would have been better to stay with Luisa. Perhaps we could have stayed up in the manhole in the roof. Like Anne Frank. It would have been better to be hungry there. Safer. Even if we had died at least we would die together.

I felt the amulet in my pocket. I got up. The man looked up. 'I need to walk for a bit,' I said, 'I'm getting the stitch.'

The man said, 'Don't go out of my sight.'

'Or,' said the woman and she smiled — and when she did I looked at her teeth, great yellow ivory like those of an old elephant found dead in a sump — 'or we'll go without you. We won't wait.'

I walked away slowly. I was aware that Mr Andreica was following me with his eyes all the time. I veered towards Naima but when I got closer the man beside her lifted up his arm and put it across her shoulders. I looked at his thick long fingers on the flesh of her arm. She had a look of complete fear on her face. I walked towards the Americans. I sat down by a family in tracksuits. I watched them eat cold McDonalds. The youngest one put down a half-eaten Big Mac. I placed my hand down casually. I put it in my pocket. I walked back to Issy. I put it down by his leg. I nudged him. His hand came out. Turning his head away, he began, like a starving rodent, to eat.

We had been flying for eight hours. We had got through the passport control, with our false passports. Mr Andreica had melted away into the crowd. The woman had not spoken to us once. She had read her novel, flicking from page to page, sighing every so often deeply, as if she agreed with what was on the page, or regretted some action. When the food came round, we ate everything they offered us. She drank a Bloody Mary, with a piece of celery as a twister. They dimmed the lights then. Mrs Andreica ordered another drink. She delved into her bag and put on my mother's earrings. Then she finished her drink and began to sleep.

She slept in a strange fitful way. Like a cat having dreams. Every so often she shook minutely and I could see her pupils running and fluttering under her eyelids. She would make a sound, not any word I could identify but as if she was trying to deny something, or say something wasn't so. I had my fingers on the amulet, I had grown used to holding it. Its smooth coolness soothed me and when it warmed up, I liked it even better.

Issy leant across with a bit of rolled-up paper and made it appear flies were landing on the huge continent of Mrs Andreica's face. She kept trying to bat them away. We laughed.

Then Issy fell into a deep sleep. I looked down at his face. So empty. It was like the clouds out the window. Just lit by our passage through the dark. He was probably dreaming of how our mother came in to say goodbye. How she wept and wouldn't let go of him.

How she said her tears would fertilise a field of flowers in which, one day, she would find him, a handsome young man, happy, a husband with children all speaking English. Or he was dreaming of how she didn't weep and hurriedly came in to say goodbye, looking over her shoulder all the time, shaking.

I looked back at Mrs Andreica. Her jacket was bulging open and inside I could see a heavy packet. The more I looked at it, I could see green notes. That old man in a wig was staring directly at me. She changed her position. She hugged the wallet into her, her hand even in sleep checking out the packet. Her lips smacked together and her body made a crude noise. A rich dense insult drifted out of her clothes. I didn't care. All I was interested in was her wallet. I waited for her to settle. Then I reached inside. I had my fingers on the wallet, I was easing it out. Her eyelids slid open. At first she was surprised to see me so close, she didn't seem to recognise me. Then she did. I stood up quickly.

'I need to get out quickly, please. The toilet.'

She got to her feet.

'A girl like you,' she said to me, 'could earn money on a plane.'

In the toilets I put the hand lotion into my pocket. I took the soap, and I took a comb someone had left behind, a blue comb and a hairclip. We would need everything now. I no longer cared. Something was happening to me. I wondered where my mother and father might be, whether they would get back to her village and if they did what might await them there. Someone knocked on the door. When I came out it was a white man. Young. His shirt, a red one, was opened down three buttons. I could see bright brassy hairs all tumbled there.

He smiled at me, mistaking me for someone else. He asked me where I was going.

'I'm going to London,' I said.

'For school?' he said.

'I've left school,' I said. 'That's finished.'

As we came nearer our destination, Mrs Andreica went into the toilets carrying a plastic Marks and Spencer bag. When she came back, she looked different. She had on a dingy-looking reeferjacket, and slacks.

The diamond earrings had gone. And the glasses were now sun-glasses, which looked like they had come from a supermarket. In the dawn light, she looked older. The air hostess, herself brushed up for landing, asked her if we needed English landing documents. When Mrs Andreica answered, she spoke as if she was a character from East Enders. She turned to Issy and me and said, 'Remember, we just ended up sitting together by accident. Got it?'

It was cold out there. As we got off the plane there was a small gap between the plane and the landing tunnel. That was my first smell of England. I shivered in my thin clothes. We were carrying with us the last smells of our country. These smells were evaporating fast. Soon we would wash them away and then, as we ate English food, so our bodies would in turn lose the smell of our country. Then perhaps we would truly be here.

We waited in long queues. Issoufou was crotchety and I had to carry his rollerblades. Slowly we inched forward to the men and women in uniforms, stamping passports. I could smell the fear. It rose in waves from behind me, from out of all our bodies. I looked at everyone and I thought: we are all escaping. All of us. Except Mrs Andreica. She looked like she was going home. She got through ahead of us. Just as she walked into the airport she turned round and glanced at me. It seemed like she was challenging me to get through.

I felt into my pocket. There was the amulet. Warm to my touch, since I had been fingering it all the time.

At the counter I handed over our passports. Only at one point did the man look at me, and it was when he was matching the photograph with my face. There was a small pause then he stamped it. 'You must be looking forward to a good kip,' he said.

I said, 'Yes. Thank you, sir,' as I took back our false passports.

'I have to go and make a phone call,' she said. 'Mr Honeysnape. Won't be long.'

That was over an hour ago. I had seen her go into the toilet. After ten minutes, when she didn't come out, I went in. There was an exit out the other side. A woman as black as myself was cleaning the floor.

'What's up love?' she said to me in a London accent. I asked her if she had seen Mrs Andreica. I described her. The cleaner said to me she had only just come on her shift. I walked round trying to find her. I couldn't see her anywhere. The place was so huge. I thought of how she told us to wait opposite the book counter, where Mr Honeysnape would come and meet us. Perhaps she had gone off to meet him. So I returned to our seats.

Another hour passed.

Issy was asleep now, slumped there, holding on to his rollerblades. Small bubbles came and went out the side of his mouth. He was exhausted. I could see that. I kept looking at the people around me, imagining what Mr Honeysnape would look like. I was surprised to see so many African people there. I could see they had all escaped too. Or had they? Some people walked towards me, smiling. I prepared myself. But they walked right past me, saying hello to the people behind me.

That felt bad.

I noticed a man looking at me.

The man kept walking past.

He was old, in his early forties, wearing brown shoes worn down on the outer side, one lace undone. He had a yellow comb in his top pocket and three buttons were undone on his knitted blue vest. Cable stitch. A white man. He was a religious man, I'm not sure why I thought that, but I was sure of it. Was he a government spy, I wondered. I felt very weary. The excitement had worn off.

I waited and then I smiled at him.

'You're looking a bit lost,' he said to me. His voice was pleasant, light. I liked the sound of it.

'I'm waiting for a friend,' I said.

'Has he been long?'

'A while,' I said.

'Why don't we wait over in the café?' he said to me. 'You can see your friend from over there. I feel like a coffee,' he said to me, smiling.

'I've got my brother,' I said.

'Bring him along too. The more the merrier,' he said, and laughed.

When we were sitting down — I had a club sandwich, ham, mustard and lettuce, Issy had a custard square, we both had cappuccinos — he said, 'And what are you doing over here?'

'Oh we're here to see the Tower of London,' I said. 'I've seen it before, myself of course, but I want to show it to my baby brother.'

Issoufou didn't say anything. He was kicking the table legs with his shoes. He was bored, I could tell. He had finished all his food.

'My parents are going to join us,' I said. 'They arrive tomorrow.'

He didn't say anything. He lifted his cup and drank, looking into the crowd.

'Is that your friend?' he said.

He pointed to an old man, carrying a broom and a kleensak. We laughed. We watched Mr Honeysnape disappear.

'Where are you staying then?' he said as he lifted a crumb on the pad of his index finger.

He hesitated at this point, before putting it in his mouth.

'A hotel,' I said.

'Where is it. Perhaps I can give you a lift?'

'Well,' I said, playing for time. 'It's over by Buckingham Palace.'

'That's out Hammersmith way?' he said.

'That's right,' I said.

'I could give you a lift,' he said. 'It wouldn't be out of my way.'

'Could you?' I said. I thought about it for a while.

I felt into my pocket, I thought I'd let the amulet tell me what to do.

'Actually we have to wait. Someone's picking us up.'

'They've probably been delayed,' the man said.

'That's right.'

We all paused for a little and looked at the crowds moving past.

'I'd like to come with you,' I said apologetically ten minutes later. 'But I feel we should wait.'

'Well,' he said, 'it's like this. I can't wait much longer. But if you want a place to sleep tonight, then I could perhaps help.'

I didn't say anything for a moment.

'I think we should wait,' I said in a low voice.

'Alright,' he said. He got up. 'Well,' he said, turning away, 'I hope you have a nice time in England.'

'Thank you,' I said.

The old man was sweeping round us with his broom. We were too tired to shift. We lifted our feet and the broom swept under our shoes.

He went on sweeping until every bit of rubbish had gone and the lino was bare of people.

Another crowd of people arrived.

The old man swept his way back to us.

He said, 'Someone's waiting for you.'

He nodded in the direction of the doors.

The kind man had come back. He was standing by the doors down the far end of the corridor. He held his car keys up.

Issy waved.

'Come on,' Issoufou said, getting up.

APIRANA TAYLOR

'Parareka' is a true story. There is a certain marae where a woman kept sitting up just as the main character in this piece does.

I like 'Parareka' because it comes from the stories, dreams and lives of people I knew or had heard of when I was a child. This is my mother and grandmother's generation. They were the generation that lived just before or were part of the great Maori urban migration. The time they represented has practically passed away. I feel I have accurately caught the way my people thought and felt. How we viewed the world. How we lived in it and tried to find answers to problems that beset us and how we tried to cope in unusual circumstances at that time.

PARAREKA

HINE ROA MATEWAI WAS a strong woman. She was the biggest and strongest woman I've ever met. I'll never meet anyone as strong and determined as her. She came from one of the rangatira lines of my tribe. The bloodlines of great chiefs ran thick in her. Lengthwise she was six foot six and she was solidly built but not fat. She had a regal air about her and she carried herself proudly. She always did a lot for other people yet she was very humble and humane and she only ever became tough and difficult under extreme provocation. Her strength came from her mind rather than her body. She never used this ability to hurt anybody and though she knew her strength she usually displayed it unwittingly, not to show off, but to accomplish whatever task she happened to be doing.

Once a calf almost the size of a cow refused to go through the gate into greener pasture and so Hine roa picked the calf up and popped it down on the other side of the fence. Frank Amoamo and myself who'd been sent by our nannies to help Aunty Hine roa stared at each other in disbelief but it was the calf who was the most surprised of all and Hine roa continued working as if nothing happened. Similarly I once saw a huge-horned stubborn ram leap the fence with its head ready to butt any fool who got in his way. Hine roa turned and balanced herself and then rammed the ram by dropping her shoulder so that she butted the rhino-like ram's head in mid-air with her shoulder. The ram fell back on its own side of the fence and was knocked out. Hine roa climbed the fence, helped the ram to its feet and then patted the creature groggily on its way. The ram never tried to take on Hine roa Matewai again.

We lived in poverty in the early nineteen thirties. We ate what we grew hunted or caught and if we were lucky we got a tiny little bit of cash off many of the small subsistence farms which made up the little left of our tribal lands. We worked hard but life was grim: one crop failure, one mistake and you starved. I've killed rabbits and eaten them raw because I was so hungry.

It was poverty that drove Hine roa's husband Te Kahu away. There were other reasons but it was mainly years and years of eating the air in your heart, as he put it, that made him decide to leave.

Their little farm was inland from the sea. Te Kahu and Hine roa raised their nine children on it. Their children lived a good life though their underwear was made of potato sacking and on early steamy mornings they stood in fresh cow pats to keep their feet warm.

Once the children were grown up and six of the nine kids left home, Te Kahu returned to live with his relations in Gisborne. He hoped life would be better there.

As a youth he loved Hine roa but the hard life changed him. He started to drink a lot. When he left he asked her to go with him, but she said no. When he left he took the horse. Their house was a long way from the seaside village. It was over hills and far far away in the back of beyond. We thought it cruel of him to take the horse and leave Hine roa stranded.

Once a month Hine roa made her way into town to get what few things she and her three remaining sons needed from the Farmers store. She strode over the hills along the river bed, through the bush and into the tiny village. 'Hey Hine roa, hey Aunty, come and eat with us,' we called to her from our doorways as she passed by. 'Haere mai. Haere mai ki te kai.' Come, come and eat.

It was our custom to share food throughout the village. If you got a sack of kina you shared it round with your brothers and sisters and your parents and your uncles and aunties and friends and first second third and fourth cousins. 'This is how we live,' we said. 'We share.' If you didn't we shunned you and your life became miserable.

The kaumatua decided that when they could they'd leave two sacks of spuds for Hine roa to pick up, out the back of Farmers, when she came into town. The kaumatua offered her a horse. This she refused because of her pride.

In June when the miro berries were ripe Hine roa sent her three remaining sons out to get the kereru. These pigeons gathered to feast on the berries and to get fat. When they were fattest they trapped the birds and killed them. Hine roa then sent the boys into town with plenty of pigeons for the kaumatua whose faces smiled with pleasure when they received the gifts. Their mouths watered and their bellies rumbled as they thought of the feast to come.

Early on an autumn afternoon Hine roa made the journey into the village and there were two sacks of spuds and some kumara at the back of the Farmers store waiting for her. After buying a little tobacco and some flour she eased the sacks of spuds, the kumara and all up onto her shoulders and turned for home. 'Kia tiaki,' called the kaumatua as she passed by. This weight is nothing to me, she replied. Besides I want to get home before it's dark. You know me, if I make up my mind nothing can stop me. If I don't get home bury me with these spuds and kumara beneath the mountain of Pae pae manu where I've worked all my life. Heh heh heh. Then I'll take this food over for our ancestors who've gone beyond.

Hine roa strode along with her load on her back. When she crossed the bridge it rained lightly. She decided to cut straight across the many winding river bends so as to reach her destination quicker. She walked into the water and waded up and across the stream. The sky got dark. It rained and rained. Up in the hills the rain water loosened an avalanche of river rocks and silt which in turn released a torrential flood and sent it charging along the river bed.

Three days later Hine roa's three sons came into town and asked if anyone had seen their mother. We replied we'd not seen her since she'd left the Farmers store. We found her later that afternoon. She was a fair way off the beaten track and she was half in the river and half out of it. She looked dead, although she still held the two sacks of spuds on her shoulders. The kumara flour and tobacco were on the side of the river to which Hine roa had been trying to cross. They were safely placed on a high rock and they were completely dry.

Hine roa was tied onto the back of a spare horse and carried back to the marae. It would be a big tangi.

When we heard the legendary Hine roa was dead we prepared for the tangi. She was so loved respected and revered by us. It was a big funeral with so many people on the marae you heard the weeping and wailing like the wind at times, Aueeeeeee tangi tangi tangi eeeeeee . . .

We placed Hine roa within the arms of the whare whaikairo on the front porch of the carved ancestral house beneath the window in the sun. Koro Hone stood on the marae before the dead woman. He cleared his throat but couldn't speak. He stood voiceless before all and the hupe flowed from his nose and the wind blew it across the marae as he stood with his eyes racked in pain. Finally he spoke. 'Tihei i te taiao tihei i te whaiao tihei te ao marama a ka puta ko au he tangata tihei mauriora. Kua hinga te rakau nui o te wao. E te whaea o te motu haere ki te okiokinga o a tatau tipuna. He whaine nui mana koe. Tangi tangi eee . . . I come in the darkness in search of light, said Koro Hone. The great tree of the forest has fallen. The mother of the land has gone. Weep, weep. He spoke of his pain at her going. All the chiefs came forward to speak and they took as much time as they wished to stand in front of the dead woman and say their farewells to the old chiefteness. We share and share and share. That's how we live, they said, and they embraced one another and wept and draped themselves over the coffin. They embraced Hine roa and said goodbye.

Her closest of kin sat next to her. They caught up on the old times and the latest news as they chatted amongst themselves and they never left Hine roa alone as they lay there. Especially at night there was always someone there to keep the deceased company. Even in such hard times there was plenty of food being cooked up in the shed out back of the marae. Everyone brought something and the community had a tangi fund saved up to help in such times.

Then we argued about where to bury Aunty Hine roa. Each thought they had the right to make the decision for everyone else and bury her where they thought best.

'Well, bury her at Ohine urupa!'

'How stupid. She never lived there.'

'Let's bury her at Titama. That's a lovely place.'

'Bugger off, she's closely related to us and we're taking her down the road to Tiki roa. It's been settled!'

'That'll be the day.'

'Hey who the hell do you think you are. Coming around here like this. This is our marae and you fellas are a pack of nobodies. Pipe down!'

This argument bubbled and boiled away all day and none of the chiefs could agree. Faces got redder and tempers got hotter and hotter as everyone claimed the right to take our beloved aunty with them. Curses and insults flew about the marae.

'Pokokohua!'

'Kaua koe e korero pera mai ki au!'

'Ko wai koe? Upoko maro.' During this time more and more people came on to the marae and the argument got bigger and bigger.

Amidst all this, some of Hine roa's distant relatives formed a group about the coffin. They picked it up and tried to make off down the road with Hine roa, in an effort to take her and bury her where they thought she ought to be buried. Hine roa's daughter Pani wouldn't let this happen; she grabbed Henry Goldsmith who'd hoisted the foot of the coffin onto his shoulder and scratched his eyes. Then a fight started. Tupaea Whanga gave Jimmy Goldsmith a black eye because of the chipped tooth Jimmy had given him. The scuffle became a full-scale brawl as people forgot the coffin and punched and cursed one another.

'Kati Kaua e whawhai. Me korero tatau . . .' Stop! Stop! we must talk this through called Koro Hone. The fighting subsided when Koro Hone rang the bell. People looked at one another and felt ashamed although one or two looked as if they wanted to keep fighting. We will talk this through, Koro Hone and the elders agreed.

As they talked a cloud of dust appeared and came storming along the dusty road. It was a posse of horsemen. As the riders got closer people saw it was Te Kahu and a group of people from Gisborne. We prepared to welcome the newcomers but before the karanga and greetings could be given, Tawhai the older brother of Hine roa made his way down to the gate and called to Te Kahu. 'Get the hell out of here! Don't bother coming in here. Just keep riding your bastard. Who the hell are you to come in here! You're bloody nobody and you caused the death of my sister by taking off with the horse and leaving her to carry all the spuds.'

'Who the hell are you to talk?' Te Kahu replied. 'Where were you when we had hard times. This woman was my wife and I loved her for years. Now get the hell out of my way.' He tried to ride his horse right on to the marae and Tawhai tried to stop him. Te Kahu raised the butt of his stock whip and cracked Tawhai across the face.

Another fight was about to break out when Hine roa sat up. No one noticed this at first as eyes focused on the fight between Te Kahu and Tawhai.

'Eeeeiiiiee . . .' All eyes turned to Pani, who sat by her mother, who rose to sit in her coffin where she once lay. Hine roa gazed unseeingly across the marae towards Tawhai and Te Kahu. 'Eeeeiiiee,' called Pani again. 'Aueeee, aueeeee,' cried the people. 'He atua, he atua. He tohu, he tohu.' A God, a God. A sign, a sign, they called.

Koro Hone could only hold his walking stick and shake. Pani rolled her eyes about in her head and looked confused and surprised, like someone who had just been shot. Te Kahu slipped from his horse and fainted and Tawhai stooped to pick him up. A child screamed and was silenced. Horses in the nearby paddock raised their heads and sniffed uneasily as Hine roa sat there like Queen of the marae for all to see.

What did this mean? What was to be done? The wind ruffled Hine roa's hair. Another child, the woman's tiny granddaughter, climbed up this seated mountain of death and lovingly smoothed her grandmother's hair into place.

'He aha ai? He aha ai?' Why why, said Koro to Hine roa who sat there with the dishevelled look of one who has just risen from bed. What the hell is going on? What the heck does this mean? we asked each other as we talked amongst ourselves.

She was bloody dead alright. The Pakeha doctor himself had certified it and you couldn't get hold of him just like that to certify death again. He lived miles from the isolated little community. A few days hard ride by horse back at least.

'Aueeee,' cried some in shock. 'Aueeee, she's dead.' She's dead, she's definitely dead! cried others in fear. Sit her down.

And so we did lay her down. You can't have corpses popping up and down any old how. We united in determination to make Hine roa lie down. We twisted and pulled and pushed at Hine roa until at last she lay, stretched out once again in her coffin, and to make sure she didn't get up again they tied her down with rope.

Then the speech-making began with an earnestness and command which made all whaikorero tangi before this seem hollow and weak. 'Takoto mai ra. Takoto mai ra. E te Whaea haere ki tua o te arai. haere haere . . .' Lie there in death oh great woman. We weep for you. Go on to our ancestors in the night. Go on to the world of the dead. Leave the world of the living. Go. Go, said the elders.

But go where? It still hadn't been decided where to bury her. 'Orewa,' some suggested. 'Mata hau,' said others. 'What about down by the church?' Even her brothers and sisters and children argued. 'We're all getting tired of this!' we yelled.

Finally we decided, this tangi had gone on too long, what with Aunty sitting up and all the arguing and people being fed throughout all this time. 'We are running low on food.'

Aunty you're dead, we said, and whether you like it or not, we've finally decided to bury you here in the paddock right next to the marae in the Poutu's plot that's the best place for you and you can lump it or leave it.

Much prayer and karakia was said and we sang our ancient songs to Hine roa and when the hole was dug we lifted her up and carried her to the plot and we laid her down in her coffin beside the hole.

We said more prayers and we were about to lower Hine roa into the grave when crack the ropes holding the old lady down broke and she sat up again.

Is she dead? Is she really dead? asked some. Of course she's bloody dead, said others. Just look at her, she's as stiff as a board and she's starting to stink a bit. This is all getting out of hand. For god's sake lets just chuck her in the hole and get on with it. Maybe she doesn't want to go here, we realised. She doesn't seem to want to go anywhere, we decided. We all looked at each other in fear and wondered what to do.

Then Koro Hone remembered what Hine roa had said. 'If I make up my mind nothing can stop me. If I don't get home bury me with these spuds and kumara beneath the mountain of Pae pae manu where I've worked all my life. Heh heh heh. Then I'll take this food over for our ancestors who've gone beyond.'

'We've got to load the sacks of spuds and the kumara and whatever else she had when she died on her shoulders and weigh her down that way, and we have to bury her at Pae pae manu where her people are buried. This is the only way she'll go into the grave quietly,' said Koro Hone.

But Koro we can't put food in the grave with a dead person. It would break our law of tapu. Disaster will fall on us if we do this.

'Kao,' not so, said Koro Hone. For in the Maori world there is food for the living and there is food for the dead. This is food in remembrance of those who've gone on. He kai ora. The spuds, the kumara, the tobacco and the flour is food for the dead, obviously, Hine roa intends to take it with her, and our ancestors want her to bring it to them.

We took Hine roa back up the river and into the hills and we buried her at Pae pae manu underneath her sacred mountain. When we put her in the grave we placed the spuds the kumara the flour and the tobacco on her shoulders. Koro Hone swears he saw Hine roa smile from the bottom of the grave when we did this. We also buried other items with Hine roa. Into the grave went a packet of lollies. A bottle of brandy. A Bible and the latest horse-racing guide. This was all to be for the ancestors. Koro Hone also slipped a note into the coffin before it was lowered into the hole. The note was a letter to God via the ancestors and it contained a list of complaints about the hard times we lived in.

As the dirt was tossed into the grave and the earth piled up on the coffin, we wept rivers of tears.

When the grave was filled with dirt and we'd emptied our hearts of the pain, we went back to the Pa where the priest lifted the tapu from us and we somehow put together a huge meal and we laughed and ate well. Then some of us went back to Uncle Tawhai's place and we got drunk for a week.

CARL NIXON

This story began as one of my first adult attempts to craft a short story. I sat down with a lined refill pad and nothing to say and then ... my mind hauled up ideas of death, alienation, and reconciliation from the depths and twisted them around the bones of a nearly forgotten story that I had heard my father tell from his days growing up in the seaside suburb of Brighton. Rereading 'My Father Running with a Dead Boy' I realise that there is a lot of my own fear and anxiety hiding behind the words. But it also has something to say about our broader New Zealand society. In its treatment of the distance often inherent in father-and-son relationships it is a story that resonates for many men. As a beginning for my writing I find 'My Father Running with a Dead Boy' both satisfying and daunting. Daunting because it has been praised and therefore has created a precedent for my work, satisfying because, for me, the story has a truth and a clarity of expression of which I am proud.

MY FATHER RUNNING WITH A DEAD BOY

AT MY FATHER'S FUNERAL an old man in a crumpled black suit gets up to speak. He rises slowly on old man's legs from among the dark suits and neatly combed heads, murmuring apologies for flattened toes and kicked handbags. For a moment I think that he is my father. The same old man's shuffling walk. But then I see that, no, they are different people. This man's nose is larger, more Roman.

It's a good turnout. Better than I would have thought for a man as quiet and solitary as my father. I close my eyes and see him coming towards me walking as he always did, stiffly, head down, shoulders hunched over as though moving into a strong wind. By the time I was ten my father was already an old man, slow and careful in his movements. No cricket on the back lawn or kicks with the rugby ball down at the park.

I dread the awkward silence which always near us. Soon I will begin to talk about the rugby or the latest rates increase although I don't really care about either and then inevitably, hating the cliché, I will work my way around to the rainy spell we've had lately. What does he think, will it be a hard winter?

I open my eyes and my father vanishes.

Someone has forgotten to turn the heating on. The church is a meat-locker despite the sunlight coming through the stained glass window behind the coffin. I stare at the colours on the pale carpet where the filtered light spreads like spilt fizzy drink — Fanta, Mello Yello, Raspberry, Lemon-Lime.

Several people have already spoken. My father's boss from the insurance office said a few words. He took a piece of paper from his pocket, smoothed it with fat sweaty fingers and, head down, mumbled into the microphone. From the front row I stared at his waist where the black suit bulged out over his belt.

'A sad day for family and friends sorely missed a diligent worker cared about his job in 30 years never a complaint punctual a good provider a great loss our condolences to Helen and Greg.'

The old man in the crumpled suit moves across in front of me. He wades into the pool of spilt drink which splashes up over his black shoes and half-way up his legs, taps the microphone with a thin finger. I see that there are dark spots on the back of his hands. Surprisingly he seems to change his mind about the microphone and steps around in front of it.

'I hope you can hear me. Never liked these things much.' His voice is deeper and stronger than I had expected. It's an actor's voice or someone who's used to telling a good yarn. A younger man's voice.

Out of the corner of my eye I think that I see my father shuffling forward to listen, shoulders stooped. But when I turn my head there is nothing. A thick drape stirred by a draught in a shadowy corner.

'I don't expect many of you know me. My name's Reginald Black but Ray used to call me Blacky and after that most other people did too. I was Ray's best mate right through from when we were about 16 to when I moved up to Napier. That was when I was 25. A fair few years ago now. We used to play rugby together on a Saturday for Brighton and we'd go to the local afterwards for a few beers. On a Friday night we'd drive to the dances in town hoping to meet a couple of girls who wouldn't mind going for a ride in Ray's car after it was all over. Most weeks we'd find a couple who were game.'

And then, amazingly, he winks, a slow old man's wink and he's looking right at me when he does it. A few people laugh nervously, unsure if this is the type of talk suitable for a funeral. The old man's skin is very brown and I have a sudden image of him down on his knees digging in rich black soil, a tomato plant in his dirt-caked hand.

Out of the corner of my eye I notice my father shuffle forward again. I don't turn to look this time and he remains there in the corner listening.

'But what I mostly remember about Ray is the time he carried the dead boy home.' I look up, not sure if I have heard the old man correctly. 'We were both still living with our parents at the time. We must have been 20 or so. We lived down by the beach and Ray was building a small sailboat in the shed out the back. Nothing fancy. Just something to potter around in on weekends, and sometimes I'd go over and give him a hand. We'd take the frame out and put it on a couple of saw-horses. It was good working outside like that. Ray's parents' house backed on to a reserve down by the estuary. Big pine trees kept the wind off and we could hear the surf as we worked if the wind was right.

'This particular day, I remember it was hot and Ray wasn't wearing a shirt. He was brown and covered in sweat and sawdust from the work. As we sanded down the hull we'd seen a couple of kids playing in the reserve, running in and out of the trees, shouting and laughing, playing cops and robbers or such like. One of them was Trevor O'Brien. His mother lived two doors down from Ray. They had a dog with them.

'Then after a while we heard the dog barking. The barking went on and on and not like when the kids were playing near us either. The dog was pretty good then. It was a strange barking, all high and excited like it had treed a possum or maybe gotten itself tangled up in a fence. After a bit of that, Ray and me looked at each other and I remember Ray said something like, "Let's go and have a look, eh?"

'It was cold in the shade of the pines after being in the sun. There was no undergrowth, just a thick mat of brown pine needles on the ground. We walked at first, a good excuse for a break, but as the dog's barks got louder Ray started running. I don't know why, I never asked. He just started running. Ray went up a trail between the lupins and I lost sight of him in the sand hills. I followed and came to a clearing with walls of sand all around. Not the sloping, dry white sand that you get down by the water but a harder mixture of sand and earth and clay that made steeper walls. It had been raining a bit that week and the sand was wet and dark. All around the top lupins blocked out the sun. It was like being in a pit. The dog was over in one corner whimpering and digging in the sand.

'By the time I arrived Ray was down on his knees with his back to me and he was digging too. "What's happening? What's going on?" You see, even then I still didn't understand. But when I got close enough to see properly I understood all right. Sticking out of the sand was a kid's foot and part of his leg. Trevor O'Brien and his cobber had gotten bored with cops and robbers so they'd dug a tunnel into the hard sand wall. They'd dug a pretty good tunnel too, big enough for them to both crawl inside. There was a good-sized pile of sand where Ray was kneeling so I reckoned they'd dug back a fair ways. A great little tunnel. Until it collapsed in on top of them.

'Ray grabbed the kid's leg and pulled. He was a big bloke, big broad shoulders and back. With Ray pulling, that kid came out of the sand like a cork coming out of a bottle. It was Trevor's friend. Ray never even looked at him. He just handed him to me like a sack of potatoes. "Get him to my place. Get a doctor." And then he was down on his knees again, digging.

'A ten-year-old kid weighs a fair bit but I ran with him bouncing up and down on my shoulder all the way to the house. Ray's mum had been a nurse during the war and she knew what to do, although she got a hell of a surprise when I crashed through her kitchen door. I watched, sucking down air in great gulps, as she cleared the sand out of the kid's mouth and then she blew into him. He was lying on the kitchen table. I watched his chest rise up with every blow that Ray's mum put into him. When the doctor finally arrived the kid was coughing up sand but I didn't wait to see what happened. I ran back through the trees to Ray.

'He was still digging. He'd had the idea of digging down from above on more of an angle. The sand was wetter higher up from the rain and didn't cave in so easy, plus the roots of the lupins held it together more. He'd dug enough so that only his legs from the knees down still showed. I hollered at him that I was there and he yelled back for me to help move the sand piling up in the entrance to his tunnel. He was pushing it back between his legs and I grabbed the sand and flung it away until my shoulders ached, but no matter how much sand I moved Ray always pushed out more. After a while not even his feet showed and I had to lean right into the tunnel to scoop out the sand.

'A long time after, I heard Ray shout something I didn't understand and he pushed out more sand and then he began backing out of the hole. I grabbed his legs and pulled. Ray was dragging the kid by the shoulders but as soon as I saw him I knew that Trevor was dead.

Mostly from his eyes. They were half open and the eyeballs were covered in sand and some ran out from his nose and the corners of his mouth.

'Ray was gasping from the digging but he held the dead boy in front of him like a baby and began to run. I ran along behind but even with the kid Ray was faster than me. He fair flew between the trees. I remember that his feet flicked up dry pine needles as he passed. The dog ran behind barking.'

The old man pauses and looks out over the people. Out of the corner of my eye my father moves again, shuffling away. He's heard enough.

'I was right. Trevor O'Brien was dead. As near as I can figure it, he was under the sand for half an hour. We went to the funeral. Mrs O'Brien's husband had died of a heart attack a few years before and she only had the one child so she took it badly. Ray took it pretty hard too — that he hadn't saved them both.

'Well, I reckon that's all I want to say. After I moved to Napier we lost touch. Neither of us were great letter writers but Ray was a good mate, a good person. For years after, he'd visit Mrs O'Brien, help out with repairs around the house and gardening and such. And you know, when he was digging that tunnel all I could think of was that it was going to cave in like the other one and then Ray would be dead too. But when I asked him about it after, he said he hadn't even thought about that. He was just thinking about the boy.'

Stepping off the carpet the old man begins the long walk up the aisle. His walking stick clicks and clatters on the stone floor. As he passes me he turns his head and nods. His eyes are the same shade of blue as my father's.

After the echo of the final hymn has faded from the rafters I help to carry my father's coffin up the aisle. It slides easily into the waiting hearse. A small river runs by the church and as we wait for someone to bring around the car I walk away over the lawn and down to the water.

Looking across to the opposite bank I see a young man with blond wavy hair standing under a tree. He is not wearing a shirt and the reflection of the light off the water plays over his tanned body. He is sweating and damp sand clings to his skin in patches.

In his arms he holds a dead boy. He cradles him gently as though the boy weighs nothing, a baby. The young man looks at me for a long moment and then smiles gently, happy to be alive and young. Turning, he begins to run. He runs along the river bank, smooth and easy despite the boy in his arms. His feet kick up dry pine needles as he passes.

I watch until my father disappears between the tall trunks of the pine trees.

ABOUT THE AUTHORS

Barbara Anderson lives in Wellington. She has written two collections of short stories and six novels, one of which, *Portrait of the Artist's Wife*, won the 1992 Goodman Fielder Wattie Award. Her new novel, *The Swing Around*, will be published later this year.

Norman Bilbrough was born in 1941. He has published five books of fiction. His latest volume of stories, *Desert Shorts*, was published in 1999. His stories have won prizes in New Zealand and Australia. 'Down on the Corner' won the *Sunday Star-Times* Short Story Award in 2000.

Linda Burgess has published three novels, a collection of short stories, and in 2000 a travel memoir, *Allons Enfants*. She has been runner-up in New Zealand's two most prestigious short story competitions – the Katherine Mansfield Award (1997) and the *Sunday Star-Times* Short Story Competition (2000) with 'Bike Ride'. She is also a scriptwriter, book reviewer and creative writing teacher.

Catherine Chidgey's first novel, *In a Fishbone Church*, won the Betty Trask Award in England and Best First Book in both the Montana Book Awards Deutz Medal and the Commonwealth Writers Prize (Southeast Asia/South Pacific Region). She is published in New Zealand, Australia and the UK and her second novel, *Golden Deeds*, will also appear in the United States. Catherine has held the Buddle Findlay Sargeson Fellowship and is the 2001 Meridian Energy Katherine Mansfield Memorial Fellow.

John Cranna was born in Te Aroha in 1954, grew up in the Waikato and lived for a while in London. He now lives in Auckland. He has published two books of fiction, *Visitors* and *Arena*, and has won a number of prizes for his work, including the 1990 Commonwealth Prize for Best First Book.

Fiona Farrell was born in Oamaru and presently lives on Banks Peninsula. In between, she studied at Otago and Toronto, had children (two), and published poetry (two collections), short stories (two collections) and novels (two). Her awards include the New Zealand Book Award for fiction (1992), a Queen Elizabeth II Arts Council Fellowship (1990) and the Katherine Mansfield Memorial Fellowship in Menton (1995).

Patricia Grace says that since the completion of her fifth novel at the end of 2000 she has been able to put thought to the adaptation of *Cousins* for film. It is a welcome change from solitary writing routines to be working in collaboration for a while. She is also working on the final draft of a book for children.

Russell Haley, born in England in 1934, moved from Sydney to Auckland with his family in 1966. Haley has an MA in English and in 1985 held the Auckland University Literary Fellowship. Russell and Jean lived in France on the Katherine Mansfield Memorial Fellowship in 1987. *Tomorrow Tastes Better*, Russell Haley's fourth novel, was published by HarperCollins in 2000.

Keri Hulme says she is glad to have made it to 54. She is a fulltime writer, painter and fisher, who is deeply concerned with local conservation issues. Of Kai Tahu and Pakeha descent, she is also profoundly interested in Kaitahutaka. A second anthology of her short stories, and a second novel, will be published this year.

Witi Ihimaera's latest novel is *The Uncle's Story*. He is a novelist, short-story writer, editor and playwright. He began his literary career in 1972 with *Pounamu, Pounamu*, and his subsequent fiction includes *Tangi*, *The Matriarch*, *Nights in the Gardens of Spain*, *Bulibasha* and *The Dream Swimmer*. He lives in Auckland.

Christine Johnston's short stories have appeared in *Sport* and *Landfall*. Her first novel, *Blessed Art Thou Among Women*, won the 1990 Heinemann Reed Fiction Award. She has written three novels for teenagers, two plays, and a libretto, *Outrageous Fortune*. Canterbury University Press published her collection of stories *The End of the Century* in 1999. She is currently working on a novel.

Fiona Kidman is a Wellington writer who has published more than twenty books including fiction, non-fiction and poetry. Her novels include *A Breed of Women*, *The Book of Secrets* and *Richochet Baby*. She has been publishing short stories for more than thirty years, and the latest of her several collections is *The Best of Fiona Kidman's Short Stories* (Vintage). Writing short stories (usually longer stories) is the form she most enjoys.

Shonagh Koea has published five novels and three collections of short stories. She had a Fellowship in Literature at the University of Auckland in 1993, where she wrote *Sing To Me, Dreamer*, which was shortlisted for the 1995 New Zealand Book Awards. A sixth novel, *Time For a Killing*, was published by Random House in 2000.

Owen Marshall is best known for short stories, but more recently has written poetry and novels as well. His second novel, *Harlequin Rex*, won the 2000 Montana Book Awards Deutz Medal for fiction.

Rowan Metcalfe was born in 1955, of mixed European and Polynesian blood, and was raised on a King Country sheep farm. She started writing early to escape the tedium of those dry hills and the smell of the woolshed. She fled the country aged 20, lived in Italy for a year, then England, where she lived in the county of Norfolk for almost twenty years, as wife, mother and political activist. She is now living at Whangamata on the Coromandel, working as a local reporter.

Michael Morrisey has published seventeen books, the two most recent being *The Flamingo Anthology of New Zealand Short Stories* (2000), a sample of the best New Zealand short stories from Katherine Mansfield to Emily Perkins, and *Heart of the Volcano* (2000), a short novel. He also teaches short story writing at several community education centres and writes book review columns for *Investigate* and *Directions*.

Carl Nixon was born in Christchurch in 1967 and has an MA in religious studies. He won the *Sunday Star-Times* Short Story Competition in 1997 with 'My Father Running with a Dead Boy', and again in 1999. He was second in the 1999 Katherine Mansfield Memorial Awards. He also writes for the theatre and his plays include the very popular *Kiwifruits and Company*.

Vincent O'Sullivan is a poet, playwright, novelist, short-story writer and critic who lives in Wellington and works at Victoria University.

Emily Perkins was born in New Zealand in 1970. She is the author of a prize-winning collection of short stories, *Not Her Real Name*, and two novels, *Leave Before You Go* and *The New Girl*. Other stories have been widely anthologised, and in 1999 she wrote a forty-part fiction serial for the London *Evening Standard*. She lives in London with her husband and daughter.

Sarah Quigley is a novelist, short-story writer, and poet. She has a D.Phil in English Literature from the University of Oxford, and has won several major awards for her writing. She is currently living in Berlin, having been awarded the inaugural Creative New Zealand Berlin Writer's Fellowship.

C. K. Stead's most recent publications are a novel, *Talking About O'Dwyer*, a collection of poems, *The Right Thing*, and a selection of essays, reviews, lectures and interviews, *The Writer at Work*. A new novel, *The Secret History of Modernism*, will appear in late 2001. Stead lives in Auckland.

Apirana Taylor is of Ngati Porou, Te Whanau a Apanui, Ngati Ruanui and Ngati Pakeha descent. He works as an actor, writer and painter. He has published three books of short stories, a novel, a book of plays and three books of poetry. In 2000 he was invited to tour Europe on a hugely successful poetry tour. His poetry has been translated into German and is being translated into Italian. His skills range from scrub cutting to journalism, and teaching drama and creative writing.

Peter Wells is a novelist, short-story writer and essayist. He also makes documentary films and dramas. His books include *Dangerous Desires*, his films *Desperate Remedies*. In 2001 he is publishing a memoir, *Long Loop Home*.

Albert Wendt is of the Aiga Sa-Tuaopepe, Sa-Maualaivao and the Sa-Patu of Samoa. He has published novels, stories and poetry internationally. At present he is Professor of English at the University of Auckland.

ACKNOWLEDGEMENTS

For permission to reprint the stories in this collection, acknowledgement is gratefully made to the authors and publishers of the following:

Barbara Anderson: 'The Girls'. First published in *I Think We Should Go Into the Jungle*, Victoria University Press, 1989.

Norman Bilbrough: 'Down on the Corner'. First published in the *Sunday Star-Times*, 2000.

Linda Burgess: 'Bike Ride'. First published in the *Sunday Star-Times*, 2000.

Catherine Chidgey: 'The Sundial of Human Involvement'. First published in the *NZ Listener*, 1997.

John Cranna: 'History for Berliners'. First published in *Visitors*, Reed, 1989.

Fiona Farrell: 'Heads or Tails'. First published in *Light Readings*, Random House, 2001.

Patricia Grace: 'The Day of the Egg'. First published in *The Sky People*, Penguin, 1994.

Russell Haley: 'Press Play Until You Find Silence' (A Spider-Web Season). First published in *Tomorrow Tastes Better*, HarperCollins, 2001.

Keri Hulme: 'Nightsong for the Shining Cuckoo'. First published in *Landfall 137*.

Witi Ihimaera: 'Life and Death in Calcutta'. First published in *Post-colonial Knitting: The Art of Jacqueline Bardolph*, Crela, Nice, France, and Massey University Press, New Zealand, 2000.

Christine Johnston: 'Funeral Shoes'. First published in *Sport 21*.

Fiona Kidman: 'The Whiteness'. First published in *Landfall 158*.

Shonagh Koea: 'Longing'. Unpublished.

Owen Marshall: 'Heating the World'. First published in *Landfall 177*.

Rowan Metcalfe: 'Perfume'. First published in the *Sunday Star-Times*, 1997.

Michael Morrissey: 'Existential Kissing'. First published in *Metro*, 1994.

Carl Nixon: 'My Father Running with a Dead Boy'. First published in the *Sunday Star-Times*, 1997.

Vincent O'Sullivan: 'Success, and the Oral Archive'. Unpublished.

Emily Perkins: 'We're Here, Anderson Says'. First published in *Fortune Hotel*, Hamish Hamilton, 1999.

Sarah Quigley: 'Only Connect'. First published in *Having Words With You*, Penguin, 1998.

C. K. Stead: 'A Short History of New Zealand'. First published in *Sport 8*.

Apirana Taylor: 'Parareka'. First published in *Iti Te Kopara*, The Pohutukawa Press, 2000.

Peter Wells: 'The Friendly Stranger'. Unpublished.

Albert Wendt: 'The Eyes Have It'. First published in *Southerly*, Summer 1998–99, Vol 58, Number Four.